PF

MW01200755

..... 1ncy Lee

"The tragic crash of a small plane sets an Oregon social worker on the trail of even greater tragedies behind it . . . A well-paced exposé of dark family secrets."

—*Kirkus Reviews*

"The plot takes many twists and turns and keeps readers guessing until the surprising end. For fans of Harlan Coben, Riley Sager, and Linwood Barclay."

—*Library Journal*

Or Else

2023 Edgar Award Winner for Best Paperback Original

"Hart remains a suspense writer to watch."

—*Publishers Weekly*

"*Or Else* is a thriller/suspense tour de force. Joe Hart has knocked it out of the park with a start-to-finish roller coaster ride of perfectly executed twists and expertly timed chills. Deep character development and rich narrative seals *Or Else*'s place as the not-to-be-missed domestic thriller/suspense of the year."

—Steven Konkoly, author of the Ryan Decker series and *Deep Sleep*

"The perfect thriller for a rainy afternoon, *Or Else* draws you into a web of small-town secrets, lies, and intrigue and doesn't let you go. Hart's well-rendered setting and characters resonate like people and places you've known. Loved every minute of this absolute page-turner!"

—D. M. Pulley, bestselling author of *The Dead Key*

"Joe Hart has written compelling stories before, but it's in *Or Else* that he shows off just how good he is. This book checks all the boxes for me: a (seemingly) quiet, small-town drama—filled with those little quirks and secrets nobody wants to talk about—that quickly blossoms into something big, sinister, and menacing. Hart doesn't pull any punches on some serious issues, either: love, infidelity, family conflict . . . there's plenty to think about right up to the explosive ending. *This* is the thriller you'll be recommending for the foreseeable future."

—Matthew Iden, author of the Marty Singer series and *The Winter Over*

Obscura

"Joe Hart is a tremendous talent, and with *Obscura*, he has taken his storytelling to the next level. This is a genius work of science fiction, brimming with thrills, scares, and most importantly, heart. I devoured this book, and you will too."

—Blake Crouch, *New York Times* bestselling author of *Dark Matter* and the Wayward Pines series

"Outstanding . . . Fans of Blake Crouch's Wayward Pines series, with its combination of mystery, horror, and science fiction, will find this right up their alley."

—*Publishers Weekly* (starred review)

I
BECOME
HER

ALSO BY JOE HART

The Dominion Trilogy

The Last Girl
The Final Trade
The First City

The Liam Dempsey Mysteries

The River Is Dark
The Night Is Deep

Nora McTavish

Where They Lie
Never Come Back
Now We Run

Novels

Lineage
Singularity
EverFall
The Waiting
Widow Town

Cruel World
Obscura
I'll Bring You Back
We Sang in the Dark
Or Else

Novellas

Leave the Living
A Hole We Crawl Into

Short Story Collections

Midnight Paths: A Collection of Dark Horror
Something Came Through: And Other Stories

Short Stories

"Outpost"
"And the Sea Called Her Name"
"The Exorcism of Sara May"

Comics

The Last Sacrifice

I
BECOME
HER

A THRILLER

JOE HART

THOMAS & MERCER

Published by Thomas & Mercer, Seattle

www.apub.com

Amazon, the Amazon logo, and Thomas & Mercer are trademarks of Amazon.com, Inc., or its affiliates.

EU product safety contact:
Amazon Media EU S. à r.l.
38, avenue John F. Kennedy, L-1855 Luxembourg
amazonpublishing-gpsr@amazon.com

ISBN-13: 9781662529740 (paperback)
ISBN-13: 9781662529733 (digital)

Cover design by Caroline Teagle Johnson
Cover image: © CoffeeAndMilk / Getty

Printed in the United States of America

She lived,
in spite of life.
   —Unknown

In my dreams there is a woman.

A woman unhindered by jealousy and insecurities. She is vibrant and free. She knows what she wants and takes it without apology. She no longer waits for words she'll never hear. She understands love is always conditional. She has been strong enough to endure what she didn't deserve, and stronger still to cast it off and leave it behind. She is everything I've ever wanted to be.

And in my dreams, I become her.

Sierra

Sometimes I ask myself where it started.

When I'm feeling especially low or missing something from before, I try pinpointing what was the first thing, the first mistake that changed everything. That put me on this course to the place where I am now. I wake sometimes in the sullen gray of dawn and can't reconcile where I am. *Who* I am. I'm adrift. Unmoored like an astronaut whose tether has broken and the only thing around them is the endless dark of space.

There are brief moments when I think I'm not better off at all. When the light falls a certain way on the simple objects in this mostly empty place where we live. Or when the clouds blot out the sun and bring long hours of rain. I sometimes think the inevitability of how it all would have played out might've been better. Or easier at least.

My mind keeps going back. It's natural—to wonder where things begin. It's an attempt to understand. To find order. If you start at the beginning, you can follow a trail forward like breadcrumbs, or drops of blood.

For me the question is never answered. I have no idea where the beginning was.

All I know is the end.

Imogen

I woke to darkness and a sickening swaying that was either in my head or the entire room.

Opening my eyes, I knew it could be either.

The cruise ship suite was lit by LEDs under the counters and cabinets, shining off the one, no, *two* empty champagne bottles beside the bed. Faint recollections of the past hours circled in a drunken swirl.

Dancing in the club downstairs. The multicolored strobes and throbbing beat.

Lev's hand in mine, on my hip, cupping my breast when no one was looking.

How the music hadn't lightened my mood like I hoped it would. The liquor hadn't helped either. Each time I thought about lunch and the sun-drenched white-stone patio overlooking the water, I'd take another drink as if the booze could wash away what I'd seen.

What I *thought* I'd seen.

Yes, always a reminder that I might be making things up. A reminder I could be unreasonable. *Paranoid.*

I hated that word. It made me sick.

Sick.

I was going to be sick.

I sat up in bed, getting my bearings. The room was still unfamiliar even after spending the better part of seven days living in it. It was spacious for a cruise suite—the front half consisting of a lounge area with a small dining table and sliding doors leading out to the balcony, the back half a bedroom hosting the king-size bed where I sat, trying to keep last night's dinner in place. My head pounded and even the low light hurt my eyes.

Mood lighting, Lev had said earlier in my ear as he turned it down until we were both softer versions of ourselves. His words had gone so deep in my head it sounded like he'd spoken one of my own thoughts. And drunkenly I'd been afraid he'd know what I was thinking. Know what kept coming back no matter how I pushed it away.

You were touching her hand. I saw it.

The image was there when he undressed me. When his mouth trailed across my skin in that delicious friction and pressure he was so masterful at applying. It was there when he pulled me on top of him and buried himself in me. It was there when I came minutes later.

Now, as the room swayed in time with my heartbeat and the wind, I realized something was missing. It took much longer than it should have, but when something so familiar is gone, you sometimes notice it last.

Lev.

My husband of only ten days wasn't in bed.

I hadn't risen yet or stepped around the partial wall separating the bedroom and sitting area, but I already knew he wouldn't be there. He had a presence I'd become deeply attuned to over the two years we'd known each other. It was as if I could sense the air he displaced. It was his breathing. How he shifted every so often even when he was comfortable. I swore sometimes I could hear the click of his eyelids when he blinked.

It was a relief he wasn't here. I was going to be sick, and the last thing I wanted was our honeymoon tainted by the memory of me retching in the toilet after five-too-many drinks, him perched on the tub's edge, holding my hair back, saying it was okay.

In the attached bathroom I spent an extended period of time deciding whether the nausea was serious or an empty threat. Something

I would have to contend with or could bluff away and pretend didn't matter.

The waitress doesn't matter. How young and pretty she was doesn't matter. How she laughed and let him touch her hand doesn't matter.

The nausea won.

When it was finished, I washed my sweating face with shaking hands, cupping the cold water and splashing myself over and over until I was numb.

Back in the main room, Lev still wasn't there. I confirmed this with a quick inspection of the sitting area and the balcony that made me uneasy, with its railing that seemed too low and the sheer drop to the water sixty feet below.

"Lev?" I said, just to say it. Like he'd answer and materialize suddenly, and the growing apprehension would just as magically disappear. "Lev?" Louder this time. Only hours ago I'd panted his name at the ceiling, the worry that someone might hear in the rooms next to ours obliterated by a second orgasm.

Now I hoped he'd hear me out in the hall where he was retrieving more ice or a snack or some other mundane thing, and everything would go back to normal. Or as normal as it could be. My worry would wither instead of growing darkened tendrils outward from my center until every inch of me would feel sick and infected. Until it would ruin what was left of our honeymoon.

But that was me. I ruined things. It was what I did best.

My clothes were a lustful trail across the floor, and I gathered them one by one and dressed. I drained a bottle of water from the room's fridge, which probably cost ten dollars, but it was so deliciously cold and clear that I didn't care. Gradually, the taste of acid retreated. I went out on the balcony and took in the view.

I'd forgotten the name of the island we were docked at. It was one of half a dozen we'd visited over the last week—all of them glowing with hyperreal beauty beneath the Mediterranean sun. White-sand beaches, water so turquoise it looked artificial, tiered buildings carved into dramatic hillsides—all whitewashed stone and blue shutters, narrow cobbled streets, and cheerful people.

This island was particularly gorgeous in the day, and at this hour of night, its port town glittered like a cluster of jewels dripping into the ocean. The bay was studded with sailboats and fishing vessels, all of them now dots of light bobbing on the water, which was choppy from a brisk wind coming off the open sea.

Our ship listed with the weather, just a little, but my stomach registered it and gave another lurch. I breathed in the fresh air, letting the breeze comb back my hair, and told myself it would be okay. It was nothing. Lev would be back any second, and I'd get past the memory of lunch.

Concessions. It was the word my mother had used regarding marriage. *It's all about the give and take, Gen. No relationship is perfect. You have to overlook certain things about each other; otherwise no marriage would last.*

I thought it was interesting she used that word. *Concessions.* A word that meant to give in.

Not compromise. *Surrender.*

Imogen

Five minutes later I stepped into the hall.

It was after midnight, and there were a few people moving along the seemingly endless corridors, their voices amplified by booze. Thankfully, they were all heading away, toward the nearest elevator lobby and not my direction. I didn't think I could make small talk now with anyone or even smile politely as they passed. Lev wasn't anywhere in sight.

I was still a little breathless from calling his phone before leaving the room. I'd told myself I was being irrational but couldn't help it. The ringtone he'd chosen for me blared from the bedroom a second later—the theme from my favorite TV show. He'd left his phone on the nightstand. This probably should've been reassuring, a promise he hadn't gone far and would be back soon. It had the opposite effect.

Now, in the hallway that looked like something out of a house of mirrors, I swallowed dryly and walked faster, determined to relieve myself of this feeling. This worry. I was so intent on getting to the elevator that I almost missed the door on the right with the pineapple taped to it.

The pineapple had been cut from a glossy magazine. It was about five inches high, and the tips of someone's fingers were visible on the edge where it had been sheared free. Lev and I had shared quizzical looks the day we boarded and walked past the room toward our own, neither of us giving it much more thought until two nights ago when a guy who bore a passing resemblance to Lev started chatting him up at the bar.

He and his wife were in the pineapple room. He'd seen us in the hall. We were neighbors! His wife, a rail-thin woman in a cocktail dress, cackled loudly at the ceiling, two empty martini glasses standing like casualties on the bar before her while she worked on a third. She wore heavy makeup and squeezed my arm whenever she spoke. Later, after I'd drifted away to the nearest window to look out at the night, Lev had asked them about the pineapple on their door. *It's an invitation for like-minded people,* the guy said. *You know, we're into having fun. Sharing. You guys should stop by some night . . .*

Lev had told me this as we made our way back to the room, both of us tipsy and laughing until our eyes filled with tears about being hit on by swingers. Lev even pretended to knock on their door whenever we passed by afterward while I dragged him away. The couple had been at the club last night and given us an overly warm wave, but by then the joke had gone flat. Deflated by lunch and how white the waitress's teeth had been when she smiled at Lev. How quickly she'd walked away when she spotted me returning from the bathroom.

The elevator was empty when the doors opened, and I stepped inside. Good. I didn't want anyone close to me; they might see something in my bloodshot eyes that had nothing to do with still being half drunk. My reflection in the polished chrome of the elevator walls was thankfully obscured. I could've been anybody.

Two decks down, the nightclub we'd been at only a few hours ago was still going strong, though the dance floor had cleared a little, which made it easier for me to see Lev wasn't one of the dozens of men grinding away against their female counterparts. He wasn't in the throngs of people lining the bar, wasn't at any of the tables or in the booths in the dim corners.

The casino he'd frequented a few times during the trip was another deck down. It was almost empty, the obnoxious digital tones and trills from vacant slots calling to bare aisles. I'd always found casinos to be some of the saddest places on earth. They reeked of desperation, of stale hope and loneliness. Lev thought it was because of what I did for a living. Risk assessment. "Of course you don't like gambling," he'd said while we were dating and I'd shot down the idea of a weekend in Atlantic City. We were living in separate small apartments, and the house on the tree-lined street with its two stories and perfect front yard was still a year away. Lev had just gotten a promotion at the firm where he was a fast-rising political adviser, and he wanted to celebrate. "The work-part of your brain won't shut off long enough to let you have fun." I didn't know if it had been an insult or not.

"You do realize the percentage of people who win is barely in the double digits," I'd retorted. "The house edge is a very real statistical fact."

"But that's what's exciting," he'd said, wrapping his arms around me, staring down into my face from his towering height. "The possibility of losing."

You mean winning, I'd been about to say, but then he kissed me and I let it go.

At the very back of the casino, an ancient couple dressed to the nines hunched over a roulette wheel like it could divine the future while a casino employee stared blankly as the ball ran in the track, around and around.

I sat down on a bench in the hall. A few people passed, happy chatter trailing behind them. The places Lev could've been on the ship were endless. But really there were only a few. He had particular tastes for eating and drinking, couldn't swim well, and normally liked to be in bed before midnight. I tried his phone again in the hope that we'd missed each other, but it only rang and rang.

Go back to the room. Drink some more water. Lie down. Yes, that was what I should do. He would come back soon; he had to—the ship was leaving the island, and we were traveling through the night to Athens. It was the last leg of the cruise.

I rose and walked down the hallway, twisting and turning through the ship until a door opened onto the main deck. The air had cooled, still almost the perfect temp, and a three-quarter moon spread itself on the water in a smear of silver. Another night in paradise. But there were clouds building farther out over the water, knives of lightning flashing inside them. I went to the railing and looked across to the city. How inviting the lights were. How beautiful the sweeping shadow of the island was against the lapping sea.

Music played somewhere inland—a party, shouting, laughter.

It should've carried me away. So what if Lev was there? He was somewhere. And I loved him. He loved me. We were married now. Vows had been spoken. To have and to hold. To trust.

Trust.

The ship swayed again, and I shut my eyes.

Imogen

The cruise employee manning the desk beside the gangway didn't look old enough to buy a drink.

He was completely absorbed in something on his phone and barely glanced up when I approached.

"Going ashore?" Toneless. Bored. There was still a scatter of acne across his forehead.

"Yes." I held out my cruise card, and he scanned it without looking at my face.

"The ship departs in two hours. Please be back aboard before then, or you may risk being left behind."

I started away, then paused, but he'd already resumed the video on his phone. I was going to ask him if he'd seen someone go ashore a while ago. A tall man with dark hair and deep-hazel eyes. A good-looking man. A smile hidden in a pleasant voice. A man he might remember. But given how he'd barely registered me, it was probably useless.

The doors opened to the gangway, and I made my way down, the concrete atop bedrock shocking in its solidity beneath my feet when I stepped off the ramp. It felt like I was sinking into it, like I weighed a thousand pounds.

On the other islands we'd stopped at, there was always a fleet of cars waiting to take tourists inland. A fervor. Buses idling in blue hazes of diesel smoke. A clamor of voices calling out the best price for a ride. But here the town started almost immediately. Easy walking distance.

Already there were smells of something deliciously fried drifting in the air, the stickiness of a drink spilled on the concrete, faint light snagging on broken glass near a trash bin.

Across the mostly empty parking lot was the main street we'd walked the day before beneath the sun. I tried returning to that moment before lunch. Tried to pretend. Lev's hand had been warm in mine, and we'd strolled along looking in the shop fronts, pausing to point something out to one another. He'd stroked the back of my neck. Spoke close to my ear. Doting. He doted on me. My mother's term. Most times she'd say it with her hand tucked close to the sagging skin of her jawline while looking at Lev across the room.

He dotes. That's not something you find every day.

Yes, he was attentive. But I'd mentally called it something else from when we first started dating.

Intuitive.

He remembered my favorite band I'd mentioned in passing on our third date and brought it up on our fifth. He complimented my eyes, knowing somehow I was self-conscious about how far apart they were. He understood by the second time we slept together exactly where I wanted his hands and mouth to linger without ever telling him. Lev wasn't just perceptive, he was instinctual.

Someone who you could meet for the first time and, when you parted, feel like you'd known them for years. Someone with charisma. Charm.

How long had I been in the bathroom at lunch? The stalls had all been full, so I'd checked my makeup and readjusted the straps on the sundress I was wearing before one opened up. Maybe long enough for him to ask our waitress just the right questions. Things he'd noticed about her in the half hour we'd been seated on the patio overlooking the endless blue sea.

Maybe all he'd needed to ask was when the restaurant closed. When she got off.

A group of people passed by on the opposite side of the street, one of the men loudly telling a story while walking backward before them.

I turned into an alleyway hemmed in by white limestone walls glowing under the streetlights and leaned against one of them, breathless from a carousel of terrible thoughts.

It wouldn't be this way. Not the way I was thinking. I was doing it again. Making things infinitely worse in my head so it was an immense relief when I was wrong. Or priming myself for the hurt so I would be ready.

"*Eísai kalá*? Are you . . . all right?" A man stood a few yards away, hands in his pants pockets, shirt half unbuttoned. His eyes were wide with concern.

"Yes, sorry. I'm fine," I said, pushing away from the wall.

"Maybe too much ouzo?"

"Yes, maybe."

"You need help . . . getting home?"

"No, thank you, I'm—" For a second I continued denying exactly what I was doing on the island, why I'd left the comfort of our suite to begin with. Deny where I was going. But then the paper-thin wall of self-deception tore apart, and resolve flooded through.

I steadied myself and said, "Do you know when Argyros closes?"

———

The restaurant was off one of the hundreds of side alleys winding labyrinth-like through the town. I found it after a few wrong turns since the walk back to the ship had felt like waking from a nightmare, one that followed you up into the light.

Argyros was a gorgeous one-level white-stone building with wide arches and triangular sail shades stretched taut above the patios. It was almost completely dark now, only a single light on in the kitchen draping across the empty bar and spilling onto the cobblestone outside. No one sat at the tables or stood by the low wall separating the terrace from the slope leading down to the sea. A lone dishwasher leaned in the courtyard smoking a cigarette and looking out at the storm.

Lev wasn't here. Why would he be? He'd had, what, five minutes alone with her while she worked? Ten at the most? It was nothing, not enough time for anything meaningful to pass between them. Even him touching her could be excused if not forgiven. A man with middle age in sight who'd only recently settled down, flirting for one of the last times. It was a death spasm of ego or lust. Something foreign to me, but completely harmless.

Except . . .

An internal constriction traveled from my stomach up to my chest as I recalled something I hadn't thought of until now. Lev had gone to the restaurant ahead of me. Had sat at the bar and gotten a drink while waiting for a table to open up. I'd been in the little shop around the corner that sold blown glass the color of the ocean, borne away by the delicacy of the craftsmanship. Floating on the cloud of my honeymoon. Afterward I'd joined him.

So there had been more time I hadn't thought of. More time for the two of them to . . . connect.

There was a bench outside the low wall I sank onto. Not for the first time I wondered if I might be losing my grip on reality.

Jealousy felt like that at its most extreme. A spider's web of conspiracy connected by insecurities. If my mother were here, she would tell me I should be ashamed. *A man who looks at you the way Lev does, and you think this of him? Shame on you, Gen.* Like I wanted to be this way. Empty and filled with acidic distrust at the same time.

The first grumble of thunder rolled in with the waves below. The storm was closer. The tide was out, and under the moon the beach was a wide white strip along the island's edge, like untanned flesh beneath a waistband. A sand path led away from the bench through the low waving sea grass, winding down to the beach. I traced its length. Saw the faint impressions of many feet there. An hour or so ago the beach might've looked more inviting. A place people might walk and talk and maybe do other things away from the darkening city.

I stood and made my way downward as thunder rolled again.

Imogen

The waves were much bigger up close.

They came in, growing higher and higher, whitening at their tops until they crashed over themselves and receded in a rush of foam. Shells clicked under my shoes, and crabs scuttled sideways in my wake to hide beneath the stones lining the beach.

The air had a held-breath feel to it preceding the storm. The anticipation of wind and rain and maybe something being changed or broken. I moved among the stones, thunder vibrating in my chest whenever it came.

The beach was empty in both directions except for a few scattered tables and chairs from some nearby resorts. Napkins drifted along with a few other pieces of trash. I moved at a steady pace, looking up every so often to confirm I was still alone. A walk. That's all it was. All it was turning out to be. Maybe a small weapon to gouge him with if he came back to the suite and found me gone. If he called, I wouldn't answer. I'd let the passive-aggressive heat fill me like a balloon all the way back to the ship. Let his worry buoy me. Let it cancel out seeing his hand on hers.

There was a corner ahead, rocks spilling down to the sea so that only a small portion of beach was visible. Part of me was already turning back. It wouldn't be long before the gangway would be pulled up and the ship would undock. But I went on, climbing over a few of the lower rocks, feet skittering on their slippery angles.

The next section of beach was brief, another corner not far in the distance. The slope above was bare, much too steep for any buildings.

Two people sat on a black square of blanket a hundred yards away.

They were only outlines against the lighter shade of sand. A woman and a man. She had a mane of hair spilling down her back. He was tall, his knees tented before him. They were sitting very close to each other.

I crouched there beside a boulder, tried to become part of it. I looked away, as if that could change what I'd seen. It would have been so much easier for the beach to be empty. So much simpler.

Lightning flashed, but I'd had my eyes closed. Any chance at seeing details was lost. And then the rain started. Pattering gently. The couple stood. She said something and pointed down the beach, away from where I watched. He took her hand, and they jogged off, dragging the blanket with them until they were lost around the next corner.

I crawled down the rocks, hands wet and gritty with silt. A creature stalking prey. It was how I felt. Because these two people could've been anyone. Just two lovers out for a romantic night on the beach who got caught in the rain.

Except the man was familiar.

His height. The way he moved. How he'd put one hand up to block the rain as he ran.

The storm came down harder, and I shivered, finding the place they'd been sitting. There were four empty beer bottles stuck upside down in the sand. Ahead, the cliff lining the beach jutted over the water, a natural shelter. As I crept closer, a shadow beneath the overhang deepened.

A grotto.

The tide was out, but when it was in, it would wash inside the cave and pile up fine sand. Comb a place there that was smooth and even as any bedspread. I made my way to the cave's opening and listened from beside it. Waiting to hear something. Anything that would confirm or deny what was stampeding through me.

A cry of pleasure from her.

Or from him.

I would know Lev's voice anywhere, especially in the throes of passion. He always inhaled shakily right before he came, and then his voice would rush out in a moan. Most times he would groan a word as well. Usually my name. I waited to hear hers.

What would happen if I went inside that darkness? What if I was wrong? Or right?

Risk assessment in real time. Except now it wasn't some faceless corporation wanting every base covered for an acquisition or building project.

It was my life. My future decided in the next moments.

Go in or stay out.

I listened for another few seconds, muscles trembling, heart thundering louder than the storm.

Then I walked away along the beach and retraced my steps up the hill.

Huge sprays of red bougainvillea draped down into one of the side streets from hanging planters. I'd stopped to smell them on the way to lunch the day before, taken in by their lush beauty. Afterward, I'd been surprised and disappointed.

I paused now beside a drainpipe splattering my feet and ankles with rainwater, and buried my face in the blooms, inhaling great lungfuls of moist air.

The flowers still had no scent.

Imogen

I kept a garden inside me, tending it whenever I could.

It was sprawling and lush, filled with plants and flowers, trees and hedges, all of it perfectly cultivated. Everything permanently in bloom. In the center was a koi pond. The water was clear and bottomless, and the koi swam, their bodies curves of vibrant color. Red, orange, white, black. Flashing.

And at the very back of the garden was a high stone wall with an iron door set in it. Behind the wall were things I couldn't bear to look at. Things that would ruin the garden. It was where I kept what I'd said to Jamie. What his face had looked like when it was over. How he'd pleaded with me, begged me not to leave.

And Marcus, he was there too. Along with the knife and how it had felt in my hand. Cutting and cutting.

I sat very still on the couch in our suite and tried putting what had just happened through the door in the wall. But it wouldn't fit. It kept slipping back through, staining the garden with oily darkness. Killing everything it touched.

The ship began to move.

I waited, breathing shallowly, listening for footsteps to approach our door and stop. For it to open and Lev to come inside. Because there'd been no postponement and no announcement when the ship finally undocked. I'd been fully expecting a call from a cruise employee asking if I knew where my husband was. Telling me he was in danger of being left behind. A short delay most people wouldn't be aware of since it was the middle of the night and they were asleep.

But the ship moved out of port into the sea without a disturbance, passing through the storm briefly as it did. Rain pattered down on the balcony, some of it splashing through the gap in the door I'd left open. I stared at the puddle gathering there, and when the rain stopped and the moon reappeared, I went outside and leaned over the railing.

The island was growing faint in the distance, the gulf of dark water eating everything up around it so it looked very small and exposed. Insignificant. Soon it was only a point of light, the city and all the people reduced to a single glimmer.

The suite door opened and closed. I stiffened. Didn't turn around. A second later, hands slid around my waist to the flat of my stomach. His chin tucked onto my shoulder, the scruff of his cheek brushed mine. I became stone.

I inhaled, searching for something. Sweat. Her scent. Their sex. But it was like smelling the bougainvillea. Nothing.

"Didn't think you'd be awake," Lev said in my ear, his breath tickling, and I managed not to recoil. I swallowed thickly and turned from the railing and his embrace, noting his clothes were dry. On the table inside the doorway, he'd set down a full bottle of champagne, the wrapper shining in the low light. "Thought you'd be sleeping last night off," he said when I only stood there looking at the bottle.

"Where did you get this?"

"At the store two decks down. Figured we needed to replenish our reserves. In fact . . ." He picked up the bottle and unwrapped it, facing partly away as he forced the cork out with his thumbs. Even with everything, I was struck by him then. Lev had a presence. Tall, sleekly muscular, dark hair, strong jawline. Traditional good looks I'd never found necessary in a relationship.

The cork popped and I flinched. He didn't notice and went to find our glasses from the day prior. He filled them and held one out to me. I kept my hands at my sides.

When I spoke, my voice was flat. "You've been gone for hours. Where have you been?"

His handsome features contracted. He set the glasses on the table. "I couldn't sleep, so I went down to the casino for a while. I . . ." He lifted a hand to rub the back of his neck and looked away.

"What?"

"I lost some money. I shouldn't have been betting, I know you hate it. Sorry."

"I looked for you at the casino. You weren't there."

He laughed. "What?"

"You weren't there." Each word felt like a punch. Something to hammer his defenses with. Break them down until he cracked and the truth came out. I needed it. Needed confirmation I hadn't imagined everything.

"Well, you must not have looked too hard." He grinned, and I wanted to hurt him then. "I mean, I was at one of the machines near the back."

"I looked there."

"When? I went to the bathroom and got a drink from the bar around the corner. Maybe we missed each other. Are you okay?" I was trembling. My hands shook, and I clenched them into fists. "Hey, I'm sorry." He tried hugging me, but I stepped away and he lowered his arms.

"You were on the island," I said to the floor between us. The space was important. Crucial. If he closed the gap and touched me, it would all crumble. I would be the one to fold. To give in and accept whatever story he told me. Then it would be my job to believe it. To make it real.

"What are you talking about?"

"I saw you."

He laughed again. "Honey, I haven't left the ship since we got back. What's the matter?"

I looked at his feet. The sandals he wore had a few specks of sand stuck to them. I could see him scrambling along the narrow streets, racing to get back before the gangway went up, before someone came to ask me where he was. He would've been holding the blanket over his head to keep himself dry; that was why his clothes weren't wet. Then to the store for more champagne, creating an alibi on the elevator ride up.

Or the specks of sand could've been from anytime. Anywhere.

"You were touching her hand," I said quietly.

"Whose?"

"Don't."

"I have no idea what you're talking about."

"The waitress at lunch. I saw you talking to her. You touched her hand."

He blinked and shook his head, looking at a spot on the wall somewhere over my shoulder. "I was telling her how great the food was. That was it."

I was drowning, and the explanation was like being thrown a safety line. So simple and straightforward. Reasonable. He always made things sound so reasonable.

"Listen," he went on, his voice much lower. "I know this is scary for you. It is for me too. But I'm ready. I think maybe it's just a self-defense thing. It's automatic after . . ." He touched the glasses of champagne as if he were going to pick them up, then thought better of it. "Let's talk. Everything is okay. I promise."

I promise. Another man had said the same words to me. Then everything had fallen apart.

Lev reached for me and I pulled away. He sighed. "Here, just come out and get some fresh air. You had a lot to drink last night. It'll clear your head."

"I don't want to."

"Please. We'll talk."

"No."

"You're being irrational. Just—" He grasped my arm, too hard, and drew me toward the balcony.

I jerked free. He was too close. Smothering. All his words piled up in my mind, caroming off one another until it was pure noise. A blinding anger birthed, whole and complete.

I put my palms on his chest and shoved.

Lev stumbled back, off-balance. He slipped on the slick balcony, arms pinwheeling, trying to catch himself.

The railing caught him in the lower back, and he tipped, his feet coming up as momentum carried him over.

His fingers grasped the railing and came free as his head clipped the balcony's edge.

He fell away into the darkness without a sound.

Imogen

The first time I saw Lev, he saved me.

My friend April had been dogging me for months about going out with her. We'd met the last year of college in an advanced statistics class that could've bored the paint off walls. She'd been rolling her eyes at the professor's repeated use of the word *quantitative*, and I'd smiled into my hand. We ate lunch together, and somewhere between there and graduation became best friends. All this was before what happened with Marcus. Before the pictures. Before the painting. Before I became someone else, even though I'd never felt sure about who I was.

But with April I was as much myself as I could be. We'd lived together for a time after I had nowhere to go. After my parents had refused to let me come home. She had opened her tiny one-bedroom apartment to me, and I'd slept on the couch and eaten her food until I found a place of my own.

"You have to come; you fucking owe me," she'd said, sitting on one of the stools at my kitchen counter, an empty wineglass before her. We were both thirtysomething business professionals working in the outskirts of DC, unattached and free. April went out every weekend and several nights a week. I stayed in. She dated a rotation of men that changed month to month. I hadn't seen anyone since Jamie more than two years before. Sometimes April would forward me some pathetic dick pic a guy had sent her, and I'd scramble to delete it and curse her even as she laughed herself silly.

"Please don't," I responded. My head was pleasantly light from the wine, my belly full of Chinese food.

"You never go out. Ever."

"So? That's fine."

"It's fine if you're fifty. Seriously, you need to have fun while you can. Pretty soon you'll be gray, and your body will be sagging where it shouldn't, and then you'll be dying, and you'll look back and your last thought will be, 'April was right. I should've listened to her.'"

"That will definitely not be my last thought," I said, cleaning up our dishes. Moxie, my pittie-mix, lifted his head hopefully from where he was sprawled on the floor as I scraped our plates into the trash. I tossed him a piece of sour pork, and he snapped it from the air and swallowed it in one movement.

"You sit here in this apartment when you're not at work," April said, motioning around at the tidy space. "You watch TV with your dog and drink wine alone and eat takeout."

"What part of this is supposed to make me feel bad?"

"Don't you . . ." April paused, then shook her head and poured herself more wine. "Never mind."

I watched her profile out of the corner of my eye as I put things away in the fridge. She never talked about my past relationships, or lack thereof. She knew better. She'd been the one to stand next to me in her tiny bathroom, helping me wash the blood from my hands as I stared blankly at my reflection. These nudges to go out with her were as hard as she'd push. I hated and loved her for it.

I bent to pet Mox's square head, smoothing his short gray fur. He looked up through calm, slitted eyes, never asking anything more of me.

"So what is it?" I finally asked.

"No, it's okay. I shouldn't have said anything."

"Shut up. Skip to where you're excited I'm actually coming out with you."

"Are you?"

"Maybe."

April squealed and poured me more wine. "Okay, so it's this super-boring work party at my boss's house—"

"You're really selling it."

"—some end-of-the-quarter-celebration shit. You can be my plus-one. Anyway, the booze will be expensive, and the food will be good."

"My caveat is—"

"I know, I know. If you get uncomfortable, you'll ghost. That's fine. I'll even pay for the Uber."

I sighed and shook my head. Took a long drink of wine.

April grinned because she knew she'd won. Her smile lit up the room. It was almost enough to make me feel good about giving in. Almost.

———

April's boss's house was in Berkley, a brick monstrosity a stone's throw from the Potomac. The neighborhood was an upscale parade of homes elevated above the street, elegant exterior lights blazing through stately trees. April and I rode together in her car, and a valet took her keys in the yard's large circular turnaround. Low music came from inside, and even before we climbed the steps, my shoulders were tightening. April must've sensed something, because she leaned over and said, "We can split in five minutes if you want. I just need to make an appearance."

I shook my head and brushed back the creeping anxiety. April was right: I needed to get out. Try to feel normal. Blend in.

The house was alive with people. Most were centered in the sunken living room directly off the entry, where a woman took our coats. Waiters in black ties and aprons circulated with trays of canapés and wine. April snagged two glasses of red, and we headed into the fray.

The lobbying firm she worked for was the third largest in the city and had connections in the upper echelons of Congress and the Senate. A few of the guests I rubbed shoulders with were familiar in the offhand way politicians are. You'd seen them somewhere before—TV, a local event, heard their voices on the radio or news cut down to sound bites. The rest were employees of the firm or quasi-business relations in the DC arena. Making my way across the room felt like wading with sharks.

I found a relatively quiet corner of the living room beside a massive fireplace roaring against the cool spring temps, and sipped my wine. April was making the rounds and had already checked in with her boss, a gray-haired man with florid skin who threw back his head and laughed uproariously at something April said. She had that effect on men. They took one look at her and lost their shit. She'd often joked about male IQs dropping in proportion to how short a skirt was.

Nearby, a group of people were having a conversation over the music. "It really goes back to the quality of home life, if you ask me," a guy with a two-hundred-dollar haircut was saying. He was holding a half-empty tumbler of whiskey or bourbon, and after a moment I recognized him as a regular commentator on several prime-time news outlets. Connor something. "We're seeing massive drops in education and huge upticks in violence, and it starts when these kids are young. There's no bedrock of values, since both parents are out pursuing careers. You look at mass-shooting numbers from sixty years ago, and they're nonexistent."

A woman wearing a slinky black dress I would've never felt comfortable in huffed a laugh and said, "Hmm, so let me think, what was different sixty years ago? Oh yeah, women were still being sidelined professionally and kept under their husbands' thumbs."

"I knew you'd say something like that, Maureen," he replied. "So typical to jump to conclusions no one was even hinting at."

"You do more than hint at it. You spelled it out two days ago on CNN." She smiled, revealing a lot of whitened teeth. "Careful, Connor, your misogyny's showing."

This earned quiet laughter from the group, and Connor shook his head. "Did I say it should be the woman staying home raising the kids?"

"You didn't have to."

"No, see, here's the problem today. No conversations can be had about real issues because if the truth veers into a region people are uncomfortable with, it gets swept under the woke rug."

"He said *woke*, everyone drink." Maureen sipped from her wine amid the laughter. "What you fail to realize, darling," she continued, "is women aren't going back to the cage they were kept in for the vast majority of history. You fucked up and let us open our own bank accounts. After that, it was all over. So no matter how you try to lay today's problems at our feet, we're just going to keep stepping over them toward what we deserve."

"Honey, no one deserves anything. We get what we work for. That's it."

"And we *are* working, so someone else will have to watch the kids." Maureen smiled wickedly, and I was surprised when Connor's mouth quirked as well. As the group drifted apart, the two of them hovered near the fire, and his arm crept around her waist. I noticed then they were wearing matching wedding rings.

This was definitely DC.

I turned to look out the floor-to-ceiling windows at the spacious backyard. It was lit by dozens of miniature streetlamps along walking paths meandering between manicured hedges and flower beds only beginning to bloom. My reflection was gauzy in the glass, the party a mingling of voices and music. The couple's opposing-aisle argument lingered like cigarette smoke. The diametric lanes people chose in life. How it felt like I'd never belonged in any of them. Like there was some other path I should be on but could never find.

"Horrible, isn't it?" The voice came from so close by, I startled and nearly spilled my wine. A guy stood a few feet away, leaning against the windows. An empty glass dangled from his fingers. He was my age, maybe younger, with the slick, lean look so many men in the city adopted. He smiled, not looking my way but still talking to me. "All this money and power in one room, and everyone's boring as hell."

"Right."

He offered his hand. "Damian DeMarco. I'm with Senator McVee's office."

"Um, Imogen. Not with anyone's office." He laughed and held my hand a second too long before letting go.

"Gorgeous name. So what do you do?"

"Risk assessment."

"Oh, you with Evans and Baker?"

"No, Stanford Management Systems."

"Haven't heard of them."

"We're out of Blanton."

Some of the shine left his eyes at the mention of the suburb, but then they crept quickly down my body, and he leaned a little closer. "I actually grew up in Upstate New York," he said like it was a guilty admission. "Tiny town. Never find it on a map. But we had fun. A lot of fun."

I nodded and searched for an exit strategy. Usually, I had one ready. This was why I avoided going out in general. The inevitable come-on. I wasn't as flashy as April, didn't dress in the eye-catching way she did, wasn't half as pretty. But nonetheless, men still approached me. My latest ex, Jamie, had given me a compliment once that stayed with me. *There's something about the way you move and how you look when you're really focused. You have a stillness that's captivating. You're alluring; it's the only way I can describe it.* It had been the nicest thing anyone had ever said to me.

But now, as Damian went on about his job at the Capitol, I started to wish I'd turned April down. I hated this dance. The back-and-forth. The flirting. The suggestion to leave the party and grab a drink somewhere. The ask for the phone number. The call for the first date. The expectation of sex after the second or third. More texts, more calls, the late nights, the dinners, the movies, the parties, the meeting one another's friends, the weekends away, the holidays, introductions to each other's families, the mention of moving in together, couples vacations, the second mention of moving in, the move-in, the sharing of personal space, the process of melding two lives into one, the hope that this would be it, the realization it wasn't. That it never would be.

I tried getting April's attention, but she was surrounded by a cloud of people. My pulse picked up speed. I looked at my empty glass, and before I could excuse myself to refill it, Damian had flagged down a waiter and was placing a fresh drink in my hand.

"So I told her it wasn't going to work," he was saying. "But that's ancient history. What about you? Ever tie the knot?"

I opened my mouth, but something was wrong with my tongue. It had retracted to the back of my throat, was pressed there, swelling my airway shut. No words would come out.

"I mean, commitment is great, but it isn't for everybody," he went on, oblivious to what was happening to me. "I feel like as an institution, marriage is having a revival, right? Like for so long it was traditional, and then it became a statement not to get married, like feminism, right? Now it's turned a corner, and it's become a rebellion through orthodoxy. I mean, I want to settle down. I think commitment is totally baller. A house, a wife, a kid or two, all that American-dream shit."

My lungs hitched as if I were holding my breath, but I couldn't get any air in. I was nodding along with him, smiling tightly to agree, all the while the room was narrowing, growing darker in its corners. I was going to pass out.

"So do you want to go grab a drink somewhere?" Damian said, leaning in. "My boss is drunk as hell now. He won't notice if I duck out early."

I tried to say no, that I was there with a friend, that I didn't want to be here at all, but nothing came out. I opened my mouth, and my jaw trembled, then locked. He was staring, eyes narrowing. Then someone's arm brushed mine, and Damian shifted back a few inches.

A man was there beside me. He was very tall. I caught an impression of dark hair and a jawline that could've been carved in granite. "Hey," he said. "Sorry I'm late. Who's this?"

Damian glanced from him to me and back again. "Oh, didn't realize you were—ah, yeah. Have a great night," he murmured and drifted away.

"The bathroom's this way," the guy said in my ear, and gently took one of my hands. He led me through the crowd, and it seemed to part before us. Everything was muffled. I still couldn't breathe. He guided us into a wide hallway off the living room and snapped a light on in an empty half bath. "Splash some cold water on your throat and wrists, it'll help," he said. I stepped into the bathroom and ran the tap. Tried swallowing again, but the muscles there wouldn't respond. Cold water splashed over my wrists, and after a second, pain bloomed there, but with it I gasped a little, and blessed air traveled into my lungs. I shuddered out a breath and drew in another. The man was a long shape in the doorway, watching. I closed my eyes and bent to press one of my coldly damp palms against my collarbone.

The tension ran out of my throat. More air came in. I brought a handful of water up to the side of my neck, and some ran down inside my dress in icy rivulets. My head was clearing. The fist of panic loosened.

"Thank you," I said, my eyes still shut. I was embarrassed, but appreciation overshadowed it. I'd been deeply uncomfortable at parties but never locked up like that before. I glanced at the doorway. "I don't know—"

He was gone.

———

April gave me a little wave and raised her eyebrows when I rejoined the party. *Everything okay?* I nodded, and she went back to listening to one of a dozen loud gray-haired men in her orbit.

As I passed by the front door, I nearly asked for my coat and left. The relief of being out and away from all the people and headed home was more intoxicating than the wine. Except . . .

The man who'd helped me wasn't anywhere in sight. It would've been easy to spot him given his height. I picked my way around the edge of the living room and peered through an archway into a smaller lounge space. A group of women milled there, exclaiming over a dress a teenage girl was holding. Prom was only a month or two off. On the opposite side of the room I glanced into an empty study before stopping near the windows again. He must've left as soon as he saw I was okay.

My luck, I thought, turning to look at the backyard. A guy who couldn't stand scenes like this as much as I couldn't, and he left before I could thank him. But that was when I spotted him standing outside near one of the lamps, his back to the house. And all at once the urge to go out the front door was overwhelming again. Because now that I could say thanks, I didn't think I'd be able to. I was too embarrassed. I'd been completely vulnerable and he'd somehow known. What did he think of me? What would he say? Still, it would be rude to just leave. *Courtesy wasted is worse than courtesy never taught,* my mother liked to say.

There were a few people smoking near the back door who moved aside as I came out, but no one else was at the end of the walk where he stood looking up at the light pollution tainting the sky. The air had dampened, and I cupped my elbows against the chill, stopping a few feet away from him beneath the nearest light pole. I cleared my throat. He turned and looked surprised to see me. For a second my simple thank-you evaporated.

I'd only gotten a vague sense of him earlier, given my state, but he was good looking in a classic kind of way. Like the men in fifties movies who always wore trench coats and fedoras. His hair was parted on the side and swept over. His eyes were very dark in the low light.

He smiled when we just stood there looking at each other. "Feeling better?"

I found my voice. "Much. Thank you."

"You're welcome. I hope it wasn't too forward butting in like that. But I could see you were struggling a little."

"How did you—" I gestured.

"I had a roommate in college who had terrible anxiety attacks. I could see the signs after a while. Cold water always helped him."

"I'll remember that."

He nodded and turned back to look at the sky. I waited, but he said nothing further. No introduction, no conversation starter. He hadn't even asked me my name. I wavered. I'd thanked him. It would be so easy to just walk away and not look back. Nothing gained, nothing lost.

"I'm Imogen," I said finally.

"Lev Carmichael." He gestured upward. "It's a pity what light pollution does to the sky. You wouldn't think it's possible—for something people made to blot out the stars."

I took a couple of steps closer and studied the hazy glow above. "It's pretty in its own way, I guess."

He nodded after a moment. "Glass-half-full kind of person, huh?"

"I wouldn't say that."

"A realist, then."

"Yes. I suppose."

"Good thing to be in this town. Probably a requirement."

"What about you?"

"Me? I'm in politics—the glass is whatever it needs to be."

I laughed. "Are you in office or . . ."

"No, God no. Advising. How about you?"

For a second I considered lying to him. Strangely, because he seemed nice. "Risk assessment."

It was his turn to laugh. "So we do the same thing."

"You could say that."

He focused on me, and it was a little overwhelming. His gaze was intense, questioning. "So who dragged you here?"

"My friend. She works for Anson. How about you?"

"My boss."

"So neither of us are here of our own free will."

"If I was that guy talking to you earlier, I'd say, 'We should both escape.'" Lev's eyes twinkled a little. "I think instead I'll just give you my card. Don't worry, I won't watch to see if you toss it before you leave." He pulled a business card from his pocket and handed it to me. Then gave me one more smile and walked away.

I watched him go, tapping the card against my knuckles. He was good to his word—I never caught sight of him again before April and I left. As we drove away from the party, I looked out the car's window at the sky. On the edge of the light pollution, a single star burned in the east.

Imogen

I stood staring at the empty balcony, waiting to wake up.

It hadn't happened. This was a dream. A nightmare. I was asleep. If I went around the wall into the bedroom, Lev and I would be there, lying close in each other's arms. We had to be.

I crossed the balcony to the railing and looked down.

Darkness.

Endless black water far below. Nothing else. No lights on the balconies underneath ours. No shouts of alarm. I tried saying his name. Tried screaming it, but nothing came out. I couldn't even open my mouth. My hands were claws, locked around the railing. The hands that had pushed him. I saw Lev tipping over the side again, heard the horribly soft sound of his head clipping the balcony before he fell out of sight.

No. No. No no no no no no.

My legs buckled.

I sagged down to the cold wetness of the balcony and sat there, pulse hammering so hard behind my eyes, it felt as if my heart were there instead of in my chest.

I'd pushed him. Pushed my husband overboard.

A thousand thoughts flooded my mind.

I needed to call someone. Stop the ship. They could send out boats to find him. Save him. Bring him back. Or his body.

A quiet keening came from me, like wind in a hollow place. What if he was dead?

Of course he's dead. He hit his head and fell over sixty feet into the water. Live people scream if they fall. He didn't make a sound.

For the second time that night, I thought I was going to be sick. I had to move.

On my feet I swayed, a fear of falling overshadowed by the sudden idea of jumping. I could swim around in the dark water until I found him. Hold him until the sun came up, and then everything would be okay. He'd be okay. I'd be okay. We'd be okay. Together.

I noted I was in shock in a very detached way. It was like watching from inside a filmy bubble hovering somewhere over my shoulder. I bit down hard on the inside of my cheek, and the pain sharpened everything again as the taste of blood filled my mouth. How long had it been since he fell? A minute? Two? No, more. Time was slipping away from me. And how fast was the ship traveling? At full speed it would reach Athens by morning. Every second I stood there he was falling farther and farther behind.

My phone was on the table inside the door near the two glasses of champagne he'd poured. They were alien, something from another world and time. They were an accusation of what had happened.

What I'd done.

It took three tries to open the phone, and when the icons appeared I stared at them, not knowing what to do. I started to dial 911 but stopped. Where would the call go? What was the local emergency number? What would I say?

What would I say?

An accident. Lev had slipped. It was true. But *why* had he slipped?

My stomach lurched as the room tilted. For a second there was an urge to call my mother, a knee-jerk reaction, then it was swept aside. There had to be someone to notify on the ship. Yes, that was right. Someone here would know what to do. People fell overboard sometimes. There were contingencies and protocols. I fumbled the cell and it fell to the carpet. I picked it back up with numb fingers, then looked around the room for some kind of salvation.

There was a phone mounted in a small alcove between the bedroom and living area. A laminated card stood beside it listing different options. At the bottom was "Emergency, dial 9." I put a hand on the wall to steady myself as the room shifted again. Then I picked up the receiver, my finger hovering over the nine. Hovering. *Push it.*

Push it.

I didn't push it.

Seconds drew out, slow and agonizing. They elongated into minutes that leaped by. Each one put more and more distance between us. Between him and rescue. Between me and discovery. Because what if he was still alive? If he recovered and told everyone what had happened. How I'd acted and what I'd said. How erratic and *paranoid* I'd been. How he'd only been wanting to talk. How I'd pushed him.

And in that split moment where I was of two minds, in two places— the now and the what-if—I thought of what was behind the garden door. Remembered the knife and Marcus and what would happen if Lev was still alive. What everyone would find out. What would come next, because this wouldn't just be an accident.

It would be attempted murder.

But it *was* murder if he was still alive and I let him die.

I was no longer in front of the phone. The receiver was back in its cradle. I was across the room on the small couch. I felt drugged. Like my blood had thickened and barely circulated. My thoughts were shapeless things trapped in amber. I was cold. Paralyzed. With each heartbeat it became harder and harder to move. To do something. To do the right thing.

And the longer I waited the more suspicious it would look if someone had seen him fall.

But there were no alarms. No one called the room. No one came to the door. It was quiet. Peaceful.

I stared at the two glasses of champagne until they quit bubbling.

After a long time, the dark outside began to gray. Far off in the east the horizon reddened. I watched the sun emerge from the sea like something being born. Its light spilled over the water, washing it clean. Everything new and clean.

I came back to myself, still holding the phone, finger hovering over the nine button. Only seconds had actually passed, but I'd seen what the next hours and days carried if I did nothing.

I pushed the button and spoke to the person on the other end of the phone as calmly as possible. Told them what I could. Left out what I couldn't.

When I hung up, I took one of the champagne glasses to the railing and poured it out before putting it on the bedside table and waited for what came next.

Imogen

High on the hill, the Acropolis caught the late-afternoon sun and held it. It grew deeper and deeper red as the sun sank on the first day of my widowhood.

I sat at the little desk near the foot of the bed in the hotel room and stared out the window. Lev had wanted to save the Acropolis tour for our return so we wouldn't be hurried. In the months leading up to the honeymoon he'd been studying Greek, wanting to be able to say *please* and *thank you* and other generalities. It had been charming hearing him repeating certain phrases aloud after dinner in the evenings or on weekend afternoons. He'd approached the language with the same steady eagerness he employed for anything else that interested him, and I wasn't surprised to hear him rattling off whole sentences to waiters and cab drivers once we arrived in Athens.

Looking at the Acropolis, I recalled how his love of architecture and history had bubbled over when he'd first seen the hilltop ruins. I'd been mostly ambivalent about it, happy to spend a few days sightseeing at the tail end of our honeymoon if it pleased him.

Now I was the only one here.

The city below bustled. Faintly there were car horns and shouts. Music rising and falling away. I sat very still watching the light change, trying to let my mind go blank.

It was something Dr. Rogers had taught me. She'd insisted I call her Helen, but being in her office with framed diplomas on the walls, talking about my deepest personal issues and shining lights on the demons, made me always think of her as *Doctor*. It felt better that way. Having someone with a title in charge of the most delicate things in your life always did.

She told me the very best way to calm myself was to empty my mind. To not think of anything. It would be the most difficult thing I would ever learn in therapy because the mind isn't a naturally quiet place. It's a street corner in the busiest city in the world. All noise and movement and clamoring for attention. To still it all would be miraculous. She said to start small, let the thoughts come and go, and if I could achieve a full minute of calm, that was enough to begin with.

I closed my eyes and tried now for what felt like the hundredth time since the last person had left the room and my phone had finally fallen blessedly silent.

Breathe in. Hold. Breathe out. There is nothing but the breaths. Breathe in, hold, breathe out.

Except after a few inhales and exhales, the mantra became something else.

You pushed him. He fell. He died. You killed him.

From bride to widow in less than two weeks.

My eyes came open, blurry with tears, and the attempted solace crumbled. Everything after calling for help that morning rushed back, looping over itself in a sickening figure eight.

Less than thirty seconds after I'd hung up the phone in our suite, a voice came over the intercom repeating, "Oscar," which I learned later was code for a person overboard. Then the ship slowed and turned, swinging back toward the place where Lev had fallen. A brief announcement followed for everyone to stay calm. There was no need for alarm.

A half dozen cruise personnel came to the room to speak with me, all crowding too close. One of them, a tall, severe woman with graying hair at her temples, asked the questions and I answered.

No, I didn't see him fall.

I woke up when I heard him yell.
Yes, he'd been drinking.
No, I don't think he jumped.

All the while I kept expecting someone to accuse me. For one of them to know just by looking at me. It felt like it was written across my face. Floating in my eyes.

I did it. I pushed him.

But all I received was quiet comfort. An offer of food or water. A different room. Murmured sympathies. Assurances that everything would be all right.

But nothing would be all right ever again.

Now a helicopter cruised overhead in the direction of the sea. It was looking for Lev. Had to be. There had been a few gray-and-white coast guard ships heading out of the harbor when our cruise ship docked. The crew person assigned to me had said not to worry. They had a good indication of where Lev had gone in the water, and now that the sun was up, they'd be canvassing. Lots of people were coming to help. I'd nodded dumbly and felt my hands shove him again and again.

My phone lit up. *Mom.* I'd called her right after checking into the hotel, knowing she wouldn't be awake yet and her phone would be off. I'd left a message saying Lev had fallen from our ship and that I was dealing with the authorities and I'd call her again as soon as I could. This was her third or fourth attempt, but I couldn't talk to her now. Couldn't deal with the sound of her voice. How hysterical she'd be. Calling Lev's parents had been bad enough.

The Carmichaels were already on their way. They booked a flight as soon as Lev's mother got off the phone with me. She'd texted me their reservation details—they'd be landing in a few hours. I would have to face them—these two deeply endearing people closing in on their seventies who had adopted me almost the second Lev brought me home to meet them. Lev's mother always hugged me first whenever we saw them. Like her son could wait a moment while she made sure this odd and quiet woman he'd found felt loved and accepted. His father made it a point to ask me about my work and really listened when I talked. He also refilled my glass no matter what we were drinking and insisted on carrying our bags upstairs to Lev's old room when we came to stay.

I would have to look them in the eyes knowing I killed their only child.

The thought got me up out of the chair and pacing. The room was well furnished but not very large. Not big enough for my sorrow and guilt. I needed to be out on the street underneath the open sky. Needed to run until my lungs burned and my blood boiled away this feeling. Until I stopped seeing him tip and fall. Stopped hearing the awful sound his head made when it hit the balcony.

Okay, okay, okayokayokay. You're okay. It was an accident. You didn't mean for him to fall.

I froze in the center of the room. Outside, the city darkened.

How often are we really honest with ourselves? *About* ourselves. People are great at judging others, but not so much when looking in the mirror. It's easier to believe you're a good person. Incapable of certain acts. But we all have an ugly place deep inside that we're aware of. A place where we keep the worst aspects of ourselves we can't acknowledge. A place we ignore until it makes itself known.

I went to mine now.

How hard had I shoved him? Had there been any intention in that split second? What had I felt?

Betrayal. Sadness. *Rage.*

And was it shock that kept me from reaching out once he started to fall? Had it all happened too fast? Or had something else held me back? Had I seen him touching her hand again, seen them on the beach together in the rain?

The phone jangled me free of myself. Mom again. I silenced the call and went on the internet, finally searching for the things I'd held off on earlier.

Could a person survive a sixty-foot fall into water?

What was the water temperature of the Mediterranean this time of year?

How long before hypothermia set in?

None of it was good.

I checked the time. Lev had fallen more than twelve hours ago.

For a long moment the side of me that was all statistics and graphs, that assessed every possible threat and outcome of each decision, reared up. Not simply regarding the fading likelihood my husband was still alive, but also everything on my search history. It was what a woman desperate for hope would look up. Nothing incriminating. I made sure before setting the phone aside. Self-preservation can be a hideous thing.

The phone was ringing again.

I ignored it and sank to the edge of the bed. A husk. Something waiting to be filled. And I would be. Eventually. Soon Lev's parents would arrive, and a part of their suffering would seep into me. My mother's disappointment would take up residence somewhere too; it already had quite a bit of real estate. After that Lev's body would be found, or it wouldn't (many times people who fell overboard were never seen again, I learned) and there would be a funeral to plan—the bitter tedium of it would find a place within as well. The condolences, the support from April, the leave from work, the "healing" that was supposed to begin. I would absorb all of it and move forward from this moment that would redefine me.

And there would always be more emptiness to fill.

I was aware of time passing. The city lighting up. The room growing dark. More phone calls. But I was outside of it all too. Floating somewhere else. Weightless. The moon high above and then swallowed by clouds with gnashing teeth of lightning. Slowly I turned onto my stomach, and the salt water burned as I inhaled it.

A knock at the door snapped me free of the nightmare. There was a cry climbing up my throat I managed to choke back. I'd fallen asleep somehow. Facedown lying on my arm, which was all pins and needles as I crossed the room, trying and failing to mentally prepare myself to face Lev's parents.

Instead of Stacy and David Carmichael, it was the police officer who had escorted me to the hotel that morning. He was a short, blocky man named Kafatos with a dark mustache and sharp eyes. Eyes that had probably skewered a number of suspects to the wall during interrogations. They'd been soft around the edges whenever looking at me earlier in the day. Now they were narrowed.

"Mrs. Carmichael, you have not been answering your phone." His English was very good.

I looked over one shoulder at where I'd left my cell, still dazed. "Oh, I'm sorry. I think I must've fallen asleep."

"I see." He glanced around the room as if searching it for something damning, then brought his gaze back to mine.

Here it came.

He would tell me I was under arrest. Someone had come forward who'd seen me push Lev. They had surveillance footage somehow. Undeniable evidence. He would handcuff me and lead me away. Everyone would know what I'd done. Know I was a liar and a murderer. I'd spend the rest of my life in prison, and I deserved it.

"They have found your husband."

For a second it wouldn't process. "What?"

"Your husband. That is what the calls were about. Please, you can come with me. I will take you."

"Uh . . ." was all I managed, still trying to reconcile what he was telling me.

Lev was gone. *Dead.* All the terrible anticipation now confirmed. I would never speak to him again. Never touch him. Never see him.

Except that wasn't exactly true. This man was going to bring me to him. They would need me to identify his body. I would have to look at him. Look at what I'd done. I couldn't . . . couldn't . . .

I took a step back, my hand coming up to my throat, and I was intensely reminded of the first time Lev and I met. How I couldn't breathe. Everything old is new again.

Kafatos had stepped back to give me room to join him in the hall. Now he moved forward, taking one of my hands gently while shaking his head. "No, oh no, no, no, I'm sorry."

"I can't," I whispered.

"No, no, you see, a misunderstanding." His wince gradually became a smile. "It's okay. He is alive. They found your husband, and he is alive."

Imogen

My mother was a dancer.

Ballet had been her life. She'd had aspirations of dancing for one of the world-class companies, but had never quite made the cut. It wasn't spoken about in our household—mom being the only one who could bring up the subject. And even then she approached it from a gentle angle of nostalgia, not failure. She'd never fallen short, only chosen a different path.

I remember the first time seeing her in her leotard many years after she'd danced in any public capacity. She used to wear it while she practiced—it was her way of staying in shape. She had long limbs and a graceful curving neck and rhythm. That early image of her was still burned in my memory. How agile and beautiful she was when she did a grand jeté. How she seemed to float above the floor, her back arched, head up. How feminine she was. How I wanted to be her.

She enrolled me in ballet classes young, and I knew from the moment I walked into the studio I would never be able to do it. All the mirrors were constant reminders of how much shorter I was than the other students. How inflexible I was. The worst part of class was always near the end when my mother would come back from running her errands and watch from the doorway. I would feel the weight of her eyes on my every move, but when I'd look she would be watching the other girls, hands clasped as if she were praying. Maybe she was.

There were long, shameful car rides home in silence, replaying all of the moments when I'd fallen out of step, lost my balance, how the teacher had to spend so much more time explaining the movements to me. I was surrounded by grace I couldn't hope to imitate, much less embody.

I tried one day to tell her I wanted to quit. She was doing the dishes, looking out the bay window on the backyard, and she paused and listened when I started to speak. I was as honest as I could be while still not wanting to disappoint her. I knew her intentions had been to get me past the anxiety I'd suffered from most of my childhood, but dancing felt like a magnifying glass for my flaws. When I was finished, she swallowed, her throat bobbing twice before she spoke. *Nothing is easy in this world, Imogen. You have to work at something if you want it. No one will give it to you.*

She never looked at me.

The recital was scheduled for a Monday evening at the theater attached to the studio where we practiced. We'd done our last few rehearsals up on the stage, and to me it felt as if we were elevated a thousand feet in the air. I could imagine all the empty seats filled, blank faces watching as I stumbled and fell beneath the hot, bright lights. And the other girls would keep dancing around me as if I weren't there. I never felt like I was.

On the day of the recital I woke while the house was still cool and quiet and used a pair of scissors to pick the stitches loose on the shoulder of my leotard. My mother had exclaimed about how beautiful it was with its patterned sequins, how it would shine under the stage lights. I worked until the shoulder gaped like an open mouth, then rehung it where it had been behind my door. I went to school with a measure of relief growing inside me.

When I got home the leotard was hanging on a chair in the kitchen. The seam had been resewn. My mother couldn't thread a needle. She must have brought it to town and paid to have it done.

That night the theater was heavy with bodies and people breathing. I could feel it where I stood at the back of the line near the far end of the big draping curtains. We were all still safely out of sight of the audience that murmured like a storm just over the horizon. The teacher had put me last as if that would somehow make my ineptness less noticeable. If she'd had a heart, she would have explained to my mother I wasn't ready. I might never be.

When the time came to go on, the line started moving, and I stood where I was, unable to take a single step toward the stage that seemed to span for miles in a wasteland of black painted planking. The teacher was touching each girl on her shoulder as they went out. She wasn't looking at me. I turned and walked between another set of curtains and crouched in a footwell of a desk far backstage. There was no delay. The music began, and the other girls' slippers tapped the floor and there was the swish of their legs in their tights, and I was a ball, curling tighter and tighter, wishing I would get so small I would collapse in on myself like a star and disappear completely. Disappear from the feeling of my mother's eyes searching for me on the stage where she had been so comfortable and adored. Searching for me and finally watching the other girls while she wished one of them was her daughter instead.

Afterward I unfurled from my hiding place and considered running away. But then the teacher found me and said in a quiet voice to go change, that she would tell my mother I'd be out soon.

It had been one of the hardest things I'd ever done—going out into the mostly empty parking lot, my mom only a dark silhouette waiting in the car. Already simmering in her silent disappointment and the shame that would be my companion for days and weeks to come.

But it was nothing compared to stepping off the elevator in the hospital and seeing Lev's parents waiting at the end of the hall.

"Oh, honey," Lev's mother said, enveloping me in a hug I couldn't permit myself to return. She smelled of faint perfume and anxious sweat. "We're here now. Everything's going to be okay." David's hand rested heavily on my shoulder. He'd been crying, his eyes bloodshot and bagged. I stood in their embrace, taking comfort from them like a thief.

"How, how is—" I tried.

"He's got a concussion and he's sunburned, but they're saying he's doing really well," Stacy said, releasing me. "He's very strong. You know that."

He was alive. The relief was intoxicating. But it was tainted by knowing what was coming. How this would end.

"Is he awake? Has he said anything?" I asked.

"In and out of consciousness," David said, his voice rusty. "The doctors called as soon as we landed. We tried getting you but . . ."

"I think I passed out from exhaustion," I said lamely. It felt insufficient as an explanation. Then again nothing I said to them would matter soon. Not after Lev told them what happened. Why he'd fallen in the first place.

"Completely understandable. We were in to see him for a few minutes earlier, but he was sleeping," Stacy said, guiding me down the hall. Kafatos trailed us. He'd spoken intermittently on the ride to the hospital—upbeat at first, then quieter until he fell silent the last few blocks. I'd barely responded. He probably thought I was still in shock. Maybe I was. But mostly I was thinking about the handcuffs hanging from his belt and how they would feel closing over my wrists.

We went to the end of the hall and turned right at a set of doors. Beyond was a half-moon nurses' station with rooms fanning out behind it. Several women in scrubs looked up as we entered, and one holding a digital tablet came forward to introduce herself as Dr. Galanis.

"You are Imogen?" she said, shaking my limp hand with her strong one.

"Yes."

"He asked for you."

My heart lurched. It felt like it had come partially loose in my chest. "So he's awake?"

"He was sedated to do some tests but should be coming around soon. He said your name to the fisherman who found him." Galanis looked me dead in the eyes. "He's very, very lucky." She led us around the nurses' station to a room on the far left. It was well lit and spacious. A bank of windows gave a panorama of Athens's lights.

Lev lay in a bed in the center of the room.

My lungs hitched, refusing to inflate. Seeing him brought a new level of understanding that this was all very real. It was happening.

He was badly sunburned, his forehead and nose blistered. Thick, shiny balm had been applied to his cracked lips, and dark stitches crept from beneath his hair to his temple where he'd hit the balcony. His long legs stretched almost to the end of the bed, and the neck of his gown was open revealing sensors and wires dotting his chest.

Kafatos cleared his throat behind me, and it was only then I realized Lev's parents and the doctor had gone to his bedside while I'd remained in the doorway. I moved forward.

Closer up his skin was worse. It looked as if he'd been boiled. The flesh around the stitches was puffy and discolored. An IV snaked out from his forearm up to a bag of saline. An oblong machine on wheels blinked silently with his heart rate and other vitals.

My eyes clouded over. Seeing him like this, the suffering and damage I'd caused, was overwhelming. Something that could never be taken back. Never forgiven.

"From what we can tell he suffered a concussion in the fall," Galanis said. "The scans we did revealed no brain bleeds or major swelling, which are both very good things. The fact he's regained consciousness several times is encouraging as well. It mostly rules out the possibility of a coma." She pursed her lips. "There is the chance of a traumatic brain injury, but we won't know for sure until he wakes fully and we can run more tests."

Stacy and David had positioned themselves on either side of the bed and were each holding one of Lev's hands. David was crying again, tears leaking silently from beneath his glasses. A memory returned to me of visiting Lev's parents specifically to tell them we were engaged. They'd been overjoyed, and Stacy had gone to open some champagne. I'd helped her and while bringing a couple of glasses to the living room had walked in on David embracing Lev tightly. Lev had to bend slightly at the waist to hug his father back. *I'm so damn proud of you, son,* David said, and kissed him on the cheek. It had maybe been the sweetest thing I'd ever seen. David had been crying then too.

"Here, honey, come here," Stacy said, scooting down the bed to make room for me. I moved forward on legs that didn't feel fully attached and braced myself on the bed's frame. He was so close. I could smell him. He still carried his own scent even after a dozen hours in the sea and amid eye-watering disinfectant. A warm masculine smell I'd burrowed into many nights in our bed.

"Physical contact is good. It lets him know you're here," Galanis said. She was staring at me. I took one of Lev's hands. It was rough and dry.

"I'm—" My voice came out in a croak. I cleared my throat. "I'm here." His corneas were outlined beneath the thin skin of his eyelids. They moved back and forth, ticking at the sound of my voice. His fingers tightened on mine.

Oh God.

Lev inhaled deeply.

"Great, that's great," Galanis was saying.

"Son, can you hear us? We're right here," David said. Lev turned his head toward his father's voice.

I wanted to run. It felt like stepping off a cliff. There was nowhere to go but down.

Lev's eyelids became slits. He blinked. Those dark hazel eyes appearing and disappearing. Reappearing.

He was awake.

"Lev? Lev, honey," Stacy said, leaning over him. "Can you hear me?"

Lev blinked some more. Closed his eyes, his forehead wrinkling. His cracked lips parted. "Wa-er."

"Water, water, okay!" Stacy laughed through tears. Her hands shook as she took a water cup with a straw from Galanis and held it to Lev's lips. He drank with his eyes closed. Long sips. He was still holding my hand but hadn't looked at me yet. Any second he would, and everything would change.

When he was done drinking, he opened his eyes again, and Galanis moved in beside David. "Lev, I'm Dr. Galanis. I've been looking after you. You had a fall from your ship and were in the water for a while." Lev squinted at her, and she glanced at his vital signs on the monitor. "You can hear me okay?"

Lev nodded. "Hurts."

"Yes, you were injured. But we're giving you something for the pain. You can have more soon, but there are some people here to see you."

David leaned over the bed again. "Hey, son, you're gonna be okay. Everything's okay."

"Do you know who this is?" Galanis asked.

Lev nodded again. "Dad."

"Good, very good. And how about this beautiful lady over here?" Stacy grinned and swiped at her eyes with the back of her hand.

"Mom."

"That's right, very good, and there's someone holding your hand. Do you know who she is?"

My heart thundered. Blood roared in my ears. Slowly Lev's eyes tracked from his mother to me. I tried to smile but it died on my face. I waited, Kafatos's presence like the heat of a furnace on the back of my neck.

Lev squinted. A shadow passed behind his gaze.

Confusion, then recognition.

His hand tightened. Squeezed. There was an almost overwhelming physical urge to pull away.

A smile tugged at the corner of his cracked lips.

"My fiancée."

Imogen

"Post-traumatic amnesia."

We were in Galanis's office down the hall from the intensive-care unit where Lev lay. It was small and cluttered but had a window with a good view of the Acropolis. The hospital was on the opposite side of my hotel, and the Parthenon glowed like a prison on fire.

"Okay, and that means . . ." Stacy said. I sat between her and David. There had only been two chairs in the office when we came in, and Galanis had dragged in a small folding chair for me, apologizing all the while. I shifted against the freezing steel uncomfortably. It must've been stored somewhere cold.

"At times memory loss occurs with a traumatic brain injury." Galanis held up a hand as David started to speak. "I'm not saying Lev has suffered such a thing, but it tracks with the incident and his symptoms."

The incident.

I kept replaying the last minutes we'd spent in his hospital room. How it slowly became clear to us all Lev didn't recall what had transpired on the ship. Beyond that he didn't remember the ship at all, our honeymoon, our wedding, or really the last six months of our lives together. He knew he'd proposed to me, but couldn't remember when or where. He knew we'd bought a house, but didn't know what it looked like. Beyond that—nothing. His memory as smooth and clean as an amputation.

"If he has this, this traumatic brain injury, what are some of the other—um, problems?" Stacy asked.

"A vast range of symptoms. There are cognitive issues like loss of speech and the ability to understand or retain information. He may have vision problems or motor dysfunction. Headaches, balance issues . . . many, many things can be affected."

"Oh God," Stacy said, sitting back in her chair. One hand clutched at her throat.

"This is not to say he will have all of them or none. It's to be aware of. So far he has feeling and movement in his limbs, he has retained his long-term memories, and his comprehension and speech patterns seem normal. All great signs."

"The amnesia," I finally said. I hadn't spoken more than a few words since entering the office, floating on a new type of shock. I wasn't going to be accused and arrested. I wasn't going to jail. At least not tonight. "Is it permanent? What can we expect going forward?"

"Usually it is very temporary," Galanis said. My stomach slithered sickeningly. "Many times people will begin to recall memories within a few hours of regaining consciousness. That's the best prognosis. But it might take longer depending on the severity of injury." A crease formed between the doctor's eyes. "What is concerning is how much of his memory is missing. Normally with this type of amnesia, the event itself or just prior to it is blocked out. Upon waking there is confusion, and the person has trouble forming new memories for a short period. But with Lev it has stretched back much further." She slid into deeper thought for a moment, then reemerged. "Again, we don't know anything for certain. The fact that Lev isn't confused about his surroundings and is accepting what happened to him is another plus."

"I want to talk about how this happened," David said. His vulnerability had retreated, and an amount of steel had returned to his voice. "Is this a type of situation we should be retaining counsel for? I mean, Imogen said it had rained and the balcony was slick. That's a liability, for sure."

"I can't really speak to anything of that nature," Galanis said. "But there are some things to consider."

"Such as?" Stacy asked.

"Like if this wasn't an accident."

I flinched and Stacy rested a hand on my arm. "What do you mean?" David asked.

"Given Lev's height and how low the banister was, this very well could be an accident. But let me ask all of you, has there been any indication Lev might've been depressed lately? Disturbed in any way?"

It took a moment for the implications to settle in, but when they did, David and Stacy both drew back from the doctor. "Absolutely not," Stacy said.

"Our son is not suicidal," David added, tapping the desk with one finger to emphasize the last word.

Galanis held up her hands. "This is nothing to bristle at. I wouldn't be doing my job if I didn't ask."

"It's not even a possibility," Stacy said. "Tell her, Imogen."

"No," I said. "He's not suicidal."

"How about drinking? I was told you both had been drinking heavily, and his bloodwork supports this."

"Well, yes," I said. There was dangerous territory ahead. Pitfalls I might not see until I stepped into them. I had to be very careful. "We were. But it was our honeymoon."

"Does Lev drink to excess on a regular basis?"

David made a sound of disgust and crossed his arms. I shook my head. "No. He'll have a couple drinks a week, maybe. A night out once in a while, but nothing major."

Galanis watched us, and I was reminded of Kafatos and his knifepoint gaze. The doctor had her own way of looking at people that was equally unsettling. In another life they might've been partners. "Talking about these things is not an affront to Lev's character. It is addressing potential symptoms of a greater problem. It is common for family to dismiss ideas like this, but no one is served by misleading me or yourselves, least of all Lev. Just because he doesn't remember the last six months doesn't mean an underlying issue won't reemerge."

"We're being honest with you," Stacy said. "We all love him and want what's best for him, but I think we all agree this was just a horrible accident."

"Imogen, tell us again what happened," David said.

I looked down at the cheaply carpeted floor. Licked my lips. "Lev stayed up when I went to bed. I was tired and . . . a little drunk. I think he might've gone down to the casino for a while." I swallowed audibly. "His yell was what woke me."

"And you don't recall anything else?" Galanis asked. She had leaned forward, her elbows planted on her desk.

"No. It took me a minute to wake up and realize what had happened—what I thought happened. I wasn't a hundred percent sure he'd fallen, but I didn't want to take the chance."

"Your quick thinking saved him," Stacy said, squeezing my arm, and I relived the moment in our suite where I considered doing nothing. Where I almost sat and watched the horizon gray and the sun rise and let him die.

We went over several more points—how long Lev would have to stay for observation (at least a few days), what the cost would be since we were outside the US (shockingly little), and what to expect going forward.

"Memory islands are very common with amnesia," Galanis said as our meeting was winding down. We'd been in her office for nearly half an hour, and she'd just answered a page saying she needed to get back to rounds. "Snapshots of certain experiences or places will suddenly return full force. Encouraging these and doing routine things will help spur more memories. Familiarity is your friend here, so do the usual things in your life. You'll be surprised how much will come back."

As we were thanking her and exiting the office, she must have seen something in my expression because she asked me to wait a moment while David and Stacy returned to Lev's room. My heart, having finally settled into its normal cadence, sped back up.

"I know you're frightened and worried," she said as we stood in her doorway. She held up a slender hand with a noticeable tan line on her ring finger. "But from one newlywed to another, please take heart. It could have been so much worse. Not many people come through like your husband. And even though his memory's been affected, at least you have your relationship to lean on and guide you. Besides, he already remembers the most important thing in the world."

"What's that?"

She gave me a smile. "That he loves you."

Sierra

I think he loves me.

That's a problem. It wasn't supposed to be this way. I made a promise to myself it would never happen again. It's too much risk. Too frightening to consider giving myself over to another person. But there's time, and there's longing, and I'm a human being with needs. Things happen even if we don't mean them to.

He looks at me sometimes like he can see the past through my eyes. As if he were stargazing. Like if he looks long and hard enough, he'll know everything about me. Where I came from. What I've done. Who I was.

I turn away then. And that's okay. He doesn't complain. I appreciate that about him. His quiet acceptance of what is. He hasn't asked anything of me. Not yet.

Now, in the earliest morning light, I sit up in bed and trace the muscles in his back with my eyes. Listen to him breathe. Savor the heat he gives off.

Steadfast is how I'd describe him. *Composed.* He never seems to be afraid of anything. And that's good too.

I'm afraid enough for both of us.

Imogen

For a split second as we pulled into it, our neighborhood was completely alien, and I wondered if everything wasn't actually reversed. If I was the one who'd lost my memory instead of Lev.

We'd been gone a total of sixteen days, which was only two more than planned, but it felt like a lifetime. The yards and homes lining the street leading to our cul-de-sac looked artificial, like stage fronts erected in place of the real thing while we'd been absent. A man was mowing his lawn and waved. He could've been an actor. A line of cars along the street in front of a garage sale. They could've been props.

I glanced at Lev, who sat in the passenger seat beside me. He was looking out the window, taking everything in. He hadn't said much since leaving the beltway, growing quieter the closer we got to home. His sunburn had begun to peel in places, and it molted onto his clothes. There was a large fleck on his collar I wanted desperately to brush away, but it would remind him of my presence, and he would look at me, and since he'd woken in the hospital, I'd found it harder and harder to hold his gaze for any length of time. I would feel myself shrinking, and if only it were true, then I could dwindle away until I was safe and unnoticeable.

Now, as we pulled around the last corner and our house came into view, I watched for a reaction. Nothing. He didn't move at all.

I pulled into the driveway and stopped before the double garage doors and turned the car off. Lev leaned forward to look up through the windshield. "So this is it?"

"Yeah. Does anything look familiar?"

His brow furrowed. "No. Not yet. Sorry." He'd been apologizing a lot since waking in the hospital, and each time it was an ice pick through my center.

"Don't apologize. It's fine. Here, let me give you the grand tour of the neighborhood." I turned a little in my seat and pointed at the low single story directly across the street. "That's the Millers'. Mrs. Miller is eighty and has advanced dementia. Her son's family lives with her now and takes care of her. They're good people. The places on either side of them we've only met once . . . and I can't remember their names."

"That makes two of us," Lev murmured.

A laugh escaped me and I faced forward again. "On the left of our place we have Steve and Tasha Benson. We hang out with them sometimes, and you go golfing with Steve."

"I golf?"

My mouth hung open, and I blinked for a second before a smile slowly quirked the corner of his lips.

"Asshole!"

"Sorry. Couldn't resist. Hey, if you can't have a little fun with a head injury, what's the point?"

I sighed and gestured at the house to the right of ours. "This is Val and Deshawn Williams. They're transplants from Brooklyn. They moved in right before us. You and Deshawn have beers pretty regularly in the backyard. But . . ."

"What?"

"You don't really like Val."

"Why?"

"You think she's a snoop."

"Is she?"

"A little. But she means well. And she's fun. She likes wine."

He was quiet for a moment. "Maybe we'll get along better this time. Fresh start, right?"

Fresh start. God.

"Let's get inside," I said.

———

Our house was a tidy two story with deep-green siding and white trim. There were accents of natural wood here and there on the exterior, like the large posts supporting the front porch. It sat on almost a full acre with a hedge on either side of the backyard hemming off the bordering properties.

When we stepped inside carrying our bags, something unlocked inside me, and a little of the coiled tension I'd carried since the night on the ship released. Home. This was home.

The spacious foyer I'd decorated meticulously to feel especially welcoming. The rugs and framed painting of a Nantucket beach above an ornate side table with its jar of sand dollars. The stairs going up to the second floor and its three rooms above. The kitchen's openness and gleaming surfaces straight ahead. A small parlor and bathroom to the right. The living room off the kitchen where we spent many nights curled in front of the fireplace or TV. The back deck overlooking a sloping yard and the mature trees beyond.

It was perfect.

I'd told Lev so the day we first saw it. He'd suggested house hunting out of the blue one morning. We'd been at my apartment and he'd slept over as had become the usual after meeting at the party nearly eighteen months prior and beginning a relationship that moved slowly at first, then plunged ahead like a roller coaster on its initial descent. We were lounging in the afterglow of an early lovemaking session when he brought up real estate.

"Why now?" I asked, playing with a coil of dark hair on his chest.

"Wouldn't it be nice to own something?"

"You mean together?"

"Why not?"

I stiffened a little, glad he wasn't looking at me. He might've seen me wince. "I mean, it's a huge step." To say I was terrified would've been like saying Everest was a steep hill. But everything about our relationship had frightened me to that point. Its whirlwind speed. How much time each day I spent thinking about him when we were apart. How utterly perfect things had been between us. All of it was too smooth. Too *right*.

And now this.

"Wouldn't it make sense to move in to either yours or mine first?" I asked. Even that level of commitment was alarming. It was another landmark on the road toward a destination I'd been to before. An exciting city skyline on the horizon with so much activity and adventure and *potential*. No one mentions that the city can be a veneer for something already old and crumbling in its foundations. No one says love can be haunted.

"They're both too small," he said, rolling toward me. "We need more space, don't you think?"

"I don't know."

"Picture it," he said, his hand trailing up my thigh. "Somewhere a little farther outside the city. I'd trade another ten minutes commuting for a quiet spot." His fingers began to move in time with his words. "Somewhere really quaint. A nice place with neighbors, but not too close. Maybe an actual yard." The picture he was painting was there, but it kept blurring around the edges with the insistent pleasure of his hand as my breathing quickened. "A front porch where we could sit in the evenings. Can you see it?"

"Yes."

"And flower beds along the side of the house?" His hand moved faster.

"Yes. *Yes.*"

"We could host our neighbors and they'd become good friends." His voice dropped to a whisper. "I could grill on the back porch, and we could have a place that was just for us, just for the two of us together. Do you want that, Imogen? Do you want it?"

I answered by pulling him on top of me and telling him yes. Over and over and over.

The second house the realtor had shown us had been this one. I'd felt a tingle of anticipation going up the walk and opening the large front door with its three little windows. Something akin to a key sliding into a lock. Knowing all the tumblers will turn smoothly.

I still felt it now even carrying this new heaviness. There was something about coming home that made everything better. A little easier to bear.

I dragged some of our luggage to the base of the stairs and turned back to retrieve more from the car, but Lev was standing in the way. He was stock-still, eyes unfocused, staring at a place on the floor.

"Hey, you okay?" When he didn't answer, a Klaxon began blaring in my mind. He was having a stroke. A delayed aneurysm. Hemorrhaging internally. The process I'd started on the ship's balcony would be finished here in the foyer of our home. But just as quickly Galanis's parting words from the day Lev was discharged came back.

You may notice some strange things. He might experience bouts of confusion or fugues. Just be aware and don't panic. It may be a memory island emerging from the fog. Don't push, let him remember on his own. More will return without interfering.

I bit back another question and stayed as still as I could, watching for anything concerning. After a few seconds his gaze came up to mine.

"Here," he said, pointing at the rug we stood on. "I proposed right here."

"That's right." I felt a little lightheaded. Like I'd drunk a full glass of wine straight down.

"We were . . ." He looked up again. "We were house hunting. You said you loved this place. You said it was perfect."

I nodded, my throat tightening. "We were standing here, and when I turned around you were down on one knee."

"I remember," he said, and hugged me so tightly it bordered on painful. I wondered if he recalled how I froze seeing him kneeling there with the ring offered up to me. Like it was a sacrifice. His love on an altar. I wondered if our memories mended themselves into something better if we needed them to.

We stood that way for a time. The front door open to the street so any passersby could see us if they looked in. Our silent house around us bearing witness. "Don't worry," he said into my ear as we swayed together. "It'll all come back."

Imogen

People can get used to anything.

It was one of my father's few observations that stuck with me. He was a quiet man with average looks and slightly above average intelligence who started out working at a branch of a local bank as a teller and moved up through the ranks until he was a manager. By the time I brought Lev home to meet him and Mom, he was a multibranch manager but would rise no higher than that. The next step up was to be an owner, and my father never owned anything outside of a house and a car. When his shift at work ended and he came home, *he* was owned.

"He's mom's hood ornament," my brother, Charlie, said one time when we were home visiting from college. Charlie was a year younger and cavalier in a way that annoyed and inspired me. He was at ease with anyone anywhere. He and worry never shared the same zip code. Nothing rattled him. Not grades or girls or even our mother.

"Jesus, they're right there," I whispered, pointing to the living room doorway where Mom and Dad had retired to watch TV after dinner. Charlie shrugged and dealt a new hand of the card game we were halfheartedly playing.

"Did you see how she shut him down when he mentioned wanting to go somewhere other than Oahu?"

Of course I had. Mom's dominance in their marriage was established like laws of physics. She was the center of their relationship. Dad orbited her. It was also so ordinary we barely noticed anymore. And if we did it was to comment on it like we were now. Like pedestrians shaking their heads and saying *what a shame* while passing an accident.

I fanned my hand out and made a quick assessment. Go for the straight or keep the two pair? I kept the two pair. Played it safe.

"I keep thinking someday he's just gonna snap," Charlie murmured. "Murder-suicide. Boom, boom. It'll be the most assertive thing he's ever done."

"Will you shut the fuck up?" I said, which made him laugh. He always laughed when I swore. He said I couldn't cuss with any kind of authenticity.

"He would have to kill her to get her to respect him."

I refused to engage and focused on the cards. It was the only way to deter him. "Two pair," I said, laying down my hand.

"Nice." He flopped down three aces and grinned, waiting for a reaction. When I said nothing and started to shuffle, he sat back and said, "Ah, the Dad response. No complaints, just compliance."

My brother wasn't wrong. I shared a weary kinship with our father despite trying to shed my subordinance like an ill-fitting skin. I understood him. Understood how easy it was to get caught in the crucibles of other people a little too long, to become soft and misshapen. *Malleable.* That didn't stop me from resenting him. From wanting him to finally stand up to mom. Stand for something. But instead he only plodded on and acclimated.

People can get used to anything.

I was so afraid he was right.

———

Lev and I got used to our new routine.

The first few days at home were deeply strange. We should have been relishing in the warmth of our commitments. Should have been settling into our new roles of husband and wife. The new us. I'd dreamed about it when I was little. How I would be when I was a wife like my mother. How I would enter the chrysalis of marriage as me and emerge as something else. I'd always wondered how marriage changes people. Because it was apparent it did. Two become one, and from that point they are bound together. Better or worse. But how does the change happen? Is it all at once or gradual?

Lev and I were both changed. Irrevocably.

The realization of what I'd done kept sideswiping me. I would forget. Never for long at first, only minutes. I'd be doing some mundane chore around the house and it wouldn't be there. I'd be this normal person just home from her honeymoon and doing laundry or taking Mox for a walk, then it would all come rushing back, and the guilt would surge through me like a brain-searing fever. The Klonopin I used to take regularly for anxiety would call to me then from the medicine cabinet. It had been months since I'd had any; I hated the way it dimmed my view of the world. But when I considered that the man sitting in the living room or across the table had almost died because of me, the lure of the pills was strong. And with the protective layer of shock worn off, it felt too large to grasp.

When those moments came, I overcompensated by checking on him. I'd taken an extra week off work, and Lev's boss had told him to take as much time as he needed, so we were both home all day. I watched closely to make sure he wasn't going to tip over getting out of bed or lose his balance in the shower. After a few times of him catching me lingering outside the bathroom door, he took me by the shoulders and said he didn't need a second shadow. To stop worrying. I needed to get back to normal. We both did.

———

I returned to work on a Friday. Easier that way since I could reestablish myself while having the escape hatch of the weekend only hours away. My coworkers were thrilled to see me. The boss, Mr. Stanford, bought me lunch and we ate in his office. He was a balding man in his late sixties with a fringe of shockingly white hair around his pate and soft eyes of fading blue. He told me how good it was to have me back and if there was anything I needed, *we* needed, to just let him know.

My office was in one corner of the building SMS leased, an open space with high ceilings and tall windows. It felt like it belonged to someone else now. The me from before. The woman rising fast through the company with a wonderful fiancé and a nice new home. The person who was always telling herself it was finally going to be okay. That she could quit walking on eggshells and waiting for the other shoe to drop.

There were dozens of emails piled up in my inbox. A new corporate assignment dealing with a major low-income housing project. It would be one of the firm's largest clients and my biggest project yet. After the first half hour of reviewing the development details, they all started running together, blurring until the words and letters themselves didn't make sense. I checked in with Lev. He was fine. How was the first day back? Great! We discussed dinner. More trivialities. Nothings in the life of a married couple.

When I got off the phone, I sat looking out one of the big windows, listening to the idle cubicle chatter on the main floor. There was a big oak outside I adored watching turn in the fall. It was still mostly green, but some of the leaves were beginning to yellow. Most people think frost kills the leaves and that's why they change, but in truth the cooler nights signal the tree to stop chlorophyll production, and the other colors start to shine through.

Because those yellows and oranges and reds are always there behind the green. Just waiting for the right moment to reveal themselves.

I didn't really recall opening the internet browser or logging on to my Facebook page. I never checked social media at work since I didn't frequent the sites much outside it. But then my fingers were typing, and the Argyros page was there glowing on the screen. Seeing the restaurant's gleaming white patio, the chairs and tables filled with relaxing diners, gave my stomach a lurch.

What was I doing?

Picking at a wound that hadn't even scabbed over yet. One that still bled freely. I scrolled down through the posts and pictures, flitting over them like a skittish bird until one stopped me with another unpleasant tilting in my center.

There she was.

As young and beautiful as the day at lunch. In the picture she was standing in a line with her other coworkers, all of them smiling. She was petite with glossy black hair and dazzling white teeth I couldn't get out of my head. Everyone in the photo was tagged in the caption below.

Lyra Markos.

Now there was a name to go with the face of the woman Lev had slept with on our honeymoon.

You don't know that for sure. You never saw if it was him on the beach.

Right. I didn't know. Wouldn't ever know because Lev couldn't tell me. But would he even if he could? And the real question was, did it matter?

I sat back in the chair, not really seeing the office walls anymore. If Lev didn't remember being unfaithful and I couldn't prove it, did that really mean it happened? It was the old question of the tree falling in the woods with no one around. I'd always thought that it made a sound but with no one to hear, it didn't matter.

It didn't matter.

I considered the days and months and years ahead. Flicked through the eventual thought processes and emotions that would accompany letting it all go. Actions and reactions. All potential outcomes. Would our marriage survive? Could I let his possible betrayal go since he'd already suffered more than he deserved? Since he almost died by my hand?

My door cracked open, and Dan, one of the other project managers, poked his head in. "Wonderful to see you in here," he said.

"Thanks. Good to be back."

"Have a great weekend."

"You too." He flapped a hand at me and was gone. I looked at the clock. The afternoon had completely slipped away.

It was time to go home.

Imogen

"There was a cat in the flower beds today."

I looked up from my plate. Lev was staring wistfully out the dining room window, a finger tracing the edge of the laceration on his temple. The bruising had faded in the days since coming home. The sunburn was mostly healed and had mellowed to a deep tan. He looked like any vacationer newly returned from somewhere warm—relaxed and healthy.

"A cat?" I said. We hadn't spoken much since I'd arrived home, both of us reacclimating to the ritual of the suburban workday.

"Yeah. A big tabby."

"Oh. What was it doing?"

He looked at me. "Shitting."

I laughed and started eating again.

"What? It was."

"No, I believe you." Lev frowned and I hid a smile behind my hand.

The cat's name was Stripes, and she belonged to Mrs. Miller across the street. I didn't tell him the cat had been named by one of Mrs. Miller's granddaughters and given to her several years back as a companion. *It's supposed to be good for people with dementia,* her son Ray told me one evening as his mother sat in her typical spot in the yard, nestled beneath blankets in the wheelchair she never left now. *The connection to an animal and petting it and whatnot. She loves her, but I don't think it's really helped that much.* I didn't tell Lev that Mrs. Miller liked to sit with Stripes on her lap and stroke her wide head with one hand as she stared at whatever passed for her reality these days. I didn't tell him our flower beds were Stripes's absolute favorite place to relieve herself. And I didn't tell Lev it had driven him mad every time he saw the tabby squatting and pawing in the soft dirt between our azaleas.

It's okay to forget some things.

"Your mom texted me this afternoon," Lev said between bites.

"I know. She called me too." Talking to Mom was a like a fencing match where I always felt like I'd forgotten some crucial piece of protective gear.

"She mentioned coming over this weekend."

"Yeah, I'm sorry. I told her it wasn't a good time. Maybe in a few weeks or something."

Lev chewed thoughtfully. "They've never been here, right?"

I'd gotten used to questions like this since the honeymoon. *I've met her before, haven't I? We keep all the laundry baskets in the closet, right?* These moments of uncertainty I'd caused. "No, they haven't. We were waiting to get totally moved in before a housewarming."

Lev looked around. "Are we going to get *more* moved in?"

"There were a few things I wanted to do. The guest bath needs new mats, and the back deck really should be restained. Plus the—" He quieted me by putting a hand over mine.

"She's going to have to see it sometime."

I withered internally. Lev had picked up on the flux between my mother and me almost instantly. He hadn't asked where it started, and I don't know if I could've told him. It seemed from birth there had always been a set of standards waiting at every stage of my life I never failed to fall short of.

Mox padded over and did an under-table inspection for any dropped food, then sat beside my chair, waiting expectantly. I gave him half a carrot he trotted away with. "I don't know, it's not a lot of notice. She wants Charlie and Beth and the kids to come, and April would kill me if she found out we had a get together and she wasn't invited. And with everything . . ." I trailed off, half gesturing at the house and him.

"It might be really good. I mean, the doctor said the more familiar things we can do the better. So spending time around people who know us might kick something loose."

I took a drink from my wineglass, but the chardonnay refused to go down. It sat burning at the back of my throat, climbing up my sinuses until it felt like I was drowning. Finally it seeped downward, and I was able to speak.

"Sure," I said. "Okay."

———

All of Saturday and most of Sunday morning were spent in a hallucinatory frenzy of cleaning and organizing. Anything I hadn't found a place for was hauled out to the garage or stuffed in a closet. Lev helped whenever I asked, constantly telling me the house looked great and not to worry. It was just a housewarming, no big deal. But men never seemed to grasp the judgment associated with the state of the home. It didn't matter if you were a CEO or a stay-at-home mom, the house was still considered a woman's domain. And whether it was passive-aggressive comments (my mother), or silently noted, there was always an underlying verdict being reached. As if a woman's housekeeping was a direct representation of her inner character.

Around three on Sunday afternoon people started arriving, April being the first. She'd already been by a couple of times in the prior months and beelined to the bathroom, throwing a complaint over one shoulder about traffic. Next came my brother, Charlie, and his family. Charlie met his wife, Beth, in graduate school, and two years later they were married. A year after that he landed a position at Georgetown teaching literature, and Beth gave birth to their first boy, Henry. Shortly afterward Nathan came along, and Beth's aspirations of her own biochemistry lab evaporated from the heat of motherhood.

The boys streamed past me into the house yelling, "Hi, Aunty Immy!" in unison, and were out of sight with Mox bounding after them even as Charlie stepped inside and hugged me.

"Great neighborhood, sis," he said.

"Yeah, so many trees," Beth said, kissing me on the cheek. My brother and his wife looked like counterparts forged from the same mold. They shared hair and eye color and had been repeatedly mistaken for brother and sister, which weirded me out a little. Even their wardrobes had started to complement one another, and I wondered if it was purposeful or another inevitable blending of a long-term relationship.

"Chewy!" Lev called from the kitchen, and my brother hustled past me to join him.

"They're pretty cute together," Beth said, glancing around the foyer, her eyes playing over my careful arrangements. "I'd be worried if we weren't all married."

I smiled and ushered her into the kitchen where Lev was setting up drinks and hors d'oeuvres. April had already parked herself at the counter with a scotch and soda as she scrolled on her phone. She gave me a quick look and I nodded. *I'm good. Everything's okay.*

The doorbell rang.

"Oh shit, get ready, sis!" Charlie called. "Momikaze incoming!" Beth swatted him as I left the room.

Mom and Dad stood on the front porch when I opened the door. Dad was dressed casually in a pair of brown slacks and dark polo looking all of the aging bank manager he was while Mom wore a sleek sleeveless dress and a shawl along with a matching handbag. She'd cut and colored her hair since the last time I'd seen her, and it swept down in an elegant bob ending just below her chin. She was nearing sixty but could've easily passed for a decade younger.

"Darling!" She swept me into a hug, then held me at arm's length. "You look so tired. I hope you didn't fuss."

"Not at all."

"Hi, honey," Dad said, embracing me with his patented one-arm hug. "Looks like the place has great bones. Good curb appeal too. Hope you didn't pay too much."

"Everyone's in the kitchen," I said.

I stood alone in the entry, pretending to tidy the small table there and arrange everyone's shoes while they chattered away in the next room. Lev was holding court, his voice carrying enough for me to hear every word, but when I realized he was talking about his injuries and the mental blankness of the last six months, I quit listening.

It could happen at any second.

A familiar voice or gesture might bring it all back. Maybe the taste or smell of the food or liquor. The play of light on the floor. Maybe someone's touch on his arm or shoulder. It was hard to say what would trip the land mine in our life.

I took a deep breath and went to join the party.

Imogen

"Everything's delicious, sis," Charlie said around a mouthful of food.

We sat at the dining room table, midway through the meal I'd hastily thrown together with ingredients I'd had on hand. There'd been no time to go shopping.

"Thanks," I said. Charlie gave me a wink and tucked back into his chicken salad. My brother could be completely over the top, but he'd always been able to take my edges off whenever I got overwhelmed. Especially when Mom was involved.

"So, Lev," she said now, taking a sip from her wine. She'd barely touched the entrée. "Tell us about Congressman Webber. How's the campaign coming?"

"Well, good, actually. Since the senate-run announcement, polling's been strong. So far all the early indications are pointing in the right direction."

Mom leaned forward. "Exciting! And so fascinating, what you do. I mean, I wouldn't even know where to begin trying to get someone into higher office."

"It's really just reading people and timing. Knowing what the constituents want when they want it." Lev went back to buttering a dinner roll.

"Will it be hard catching up now with your condition?"

"Mom . . ." I said.

"I'm just asking, I mean we already addressed the elephant in the room. No secrets with family is what my mother always said."

"Grandma also said the moon landing wasn't real, so . . ." Charlie raised his eyebrows and shrugged. "Just saying." April laughed into her napkin.

"Charles, please."

"Um, it's been a little rough," Lev interjected. "But my team's been great about keeping me up on everything, and my beautiful wife's been so attentive. That's made all the difference in the world." He squeezed my hand and I smiled tightly.

"Well, that's what spouses are for, right?" Mom said. "I mean, where would we be if we didn't support one another. Right, Ted?"

My father looked up from his plate like he'd been ambushed. "Um, right."

"I just think it's so soon for you to be working again."

"I'd go crazy if I didn't have something to occupy my mind. But working from home's been nice," Lev said.

Mom turned her sights on me. "And doing the same wasn't an option for you?"

"Not really, no."

"Well that's a little cold of them, don't you think?"

"Actually, Mr. Stanford's been very accommodating."

"So someone else could've kept doing your guesswork while you stayed home and looked after your husband?"

Guesswork. It was always how she referred to my profession. I didn't know if she didn't actually believe risks could be assessed and avoided if you stopped to take in all the available information, or if she couldn't imagine not blundering forward without caution toward her own interests.

April must've seen or sensed my hand tightening on my fork because she said, "Oh, I don't know, Cora, I think he's more of a modern man. You don't expect your wife to wait on you hand and foot, right, Lev?"

Lev's face colored a little. "Not at all. I'm fine, really. More and more is coming back each day, and Imogen's filled in all the gaps, so I don't really feel like I'm missing anything."

"We're all just so glad you're okay," Beth said, standing to attend to the boys, who were gradually spreading their dinner across the kitchen counter where they sat.

"That's the main thing," Charlie said, slapping Lev on the arm. "Besides, you can't get out of marrying my sister that easy."

Lev stroked the back of my neck. "I wouldn't dream of it."

———

When dinner was over, April helped me clean up while Lev finished giving everyone the grand tour.

"Is it bad to say your mom's a fucking beast?" she said, scraping a plate into the garbage.

I sighed and rinsed a glass before putting it in the dishwasher. "Total beast."

"Relentless. My mom's bad, but . . . wow."

"There's no stopping her once she smells blood."

"Should I slip some ketamine into her wine? I literally have some in the car."

"That's okay. I can make it another hour or so."

"This isn't a sleepover? I saw her with an overnight bag." I threw a towel at her as everyone came down from upstairs.

"Gifts?" Charlie said, poking his head in the kitchen.

We opened the housewarming presents everyone had brought in the living room. There was a lovely antique salt-and-pepper-shaker set from Charlie and Beth they'd picked up on their most recent trip to Germany, and a wooden boxed dinner kit from April complete with wine, spatula, tomato sauce, colander, and pasta. Lastly my mother held up a finger as dad went to their car and returned with a large engraved sign boasting THE CARMICHAELS in dark, bold letters.

"Isn't it wonderful? We had it commissioned by one of our neighbors. He's retired and does this in his spare time."

"Thanks, Mom," I said, passing the sign to Lev.

He looked it over and nodded. I could tell he hated it as much as I did. "It's lovely, thank you both."

"So where are we thinking?" Mom said. "Maybe above the front door? Or you can put it in the foyer; it's a little bare in there."

"Right." It was all I could manage through clenched teeth.

"Come on, let's go take a look." She gestured Lev up from his seat and herded him toward the entry.

"Mom?" I called after her, but she was already out of sight. My father had become deeply interested in a stain on the belly of his shirt. Charlie clapped his hands to his cheeks and mouthed *oh no!* I flipped him the bird and went out to the foyer to find Mom eyeing the large framed beach picture on the wall. "Mom, we'll figure out a spot for it, okay?"

"I'm just envisioning." She turned in a circle, studying each wall as April joined us. "Here, let's move this and try it above the table." She grasped the beach picture and unhooked it from the wall.

"Mom, stop," I said, grabbing the other end of the large frame.

"Imogen, it's not permanent. I just want to see how it looks there."

I tried easing the picture from her hands, but she held tight. "I like this where it is."

"You're being silly. Let's see the sign here, and then you can put this back up if you want."

"Mom, *no*."

I tugged again and she lost her grip.

The picture's full weight caught me off guard, and it slipped from my hands, spun partway around, and crashed to the floor.

Glass shattered and sprayed our feet.

"Fuck!" I couldn't help it. I stood looking at the picture face down on the floor surrounded by glittering shards, and my eyes clouded over. "You can never just leave it be. Why can't you leave things alone?"

I knelt and began gingerly picking up the largest pieces of glass, my mother's feet watery swirls in the corner of my vision.

She drew in a long slow breath as Lev bent beside me. "Well, at least this one won't cost your father and me fifteen grand."

A shard sliced into the palm of my hand.

The pain was sudden and uniquely bright the way cuts always are. That shocking parting of flesh. Blood springing up in response. So quick and intimate. Like whatever did the cutting was made specifically for it.

Lev hadn't noticed. He was looking up at Mom, brow furrowed. Confused by what she'd said. Of course he was. He didn't remember.

"Jesus, Cora. Really?" April said quietly. Then she was hoisting me to my feet and guiding me upstairs and into the bathroom. "Where do you keep the bandages?"

I settled onto the rim of the tub. "Third drawer down on the right." I stared dumbly at my hand, the blood seeping from the wound in ruby droplets. April knelt in front of me and cleaned the cut with some peroxide, then laid a bandage gently across it. All the while I studied her. My friend. My protector. It could have been ten years ago in the bathroom of her apartment. Everything old is new again.

"He doesn't know?" she asked as if reading my mind.

"I told him. Right before the wedding. He doesn't remember."

"Christ."

"Yeah."

"Goddamn her."

"Yeah."

"Say the word and I'll clear everyone out down there."

"It's okay. Just give me a minute."

"You sure?"

"Yes."

She cupped my face with a cool hand, then left me in the quiet emptiness of the bathroom.

I tried clearing my mind. Letting it all go. Breathing. Just breathing. Simple. Easy. But my mother's voice was there, needling away inside like it always had. Bringing images up from the past like bodies rising with bloat to a lake's surface.

The knife.

The cutting. How right it was. How *good* it had felt.

How Marcus's blood had looked, seeping over the blade. The shiny fear in his eyes reflecting the rage in my own.

The pain in my hand. Then and now.

When I looked down, my thumb was digging, digging at the wound. The bandage was a twisted curl on the floor, and both my hands were sticky and red.

Imogen

When I'd cleaned up, I went back downstairs to find the house mostly quiet and empty. The broken picture was gone, and the foyer had been swept. The sun was setting, and the light coming in through the west windows was a deep Halloween orange. Beth was at the counter with the boys, who were quietly coloring in some books she must've brought along just in case.

"Hey, are you okay?"

"Fine," I said, finding my glass of wine and refilling it. Mox came and sat at my feet, staring up at me in his questioning way. *Okay, mom?* I petted his snout and kissed him between the ears.

Beth lowered her voice. "I'm really sorry."

"Thanks. Where is everyone?"

"Lev took your parents on a quick tour of the outside. They were going to leave after that. They might be gone already."

"Charlie?"

Beth rolled her eyes. "Out in your backyard smoking one of his god-awful cigars. I told him not to bring them, but he insists whenever there's somewhere he can light up."

"Daddy smells bad after," Henry said without looking up from his picture.

"Your daddy always smells bad, though, right?" I said. He grinned at me as I pinched my nose and fanned the air. "He's stinky." That got both the boys laughing, which buoyed my spirits a little.

Outside, the air had taken on a chill and was filled with the scents of turning leaves and freshly cut grass. But there was a hint of cigar smoke, too, and after a second I spotted Charlie at the far end of our yard inspecting a young silver maple Lev had planted shortly after we moved in.

"You're stinking up the joint," I said, coming even with him.

"No more than Mom already did. Jesus, you okay?"

"I'm fine. Little cut from the glass."

Charlie shook his head. "Seriously, that woman. Sometimes I can't believe she's our mother. Like maybe we were both adopted. What a relief that would be."

"Explains why you and your wife look more alike than we do."

"Fuck off."

"And if we're adopted, there's a chance you and Beth actually are related. Wouldn't that be something?"

He grinned and puffed on his cigar. We stood in the chill silence as the evening deepened. Some more of the stress drained away. Just being around Charlie usually did that. After a while Lev appeared at the side of the house. He was alone and poking through the flower beds. Probably looking for souvenirs Stripes had left behind.

"Lev actually got Mom to apologize," Charlie said.

"Really?"

"Yeah. He worked his political magic on her, and pretty soon she was blushing and telling him sorry she'd pushed hanging up the sign."

I laughed. "Of course she apologized to *him*."

"She'll call you."

"I won't hold my breath."

Charlie nodded to Lev, who was only a shadow now, bending and picking at some of the shorter bushes. "You got a good one there, sis." I studied Lev's outline and must've been quiet too long because Charlie said, "He's gonna be fine. You know that, right?"

"I know."

"I can't imagine how scary it was for you. If something like that happened to Beth . . ." He let a stream of smoke hiss out from between his teeth.

We were silent again for a beat. Lev disappeared back around the side of the house. I toed at the lawn and said, "You'd tell me if he wasn't, right?"

"Wasn't what?"

"A good one."

He laughed. "Of course. What are you talking about?"

"Nothing." I hesitated, completely unsure of myself. But now that I'd started down the path, I kept going. "You never noticed him being . . . lewd."

"Lewd?"

"Like, with women. You guys have hung out quite a bit since we started dating. He never did anything, I don't know—"

Charlie waved a hand at me. "No, God no. He loves you." But he'd spoken too quickly. Years and years of hearing my brother's voice, his tone, his choice of words had attuned me to whether or not he was telling the truth. Or at least the full truth.

"What?"

"Nothing."

"Charlie, what?"

"Jesus, it's absolutely nothing. Completely innocent."

"So if it's innocent, tell me."

"You should've been a lawyer. Or a cop." I waited and he finally shook his head. "The one time we took dad golfing over at Cedar Ridge—you guys had been together maybe six months then? We hit the clubhouse bar afterward, and there was this waitress who was giving Lev the eye. Like, obviously flirting. Lev thought it was funny and leaned into it a little. By the time we left she'd given him her number. He showed me and threw it away when we left. Nothing happened."

"Uh-huh." An oily ribbon laced itself through my stomach.

"Seriously. It was a joke more than anything. Besides, that was before you guys were together-together."

"What's 'together-together'?"

"You know . . . engaged."

"So before that, everything's fair game?"

"See, this is why I didn't want to tell you. I knew you'd blow it out of proportion. It was guy stuff. Stupid guy stuff."

The outdoor lights came on, flooding the darkening yard, and a second later Lev stepped onto the deck and leaned on the railing, studying us. He was only a silhouette.

"Don't worry," Charlie said under his breath as he put his cigar out. "He's not like other guys."

We started back toward the house. Lev watched us approach, his features still hidden by the glare of the light.

"You sure you're okay?"

We stood at the matching sinks in our bathroom brushing our teeth. The housewarming wound down quickly after my parents' departure. Charlie and Beth needed to get the boys home for bedtime, and April had a date because of course she did. We'd spent the last hour tidying up in separate rooms, neither of us yet ready to discuss the evening.

"I'm fine," I said, spitting toothpaste into the sink. "I'm sorry you had to see Mom at DEFCON 2."

"She apologized."

"Charlie told me."

"She was sorry."

"Yeah."

"Really."

"She was sorry it didn't go exactly like she wanted. That's all mom's ever sorry for."

He put away his toothbrush and came to stand behind me. His hands settled on my shoulders and squeezed. "It's really my fault." Our eyes met in the mirror.

"What do you mean?"

"I knew you didn't want to do the housewarming, but I thought it would help me . . . you know . . . and that was a little selfish." His hands increased their pressure, finding the knots of tension and kneading them away.

"It's not selfish to want to remember," I said quietly. He made a noncommittal sound, and I tilted my head. His fingers kept working. "Did it?"

"What?"

"Help?"

He was quiet for a long time. "There were flickers. Like when we were all eating dinner together. We'd done that before, right?"

"Yes. Quite a few times since we got engaged."

"So not really memories, but shadows of them if that makes sense?"

"Sure. But nothing else?" He must've felt me stiffening because he paused in his movements.

"Like what?"

"Like anything."

He resumed. "No. Not really." It was his turn to be quiet. I watched him in the mirror, his head turned slightly away, eyes distant. I wondered if he was thinking about what my mother had said. If he was considering asking me. And what would I say?

His hands kept working, my muscles becoming liquid beneath them. God, he was good at finding pressure points.

"So that sign," he finally said. "On a hideous scale of one to ten?"

"Fucking twelve."

Our eyes met again in the mirror, and we both burst out laughing. And for a moment it all fell away—the worry, the suspicion, the guilt—and we were just us again. The us from before, when I was finally letting myself believe I could have this level of fulfillment and happiness. That I deserved it.

He leaned close and his lips brushed my neck. The spot he always started with. I shivered. "You know," he said, pausing to kiss me again. "We haven't since I was in the hospital. And I know you've been afraid I'm not up to it, but I can assure you—" He turned me partially around and kissed above my collarbone, letting his lips drag down to my chest. "I am."

His breath was cool with mint. And even though he was wrong about why we hadn't been intimate, the effect was intoxicating. My few remaining inhibitions wavered and collapsed, and desire rushed through, flooding both of us.

We made it to the bed and it was new like the first time with a frantic edge to everything, our motions hurried and eager. His hands and mouth were everywhere, all the places I craved them. I stroked him until he was begging me, pleading, then pulled him inside. Couldn't get him deep enough.

While he moved above me her name kept repeating in my head. *Lyra Markos. Lyra Markos. Lyra. Markos.*

Had he fucked her like this? With this kind of abandon? Or was it different? Hollow and unreal, a stranger in the dark of a cave on an island he would never set foot on again.

I rolled on top and rode him with deep plunges that made the cords in his neck stand out as he tried to hold on. I stared as his eyes clenched shut, felt his fingers tightening on my hips. I was in control. Me. Not someone else lost in the roar of a distant sea who could've been anyone. Me.

His wife.

Our climaxes were seismic. We sprawled within them, holding each other through the aftershocks until we were both still.

He kissed my shoulder and muttered something that could've been *I love you.* I didn't say anything back. Just watched him drop into sleep like a stone.

For a long time I lay staring at the ceiling, watching the shadows shift and dance. Thinking of the depths people carry. How maybe we're not supposed to know how deep they go. It was foolish to think we could know someone else when we never understood ourselves.

Sleep caught me off guard and drew me under. There were charcoal dreams of the island beach. Lyra Markos and my husband hand in hand, running not from the storm, but from me as I chased them, gripping something long and glinting.

I woke clutching the sheets, teeth clenched, the cut in my palm aching. I turned my head to the side, releasing a held breath.

Lev lay facing me, his eyes open and staring.

We stayed that way, inches apart for a strange moment that lengthened into something else. Then he rolled away and his breathing became deep and even.

How long had he been watching me? Had he even been awake? Had I cried out in my sleep, said something?

My throat was rusty, and I rose and got a drink from the bathroom faucet, wiping my mouth on a towel when I was done. I stood looking at myself in the mirror and was reminded of Lev earlier on the deck, his face hidden in shadow.

Back in bed, settling beneath the covers, the house quiet except for the brief jangle of Mox's collar as he scratched, then fell still, I willed sleep to come, but it kept darting away. Lyra's face swam in and out of the dark.

And then the answer came as bright and clear as the sun breaking through clouds. There was one person who could tell me the truth.

I fell asleep again and there were no more dreams.

Imogen

Hello, Lyra. You don't know me, but you might have served my husband and me lunch at Argyros a few weeks ago. This may sound strange, but I have something to ask you. And you might already know what it is, but please don't be afraid—I'm not angry. I just need to know. From one woman to another. Please respond when you have time and we can talk.
Hoping to hear from you,
Imogen Carmichael

I read through the direct message a dozen times.

Added a line. Deleted it. Read it again.

Brought the mouse over the "Delete Message" button. Let it sit there. I was sweating.

What the hell was I doing?

The idea in the prior night's darkness seemed like the perfect solution. Reach out to the woman herself and simply ask her. *Did you sleep with my husband?* No recriminations, no anger, just a simple question. Like I'd said in the message, one woman to another. And she might lie to me, but why? What was I going to do to her? She was half a world away, living her own life. Probably moved on to the next guy, with Lev fading fast in her memory. What did it hurt to tell me the truth?

But the thought of her doing so caused my heart to kick in my chest. If she confirmed they'd been together, what then? It would be my choice to broach the subject either now or down the road when Lev regained his memory. And from that point it was blank emptiness. I had no idea where to go.

"How's the Roy assessment looking?"

I startled and spun in my chair to find Mr. Stanford standing in the doorway, eyebrows raised.

"Oh, good." I minimized the social media page and clicked through to the spreadsheet I'd been absently adding to all morning. "I finished the projected tax analysis, and I'm starting on itemized incentives."

"Great. Is the end of the month still realistic?"

I pretended to squirm a little. I could definitely have it done by then. Even beforehand if I put all of my faculties toward the project. But in reality I was divided. Split a dozen ways by what was going on inside me. I was barely working at half speed, and if I wasn't careful, it would become apparent.

"If you need more time, it's no problem," Stanford said. "Just say the word."

"No, I'll be able to finish by then."

"Great. Big project. Big, big project. Next-level stuff here. Exciting." He flashed a smile and rapped the doorjamb with his knuckles and was gone.

I looked at the spreadsheet, not seeing it at all, before finally clicking back to the message page. My words floated there. The rest of my life potentially decided by the movement of one finger.

And in that moment I was back in the apartment I'd shared with Marcus. I was picking up his phone and punching in his code. There'd been a point where I could have stopped. There always was. I could have kept myself from looking. Could've told myself anything to keep from knowing. But I always would have wondered. And doubt is an acid that will eat you inside out if you let it.

I sent the message and leaned back in my office chair and turned to look out the window.

The oak was on fire with color now. Sizzling orange and ember red. It wouldn't be long before the parking lot would begin to fill with fallen leaves and the air would cool and the promise of frost and snow would whisper in the bare limbs and dying grass.

Soon everything would change.

Sierra

I rise and dress in the near darkness, knowing where all my clothes are by touch.

They're both still sleeping. Before I go, I linger in the other bedroom doorway, listening to his soft and steady breathing, absorbing it like a drug.

Outside, the mountain is still. Dark. Nothing moves except the breeze. There are eyes on me but none of them human. Nothing that will hurt me. I call out a few times, hoping to see a familiar four-legged shape amble out of the dark, but there's no response. Only silence. Except for the people in the cabin, there isn't another person for nearly seven miles in any direction.

It rained in the night, and the ground is still damp and quiet as I make my way along the path beside the leaning shed I keep meaning to tear down. There is a solid foundation beneath it, but what I'd build in its place I don't know.

A dozen steps into the forest and the narrow drive leading to the cabin is no longer in sight. A dozen more and neither is the building and the clearing it sits in. I could be anywhere in the wilderness now. Lost and alone. But safe. Alone and safe.

Some gray light seeps from the east. Enough to see by. The great trees loom overhead and droop garlands of moss down to the forest floor. Everything wet and green. A deer spooks ahead and sprints off with a flash of tail and springing brush. My heart pounds, and I move faster down the slope.

I speed up to a jog. Then a run, imagining something is chasing me. *Someone.*

Tree trunks flit past. Logs are hurtled. Feet sliding, finding purchase. Down. Down. Down.

Branches scratch at me, but I lower my head, one hand out as if reaching for salvation. And it's there in the near distance.

The lake.

Its bank is even steeper, and I turn sideways when I reach it, skidding over loose dirt and stone until I stand on the shoreline, breathing hard. Fog hangs over its flat openness in gauzy curtains, and I take in its shape.

It is a half mile across but at least five times that in length, its far ends still lost in gray mist. It would take someone an hour or more to circumvent it on land through the heavy cover. Longer if they tried to move on the unforgiving slope.

I undress. Underneath my clothes is a sleek one-piece swimsuit. I swing my arms to warm them and put one foot in the water. It's freezing. It always is. I click a button on my wristwatch, take two deep breaths, and dive in.

The water sinks its teeth into my nerves. Cold fire. But it is a familiar pain. A welcome one. Completely submerged, water humming in my ears, and I'm free.

Weightless and gliding. My body already moving in an easy rhythm, slowly picking up speed. Stroke. Kick. Stroke. Kick. Breathe. Again.

The water tastes clean and clear. Glacier melt this high up. There are fish here, but no one comes to catch them. This place is mine and has been for the last two years.

Head up to look around. The sun is peering toward the mountain, the light gaining color. I'm halfway across.

Stroke. Kick. Breathe. Stroke. Kick. Breathe.

My muscles burn and the water's no longer cold. I'm a part of it. Cutting through it. Through myself. There is nothing but the movement and the breathing and the other side of the lake slowly coming nearer and nearer.

I feel him behind me, watching from wherever he is, and it drives me faster. Knowing he still exists in this world.

The shore is closer. A dozen strokes.

Seven.

Three.

Gravel beneath my fingertips and I stand, wading out, panting, breath pluming.

Turning, I look back, hands on my hips, trying to lower my heart rate. I click the timer on my watch. Nineteen minutes, forty-nine seconds. Faster than last time by two seconds. Better. Always better.

The day brightens, and the first rays of sunshine break through the cloud cover and burst on the water's surface in a thousand points. It holds for a tenuous, stunning moment. Then the light fades. The lake is flat steel again. I shiver.

There might come a day when this isn't routine. Isn't practice. And I'll have to be faster than I've ever been before. I wish it wasn't so, but it is.

When my heart returns to its lazy pace, I reenter the water and now it's warm. Welcoming. It is my ally, and I cross it with thanks back toward the waiting shore.

Imogen

"I'm home," I called, coming through the doorway.

Mox hustled across the kitchen, nails clicking on the floor, and danced around my feet as I set my purse and laptop case down to greet him.

"Such a good boy, Moxie. You're the best boy." I scratched his head, and his tongue lolled happily. I stepped out of my heels, transferring my things to the foyer table, and noticed a strange smell. Almost like the inside of a car on a blazing-hot day. Like something that wasn't made to cook slowly heating. "Honey?"

No response.

Lev wasn't in his usual place at the kitchen counter. He'd taken to working there instead of in the upstairs office, citing the space had too much of a closeted feel. His laptop and a few documents were spread across the granite, and I poked through them, looking for a note. Nothing.

"Where'd he go?" I asked Mox, who tilted his head in response. The garage was empty, Lev's Audi gone from its place. He hadn't really driven anywhere since arriving home, only up to the grocery store a couple of times. Other than that, I'd taken care of the errands.

My fingers tapped the kitchen countertop, and I sniffed the air again. The smell was gone. Or maybe I'd just gotten used to it. I tried recalling another time I'd been home alone since coming back from the honeymoon and couldn't. The house had a different feel with him gone. A visceral emptiness. The same as the suite on the ship when I'd woken to his absence.

Don't think about that.

I made myself a snack and ate it at the counter, half my mind retracing the meager progress I'd made on the Roy project, the other half resisting the urge to check my Facebook account.

It had been two days since I'd reached out to Lyra Markos. Two excruciatingly long days without a response. When I looked back through her posts, they'd tapered off over a period of months, as if she'd become disenchanted with social media. Prior to that there'd been a smattering of pictures of her with a young dark-haired man with full-sleeve tattoos on both arms, a couple of shots of tropical birds high in trees, and a tall glass of wine with a caption in Greek I had to look up and translate. *I deserve this.*

Now I pictured her opening my message, reading and deleting it without a second thought. Or maybe she'd even laughed, then trashed it. Some poor silly woman yearning to know the truth about her husband. I couldn't help but imagine what kind of person Lyra Markos was. Was this the type of thing she did a lot, or was it spur of the moment and completely out of character? Did she feel any sense of guilt, or did she approach trysts the way she did big glasses of wine? *I deserve this.* What did it feel like to have that kind of power—to catch a stranger's eye and succumb to seduction like slipping into a warm bath? Besides her youth and beauty, what had drawn him to her in the first place? Was it simply carnal attraction, or was there something elemental about certain women that men couldn't resist? Did she possess an undeniable hidden quality, the kind of lure I'd always felt lacking in myself? And if so, why? Why *didn't* I have it? Why was I the type of woman to be betrayed?

Why wasn't I enough?

I swiped at tears threatening to spill free as Mox pressed his jowls to my leg. "I'm okay," I croaked. Maybe I was and maybe I wasn't. And maybe the answer to my question was the same as Lyra's.

I deserve this.

My phone chimed and I picked it up. A message from Lev.

Ran in for a quick meeting with Carson and the crew. Hope I didn't worry you. Sorry I forgot to text.

A level of relief settled over me. What had I expected—that he was out carousing in the early evening at a local bar? I typed a quick response—totally fine, no worries!—and set to cleaning the streaks of mascara drying below my eyes.

Mox padded out to the foyer, and I heard him woof once, then fall quiet. "Moxie, come here." I sniffled and rose to scrape the last of my snack into his bowl, no longer hungry in the slightest. "Got a treat for you."

Out of the corner of my eye something moved. I was no longer alone.

I spasmed, arms coming up to deflect a blow, and took a step back. There was something in their hands, a blunt object they were going to smash my skull with, and they were smiling insanely.

My breath whooshed out in one long exhale. I sagged.

"Easy, girlie," Val Williams said, holding out the bottle of wine. "It's hump-drink-day, remember?"

———

We sat on the side patio between our homes and sipped the cab sauv I'd thought I was going to be murdered with.

"Sorry to just barge in," Val said, adjusting her sunglasses.

"No you're not."

"I mean it! I knocked; you didn't hear me?"

"I guess not."

"Should get that checked; you're too young to be hard of hearing. My mother-in-law? Can't hear a damn thing anymore. Speak right in her ear—nothing. I think she fakes it half the time, though. Does it to piss me off. Works like a charm." Val shifted on the chair and recrossed her legs. She was five years my senior with voluminous curls of dark hair she always wore down and a Boston accent so thick some words took me a few seconds to understand after hearing them. She was loud, nosy, foul-mouthed, opinionated, and one of the funniest people I'd ever met. I loved her.

"Anyhow," she was saying, "I wasn't going to let you dodge me again. It's been three weeks of standing me up."

"Val, my husband almost died on our honeymoon."

"All the more reason for wine." She threw back her head and cackled, and I felt some of the strain of the last two days slacken.

A pleasantly cool breeze glided through the neighborhood, swinging the changing leaves like ten thousand little bells. Mrs. Miller was out in her wheelchair, a blanket draped over her lap, staring at a place on the ground a few feet in front of her. Two girls cruised by on a pair of scooters, their hair trailing behind them, and a dog barked somewhere up the street.

Val must've been noticing all the same things because she said, "Kinda perfect, isn't it? Like I never knew places like this really existed until we moved here. Goddamn modern-day Norman Rockwell painting. *Saturday Evening Post* in suburbia or some shit."

"For sure." I checked my phone for notifications. Nothing. Took a drink of wine.

"You okay?"

"Yeah. Definitely."

She sat forward. "I mean really. How are you holding up?"

I shrugged. "It's super weird."

"Honey, I can't imagine. Like, is he having to relearn everything?"

"No, he's got all his long-term memories. Just the last six months is basically . . . gone." My throat tightened, and I shook my head. "Sorry."

"For what? You didn't do anything wrong." I choked out a small laugh, and Val eyed me over her sunglasses. "Seriously, are you okay?"

"I'm fine. It's just been hard trying to get back to normal. Work's been crazy, and—" I gestured at the house, unable to sum up that none of this had been how I pictured us beginning our life together. How nightmarish the last weeks had been.

"Well you need anything, just say so. We're here for you."

"Thanks. We really appreciate you watching Mox for us while we were gone."

She waved one hand. "He's such a sweetheart. I didn't want to give him back."

"Here, kitty-kitty!"

Both of us turned toward the Millers' place. Mrs. Miller called out again in a faint wavering voice so melancholy it played across my heartstrings.

"She's been doing that all afternoon," Val said. "Saddest goddamn thing."

Ray Miller appeared from around the side of the house and knelt beside his mother. She waved a frail hand, and he nodded, then guided her chair across the yard and up the ramp to the house.

My phone screen lit up, and I grabbed it, but it was just a random email notification.

"What's with you?" Val said. "Never seen you so worried about your phone before."

"Work and whatnot." I toyed with my wineglass, watching the red liquid swirl below the rim. "Actually I'm waiting to hear from a girlfriend of mine. She's going through some things."

"Oooo, unspilled tea? Do tell."

"She thinks maybe her husband's cheating on her." I kept my eyes on my glass, afraid Val would see something in them if I looked up.

"Is this your girl, April?"

"No, God no. I don't know if she'll ever get married. No, it's . . . someone else."

"So what's the deal? She catch him texting or something?"

"No. She thought she saw him with another woman. But she wasn't sure it was him."

Val scowled. "She confront him?"

"Yeah. He denied it."

"'Course he did. How long they been married?"

I started to answer and caught myself. "A few years."

"And what was he like before they got together?"

"Normal. Average, I guess. I don't know."

"Can tell a lot about a man from his exes." She leaned forward conspiratorially. "I did the full deep dive on Deshawn before we set a date. Stalked his prior girls online, talked to a few of his old friends and relatives who I knew would tell me the truth, everything."

"Really?"

"Of course! I wanted to know what I was getting into." She sat back and sipped her wine. "He wasn't too broke to fix, so I did the deal."

I laughed. Couldn't help it. "Don't tell me you never snooped on Lev before you tied the knot."

"I mean . . ."

"Uh-huh, good on you. Can't leave stones unturned—snakes know how to hide."

My face heated with the memory of searching through Lev's phone one night after he'd fallen asleep, breathless and heart thundering. Any second I'd expected to come upon some scandalous picture of a past girlfriend he'd been saving or something even worse. But there'd been nothing. Later I'd scrolled through the last couple of years of his social media profiles and everything he'd told me was there, more or less.

"But seriously, tell your girl to do some digging. Men are like dogs at the racetrack chasing the mechanical rabbit. If you watch them long enough, you realize they're just going round and round."

A text from Lev lit up my phone.

Going out for a couple drinks. All good?

All good! Having a drink with Val myself.

Cool, tell her hi.

"Hubby?" Val asked, refilling our glasses.

"Yep." Mox padded around the side of the house and sat beside my chair. I absently stroked his ears. "So what would you do if you caught Deshawn?"

"Cheating? Well let's just say he'd never have to worry about doing it again." Val laughed her usual laugh, but it didn't reach her eyes. I wondered if there was something there behind the joking. Some near miss or course correction in their past. There always seemed to be in every relationship. No marriage was perfect. No matter what it looked like on the surface, there was always something beneath it.

Imogen

It was almost midnight when Lev stumbled through the door.

I rose from my place on the couch where I'd been half watching some stupid reality show with Mox curled beside me. Lev slouched in from the entry and braced himself on the kitchen counter.

"Whoa," I said. His eyes were bleary and bloodshot, and his hair was mussed as if he'd been in a high wind. "A couple turn into a dozen?"

"I know, right? Carson is almost as good at drinking as he is at giving speeches. Your husband, not so much. Especially after a pretty dry month." He gave me a sheepish smile and tried smoothing his hair, which only made it stand up more. For a second he looked so young and boyish it was hard to reconcile all my worry and suspicion. It seemed like someone else's life.

"You didn't drive, I hope."

"No. Definitely not." He shrugged out of his coat and slung it over the back of a stool before opening the fridge. "Got an Uber that cost us a second mortgage, hope you don't mind." He started pulling out ingredients for his patented hangover cure. He'd made it for me one of the first nights we'd had too much booze together at my apartment. *See the trick is getting ahead of it,* he'd said, swaying a little in my tiny kitchen. *You preempt all the nastiness with something super healthy. It makes your body think everything's okay.*

I watched closely as he set up the blender and dropped a handful of blueberries and a banana inside along with some almond milk. A dollop of turmeric extract, and without pausing, he pulled open the spice cabinet and reached to the very back behind all the other bottles and fished out the ground ginger. *That's the secret ingredient,* he'd said. *The ginger does all the heavy lifting.*

He turned the blender on, and the contents went from a splotchy Jackson Pollock to a solid dirty orange. He poured it into a glass and guzzled it down, hip leaning against the counter. When he finished, he noticed me watching him intently and looked around. "What?"

"Nothing," I said. "I'm going to bed."

———

We lay side by side in the blue-black of early morning. Every third or fourth breath, Lev produced a quiet snore, the only indication he'd had too much to drink.

For the first part of the night I'd attempted to sleep, feigning it when Lev came to bed a half hour after I'd lain down. He was usually horny after drinking, and I didn't want to go through the motions of gently rebuffing him, seeing the disappointment or hurt on his face. Instead I'd waited until he'd drifted off, then risen and pulled his clothes out of the hamper, and stood smelling them in the dark.

Just his cologne and a whiff of beer. No perfume. At least none I could detect.

It was a pathetic thing to do and a weak comfort, because it only began another parade of thoughts instead of quieting them.

Lyra Markos.

Charlie's admission about the waitress Lev had flirted with.

The easy way he had with everyone and the lingering looks I'd seen women give him.

My jealousy and suspicion were two edges of the same blade. One that cut me and whoever else was within arm's reach.

I turned over, closing my eyes, then opening them to look at my phone. Almost three in the morning. No new messages. She wasn't going to answer me.

I climbed out of bed, unable to lie still any longer. Lev slept on, oblivious, and all at once I was furious with him. His casual relaxation, his ease, and even the sympathy he'd received. For a brief second I saw him tipping over the railing again, and a note of satisfaction chimed within me.

Just as quickly it became discordant and my stomach churned.

I left our bedroom and padded down the hall, telling myself I hadn't felt it, hadn't thought it. Hadn't meant for him to fall or float, sunbeaten, in the water for a day. But was that why I was so intent on knowing? Because if he had been unfaithful, would it relieve some of the guilt? Would some part of me feel justified in what I'd done? Maybe even *glad*?

Deep cleansing breaths, in and out, trying to hyperventilate the thoughts away.

My shoulder brushed the wall and the whole house seemed to tilt.

I pressed my forehead against the cool trim of the office doorjamb and inhaled again and again before stepping inside the office and sitting down at the desk. I stared at the desktop computer's blank screen. My reflection there a hollow darkness. As my heart rate slowly returned to normal, Lev's words floated through my head again.

The ginger does all the heavy lifting.

He'd known exactly where the ginger was. Despite not having made his hangover cure since we came home, which was the only thing he used ginger for, he hadn't paused when reaching for it. Like muscle memory. And maybe that's all it was. A reflex.

Or maybe everything was starting to come back.

I opened my cell's browser and pulled up Argyros's page again. The phone number hovered along with the other contact information. Greece was seven hours ahead, the restaurant would just be opening. If I called now I'd probably get a manager, or maybe Lyra herself. I could hear her voice, ask my question, and even if she didn't answer me, I'd know.

My thumb drifted over the number. Touched it.

The phone was at my ear. My heartbeat thudded against it.

The call connected. It rang.

Every cell in my body felt like it had been filled with helium. I was light. Floating away.

Another ring.

Another.

They weren't open yet. No one was going to answer. I started to pull the phone away with a flood of relief.

The other end of the line clicked.

"Argyros, Αργυρώ πως μπορώ να σε βοηθήσω?" The voice was serene and most definitely male. "Hello? Can I help you?"

My throat wouldn't work. I swallowed and sat forward, pinching my left earlobe as hard as I could. The pain got everything moving again. "Yes, sorry, I'm wondering if I could speak to Lyra? Lyra Markos? Is she working today?"

There was a long pause from the other end. "Who may I ask is calling?"

"Um—" I hadn't planned on explaining myself to anyone besides Lyra. I felt small and childish. "My name is . . . Jen, Jennifer. I'm a friend of Lyra's. We met while I was on vacation. I'm having trouble getting a hold of her and wondered if she's there."

Another pause, only my heart hammering in my ear. "No, she's not here. And actually, perhaps you can help me."

"O . . . okay?"

"When was the last time you spoke to her?"

"I'm—I'm trying to think. Maybe a couple weeks ago?"

"And did she say anything to you about her plans?"

"Plans? I . . . no, I don't think so."

A grunt from his end. "These kids, you cannot count on them for anything."

"I'm sorry, I don't understand." My apprehension had receded, confusion taking its place.

Another grunt, and it sounded as if he'd switched the phone to his opposite ear. For a second I swore I could hear the sea in the background, crashing hard on the white beach, could finally smell the bougainvillea. It was a bitter scent. When he spoke again his voice was distant, as if all the miles between us were trying to sever the call.

"Lyra hasn't been in to work at all. I haven't heard from her for weeks."

Imogen

It rained on our wedding day.

They say it's good luck. But not this kind of rain. This wasn't intermittent showers or a gentle mist that looks so pretty on a filtered video. It started in the early morning hours and just got heavier as the day went on. It came down in rashes, soaking anyone in seconds who stepped out into it. Flood warnings were issued, and lightning stitched the sky in jagged white-blue threads, pulling thunder behind it.

I was finally alone after hours of preparation, pictures, primping, and nervous pacing. The church's bridal suite was a long narrow room adjacent to the sanctuary, where the thrum of hundreds of voices drifted through the wall. I stood looking out the single window at the rain and thought how fitting it was. How *biblical*. A sign. One that could trigger a decision that would make the storm outside look like a spring shower.

I surveyed the back parking lot below the window, then moved to the full-length mirror to study my gown. It was sleekly strapless, and like nearly all soon-to-be brides, I'd put in the hours at the gym to tone my shoulders and arms and tanned so my skin popped against the white dress. My hair and makeup were flawless, and my teeth had been whitened. I could've stepped off any of the magazine covers polluting my mother's coffee table. Could've been anyone.

I checked my phone and was going to look at the parking lot again when the suite's door opened and my mother stepped inside. She was decked out in a dark-blue satiny dress showing off her dancer's physique she continued to maintain.

"Oh, honey." Mom stood there, hands clasped under her chin, taking me in. I wondered what she saw—the made-up and brushed woman in a $3,000 gown, or me. "You look absolutely stunning. This is going to be so beautiful. Such a beautiful day." I threw a glance at the moisture-flecked glass. "Don't give the weather another thought. It's good luck, you know."

"That's what they say." I sat down on the little couch against the one wall and checked my phone again. It was almost time. Mom came and sat beside me, smoothed her dress and then smoothed mine.

"I saw Lev out in the hall; he looks . . ." She let out a sigh that crossed the line between admiration and desire. "You really got yourself something there, Gen." I didn't reply. Was beginning to find it hard to speak. Hard to think of words at all. She must've seen me struggling. I wasn't good at hiding my emotions, and my mother was like a hawk, circling miles above, always able to spot an insecurity and swoop down on it, talons exposed. "What is it?" No *honey*, or *Gen*, this time.

My lips were dry when I licked them, tasting the gloss April had helped me apply a half hour ago since my hands were shaking too badly. "I'm not sure . . ."

"No one is, not really," Mom said. "This is a big day for you. For any woman. But marriage isn't something to be afraid of." She reached out then and touched my cheek with the back of her knuckles, gentle enough not to smear the foundation there. "You've always been afraid of something. Ever since you were little. Scared of the dark. Of the Browns' dog. Of your first sleepover, but you were always okay afterward."

I wanted to tell her no. I hadn't always been okay. That she just chose to believe I was and there was a difference. Once when I was seven, she had taken me and Charlie to a children's hour at the local library. The book they read to the kids was one of the *Little Bear* books, and the librarian had dressed up in a bear costume. It wasn't a particularly convincing getup and hung loosely on her. The hood, which made up the bear's head and mouth, framed her face so it looked like she'd already been eaten. All the other kids loved it, but it had made me cry. Once I started I couldn't stop, and Mom had brought me to the empty girls' bathroom out of embarrassment. When I still couldn't calm down, she slapped me on the mouth. Not hard, but hard enough to shock me into silence. As the years went on she continued the tactic, shifting from physical reprimands to emotional ones. I never could decide which hurt more.

"I think it's why you chose the career you did," she went on, sniffing a little as she sat up straighter. "I never thought it was healthy to embrace something like that."

"Risk assessment isn't about being afraid. It's being prepared."

"But that's neither here nor there," she said, not seeming to hear me. "You're doing well, and now you've got a good man. In today's world women like you could do a lot worse."

Women like me.

She smiled, and I could see some of the wrinkles around her mouth the makeup didn't cover. They looked like long-dry tributaries. "We were worried for a while. But you're on the right track now. Someday there'll be little ones running around, and you'll look back at today and laugh at how anxious you were." Mom patted my hand and rose from the couch.

"I don't think I'm ready." I blurted it out before she could turn away, believing she'd done her motherly duty.

"You've got cold feet, that's all. They'll warm up."

"It's not . . . I feel like maybe Lev—" *Like maybe what?* It was something I'd asked myself over and over in the months since he'd proposed. April had said I was waiting for the other shoe to drop when I'd voiced my concerns to her. Maybe that was true. Maybe I'd been waiting my whole life. It was why I'd walked away from Jamie—the way we'd been together, how much he'd meant to me—it felt like a fragile vase teetering on the edge, about to fall and break. And it was also why I'd said yes to Lev's proposal. I didn't want to make the same mistake twice.

"Lev's what?" Mom asked. She wasn't bristling yet, but her patience was thin enough to see through. "What's wrong with him?"

The answer was simple—nothing.

I'd searched for flaws in him but came up empty except for the small annoyances any decent person overlooks when they love someone. And I did love him. He was everything I wanted. Everything any woman could want. Except . . .

"Nothing's wrong," I said, and Mom visibly relaxed. "But if nothing is ever wrong . . . is everything wrong?"

My phone chimed then. It was on the table beside the couch, and Mom glanced down at it. She stared at the screen until it went dark again. Then she walked slowly to the door as if the marble beneath her elegant shoes was glass. She paused there, hand on the knob, not looking back. "Nothing is perfect, Imogen. If you search for perfection, all you'll find is pain. I thought you knew that by now."

Then she was gone.

I couldn't stand the first time I tried but made it on the second attempt. I picked up my phone and flicked open the Uber notification, then went to the window and looked down at the car waiting outside. Its headlights illuminated the rain in cold white cones.

Someone probably made up the good-luck thing on the spot a long time ago to comfort some devastated bride as all her carefully laid plans became a sopping mess. It's what we do when something upends our expectations—we try spinning it into something else. Make believe until it conforms. Becomes something familiar enough to put faith in when it happens to you.

Rain is good luck on your wedding day because a wet knot is so much harder to untie.

I canceled the car, then opened the bridal suite's door and stepped into the rest of my life.

Imogen

The air in the empty conference room was still and cooler than my office. I sat at the long table with its dozen chairs tucked neatly around the edge and a single wireless speaker in the center. The rest of the room was featureless except for a drooping ficus in one corner next to the tall windows. Everything in its place. Except for me.

I rearranged the Roy files again, the pages not making any kind of sense. The numbers washed together, and the words looked like another language. My mind skipped across them, unable to sink in and absorb what was required.

Part of the problem was exhaustion since I hadn't been able to sleep after the phone call to Argyros. Upon hanging up with the restaurant manager, a weight had settled into my stomach—a sick heaviness that accompanies the whipsaw of uncertainty about what you thought you knew. I thought I knew Lev. At least before our honeymoon. Then after the night on the beach, I wasn't sure. And now . . .

I pushed back from the table and paced to the window, needing to move. The street below was pitch black with moisture, fallen leaves bright splotches plastered to its surface. I stood looking the ghost of my reflection in the eyes.

Some would argue infidelity was built into us. Part of our basic biological imperative, especially in men. Go out and spread your seed. Multiply. Pass on your DNA. The temptation was there, anyone who said otherwise was lying to themselves. But it could be tamed. Fenced in by vows and tethered by rings on fingers. Promises.

But what about other needs? Darker ones?

I realized someone was saying my name, and not for the first time. One of the interns stood watching me in the doorway with open concern.

"What?" I said, as if I'd been caught doing something filthy.

"Everything okay?"

"Yeah, for sure."

"You must've been miles away."

"Just tired."

She nodded. "Lucas Roy is here."

"Right. Send him in."

Time to work.

———

At some point between the lunch I couldn't eat and arriving home, I convinced myself there was nothing to worry about. The initial shock and assumptions had been worn down by constant mental gnawing and by concentrating on work as hard as I could. When I'd resurfaced from the Roy file, what met me was a calm rationality I embraced wholeheartedly.

So Lyra Markos hadn't been to work—did that mean something terrible had happened to her? Not likely when I stopped to really consider it. It was nearly laughable. The world has a way of skewing when you're paranoid and tired and anxious. It becomes an unfamiliar place where everything is dangerous and hidden motives move the pieces when you're not looking.

In reality a woman of Lyra's age probably got bored with her position and decided to move on without giving notice. End of story.

Then why hasn't she responded to your message?

A thousand reasons. A million. This wasn't her issue, it was mine. Mine to let go.

I decided I would as I climbed from the car and went inside our home. The place where we were making a life for ourselves. One that couldn't be built on a foundation of suspicion.

Lev was in the kitchen wearing a nice pair of slacks and a dark button-down. His good jacket hung from the back of a barstool. "Where are you going?" I asked before kissing him hello.

"We," he said. When I just stood there blinking, he cocked his head. "Dinner? With Chewy and Beth?" Right. We'd set up a dinner date with them before they'd left the housewarming. I'd completely spaced it.

"Shit, okay. I'll get dressed."

"Or—" Lev pulled me close as I started toward the stairs. "We could cancel and stay in." His hand slid down the small of my back, and he pressed his lips to my throat. I stiffened. He felt it and straightened. "What's wrong?"

"Nothing, just a long day, and now I'll have to rush to get ready," I said, hurrying toward our room. I undressed quickly in our walk-in closet and weighed which dress to wear. Charlie had booked a table at one of the nicer restaurants in Logan Circle, which meant putting on something I wasn't truly comfortable in. When I turned to go back into our bedroom, Lev was standing in the doorway watching me.

I flinched, covering myself with the dress. "Jesus!"

"Sorry. Thought you heard me come up."

I sighed, pushing past him. "That's a no."

"Hey, are you okay?"

I turned my back to him, trying to find a pair of heels that would work. "Yes. I told you, work sucked."

"And you didn't sleep well."

I froze, one hand on a pair of black pumps. "Tossed and turned." I held the shoes close to the dress, feigning interest if they matched or not. Lev crossed the space between us and let one finger drift up the bare skin of my back. I broke out in goose bumps.

"You're so beautiful." His lips skimmed the nape of my neck. "I know you don't think so, but someday I'll make you believe it."

He lingered for a moment, then made his way downstairs. When he was gone I dressed, slowly shimmying into the dress. Stepping into the heels. I stood looking at myself in the full-length mirror, still feeling the warm brush of his lips against my skin.

As we were climbing in the car to leave, Ray Miller came jogging across the street, the skin near his receding hairline red and beaded with sweat. "Hey, guys, sorry to bother you, but you haven't seen Stripes around, have you?"

Lev frowned, glancing at me over the top of the car. "No, not lately," he said.

"Been gone for the last couple of days. Sometimes she disappears for a while, but never this long. Mom's pretty upset." Ray squinted down the street. "Looked everywhere but no sign."

"I'm sorry," I said. "We'll keep an eye out for her."

"Thanks. Looks like you're out for a night on the town. I won't keep you." Ray waved over one shoulder and made his way back across the street. As we were backing out of the driveway, I glanced into Ray's yard. Mrs. Miller was in her wheelchair, swaddled in blankets like usual. Her mouth was moving.

She was talking to herself again. But for some reason it felt like she was speaking to me.

Imogen

The hostess sat us at the back of the restaurant—a place called Winthrüm, self-described as "a collective cuisine experience."

"This is great," Lev said, taking in the pendant lighting and the long lengths of silk draped overhead. The airflow made the ceiling undulate as if we were underwater watching the ebb and flow of currents.

"Food's even better," Charlie said, opening the wine menu and ordering a bottle for the table when the waiter breezed past.

"This is so fun," Beth said, squeezing my hand. "We haven't seen you guys in forever."

"We were just at their place," Charlie said.

"I mean like a real night out. Without the boys."

"Where are they tonight?" Lev asked.

"With Beth's mom," Charlie said as the wine arrived. "She'll stuff them with sugar and keep them up late. Completely fucks their sleep schedule."

"She likes spoiling them a little, that's all," Beth said, looking down to smooth her skirt. Charlie rolled his eyes at Lev, and I suddenly wished my brother was sitting opposite me so I could kick his shins raw.

The appetizers Beth raved about were shiny pastry-like shells filled with shrimp, cream, and herbs. Conversation began to flow along with the wine. When Lev finished telling a story about work and Beth and Charlie were laughing almost to tears, his eyes met mine, and the solid connection felt right. Real. Like it should be.

"So let's get business out of the way," Charlie said, interrupting Beth and my discussion of the novel we'd recently buddy-read.

"What business?" I asked.

"The food for Mom and Dad. We all good?"

For an uncomfortable beat I had no reference point—then it clicked. We were in the final planning stages for our parents' fortieth wedding anniversary in a couple weeks. We'd rented out the small seaside resort where Dad had proposed. The guest list was fairly extensive. I was in charge of meals, which I'd completely forgotten. "Uh, yeah. Yes. It's . . . the caterer's getting back to me." I took a long swallow of wine.

Charlie frowned. "What does that mean?"

"It means they're checking their schedule to see if it will work. What else could it mean?"

"It could mean you dropped the ball." I flipped him off. "That's nice. But seriously, what're we going to feed everyone? Hot dogs? I nailed down the venue, you were supposed to do the food."

"Because reserving a resort and planning a menu for two days is totally the same thing."

Lev waved his napkin like a white flag. "Guys, let's not fight. I'm sure it'll work out."

"You okay?" Charlie asked, eyes narrowed. "You seem off."

"Leave her alone and pour me more wine," Beth said.

The entrées arrived and mine was delicious. As we ate the mood at the table lightened. Charlie ordered another bottle of wine, and Beth pretended to be mad about it as she excused herself to go to the bathroom.

"So how did you hear about this place?" I asked Charlie, wanting to smooth the anniversary-plan rift.

"Actually the dean suggested it at the last department meeting. His nephew is a sous chef here. I might be able to get us a tour of the kitchen if everyone—"

Charlie's voice faded away. I could no longer hear him.

I was watching Lev.

A woman was crossing the room. She was young, maybe mid-twenties, wearing a stunning backless dress. In my periphery I could see the slight turns of nearly every male head in the room, tracking her progress. My husband was one of them. He stared, lips parting slightly as if he were about to receive a spoon-fed delicacy.

My dinner tried reversing.

Charlie was still talking but there were longer and longer pauses between his words. When I glanced at him, he was throwing furtive looks between Lev and me. The woman sat at a booth among a half dozen other people in the corner of the room, and Lev continued to stare, something leaving his gaze. A faint sense of déjà vu drifted through me.

This was how he had looked the night when I'd woken to him staring at me in bed. His eyes were glazed. Dead.

"God, even the bathrooms are gorgeous," Beth said, settling back into her chair, which should've broken the spell. But I couldn't look away from Lev. He couldn't look away from *her*. "What'd I miss?" Beth asked. I opened my mouth to reply but Lev beat me.

"Pretty cute."

"What?" I said, my voice strained.

He motioned in the woman's direction. "The twins."

Until then I hadn't noticed the twin boys in double high chairs beside the booth. They were perhaps a year old wearing matching outfits, bibs stained with dripped food.

"Super cute," Beth said. "But my God, I couldn't imagine having two at once. Their poor mother."

"On the flip side it's one pregnancy and done," Charlie said.

"Oh yeah, walk in the park."

"I'm just saying, the body only has to go through it once versus twice. Has to be better overall, right?"

"Whose body?" Beth asked.

Lev came back to the conversation, glancing between Charlie and Beth like a tennis match, smiling faintly. I watched him, wondering if he even noticed what he'd done. What had happened.

"You know what I mean. And I'm sorry women are the ones who bear children," Charlie said. "I forgot it was men's fault."

"The fault is pretending the playing field is even." Beth shook her head and drank more wine. "It's not."

"Lev, help me out here," Charlie said, half bemused, half irritated.

"I think parenthood is a big deal. Definitely bigger for women since they're the ones with the physical responsibility," Lev said slowly, fully there again, back from wherever he'd gone. "But I envy you guys. I can't wait to be a dad."

"Think you'll start trying soon?" Charlie asked. "Mom would be fucking ecstatic."

"I don't know," Lev said, reaching out to take my hand. "But we don't want to wait too long. Time has a habit of slipping away." His fingers rubbed mine.

I swallowed thickly. "We don't want to hurry it either. It's a huge decision."

"Biggest decision you'll ever make. You definitely want the timing to be right. If I could do it over again . . ." Beth said, trailing off.

"What?" Charlie asked, wineglass halfway to his mouth.

"No, it's just—" She shrugged. "I had funding for the lab, and the last paper I published on enzymes was really well received."

"But it's all contingent. If we didn't get pregnant when we did, the boys wouldn't be the boys."

"Maybe, maybe not."

Charlie laughed without humor, looking around the table then down into his glass. "Well, I wouldn't trade anything for the boys."

Beth cupped her chin in her hand and stared across the table at him. "You didn't have to."

Imogen

The beltway's streetlights cut through the car's darkness like blades as we passed beneath them.

Dinner had ended with a quick tour of the restaurant's kitchen and a dessert I couldn't get myself to partake in. Charlie had given me the eye in the parking lot after we hugged goodbye but kept his comments to himself.

"Dinner was fantastic," Lev said, moving into the right lane. Our exit was coming up.

"Yeah, really good."

"You didn't eat much."

"I wasn't hungry."

"Are you okay?"

"I told you—"

"I know, work. But you were up in the middle of the night and now you don't have an appetite. I just want to make sure everything's all right."

I looked out the window. "What you said tonight, that's not what we talked about."

"What?" I could feel the heat of his eyes on the side of my neck. "You mean having kids?"

"We said we'd wait until everything was steady. Secure."

"Aren't we? Our jobs are good. We have a house now with plenty of room."

"It's not something we decide over dinner with my brother and sister-in-law."

He laughed. "We were just talking."

"And talk gets back to my mom. If she thinks we're trying to have a baby . . ." I trailed off, the notion a little too much for me to consider. Lev guided the car smoothly onto the off-ramp and turned right in the direction of our development. We rode in silence, the soft thump of seams and potholes in the road steady background noise.

"I think," he said as we pulled into our neighborhood, "the accident did something to me." He stared straight ahead at the road. "When I woke up in the hospital, I realized things could've gone completely different. What if I'd hit my head harder? Or that fisherman who found me decided not to go out that day? Anything could've changed what happened. And it terrified me. It still does." We glided around the gentle curves in our neighborhood, homes and cars there and fading in the headlights like illusions. "Everyone knows life is short and fragile in the abstract, but then something happens to you, and it's real."

He pulled into our driveway and parked. Shut the car off. We sat in the darkness, both of us outlines of who we were. "I was drifting before—through life." He took one of my hands again, his skin so warm, mine cold. "The accident clarified it all. Now I know what I want." He leaned close, his breath against the side of my face, lips pressing there gently, whispering.

"I want us to have everything. I want it to be perfect."

———

I followed the woman from the restaurant down the street, staying a good distance behind her. The clack of her heels echoed off the buildings, drawing the looks of men we passed while she continued on, oblivious.

There was something in my hand. I was gripping it so hard my fingers ached, each heartbeat there, pulsing with intention. As we walked, the streetlights became farther and farther apart, the other people on the sidewalk drifting away. Soon it was just us, the street empty and stretching into endless night. Fog gathered at the edges of my vision, and each time I looked down there was nothing but swimming gray.

The woman stopped walking, and the distance between us closed. One of her arms came up and she pointed ahead into the darkness. She was repeating something, her voice rising and falling like a cosmic volume knob was being turned up and down. When she was close enough to touch, I grasped her shoulder and spun her around.

It was Lyra Markos. Her eyes were wide, staring past me, still trying to point at whatever she saw, which was now behind me, I could feel it coming closer, looming at my back like a crumbling mountain. But that didn't matter. Nothing mattered.

Lyra smiled and her teeth were red. Blood seeped between their gaps, and only then did I feel my arm moving like a sewing needle, shoving the knife I held into her stomach over and over and over and over and over and over—

My breath wheezed out as my eyes opened to our bedroom ceiling.

My back was seizure-arched, mouth gaping, yearning to release the shrieking in my head. Something wet slid along the side of my leg, and I coughed out a feeble cry.

Mox.

He stood at our bedside, licking my calf where I'd kicked free of the covers during the nightmare.

Nightmare. It had been a nightmare. I sagged into the sheets, feeling how sweat-damp they were. Mox came closer, pressing his nose against my arm, and I petted him weakly. Lev turned over in bed, facing away from us, his breathing soft and even. I lay there, the dream fracturing, Lyra's beautiful smile stained with blood the only real image remaining.

It hung there in the dark like the Cheshire cat's as I climbed out of bed and went to the medicine cabinet. I took the bottle of Klonopin from where it sat beside my birth control and shook a couple of pills out, gulping them down with a glass of water. There was less of the medication than I recalled, and I started to count the pills out of habit before putting them away. I didn't need them anymore. Not really. I'd prided myself on not using them for so long. But now I was infinitely glad they were there. Even though the details of the dream had thankfully evaporated, the terror lingered, following me down to the kitchen where I heated water for tea.

It was seeing the woman at the restaurant and Lev's reaction to her that had spawned the nightmare, of course. The conscious mind loads the gun, and the subconscious pulls the trigger. After we'd gotten home, I'd wanted to ask him about her. Why he'd been staring. If she'd seemed familiar in any way. How her dark hair had looked in the light, the roll of her hips beneath the dress—if any of it had bloated a memory and caused it to rise to the light.

Because from the right angle she could've been Lyra.

The kettle began to steam, and I filled my cup, pausing to grab my laptop and a blanket before going outside onto the deck. The night was crisp. Cricket song sawed the still air. I settled into a chair, the blanket wrapped tightly around me. Sat looking off into the dark.

Memory islands, Dr. Galanis had said. Glimpses of things through the fog of amnesia. That was what was happening to him.

He was remembering.

The fugues were memories clawing their way to the surface. How long would it be before everything came rushing back?

I drank some tea as Mox padded across the deck and settled beside me with a prolonged groan as if to ask what we were doing up in the middle of the night. I made sure the house was still dark, then opened my laptop and gave in to the idea that had occurred to me shortly after speaking with the manager of Argyros.

After ten minutes I'd set all the alerts I could think of regarding Lyra Markos; her name along with keywords like *disappearance, missing person, investigation,* and even *death* and *body.* When it was done it felt like completing a filthy but necessary job. I wanted to scrub my hands, take a long hot shower. But you can't wash away suspicion. It's a stain removed only by resolution.

Across the yard Val and Deshawn's house was silent and still like the rest of the neighborhood. Our last conversation returned to me then, drifting up until her words felt tangible enough to grasp.

Tell your girl to do some digging. Men are like dogs at the racetrack chasing the mechanical rabbit . . . just going round and round . . .

Before I could stop myself, I'd opened up my social media page and clicked on Lev's profile. He'd dated more extensively than I had but was in only one serious relationship shortly before meeting me—a woman named Jasmine, who he'd been with for over six months before breaking it off. *It was inevitable. We were going in separate directions,* he'd said. *She had no plans for the future, no drive. It was never going to work.*

Now Jasmine's face appeared on the screen—dark hair, brown eyes, pouting lips. Lev had taken the picture and posted it, the caption beneath it reading: *How lucky am I to be with this woman?*

How lucky.

I continued scrolling through his posts, his history flowing upward across the screen, time rewinding to before I'd known him. Through different jobs, trips, friends, family, dinners—it all became a blur. Years and years when he was a stranger set on a course toward me, toward the night we met at the party. Where he'd saved me from myself.

And here I was picking through his past when I hadn't been honest with him until the last possible moment. Had held off telling him about Marcus and the painting and the faint scar on my hand. I'd been so afraid he would walk away, but he hadn't. He'd listened with a calmness I found almost disconcerting and comforted me when I eventually broke down. *It's okay. I understand. That's all in the past now. It's done.* The relief had been palpable. The reassurance of love overwhelming.

On the laptop I was six years into his history, deeper than I'd ever gone, and there was nothing. No red flags, no lies, no secrets. Just a man living his life online like millions of others. There was nothing here. A dead end within a dead end.

My hand left the track pad and was reaching for the screen to close it when a picture drifted into view.

It was Lev with a woman standing near the ocean's edge, flaring whitecaps behind them. Their arms were wrapped around one another, and a large heart had been drawn in the sand at their feet, their names carved to either side of it.

I stared at the picture. It was the first one I'd come across featuring Lev with another woman before Jasmine. The woman was blond with a wide striking smile below the dark sunglasses she wore. I scrolled down. She was featured in the prior picture, a side profile of her behind the wheel of a car taken from the passenger seat. The one before that was her again. And again. And again. Six shots in all, each with a different caption and location. Lev had never mentioned this woman before, even though they'd been in a relationship for over a year judging by the post dates.

I sat motionless for a moment, a many-legged crawling sensation in my stomach. I was about to click into her profile when there was a flash of movement at the top of the screen—I'd received a new message. Dragging my gaze from the woman, I clicked the flashing icon, and my heart stuttered.

Lyra had responded.

Imogen

Hi, Imogen.
I do remember you. I think you are writing about
your husband and me? Is your husband gone?
Do you know where he is? Please tell me and I
will help you.
Lyra

"What the fuck?" I said quietly.

I read through the message again, going much slower, sure I'd
missed words in my rush or overshot the meaning somehow. But it was
the same. No—worse this time *because* it was the same. Worse because I
had absolutely no idea what to make of it. Mox rose and ambled to the
sliding door, but I barely registered him. I was lost in what she'd written.

I think you are writing about your husband and me? That was a gut
punch in itself. It confirmed what I'd suspected all along. It had been
them on the beach. He had fucked her. The hurt was there, but it
was a dull burning like a spreading infection. I think I'd known down
deep somewhere all along, primed myself for its eventuality. But there's
always impact in a crash even if you brace yourself.

Is your husband gone? Do you know where he is? Was something getting
lost in the language barrier? Or was she speaking in a metaphorical
sense? Did she mean, *Has your husband not been the same since he was
with me? Do you know how to get him back?* I didn't think so. It felt like

she was being literal. Like she thought Lev had disappeared and I was looking for him.

"What are you doing?"

An electric jolt shot the length of my spine. Lev was a dark shape in the doorway. He hadn't turned any lights on, and I hadn't heard the door open.

"Work," I managed.

"It's four in the morning."

"Couldn't sleep again."

He rubbed his eyes and stepped outside. I x-ed out of the web page and closed the laptop as he settled into a chair opposite me. He shivered. "It's like fifty degrees out here."

"I . . . had a bad dream. The air felt good."

"Want to tell me about it?"

"No."

He nodded and looked away across the yard. "You don't want to tell me much these days."

My mouth was painfully dry. "I've been struggling, I think." He looked at me again. "After the cruise. It's . . . it's like what you said last night—I'm afraid."

"Of what?"

Of you, I almost said. Or had it actually been *of me*? "It feels like everything's moving too fast sometimes. Like our life's picking up speed, and there's no brakes. I want kids, but not now. I'm happy with our careers, but I've seen people burn out in their jobs trying to rise too quickly. Other couples"—I hesitated, then plunged ahead—"they get divorced even though they look happy on the outside. But inside they're . . ."

"Inside they're what?" His voice had dropped so low I barely heard it. I couldn't tell if he was looking at me or not.

"They're fighting to hold on."

"Or let go."

I didn't say anything. Lyra's message hung behind my eyes like a chyron. *Is your husband gone?*

Lev sat statue-like for another long moment, then rose and went to the door. He stopped there, his back still to me. "Are you coming to bed?"

"Pretty soon."

He went inside, his shadow gliding through the darkened kitchen and up the stairs. I sagged, releasing a long slow breath. When the tingling in my fingers abated, I opened the laptop and brought up Lyra's message again. Read through it a dozen times until the words blended together and formed a noose in my head, strangling all other thoughts.

I wondered what Lev really thought about me being out here. What he suspected. What he remembered. And what else he was hiding.

I took in Lyra's message one more time and realized something I'd initially missed. The surprise and utter strangeness had eclipsed its greater meaning.

Lyra was alive.

Regardless of what was happening between Lev and me, that was the most important thing. She was alive.

I stood, intending to carry at least that much with me and try to sleep again when I remembered the woman deep in Lev's past. The one he'd never mentioned even though she'd been someone important enough to take up over a year of his life.

When I'd navigated back to the pictures and found her profile I learned two things. One didn't mean anything, and the other chilled me even more than the night air finding its way beneath the blanket to my exposed skin.

Her name was Sierra.

And she'd disappeared three years ago.

Sierra

When I return to the house the smell of bacon permeates the air.

He's awake at the stove, smoke curling off the pan. He shoots me a look over one shoulder as I come in.

"How'd you do?"

"Just under twenty minutes. Is he still asleep?"

"Mm-hmm." He scoops the bacon onto a plate and starts cracking eggs into the pan. They sizzle in the grease. "No sign of the dog?"

The dog. It's always how he refers to Zee. He doesn't like dogs, and I understand his aversion since he wears the scar on his face where one bit him as a child. But not all dogs are the same. Not all of them bite. "No. Nothing."

"Want me to—"

"No." I say it too sharply, and he gives me a look before going back to cooking. I'm worried about Zee but desperately trying not to be. He's run off before but has always come back within a day or so. I keep catching myself glancing out the window, expecting to see him loping across the yard. "I'm going to drive around after work again. I put word out at the bar too. If someone sees him, they'll let me know." He shrugs as if to say, *Suit yourself.* He's mostly passive—the kind of man who's satisfied and relaxed as long as the sex is consistent. But lately he's made some comments about fixing up the cabin's siding, buying new tires for my truck, repairing the back steps. All things that move him closer to us. All things I can take care of myself. I've been mostly ambivalent, but soon we'll have to have a conversation. Lines will have to be drawn, and I'm always the one drawing them.

I start to walk past him to go change into dry clothes when he says, "He called me 'daddy' last night."

I stop, one hand braced against the hallway doorjamb. "What? When?"

"Was just saying good night, and he said, 'Good night, Daddy.'"

There is dead space in my chest where my heart should be. "And what did you say?"

"I said good night." My fingertips dance on the doorjamb, rapping out a quiet rhythm. "You want me to—"

"I want you to go home," I say. I meet his eyes, and he sees there's no sense in arguing. No point in even asking. He nods and shuts the stove off, setting the eggs on a plate before going to put on his boots by the door. He pauses for a second like he's going to say something, then thinks better of it and steps outside. His Jeep rumbles to life, and a second later it jounces away down the rough drive and is lost in the morning mist.

———

I watch him eat.

It's something I never saw myself doing or taking an interest in. But then again for much of my life, motherhood was an appealing but distant city I hoped to visit someday—the layout and landmarks known only secondhand from those who had been there. No one tells you how much satisfaction there is in watching your child take sustenance. Maybe it's more common among mothers—a seed planted by nursing and the lifegiving of your own body flowing into theirs. Their hunger a sign of health and growth. Of their need for you.

He grasps another piece of bacon with chubby, grease-stained fingers and munches it, studying an ant trundling slowly across the wall. He points. "Bug."

"That's an ant. Mom will get it." I scoop the ant up and open a window to place it outside. When I sit back down across from him, he's drinking orange juice out of the glass, holding it with both hands. His hair is still bedswept, and he smells like sleep. I could breathe him in all day.

He burps and smiles slyly. "Scuseme." He runs the words together like he's in a hurry even when sitting still. He leans to the side and looks past me down the hallway. "Where Daddy?"

The same emptiness fills me. I knew something like this was coming, but it still catches me off guard somehow. "Not Daddy. That's Tyler. Remember?"

"Tyler."

"Right."

His small face scrunches as he thinks, tiny wheels and gears spinning in his head. Not yet three years old, and he's problem solving, working things out on his own. "Kai has a daddy."

Kai is his best friend at the little day care half a mile from the motel I manage. "Yes, Kai has a daddy. His name is Andy."

"What my daddy name?"

I look out the window, wondering if there's any answer I could give him that would be close to the truth. Something he could understand. Something I could relay when I can barely get myself to face it in the nether hours of the morning when I'm alone and all the world feels empty.

"Wash up, okay? It's time to go."

———

To find Maynard, Washington, on any digital map, you'd have to zoom so far in your screen would blur. It's situated on the seaside of the Cascades, over two hours' drive from Seattle. Nestled. It's the first thought that came to mind when the town appeared through the intermittence of my windshield wipers shunting the heavy sleet. The buildings grow out of the little valley as if they'd been planted instead of built. Mature stands of trees separate uptown from downtown, so they feel like two completely different places. And they are to some extent. Uptown has three of the better restaurants as well as the mercantile, which sells everything from drill bits to diapers. But downtown is where the only motel is. The Nodding Pines hosts twenty rooms and a modest lounge that does good business most weeknights and overspills into the lobby on the weekends.

I pull into the motel's lot and park in my usual place farthest from the office. The weather is mild and fair for a late-spring day in the Pacific Northwest—no rain yet. But there will be. The latest night girl folds her paperback up and heads out the door with barely a "seeya" over one shoulder when I come in. She's bored and I can't blame her. Only one of the rooms has a guest, and I do the cleaning during the day, so at night there's only the phone and the door to watch—both of which are usually quiet outside of ski season.

The bar is empty and dark, upturned legs of chairs on the tables like those of dead insects. I go behind the counter and get a pot of coffee going, pouring a strong shot of bourbon into the cup before filling it. I sit there on a stool, letting my eyes unfocus and my thoughts drift. I put two fingers up and touch the place where my son kissed me when I dropped him off. There's a hint of grease there from where he missed washing the corners of his mouth.

There was a time when the notion of having someone who depended on me for nearly everything was the most terrifying thought in the world. To be that responsible for another heart and mind was overwhelming. But now I understand that's what provides the will to do so. The love is intrinsic the moment you hear the first cry and know they're yours. That they are *of* you.

That you would gladly die so they could live.

"Sittin' with all your friends, I see."

There's a shape in the doorway watching me. Marlene Tanner, owner of the Pines, is a stout woman of sixty with coils of gray hair she ties back in a tight ponytail. She's worn nearly the same outfit everyday I've known her—zip-off khaki cargo pants and a hoodie of some nature—and today is no different.

"Best company is usually your own," I say.

She grins and sidles down behind the bar to pull a cold beer from the cooler. "Cheers to that."

We sit sipping our drinks, a brief nudge of wind against the curtained glass. It feels safe in the near dark with my friend close by, in this town nestled high in the mountains of a state I'd never been to until three years ago. But safety is temporary like everything else.

"Found your dog yet?" Marlene says as if my thoughts are like moths, easily plucked from the air.

"No." I put fifty miles on the truck the day before looking for him, my son happy to ride with the window down, calling out in his little-boy voice when the urge took him.

"I asked around over at the café, but no one's seen him. Be pretty far for him to come into town anyway," Marlene says.

"Yeah. My guess is he chased a rabbit out behind the cabin and got turned around. I've been leaving his food out. He knows his way home. He'll come back," I say with more confidence than I feel.

"Careful with that food something else doesn't come looking." If Marlene notices how quickly I glance at her, she doesn't show it. "All kinds of predators up in the high country."

Yes, all kinds everywhere.

We talk for a bit about the motel. Its upkeep, repairs, orders for the bar, if the night girl is working out (she is), if the wallpaper Marlene insisted on in half of the rooms is growing on me (it isn't). It's a comfortable ritual we do a few times a month, a time we enjoy since the motel is something we saved together. Salvage, I've found, is a bonding agent rivaled by little else.

Marlene drains the last of her beer and sets it in the recycling bin. "Well, I'm off to Dickson for a couple days. There's a sale I'd never forgive myself if I missed." Marlene's other passion outside of hideous wallpaper is estate auctions. She's a bit of a pack rat—always purchasing things with the intention of reselling them, but never does.

She pauses on her way out, looking back at me. "You know I owe you these trips. Wouldn't be able to go at all if you hadn't come wandering in here. Can still see you sitting on that very stool the first time. You looked like"—*like something was after me*—"you were meant to be there," she finishes after a beat. "I don't put much faith in fate, but gratitude's something I practice on the daily. Love ya, honey."

Then she's gone, and it's a good thing because her kindness and warmth still blindside me. After leaving my entire life behind and coming to understand every facet of the word *alone*, another's compassion is like a wellspring in the desert.

I swipe the tears away and refill my cup—just coffee this time—then go to the desk in the lobby and start to work, telling myself I will only look out the windows a few times before lunch, and only to see if it's raining. I won't check the back exit's locks at all. Won't make sure the pistol is in its box beneath my truck's seat. Everything is where it should be. We're safe.

Safe for now.

Imogen

The hotel's rooftop bar overlooking a back channel of the Potomac was mostly empty given the overcast sky and cool breeze. The hostess who sat me said they were a week away from closing the space for the season. I put my hands out to warm them over the gas fireplace she'd turned on after taking my drink order.

It had been two days since Lyra's message. Two days since I discovered the existence and disappearance of Sierra Rossen. Two days of her face and vivacious smile there in my mind when I went to sleep and waiting when I woke up. There when Lev asked me a question I barely heard. There when my boss startled me as I stood at the vending machine staring into nothing.

"Sorry I'm late. God, the fucking traffic was insane." April settled into the seat across from me looking chic and gorgeous in a dark peacoat and creamy cashmere sweater. Her cheeks were aglow from the brisk weather, and I didn't blame the waiter for stammering when he came to take her order. After sipping deeply at a tall gin and tonic, she said, "Okay, what's going on, you sounded really weird on the phone."

I bit my lip to keep it from pouring out all at once. In the early morning when I couldn't sleep, telling my best friend everything had seemed like the answer I'd been searching for. Someone to provide some perspective. But now, faced with exposing the labyrinth of my paranoia, I wanted to tell her it was nothing. That I'd just wanted to see her and have a drink.

"Listen, I know the dance you're doing right now. You're debating whether or not to actually say what you called me here for. But we both know even if you hold off now, you'll end up doing it later anyway. So come on, spill that shit," April said.

I took a breath. And told her.

Everything. Starting with the unease at the flawlessness of Lev's and my relationship before marriage, then the events of our honeymoon, and ending with Lyra's message and Sierra's disappearance. All except what had happened in our suite on the ship. How Lev had actually fallen. That I kept locked safely behind the door in my inner garden.

When I was finished, April sat staring at me for a long time. So long I fully expected her to get up and leave without looking back regardless of our friendship and her long-standing role as my quasi guardian. Instead she surveyed the water far below, finished her drink, and said, "What do you know about this Sierra?"

"Not a lot. There wasn't much online about what happened to her. Around three years ago she didn't come home when she was supposed to. Her boyfriend at the time reported her missing, and the cops found out her car had been abandoned in a parking lot south of the city and impounded."

"Foul play?"

"Wasn't mentioned anywhere."

"What about friends, family?"

"Couldn't really find a lot—there's quite a few Rossens in the area. Without reaching out to all of them . . ."

"So since you think Lev cheated on you, your concern is . . . what?" She laughed nervously. "He killed a former girlfriend?"

Hearing my greatest fear aloud was disconcerting, but at the same time it sounded foolish sitting here across from my friend in broad daylight. "I don't know. It's just . . . really strange."

"Is it, though? Correlation doesn't equal causation."

"Thank you, I'm pretty familiar with the idea."

"Right, sorry." She tapped the tip of a fingernail against her empty glass. "Can I read the message?" I gave her my phone. She studied Lyra's cryptic note while the waiter replenished our glasses. "That's super fucking weird," she said, handing it back. "And a little creepy."

"Not just a little."

"So what do we know? You think he fucked around on the cruise."

"That message confirms it, right?"

"Maybe? It's bizarre, but she doesn't come right out and say it. You didn't respond, I take it?"

"No. Would you?"

She shrugged. "Either way, Lev falls overboard and his memory gets fried. Now you find out one of his exes disappeared a few years after they dated." I nodded. "Have you considered just asking him?"

"Of course."

"But . . ."

"But he's not going to be honest."

"How do you know that?"

"Well—"

"If he tells you they dated and broke up and then she vanished and it's the truth—" She shrugged. "Case closed."

"But I don't know that's the truth."

"Look, not saying the police are total wizards around here, but they were involved and never classified her as a victim of a crime, right? So that's something. I bet they even questioned him."

"Sure, but—"

"And if they checked him out and didn't find anything incriminating, that's another vote of confidence. I mean, sometimes people just up and leave, right? Maybe she ran from her last boyfriend—who knows what she was dealing with personally? She wouldn't have been the first woman to pull up stakes and take off for greener pastures."

April wasn't wrong. In fact, right now the idea was alarmingly appealing. I could pay the bill, get in my car, hit the beltway, and be two states away by the time the sun set. Leave everything behind. But would that solve anything? I knew it wouldn't, because I would still be me.

"Please don't take this the wrong way . . ." April said. "But are you sure this isn't all because of the stress you've been under? With his accident and work and now this Greek weirdo? Or could it be you're . . ."

"What?"

She squirmed in her seat. "Looking for something to be wrong when there isn't anything? That you're trying to find a way out before you get hurt?"

"It's not like that." *Was it?*

"All I'm saying is the past can overwhelm you sometimes, and you have to fight it. With everything you've gone through, maybe it's creeping in again."

"No." I said it like a slap.

"Okay. Okay."

We fell silent, each retreating to our drinks. I felt like a shit snapping at her after everything she'd done for me. She'd been the only steadfast person throughout my adult life. A better friend I couldn't ask for. But some injuries are too tender to be touched even by the gentlest of hands.

She cleared her throat. "So you have to ask yourself what you really want. As far as I can see, you've got two choices. You can either try letting it go, or you can dive in and find out more about Sierra. At least enough to satisfy your curiosity."

Curiosity. It went well beyond that. *Compulsion* was a better word.

Following impulses went against everything I'd built my life around, against who I was. There was safety and security in learning all the metrics, of assessing risk versus reward. On the one hand April was most likely right: In all reality, Lev probably had nothing to do with Sierra's disappearance. It was happenstance coinciding with my earlier worry about Lyra's safety. On the other hand, there was my state of mind to consider. My own comfort. No one else, including April, had to go home and sleep next to him with the questions hanging over them.

"You never found out who . . . you know, with Marcus . . . and you were able to let that go," April said quietly, trailing off.

The pictures on his phone swam through my mind, carnal and still so sharp. So cutting. I wasn't sure I'd let anything go.

"But come to think of it," she said, her tone shifting, "there is one person who could find out about Sierra for you. He literally digs up dirt on people for a living. All you'd have to do is ask."

For a brief moment the gears of my mind spun freely, and then they meshed. I sat back. "No. Absolutely not."

"I saw him last week at a fundraiser thing. He asked about you."

"April. No. I could never . . ."

"He looked great."

"You're not helping. Like, at all."

She smirked. "Sorry."

"You're not."

"Not really." I breathed out half a laugh, and she reached across the table to hold my hand. "Seriously, I want you to feel good. Whatever it takes. Whatever you need."

We sat that way for a beat. I studied our two hands linked in the center of the table.

What do I want? What do I need?

Imogen

I tried figuring that out over the next few days.

What I wanted was easy. I wanted to go back to our honeymoon and linger in the bathroom at lunch for an extra thirty seconds so I'd never see Lev touching Lyra's hand. I wanted the hesitant but undeniable bliss I'd felt before our wedding to return. The cautious hope each morning I woke next to him that this feeling wouldn't ever go away—that it would only continue to deepen as time passed. That I deserved to be this happy. This fulfilled.

What I needed was to know.

After meeting with April, I found myself daydreaming at my desk when I should've been putting the final touches on the Roy file for the upcoming presentation. I fantasized Lev was telling the truth—that he hadn't slept with Lyra and that Sierra had simply pulled up stakes and left her life behind. I imagined all my suspicion was simply my own insecurities rearing their ugly heads and basked in what a relief that would be.

Except pretending was a false and fleeting comfort, especially since I knew how darkly seductive lying to yourself could be. I'd prided myself on knowing all parameters, weighing out decisions based on facts, not assumption. I revered the cold clarity of data and statistics.

But I also knew that when you built your perspective of reality by measuring every possible threat, the world began to look like it was made of knives.

All of this cascaded through me as I drove home and went inside. Mox padded to meet me as usual, but otherwise the house felt vacant. After a period living together, you know when your significant other isn't there. Their absence is like an echo waiting to be heard.

I checked my phone. No messages, but it was Friday night. Lev's client, Carson Webber—the US Senate hopeful—liked to take everyone out at the end of the week. Let them blow off steam, especially since the election was nearing and the finish line was in sight, for better or worse. I double-checked the garage, verifying his car was gone, then grabbed a beer and sat down at the counter with my laptop.

For a second I resisted the urge to resume my research about Sierra, then crumbled and dove in. There was little more to glean. She was a year older than me and had worked for some time at a medium-size corporate insurance firm before starting her own travel agency. When I clicked on a link to her website, an error message appeared—**PAGE NOT FOUND**.

Not found.

I went to Sierra's social media page and studied her profile pic, sipping at my beer and petting Mox while a gust of wind pried under the eaves. I considered sending her a message but just as quickly dismissed it. Like anyone else in her life who cared about her, I'm sure that was the first thing they did. Before closing the laptop, I checked my own messages even though I'd looked at them earlier in the day and there were no icons indicating anything new.

But there was.

A new message sat at the top of my page though it was already marked as read. It was simple, a one-line plea that turned my stomach.

Please tell me where he is. I promise I'll help you.
Lyra

What the hell was this? I looked around the empty kitchen as if an answer would materialize. I reread the words, turning, twisting them in my head, but there was no way to make them anything else.

My fingers were on the keys, cursor blinking in the empty field.

I stood and walked away. Paced behind the counter and to the back door. Looked out at our empty yard, which was gathering with night shade. I sat back down, shaking my head, mouth open slightly like a dog who's tasted something rotten. What would I say to her? Tell her where Lev was? That he was here with his wife, exactly where he should be? That she should leave us alone?

But I wanted more than that. I wanted to know.

Did you sleep with my husband?

I hit send before I could stop myself and flicked back to Lyra's page. Stared at her image as if I could glean something from it. Then I went to the laundry and found one of my shirts, held it to my mouth and screamed into it.

I was shaking, heart rapping against my ribs hard enough to hurt. The walls swam and swirled. I braced myself against the washing machine and took deep cleansing breaths until I slowly became aware of sounds coming from the kitchen.

Lev was at the counter, putting away a couple of bags of groceries. "Hey," he said when I stepped into view. "Swung by the store and got everything to make chicken marsala. Sound good?"

I nodded, eyes glued to my laptop that was open to Lyra's page on the counter.

I'd shut it.

I knew I had. Could remember closing it before hurrying to the laundry room.

Hadn't I?

Lev finished putting the food away and rounded the counter. "How was work?"

"Fine," I said, eyes flicking helplessly from him to the laptop. He followed my gaze and stood staring at the screen for a second that elongated into something unnatural.

His lips parted. He blinked. I waited, pulse shuddering my vision. "Who's this?" he finally said.

I swallowed what felt like crushed glass. "Do you recognize her?"

His brow furrowed. Horrified, I watched him reach up and touch the nearly healed wound on his head. "No, don't think so."

"We met her on the honeymoon."

"Oh. Well, that explains it."

He loosened the collar of shirt and started to turn toward the stairs.

"Do you think she's pretty?" The words hung in the air as if someone else had spoken them. For a moment I thought I could grasp them, pull them back.

Lev's brow furrowed. "What?"

"Do you . . . think she's pretty."

He looked at the screen again as if to assess it and decide. As if he hadn't already. "She's young."

"That's not an answer."

"It's to say, yes, she's pretty," he said, as if speaking to a child. "But she's young. Too young."

We stood surveying one another, then he turned away and went upstairs, calling back over his shoulder as he went. "She doesn't hold a candle to you."

———

Firelight danced across us, brushing back the shadows so that we sat in a cocoon of light. Everything beyond was solid darkness.

Lev had cooked, opening a bottle of wine and pouring us each a glass, but there'd been little conversation to go with it. The tension in the room was suffocating. At the end of dinner he suggested finishing the bottle around the fire outside. *It's such a nice night.*

It was.

There was a chill, but the fire beat it back. The sky was stained with light pollution, but it was quiet in the neighborhood, only a few homes lit like beacons in the distance.

I rewrapped the blanket around me and sipped my wine. I'd been light-years away since putting the uneaten half of my dinner in the fridge, and Lev had said little after getting the fire roaring. Now he leaned forward, his features emboldened by the flames.

"So I know things have been . . . weird," he said haltingly, looking down at his glass. "And I think it's my fault." I straightened. "The accident changed my perspective, but I got so caught up in how I felt, I didn't take into account how it would affect you." He cleared his throat. "I started going to therapy."

"Therapy?" It was all I could think to say.

"I realized I needed help adjusting. Trying to remember things that aren't there is frustrating. I've gotten angry. And this zest for life and wanting . . . well, everything—I thought about what you said the other night. About moving too fast. Burning out. When I told the therapist, she agreed you were right." He hunched closer to the flames, eyes finding mine. Embers glowed in them that didn't seem to have anything to do with the fire. "I do want a family. I want an amazing career. I want a life overspilling with joy and love. But more than anything, I want what makes those things possible. I want you."

There was a faint vibration in my chest separate from my heart. It was longing. In that second I saw myself leaving all of it behind. Forgetting the jealousy and doubt. I could imagine it receding like murky floodwaters as I stepped back into his arms and gave myself fully over to him.

He was waiting. Waiting for me to respond.

I opened my mouth, not knowing what would come out, as someone appeared from the darkness behind Lev and grasped his neck.

Everything slowed down and sped up all at once.

Lev released a grunt of surprise and leaped from his seat, his wineglass flying into the fire and exploding there with a hiss. The person behind him stumbled forward, barely catching themselves on the back of his chair. I was suddenly standing, the blanket falling away, flight or fight warring within me.

"You," the figure said, pointing at Lev. "Where is she?" Lev had sprawled away to the edge of the firelight and was breathing hard. Now he stepped forward, squinting.

"Mrs. Miller?"

I saw then he was right. It was our neighbor sans wheelchair. I hadn't known she could walk, but somehow she'd made it all the way from her house across the street in bare feet and a shapeless cotton gown. Her white hair shone dully, and her eyes were widely rounded and fastened on Lev. She was still pointing. "You."

I got moving then. Shook off the shock and fright and rounded the fire to the old woman who was beginning to sway. I wrapped my blanket around her, but she didn't seem to notice. "Here, Mrs. Miller," I said, trying to ease her down into a chair. But she shrugged my hands away, still a lot of strength in her aging body.

"I saw . . . you," she whispered. Lev glanced from her to me, stricken, hands held out as if he had no idea what to do with them. "What did you do with her? Where is she?"

"I think—" Lev started, but then patted his pockets for his phone. "I'll call Ray." He set off for the house, and we were alone.

"Let's sit down, okay?" Gradually she turned toward me. The rictus of her mouth relaxed, and she blinked at me in the dimness.

"Sandy?"

"No, it's Imogen. From across the street."

Mrs. Miller wavered in place, then shuffled into the dark. I followed her. When I placed an arm gently around her waist to steady her, she didn't pull away. She was saying something under her breath I couldn't quite make out as her house came into view.

"What was that?" I said.

"Hurt her," she said, eyes fastened on the grass her fish-belly-white feet were sliding through. "In the moonlight. Saw him hurt her in the moonlight."

Gooseflesh rippled across my skin. "Saw who?" I asked. We stepped off the curb and began crossing the street. "Who did you see?"

She slowed, then stopped at the entrance of her driveway and looked back at our house. Lev was a shadow in front of the garage. Motionless. Watching.

The Millers' door swung open, and then Ray was running toward us. "Who?" I asked again, lower this time. Her cataract-laden eyes swung across me to her approaching son. She pointed in his direction as he neared us.

"Him. It was him."

"Jesus, Mom, what're you doing?" Ray said breathlessly, taking his mother's arm.

"Don't touch me," she hissed.

"I'm so, so sorry," he said. "I don't know how she got out of the house without us knowing. She was asleep last time I checked on her."

"It's okay," I said. "Don't worry about it."

"Where is she?" Mrs. Miller said.

"I don't know, Mom. But we'll find her, okay?" Ray mouthed *Stripes* to me over his mother's head, and I nodded, still feeling as if I were watching everything from far away. "Let's get you inside, Mom. I bet you're cold."

"Do you need help?" I asked.

"No. Thank you—and so sorry again."

I watched until they had managed to get up the wheelchair ramp where Ray's wife, Sandy, was waiting with the chair. Then I headed slowly back across the street. Lev was gone from the driveway. Leaves clicked in the breeze. The night was quiet again.

Where is she?

I stood at the base of our steps with the same question echoing inside me. Through the door's glass Lev was a muted shape moving across the kitchen. When he was out of sight I called April. She picked up on the first ring.

"Do you have his number?" I said before she could ask anything. "I think he changed it." To her credit she knew exactly who I meant.

"Yes."

I felt something shift internally. A line being crossed I couldn't retreat from.

"Okay. Send it to me."

Imogen

Rain lashed the windows of the little café, and I curled my hands tighter around the mug of coffee, partially for the warmth but more to keep them steady.

Outside, the world was a gray-streaked blur. Traffic trundling by, people hurrying beneath umbrellas. I checked the time. It had taken me ten minutes to get here from work, and he was late. We wouldn't have much time if he did show up, and I was starting to have second thoughts. No—these were fourth and fifth thoughts. It had taken me days to work up the nerve to call after April had sent me his number, and I'd almost hung up when he'd answered. I'd rushed past his surprise and confusion saying I'd explain everything if he'd meet me for lunch. Any other person would've told me to go fuck myself, but he was different. I hated to admit I'd always known that. Especially now.

My fingers drummed on the table. I checked the time again. I couldn't do this. Couldn't face him for any reason. I had to go.

As I stood the door opened and the sounds of the storm rushed in. A man in a long dark coat stepped inside, brushing the water from his shoulders and hair.

Jamie Flanagan.

I hadn't seen him since the day at his apartment when I collected the few items I'd begun leaving there in the ceremonial act of the slow move-in. Him following me from room to room, pleading—asking just to talk. For me to explain what was happening. But how could I? How could I tell him I'd never been happier, and that was why I couldn't see him anymore?

Now the world swam a little around the edges as he clocked me and our eyes met. April hadn't lied—he looked great. He still wore a scruff of beard accenting his jaw, and he'd let his hair grow into messy curls, which definitely suited him.

He smiled hesitantly and crossed the room. We stood on opposite sides of the table, taking each other in.

Jamie shook his head. "You look exactly the same."

"Your hair's longer." He touched it as if he hadn't noticed, and we both laughed a little at the overpowering awkwardness.

"So . . ." he said, glancing around. "The old stomping ground."

I nodded. I'd picked this meeting place on purpose since it was just around the corner from his old apartment where we'd spent countless lazy Sunday mornings lounging in bed before walking here to have a late lunch. Then back to his place, almost always finding our way back to bed for the remainder of the afternoon.

"Hasn't changed much," I offered. We sat and he ordered a coffee. The café wasn't overly busy, but quiet conversation strummed the air, filling the silence between us.

"How have you been?" he asked.

"Good." It was a knee-jerk response. It didn't matter how much I was struggling, I always said the same thing. "Busy. How about you?"

"Same. Good. Busy. All the usual suspects."

I waited until his drink arrived before starting. Not knowing how, just starting. "I know you probably never thought you'd hear from me again."

"Was sure of it, actually." He flashed a smile, and it was like no time had passed at all. "I've had some bigger surprises in my life, but you calling is near the top."

"I know, I'm really sorry. This is . . ." How did I explain what this was without confirming what he probably already suspected. I faltered and shook my head. "I shouldn't have bothered you."

He sat back in his chair, assessing me. Another aspect of him I'd forgotten—his quiet focus. It was what made him extremely good at his job. "Why don't you let me decide that. Tell me what's going on, then I'll either tell you to go to hell or not." Another smile, daring me.

I took a breath. Then started to talk.

I told him less than April but enough that he got the picture. I could almost see his mind working, already pairing and discarding connections. Gauging whether there was anything to find or not. Whether he could help or if I was as delusional as I'd felt over the last weeks. When I finished, he looked down at his hands folded on the table and said, "April told me you got married. I purposely didn't keep track of you online afterward. It was too—" He glanced up, then away. I knew what he was saying. I'd been tempted to check in on him countless times since we broke up but knew it would be like probing a wound that definitely wasn't healed. There were a hundred questions I wanted to ask him; was he seeing someone, how was his family, did I still cross his mind as much as he did mine? But then he said, "So you want to know more about this Sierra. That's it?" and everything else receded.

"I think if you looked into it and gave me your opinion it would go a long way."

"And if there's something there? Then what?"

"I don't know."

A few patrons left, and a damp draft swept across us. Jamie stared out the window. "I'm good at figuring things out. I have a knack for finding what's been hidden. But as hard as I tried, I couldn't understand what I did wrong. How I managed to screw up the best thing that ever happened to me."

"Jamie—"

He held up a hand. "Please. I probably won't ever see you again after this. Consider it my price for meeting today." I quieted, bracing myself. "I knew trust wasn't easy for you and you needed to take it slow. I thought that's what we did. I thought you were comfortable with me."

"I was." It came out as a whisper.

"Then I just need to know—why?"

I couldn't breathe all the way in; the air clotted in my throat. "Because—" I closed my eyes, and when I opened them, it could've been any day of our relationship. Him sitting there, probably at this exact table, looking at me the way he always did. Like I was something completely new. "—it was too right. *You* were too right. I was terrified of giving myself fully over, and losing everything again."

He stared at me. *Into* me. That familiar penetrating look, the intensity he carried about him like a live wire. "That's the truth?"

"Yes."

Finally he nodded, clearing his throat. "Well, I'd like to help, but I do oppo research almost exclusively these days. Not really into missing persons."

"But you know who my husband is. Who he's currently working for."

Jamie waited. "What're you saying?"

"If you won't do this for me as a favor, you could bring whatever you find to the opposing campaign."

After a drawn moment he barked a laugh. "Well, that answers one question."

"What?"

"If you've changed."

I wanted to know what he meant. If I had or hadn't.

"I just don't want to make the same mistake again," I said finally.

Something glinted deep in his eyes, and he bit at the corner of his mouth. The waitress came by with the bill, breaking the moment. Jamie paid before I could, and when she was gone he stood, shrugging into his coat. "I'll send you anything I find," he said. "But if there's nothing, I hope you can move forward." He started to take a step and stopped. "All I ever wanted was for you to be happy. I still do."

I watched him go, a thousand things running through my mind I couldn't get myself to say.

Imogen

There was a gift basket on the front steps when I got home from work.

A nice bottle of wine, a meat and cheese spread, assorted chocolates. The card attached read:

So sorry for the other night, and thank you for looking out for Mom. You don't know how much we appreciate it. Love, Ray & Sandy

The rain hadn't let up, and the Miller house was mostly lost in the drizzle along with the rest of the neighborhood. I went inside and fed Mox, watching him wolf down his food before changing into dry clothes. Lev wasn't home yet, and I was thankful since it felt like my meeting with Jamie clung to me like a modern-day scarlet letter. *A* for *accusation* instead of *adultery*.

Jamie.

It had been strange seeing him again. Not just because of why we'd met, but also how I'd felt. There was the expected jolt of reuniting with someone you'd been deeply intimate with, but there'd also been an undercurrent of connection the second he stepped into the room. Like some invisible tether had been tied between us all along.

I suppose that's what happens when you end something that doesn't deserve it—a part of it continues on.

Downstairs, I double-checked the Roy files on my laptop, assuring everything was in place. The presentation was looming, and Mr. Stanford was as nervy as I'd ever seen him. The same went for me. It was no secret around the office that this was my proving ground. If I nailed the Roy job, there would be a promotion ahead with the eventuality of my name being added behind Stanford on the company title. I'd been there for years and had risen through the ranks consistently—the very model of the modern businesswoman. But even the promise of advancement didn't hold the sense of accomplishment it should've. It felt like yet another milestone on someone else's path I was dutifully following. Another box in need of checking. I'd been waiting all my life to feel like these aspirations were my own. Was still waiting.

With the Roy file saved, I checked my messages, hoping and dreading Lyra had responded. She hadn't. There were no new updates on her page and no Google notifications. It was like she'd disappeared again.

Where is she?

My phone chimed, snapping me back. Charlie. The text was one word. Caterer???

"Ffffffffuck!" I yelled, startling Mox so badly he leaped to his feet and spun in a quick circle. Mom and Dad's anniversary was this weekend, as in four days from now, and I'd forgotten to book the caterer. Again. Charlie was going to crucify me. And Mom . . .

I scrambled through an online listing in the resort's general vicinity, calling number after number in a widening area until the grim certainty fully sank in. There was no one available on such short notice. We were having a fortieth wedding anniversary without food. I could see the look on my mother's face—a disappointed but unsurprised expression she'd honed to a razor point over the years. Could feel myself squirming on its impalement already.

The sounds of Lev arriving home intruded, but I could barely raise my face from my hands.

"Hey, how was . . . Oh, what's wrong?" he asked, suit jacket hanging from one fingertip.

"I—" I started, but my voice cracked. "I forgot to book the caterer."

"Oh shit."

"Yeah. I don't know what I'm going to do."

"Assuming you called all the—"

"Yes."

He hung his jacket from the back of a stool, stood staring off into space. This was one of his thoughtful looks, not the deadened expression I'd come to dread. Mox padded to him, and Lev scratched behind his ear without breaking concentration. "How desperate are you?"

"Scale of one to ten? Fucking twelve." We said the last in unison, and I released a laugh that threatened to become a sob.

"I have an idea. It's a long shot, and even if it works out, your mom's going to hate it."

"Cherry on top."

He smiled, pulling out his phone. "Let me make a call." He started toward the back deck, then paused at the door. "Did you have lunch somewhere over in Shaw today?"

My stomach clenched. I was supremely glad I was looking away so he couldn't see my face. Truth or lie? "Yeah. Why?"

"Greg was over that way, and said he thought he saw you in a café with someone."

My pulse slammed in my ears. So loud I wondered if he could hear it. "I met up with an old friend."

"Cool." He started out the door and I turned.

"It was actually an ex."

He stopped, one foot outside on the deck. "Oh. Okay."

"We hadn't seen each other in years and . . . he reached out. So we had a quick bite and caught up."

He surveyed me for a beat, a cautious smile forming. "Should I be worried?"

"No," I said, my voice steady. Sounding like someone else. "Not at all."

Imogen

Seven sets of male eyes watched me from around the conference table.

Equality is vaunted in business. Held up like a badge of honor doubling as a shield from criticism. In today's world women have every opportunity that men do. They're given the same respect as their male counterparts. Everything's dealt equally across the board regardless of sex. We're told the same thing over and over. But it begs the question of why something as basic as equality needs to be defended so vehemently and propped up so much. You'd think if it was what they say it is, it would be self-evident.

Not that there hasn't been progress, and it looks good on paper, but tell that to any woman who's stood up in front of a room filled with men.

I tried not to focus on each individual of the Roy team as I relayed my report and pitched the corresponding plan of action. But it was impossible not to notice certain body language or expressions. Some of them appeared to be listening raptly while others seemed to drift. And of course there were the glances at my body, gazes lingering just a little too long in certain areas before moving on.

I was a business professional. I was a little girl playing dress-up. I was a piece of meat.

And all this comingled with a knee-jerk self-dismissal. *You're being oversensitive. Reading into things. Not giving them credit. Not all men are like that. Don't overreact.*

But I wondered how much of this was my own rationalization, and how much had been drilled into me since I was old enough to understand there was a difference between boys and girls.

"So that brings us to cost analysis for site evaluation," I said, flicking to the next slide on my laptop, which was paired with the large display screen on the wall. "As you can see, I've compiled comparative real estate averages for the last five years alongside boring samples for neighboring construction projects that were encouraging for your proposed building zone. And I think you'll find this very interesting." Mr. Stanford sat in the very back of the room, nodding his approval. Despite the last month, despite my distraction and raging personal turmoil, despite being the only woman in the room—I was killing it.

I tapped the next slide. Nothing happened.

I hit it again. No response. I cleared my throat. "Sorry, think my laptop froze. Hold on just a sec . . ." I disconnected from the display and went to the broad overview of my file.

The last four slides were missing.

No.

It wasn't possible. I'd checked and double-checked everything last night. It had been fine. Nervous sweat that had been beading between my shoulder blades began to trickle. It was okay. I had a backup just in case something like this happened. I clicked through to my cloud folder as some of the Roy team stirred in their seats. Mr. Stanford crossed his arms, brow wrinkling. For a second as I scrolled through the folder, I thought I'd gone too quickly. But starting over and going first alphabetically then performing a quick search confirmed my fears.

The backup wasn't there.

It wasn't in any of the other adjacent folders or on the desktop or in the trash. It had vanished.

My throat closed to a pinhole.

"Do we need to take a break?" Stanford asked.

"No . . . no hold on just a second." One of the Roys shot a subtle look at his brother that confirmed everything I'd been thinking earlier.

I took a breath, but the air was warm and stifling, too close. I could see this all playing out—having to reschedule the meeting, a reprimand by Stanford, the Roys going with another management firm, the promotion slipping away—a greater part of my confidence and credibility with it.

No.

I swallowed past the tightness in my throat and navigated to my work email. I'd sent myself a copy of the presentation near the end of its completion as a fail-safe. It had to be here. If it wasn't, there was something seriously—

There.

The email with its attachment appeared, and with it relief bordering on salvation. I opened the file, skipped to the proper slide, and reconnected to the display. "Sorry about that. I guess even risk analysis doesn't come without hazards." Half the room chuckled appreciatively. I smiled with gritted teeth and waded back in.

"Thank you so much. Thank you. Thanks. Thanks very much."

I shook hands with the line of men as they filed out of the conference room. Most of the Roy team were affable, smiling, returning the thanks, some doling out a quick compliment with their handshake. When they had all exited the room, I shut the door and leaned against it, head down.

The rest of the presentation had gone smoothly. All my slides were current, and I'd only had to wing one portion at the end that I'd rewritten since emailing myself the file. The Q and A had been lively but not overly long—a good sign my work had landed near the bull's-eye.

"How do you feel?"

I'd almost forgotten I wasn't alone. Stanford still sat in his chair near the back. He'd loosened his tie and unbuttoned the top of his shirt. I took a seat at the opposite end of the table.

"Wrung out. But good. I think they were very engaged."

He sat forward. Took off his glasses and cleaned them. Put them back on. "Is everything okay?"

I was beginning to detest that question. "Yes. Sorry about the glitch."

"I'm not as worried about the presentation as I am about you." *Bullshit.* "Since you came back it seems like you've been very distracted. Withdrawn. Not yourself at all. The Imogen I know never would have made a misstep like that. Some of the staff have been . . . concerned."

"They don't need to be."

"Do I?"

The paternal tone in his voice was sandpaper to my eardrums. All at once I was furious. I'd worked my ass off on the presentation, and other than a technical blip, it had gone great. I *was* distracted. But I hadn't let it interfere with my work. At least not to the extent Stanford was insinuating. All that aside, he didn't have anyone else who could've put the presentation together as well or on the same timeline. "I'm fine," I said evenly and started packing up my computer and papers.

"Because there's no shame in needing help. All you need to do is ask."

I stopped cleaning up. "Was the presentation satisfactory?"

"Yes, but this is more about—"

"Do you think we lost the project today?"

"What? Well . . . no, I don't—"

"Then if my performance isn't being questioned, I'd rather you and everyone else keep your opinions about my personal behavior to yourselves."

"Imogen, hold on—"

But I was already gone. Out the door and walking down the hall. Part of me was turning around to apologize—the polite part instilled by a lifetime of etiquette. But I forced myself to keep going, focusing on how good it felt to give Stanford the brushback. To defend myself against all the passive-aggressive concern.

It was only midafternoon, but I left the office and drove across town, not really knowing where I was going while knowing all along.

The parking lot was a few miles off the beltway not far from the river. It abutted a growth of skeletal trees on one end and wrapped around a condemned building on the other. Several cars were parked sporadically, most covered in a layer of grime. One was missing its wheels. Long strands of dead grass grew from the fractured asphalt. I pulled into a spot at the far end near the trees and sat listening to the wipers swipe away intermittent rain.

This was where Sierra's car had been found after she'd gone missing.

It was about as lonely a place as I'd imagined, even though the neighboring properties were mid-level office buildings with a busy Chinese takeout place down the block. I imagined her sitting exactly where I was. Shutting off her car. Climbing out and . . .

"Disappearing," I said.

Did that really feel right? There were a lot of other scenarios— much darker possibilities. I brushed up against them as my thoughts turned to the missing slides of my presentation. In my current state, had I somehow inadvertently saved an older version over the newest? It was possible. Unlikely, but possible. Or had my work been sabotaged?

The night before had been one of the better ones since the housewarming. We'd talked some, laughed a little, watched a movie. He'd tried to initiate sex, but I played the tired card, then lay awake for half the night. At no point did I recall him out of bed. And he'd left the house before I did. Besides, my work was password protected. So . . .

"So what." More questions without answers.

A text from Lev lit up my phone. Still getting off early? I got the car mostly packed.

I gazed out at the rain-smeared view of the world, wondering if my internal outlook was any clearer. Wondering what Sierra was seeing now. If she was seeing anything at all.

Sierra

There's a comfortable rhythm to my days.

Rising before the sun. My swim. Breakfast with my son. Our combined silliness on the way to day care. A moment of quiet before I start work. Work itself.

This time of year is what Marlene calls "the lulls." Ski season behind, hiking season ahead. Though for the next six months we'll get few tourists. Fewer still actually staying the night at the Pines. That's fine by me.

When I'm caught up on any paperwork at the front desk, I clean the rooms whether they need it or not. Even if no one's stayed I turn each of them once a week. Dusting. Vacuuming. Wiping down surfaces. Clean the toilet, the shower, the little TV, change the sheets. I fall into my own personal lull. It's comfortable and peaceful in the quiet, empty rooms. The tidiness when I'm done satisfies something internally. Some simple yearning for harmony I've been chasing all my life without knowing its name.

Outside on the walkway fronting the rooms, I pause with my cart full of cleaning supplies. Adjacent to the motel is a sweeping drop populated by silver firs two hundred feet tall. Their branches nod in the breeze, massive lengths swaying but strong.

As I watch, the clouds ease apart, allowing sunshine to cascade through the forest. The moisture on the needled branches glows white, and I feel each point of light flaring inside me. Warm. I'm captured all over again by the beauty of this place. Overwhelmed by the gratitude of bearing witness. Thankful I'm alive.

There was a time when my life was set to a speed unconducive to wonder. When I missed moments of brilliance like this because of exterior pressures forcing me in directions I never intended or wanted to go. I was molded into a shape pleasing to others. But that's all gone now. Fallen away, leaving me who I've become. Who I was meant to be.

I close my eyes and breathe in the damp air laced with sunlight before it can disappear, and I go on to the next room.

There are people who love me who are looking for me. Who wonder where I am. I feel their yearning and sadness across the distance like radio waves searching for a beacon.

But there is before and there is now.

And in my heart I know that even if we weren't being hunted, even if I could step back into my old life and everything I knew, I could do it no more than a butterfly could return to its chrysalis and reemerge in the form it once was.

Imogen

"Soooo . . . how was seeing Jamie again?"

I looked over my reflection's shoulder and found April leaning casually in the bathroom doorway, a gin and tonic dangling from one hand. "It was . . ." I went back to trying to get my eyeliner right. "Fine."

"Fine. Jesus."

"What?"

"It's okay to say he looked gorgeous. You're not dead, just married. Though I guess it's kinda the same thing . . ."

I sighed. "He looked—good."

"Moving on. What did he say about your quest?" April sauntered into the bathroom and leaned against the other sink.

"He said he'd do it."

"Well of course he'll do it. I mean what did he think?"

"He probably thinks I'm crazy. Just like you do."

"I don't. Well, maybe a little."

"But overall he wants me to be happy." I could still see the mixture of concern and longing in his eyes. It was a heartbreaking combination.

"You know—" April started, then shook her head and took a sip of her drink. "Never mind."

"Like I'm going to let that go?" I put the eyeliner away and fished my birth control out of the bottom of the toiletries bag. "What?"

She chewed her lower lip. "He bought a ring."

"What?"

"Jamie. He told me the last time we saw each other. We got talking about you, and he'd had a couple, and he said before you broke it off, he'd bought a ring. He was just trying to figure out how to ask without spooking you."

"Oh." It was all I could think to say. Jamie. Poor Jamie. Unlucky enough to cross paths with me.

"I mean, don't beat yourself up about it. It's in the past. We have to let things go, otherwise they'll eat us alive, right?"

"Right." I was holding the packet of pills tightly, trying not to imagine Jamie before me down on one knee, holding out his hopes in one hand. Tried not thinking about how choices are rivers, running ahead and through us. From us.

I punched one of the pills out, the plastic crackling. I bent the package one way, then the other. "Does this feel funny to you?" I said, handing it to April.

"Funny?" She twisted it, gave it back. "It feels like plastic."

"It's crackly. Brittle." I brought the pill closer to my face. Turned it over. "Does the color look off?"

"Oh my God, just take the fucking thing so you don't get knocked up, but more importantly so we can go downstairs and I can get another drink. This is going to be a long fucking weekend," she said over one shoulder as she left the bathroom.

The pill lay in the palm of my hand. I turned it over once more, then swallowed it. April was right. It was time to go down.

———

The inn where my dad had proposed and sealed his fate was directly on the beach. A quaint seaside retreat built a hundred years ago and added on to in the last ten, which boasted seventy rooms now instead of its original forty-five. There was a nice courtyard facing the ocean, and this was where the main celebration was being held for their anniversary.

The yard was partially hemmed in by tall hedges on each side, forcing the eye out to the water while giving a sense of privacy. Strings of lights had been draped across the space over a few dozen tables, several of which were still being set up by Charlie and Lev, who'd volunteered earlier.

April and I watched them from the bar off to one side. They looked like boys with their dress shirts rolled to their elbows, laughing and joking, racing one another to set up chairs the fastest. Lev himself was in much better spirits today. Mom and Dad had chartered a sailboat for the day before and we'd gone out in the afternoon. All of us except Lev. When he'd heard the plan he'd been good-natured about it, but I could see his discomfort at the thought of going out on the water. Mom was mortified. *How could I have been so thoughtless?* She'd apologized to the point of embarrassment. I'd given him a small wave as we cast off. He'd waved back from shore.

Now he caught my eye and grinned, shouldering Charlie out of the way to set up the last few chairs. The clouds were gauzy, and wind shot over the ocean. The evening was mild with a gentle breeze. And beneath the soft lights dressed in his dark slacks and white shirt, Lev had never looked more handsome.

"Glad they have something to occupy them," Beth said, coming up to the bar. "Between the boys and those two, I thought was gonna lose it. Martini, please." While the bartender made her drink, she cast a look for her sons, who were on the other side of the courtyard playing an alternating game of tag and shove-the-other-in-the-dirt. "There should be an entertainment section for kids and husbands at every function as far as I'm concerned."

"Who would take care of all the grunt work then?" Charlie said as he and Lev approached.

"Us," Beth replied. "You'd be surprised what we're capable of if you got out of the way."

"Oh yeah?" Charlie swept her into his arms.

"Yeah." Beth giggled, blushing as he said something into her ear. Lev leaned in and kissed the side of my neck, cologne and a hint of sweat about him. My skin tingled not unpleasantly.

"Literally fifth wheel over here," April said, sipping her drink.

"Couldn't find a date?" Charlie said.

"Why would I subject another human being to this?"

"It should be fun," Lev said, ordering a beer.

"Mom explicitly said no speeches, so you know she's absolutely expecting speeches," Charlie said.

"Hope Dad has his note cards," I said.

Charlie pitched his voice down, doing an eerily good impression of our father. "The last forty years have flown by, and I'm hoping to be released soon for good behavior. To the warden!"

"What were you saying, Charlie?" Mom said, coming even with the group.

Charlie nearly spat out the sip of beer he'd taken. "Nothing. Gorgeous night, isn't it?"

"Perfect. Everyone doing okay?" We all rumbled agreement. "Imogen, the concierge informed me the caterer has arrived."

Lev and I shared a brief look. "I'll go check with them."

"Can't wait to see who you got, sis," Charlie said, eyes gleaming.

———

"Big Bill's Bodacious Barbecue," Charlie read aloud off the side of the truck backed up near the courtyard.

Big Bill himself had already unloaded the food and equipment, and there was steam rising off several heating trays filled with pork, beef, and chicken. Another chef was spitting a large ham hock over charcoal. People were beginning to gather in the courtyard, predinner drinks in hand, a hum of voices smattered with laughter.

Charlie slowly rotated until he faced me. "What the fuck?"

"The other caterers fell through. They were the only ones available." If only Charlie knew how close we'd been to having no caterer at all. Big Bill was from North Carolina—a close college friend of Congressman Webber. Lev had called in the favor the night before my presentation, and Webber had come through.

"I don't understand—you had months to book someone."

"Relax," Beth said, coming up beside us with Lev and April in tow. "I just heard someone say it's refreshingly unpretentious."

"That's the most pretentious thing I've ever heard," April said.

"All that aside," Charlie said, "Mom hates fucking barbecue."

Mom was standing at the opposite end of the courtyard eyeing the food as it was being set up, one hand clutched below her throat, the other holding a tall glass of white wine she kept swirling.

"It was the best I could do," I said, a huskiness to my voice. I couldn't cry now. Not in front of everyone. Couldn't let them see how unbalanced I was. How ready to break.

"Well, why didn't you—" Charlie began, but then Lev reached out and gripped his elbow.

"Hey, man, leave it alone." Lev's demeanor had shifted. It was like the air had tightened around us. Charlie sensed it too. Something passed between the two men.

"Yeah. Yeah, sure," Charlie said. "Sorry, sis. It's fine."

I shook my head—in dismissal or denial, I wasn't sure.

"Well, it smells great," Beth said, breaking the quiet. Her effervescence and attempt to smooth over something that most definitely wouldn't smooth over was suddenly beyond funny. I put a hand over my mouth as if to catch the wild laughter that came out. Lev appraised me, then started to chuckle too. Soon we were all leaning against one another, everyone a little drunk, the tension dissolving within the absurdity of it all.

Big Bill dinged a wineglass with a spoon. The courtyard hushed. "Hey, y'all! Wanted to let everyone know, the buffet line is open. Dig in!"

I bit back another scream of laughter, and we lined up for the food.

―――――

Charlie was right. Mom wanted speeches. I'd been prepared for this, the spectacle she needed to fill some vacant part of her that never stayed full for very long. At one time I thought I could be that for her—a piece of herself she'd pushed out to the world but needed to absorb again. Later I knew the emptiness was too large for me. I would get lost inside it.

On cue, Dad rose from his seat when everyone was midway through the meal, holding a small microphone, his voice coming clearly from some wireless speakers hidden somewhere in the courtyard.

"Thank you all for being here with us tonight," he said, nudging his glasses into place. "When the kids asked us what we wanted for our fortieth, we said 'to see our friends.' And since they couldn't make it—" Everyone laughed. I smiled. "But in all seriousness, I'm honored to be standing here beside my wife not far from where I proposed all those years ago. And they've been good years." Mom was looking up at him, basking in the moment, head tilted, eyes shining. "They've gone fast, which I think is a sign of living well. If I could do it all over again, I would only do one thing differently. I'd get down on one knee and ask sooner."

I was touched to see a tear at the corner of Dad's eye as he bent and kissed Mom. Applause from all the tables, then the microphone was passed on. People began to offer their congratulations and quips and sweet anecdotes about the couple of the hour. Charlie caught my eye at one point and pretended to be sick. I didn't know if he was goofing on the moment or commenting on the food. I gave him the finger and took another bite of smoked turkey. The food was excellent no matter what he thought. Mom had taken a polite helping of mashed potatoes and salad and touched neither. She hadn't looked at me all evening.

Soon the microphone had traveled to our table, and while I was still cobbling together something to say, Lev was standing and clearing his throat. I craned my neck to look up at him.

"Hi, I'm Lev—Imogen's husband if I haven't been introduced yet—and I'm obviously very new to the family, and to marriage itself. Like most of us, I always had an idea about what marriage would be like from watching my parents. They're the blueprint you can't help but build from and compare your life to. You find yourself wanting that connection they share, the way they understand each other. And if you're observant you see that not everything is perfect in a marriage. There are challenges. Ups and downs. Doubts." I reached out to take a sip from my champagne, but there was a tremor in my hand. I put it back in my lap. "But if a marriage is meant to be, those trials deepen the relationship. And that depth is where the strongest love forms. Not so much in the easy days, but in the difficult ones. Seeing a marriage like Ted and Cora's is a testament to trust and dedication and respect. Everything I could ever want for my own." He touched my shoulder gently, and I found myself putting a hand over his, audible murmurs of appreciation from several tables. "So that's all to say, I'm so happy for you both and I—"

I was looking down when he stopped speaking, so I thought he was just gathering his next set of thoughts. Or maybe getting choked up himself. The sound of the incoming tide filled the empty space. Then I heard Charlie quietly say, "Hey, you okay?" I glanced up at Lev.

He was staring down at the table, eyes glazed. His mouth had slackened and the microphone was at his side. A familiar plunging sensation filled me, as if everything inside had dropped through a trapdoor. I followed Lev's gaze down to our champagne glasses side by side.

The golden liquid.

The bubbles sliding up the glass.

Seeing what he was seeing. Knowing what was happening.

The champagne he'd poured right before he'd fallen overboard.

The last thing he'd seen before I pushed him.

The microphone fell from his hand, making a terrible thud when it hit the grass. Like a crumpling body. His jaw was working, chewing back something trying to emerge. Slowly his eyes slid to mine. "You . . ." He breathed the word but it was enough to know.

He remembered everything.

Imogen

Lev's chair tipped over and he stumbled away from the table.

I watched helplessly. I was being sliced open. Vivisected by all the questioning eyes, the murmurs of concern. I didn't know what to do. Lev hurried out of the courtyard and slipped inside the inn. I reached down and picked up the microphone.

"Sorry. He's . . . Excuse us." I handed the mic off to April, who accepted it like it was a stinging insect. Then I was moving, floating on legs that weren't mine, barreling through a jungle of thoughts with no visible path. My mother flashed me a look as I passed and went inside. April's voice came from the speakers, muted and strained as the door swung shut behind me.

The inn's rear foyer was empty. For a drawn moment I thought he'd gone up to our room. Was already packing. Would leave me here to explain what happened to everyone. A poetic punishment.

He knows. Knows what I did. Why he fell.

The fact nearly unhinged my knees. I'd half believed this would never happen. That his fall would remain safely forgotten, and I'd have all the leeway I needed to put my concerns to rest. But this was reality. He'd remembered.

I was so absorbed I almost didn't notice him standing in the adjacent hallway, one forearm on the wall, his forehead pressed against it. Like a child counting to play hide-and-seek.

I approached him, stopping a safe distance away. Every nerve sang in disharmony. I wanted to run. Wanted to say I was sorry. Beg forgiveness. I even hoped I was wrong—that there was a chance he hadn't recalled everything.

But I knew that was a false hope when he finally straightened and turned to face me. His features were flat and gray. He studied me with the cold detachment of a stranger.

The seconds ticked out, three of my heartbeats in each one.

"I'm . . . I'm sorry," I finally said, voice failing on the last word. He stared back, unblinking. "I didn't mean—" Tears cinched off the rest of what I was trying to say. And how much was it worth anyway? How could an apology make up for almost ending his life? I could see him reliving the hours spent floating in the ocean, sunburned and bleeding. Imagine what he thought of the woman he'd chosen to marry. The speech he'd just given bitter and curdling on his tongue.

"Why?" he said at last.

"It was—" He waited as I wrestled with an explanation. Anything bordering reason. There was nothing.

"Because I talked to another woman? You thought since I touched a waitress's hand I was cheating on you?"

"No . . . that's not . . ." I shook my head. How could I voice something I'd never come to terms with personally?

The silence stretched out. Became corrosive. "What you told me about him before the wedding, I thought I understood. But maybe I didn't." He made a weak gesture. "Maybe I don't."

Marcus.

Another secret lost until now. There was a faint pounding somewhere in the inn. Like someone banging insistently on a door.

"Did you mean to do it?"

I couldn't tell what he was asking about. Marcus or himself. I was losing sense of place and time. Split in two. One part watching him fall over the railing, another holding a bloody knife.

"No, of course not," I said. But hadn't I felt some sense of righteous vindication both times? Two men getting what they deserved for once. "It was an accident." The pounding was louder. As if it had moved closer. I shook my head, trying to clear it. "Please, just listen—I didn't mean for you to fall. I never wanted that to happen. Never."

Lev released a long breath. "I want to believe that. But what you did to Marcus . . . it scares me." He swallowed. "*You* scare me."

Something was coming apart inside me. Bending and breaking. The distrust in his eyes was like a physical thing, filling the space between us. Shoving us apart.

Lev started down the hallway. "Where are you going?" I asked.

"Home," he said. "Can you get a ride back with April?"

"Yeah," I heard myself say.

"I think . . ." Lev paused, then shook his head.

I started to say something to mend what I'd done. Anything to make this feeling go away. But Lev was already striding along the hall, head down. Then he was gone. There was a chair near the foyer and I moved to it, needing to sit down, but when the rest of the room came into view, I froze.

I wasn't alone.

My mother stood just around the corner, arms folded tightly. As soon as I saw her, I knew two things. One, she'd heard our conversation—the look on her face left no room to think anything else. And two, I knew where the pounding was coming from.

It was inside me.

The garden door was breaking, all the things I'd kept within fighting to get out.

"Imogen," Mom said, her voice so low it was hard to hear. "What did you do?"

The door burst open.

Imogen

What did you do?

The same thing she had said as I stood cold, bloody, and alone on the doorstep of my childhood home all those years ago. I reflected later that her first response hadn't been *Are you okay?* or *What do you need?* It had been accusatory. Mom knowing me so well. Seeing it on my face. Knowing I was to blame.

I'd told her what I could. Enough so that she got the picture and knew I wasn't going to bleed to death. She'd handed me a towel for my hand and shaken her head. *Go to the emergency room. We'll talk later.*

Then she'd closed the door.

I'd stood and stared at it for a long time. Long enough for it to materialize inside me. For me to imagine the door set in a stone wall, a garden growing round it. I took everything that had happened in the hours before and pushed it through the opening, then shut and locked it tight.

It had stayed closed until now.

————

You were perfect.

I saw you for the first time in the art history class I'd taken on a whim as an elective. I'd always been interested in art but had found out relatively quickly I valued more how it made me feel versus knowing its origin and mechanics. I think that's true for most good things—if you try too hard to understand them, you kill what makes them special in the first place.

You were sitting two rows down, off to the right. Your hair was what I noticed first. How dark and lush it was. How you kept brushing it behind your ears. Your smile came next. You smiled often and it was dazzling. I wondered those first days before we'd met what it would feel like to have you smile at me. You moved your hands a lot, especially when you were excited. You answered questions no one else knew, but you weren't arrogant. You had a way of drawing people in, even the professor. I think I might have loved you a little before you ever looked at me.

But you did. One day we were both early to class, and I caught your eye somehow. We exchanged a glance. Then another. By the time the lecture hall was full, you'd looked at me five times, smiled on the last two. I'd smiled back. You came up to me after class and asked what my name was and why I was hiding near the back. I lied and said I wasn't hiding.

I'm Marcus, you said. *But everyone calls me Marcus.* Even your stupid joke was charming. It disarmed me. Maybe even then you could tell I was nervous about every aspect of myself. We got coffee together. You were a year older, an art major. Not because you were an artist, no. You said you couldn't be. You'd tried but didn't have the necessary talent. You loved art for what it was, how it affected people. How seeing a great painting could change something integral about yourself. You wanted to open a gallery someday. Jet around the world and collect pieces from emerging painters and sell them. You were like some exotic creature I'd only read about.

I was swept away.

You were confident, but not overly so. Smart and well read. Considerate—you always asked what I wanted to do, where I wanted to go, before voicing any of your own ideas. You had an intensity about you, especially when viewing art. It was like your eyes were seeing things no one else was. I suppose that was true. You looked at me the same way, and it undid something inside me.

You weren't my first, but your intimacy was something transcendent. You were experienced and patient. So unlike the two other high school boys I'd slept with. As a teenager, I'd felt pressured to slough off my virginity as quickly as possible while maintaining a sense of self-respect. But afterward, when the boy I'd been with rolled away to leave me to clean myself up as best I could in the back seat of his car, I felt nothing but dim relief tinged with embarrassment. Another task accomplished. Pleasure would come later, mostly by experimenting solo. But with you it was different. Beneath or above you, I felt like someone else. Like I was a piece of art you were penetrating, not only with your body but with your mind as well.

Your family was affluent, old East Coast money. Your father in finance, your mother a former tennis star. You were their only child, and they prized you and your future above all else. I remember the first time you brought me home to meet them. We'd been dating three months, and things were much more serious than I'd anticipated. The trip to see them at their summer home in the Hamptons was one of unending questions and prolonged assessment. They wanted to know everything about me, and as nice as they tried to make it, it still felt like an interview for a position I was deeply unqualified for.

They'll love you like I do. I promise, you'd said as we drove away after. Internally, I bloomed colors there were no names for. It was the first time you'd said *love.*

My mother became a different person overnight after learning of you. I'd been very hesitant to mention I was seeing someone, unsure of how she'd react. In the past she'd been polite but cool to any of the boys I dated. Maybe she knew it was merely tryouts in preparation for the big leagues. Or maybe she had so little confidence in my judgment, she couldn't be bothered to care. But with you she was different.

After our first family dinner together, she came alive. Calling me. Texting me. Suddenly very interested in the small details of my day-to-day. It was as if your looks and charm and money woke something up inside her. A long-dormant fantasy of dancing with a ballet company in Russia and meeting a handsome and mysterious stranger who happened to be rich. A life born out of passion and chance that became a waking dream. Elegance and wealth and the world at her fingertips. Maybe she saw the future she never had in you. An avenue finally opening to live vicariously through me.

When we'd been dating six months, you asked me to move into your penthouse apartment. You told me you wanted me closer. Didn't want to spend any more nights apart. I was thrilled and taken aback. Afraid. Moving in together was another level of commitment, a large leap in preparation for an even bigger plunge. I called my mother to ask her advice, not because I didn't know what she'd say, but to hear her reinforce the preordained steps in the progression of my life. She was excited but sensed my apprehension and tried snuffing it out like a spark that could ignite a forest fire. I would be a fool to turn you down. What didn't I like about you? Could I name a problem?

The answers were no. But that didn't mean I wasn't afraid.

Fear and I had been close acquaintances all my life. Anxious hesitation hindered most of my decisions, while other people I knew embraced experiences and opportunities with joyous abandon. For me, calculation was a comfort. A spreadsheet of pluses and minuses totaling either red or black. Even as my mother urged me forward and I began merging my belongings and thus my life to yours, I was running risk assessments and creating redundancies. I renewed my lease for the next year for a place to move back to. I kept my possessions localized to one area of the apartment in case I had to gather them quickly. I maintained my GPA even though you took up a huge amount of my bandwidth. But even with the built-in caution and conscious insurances, I couldn't deny what was happening.

I was falling in love.

We went almost everywhere together. We cooked on the weekends and spent rainy Saturdays in bed. We saw films and frequented clubs with your friends. We talked for hours over morning coffee, having deep conversations about important and trivial things alike. We agreed on politics and our lack of enthusiasm for any organized religion. We took walks at dusk, enjoying how the sky changed colors right before the sun dropped below the horizon. You enchanted me with your subtle wit and your carefree whims. You moved through the world like it could never hurt you. I envied you so much.

For our one-year anniversary, you booked a trip to Paris. I'd never been out of the country. We spent a week sightseeing, eating dishes I couldn't try to pronounce, drinking wine on busy street corners, listening to people talking like it was music.

When you took me to the Louvre, it was like bringing me to your church. You led me silently past pieces with a reverie bordering on rapture. We considered Mona Lisa's smile and Géricault's tragic *Raft of the Medusa*. While I was studying *Psyche Revived by Cupid's Kiss*, captured by the lovers' intensity, you got down on one knee behind me. There were gasps and exclamations. People filming and taking pictures as my hand stole up to my mouth. You were so beautiful there, down on one knee—the first time I'd ever seen you truly vulnerable.

I had to force myself not to run.

All at once the gravity fell on me. Crushing down. This was the rest of my life. All of it laid out if I said yes. Because for all your charisma and intensity, you were our center. You were going to open a gallery with the trust fund your parents had set up. You were going to travel and collect art. You were going to write insightful articles that would send shock waves through the creative community. Your insight. Your passion. Your dreams.

And of course, I would be there, too, on the periphery.

I would come along for the ride and do what I could in the shadow of your aspirations. All I had to do was say yes. And with you there before me, with all the people watching in that very public and perfect setting, how could I answer anything different? How could any woman?

Afterward, we went back to our hotel and made frantic love. When we were both spent, I went in the bathroom and shut the door. Stood looking at the heavy ring on my finger. Wondering how long it would take for me to become the person I was expected to be. I hated myself then for dimming what should've been the brightest day of my life.

My mother was ecstatic.

She lit up like a supernova and became a fixture in my life. Even though we'd both agreed to hold off on the wedding until we were well established in our careers, she insisted on starting to plan. We visited venues, went dress shopping, looked at flower arrangements until I saw them in my sleep. There was food to decide on and a guest list to compose. Whenever I told her there was plenty of time, absolutely no rush, she would wave the idea away. Planning was never in vain. In every other reality, I agreed with that. She ingratiated herself with your mother and they began spending weekends shopping in the city together. As an engagement gift, your parents gave "us" one of your favorite paintings. It was an original by a Swedish artist named Ğ. A six-foot-tall oil done in dramatic sweeps of black and red depicting the abstraction of two figures locked in an embrace. It was titled simply *The Lovers*. You hung it on the wall in the living room where it would get the best indirect light. I'd catch you studying it at least once a week, hand on your chin, eyes flitting from one brushstroke to the next.

Time went on. You graduated. I took on an unpaid internship at Stanford Management Systems. I felt the owner saw something in me. After a few months of digital filing and coffee runs, he began sending me to conferences he or his employees lacked the time or will to attend. We would FaceTime while I was away. I began noticing a distance between us that had nothing to do with how far apart we were. You were still exuberant about the plans for the gallery, but I could tell it was more than you'd anticipated. The first real challenge you'd faced. Everything else had fallen so easily before you. Including me. I told myself that was all it was.

On those trips, I used the time alone for self-reflection. Asked myself what I wanted that I didn't possess. Why I felt a longing for some aspect of myself I was missing and couldn't name. I traced the route of my life and knew it would be the envy of many. By all appearances, I had everything I needed. And I was grateful. Grateful for you and for the privileges I was born into. Yet I felt trapped, hemmed in by expectations on every level. And mingled within it all was the shame from resenting the attention and approval I was now receiving from my mother, while basking in it nonetheless. I feared retribution and disdain for wanting to deviate. Especially since I had no clear goal outside of those presented to me.

But sometimes I saw an open road winding away through an empty valley, heat shimmering across it, the sky above an impossible white blue. My only companions the will to see what was over the next hill and the freedom to do so.

I told myself most people probably felt this way when faced with their place in the world and the path forward. I decided the unnamed longing would be smoothed away by time and enough trust in the future. That it was the discarding of impractical dreams all women eventually set aside to focus on what was reasonably attainable.

The day it happened, I decided to surprise you.

The conference I was at in New York ended early, and I caught a train home instead of staying the extra night. You texted you'd been out with some friends and were recovering. On the way home I stopped at our favorite Thai place and picked up dinner and a bottle of wine. You were in the shower when I came in. You adored long showers, and I knew I had time to set the table and pour us glasses of merlot.

Your phone was on the bed along with a few balled-up tissues. At first I thought you'd caught a cold, but when I picked the tissues up to throw them away, I noticed a smell. It was you. Your most intimate scent. I could almost taste you.

I looked from your phone to the tissues, putting two and two together. I'd never been aware of you using porn before and hadn't thought you'd required it, given our healthy sex life. But I was mature enough to accept you might have been struck by need and satisfied yourself while I was away. Out of pure curiosity, I picked up your phone and punched in your code.

For a second what was on the screen was so shocking, it wouldn't compute.

At first I thought I'd been correct. It was just an explicit still shot from some website. I was somewhat disappointed but not completely surprised. But then I noticed details in the background beyond the photo's centerpiece.

Like the pattern of the bedsheet and the lamp on the table. The color of the pillowcase.

It was our bedroom.

And when I refocused on the subject of the picture, of course I recognized the sweep of your hip. The small scar on your side where you'd fallen from a skateboard as a teen. How could I not know your body after such sustained intimacy? All at once the horror of what the picture meant descended upon me.

You had been in our bed with another woman.

Her flesh on the screen pressed against yours.

I found myself swiping to the next pic. Another angle of her body from the shoulders down. They were taken awkwardly, as if you'd been trying to snap them without her knowing. I studied each one as if I were looking at photos from a car crash. But the crash was happening now inside me.

I realized where I was sitting on the bed. Almost on top of where you'd fucked her. Where we'd fucked countless times. Probably sitting where you had masturbated to the pictures before showering.

I was sick and shaking. Lost in the avalanche my life had become. I set the phone down and left the room. You were singing something in the shower.

I stood in the center of the apartment, looking around, unable to think past how reality had shrunk in the last few minutes. How things I'd accepted and taken for granted were small, thin lies. The space I'd begun thinking of as home was now completely alien. All your belongings betrayals. Everything felt sharp and poisonous.

My gaze landed on *The Lovers*.

I don't recall getting the knife from the butcher block. Only later, when it was stained with blood, did I notice it was the expensive chef's knife I'd gotten you for Christmas. I stood before your beloved painting. But now it was different. The two figures embracing were no longer abstract. They were you and whoever you'd brought home to our bed.

I slashed the canvas diagonally from left to right.

Cut through the lovers. Cut them in half.

Pushed so hard, the blade bit into the wall behind.

I kept cutting and cutting, watching the painting gape open and hang in shreds as my arm began to burn.

Then you were there, soaking wet, a towel around your waist, shouting. You grabbed my shoulders and hauled me away from the painting so violently that I hit the wall and fell. You realized what you'd done and tried helping me up, but then I was standing and had the knife to your throat, the soft skin there popping open against the blade's wicked edge. Your eyes bulged, staring into mine. Terrified. Pleading.

And in that moment I wanted to jerk my arm. Slit the throat that had produced the lies I'd believed.

But within the same heartbeat, I saw everything from outside myself. Saw what I was about to do. What I was capable of. What I was about to become.

I took the knife from your throat and stepped back. A little blood leaked from the cut on your neck. It was barely a graze, but when you swiped at it and saw you were bleeding, you let out a cry like a little boy who'd had his first accident. Discovered he wasn't invincible and was horrified by the fact.

I felt wetness in my hands and at my feet, and when I looked down I realized I was gripping the knife blade and it had sliced deeply into my palm. Blood pattered onto my pant legs and stained my socks. Dribbled onto the hardwood floor.

After that was mostly a blur.

Wrapping my hand in one of my T-shirts. Packing my things while you locked yourself in your office. Leaving the penthouse with the sound of you speaking to someone on the phone.

After the brief stop at my parents', I went to April's. She took me in without question. Helped dress my wound. Gave me tea and something to eat. Held me while I cried and eventually fell asleep. I stayed with her during the fallout.

Our parents got involved, and as the story gradually came together, it was decided the best outcome (for all parties) would be not to involve the police, on one condition—if the cost of the painting was reimbursed. Fifteen thousand dollars, which I didn't have. My mom and dad wrote a check, and you mailed me the last few items I'd left behind. There were no more words, and I only saw you one more time. It was a year later, at a coffee shop. You were with a pretty woman at a table near the back. I thought she might be the one from the pictures. Seeing the two of you together didn't reawaken the loss or anguish I expected. All I felt was a dull throb in the scar on my hand.

I left without looking back, holding the coffee cup tightly, letting the heat sear deep into the healed wound.

Sierra

The bar is just starting to liven up when the evening guy comes in to relieve me.

He's a college kid only a few years into his twenties, here for the hiking and mountain biking. Shaggy hair and a good-natured smile. He tries flirting with me in the brief overlap of our shifts. Harmless flattering stuff. I'm nearing forty, so I take it as a compliment and tell him to focus on his bartending skills so I don't have customers complaining about weak whiskey-Cokes anymore.

The rain has gotten a little more serious in the afternoon hours. I jog to my truck and brush the wet from my shoulders and hair and start thinking about Zee again. I take out my phone to call the sheriff and check if anyone's brought him in when I see a text I'd missed earlier from Tyler. It's a picture of Zee on my front porch with a message beneath: Look what I found.

The relief is overwhelming. Where was he? I text quickly.

Tell you later . . . is his reply.

Elated, I start to head across town to the day care, but for once I'm off early and not due to pick my son up for another half hour. Instead, I coast down Main Street and park in front of Folded Corners, our one and only bookstore. Besides the lake at dawn, this is my favorite place in Maynard. It's a cozy, squarish space with four freestanding shelves, a coffee counter at the back, and a sitting area in front of the big windows looking onto the street. I get a small light roast with cream, snag a copy of *Songs of Innocence and Experience* by Blake, which I've been working my way through, and sink into one of the battered but undeniably comfortable armchairs.

I get lost in the words for a while. The coffee is good and strong. The rain streaks the windows, turning everything outside into a watercolor that hasn't dried yet.

Tonight there will be dinner to make, stories from day care to listen to, bathtime, and bedtime. Nothing asked of me I'm unwilling to give. But for now, this moment is for me, and I savor it.

It's time to pick him up, but first I finish the poem I'm on.

> Graze after thee, and weep.
> For, wash'd in life's river,
> My bright mane for ever
> Shall shine like the gold
> As I guard o'er the fold.

I close the book and hold it for a moment, letting the words toll like a bell inside me. Listen to its soft pealing. I start to rise from the chair when something stops me.

Someone is standing across the street in front of the post office, which is closed and dark at this hour. They're a blurred shape through the streaked glass, but the sight of them makes me pause.

They're staring at the bookstore. Staring at me.

I shift, trying to get a clearer look through the glass, but everything beyond is watery and smeared.

"Need anything else, Sierra? I'm gonna shut the coffee down in a minute."

I glance up at Kim, the owner. "No . . . no, I'm fine."

"You sure? You look like you just had a bad thought."

I blink, looking back out the window.

The person is gone.

"I have to—" I say, but I'm already standing, setting the book back on the shelf and heading for the door. Kim says something else, but I don't hear it. There's a faint buzzing growing in volume, drowning out everything else. I step out below the store's awning. Rain drifts down the street in curtains. There are a few cars parked along the opposite curb, and I head across to them, considering getting the handgun from my truck along the way and dismissing it just as quickly.

There is no one hiding behind the cars or tucked beside the post office. No sign of anyone on the street. I look both ways, then head downtown through the rain, swiping it from my eyes. The street curves through a brief stand of trees, and I stop beneath them, peering into the dripping shadows. Waiting for movement. Searching for a shape that doesn't belong. An exhaled breath.

Nothing.

I'm alone.

Back at my truck, I climb into the cab and start the engine. Crank the heat on high and hold my shaking hands out to the vents. My eyes creep to the mirrors.

I'm overreacting. There are a thousand explanations for what I saw. It could have been anyone standing there. Except there was a hint of recognition branded in my mind by fear.

The shape of his shoulders. How he held his head. The way he stood.

No.

It's not possible. There is no way he could have tracked us here. Especially after all this time.

But in truth, time is his friend. Each day is another chance to continue his search. And I know he is looking. Can feel his pursuit every so often like a cold spot in a warm lake.

I'm starting to hyperventilate. Have to calm down. I breathe. Think of the lake and the motion of my arms and legs propelling me through the water. When my mind is still again, I go back over every precaution I took. Every step that led me here. Retrace each decision and hunt for the smallest flaw, asking myself the same thing again and again.

Is there anything that could've led him here? Anything I missed?

No. There is nothing.

No one knows where I am. No one would think to look for me here. I've left no digital footprint in three years. I've cut every tie. I have never seen a familiar face here. Never had anyone recognize me. People may have suspected I'm running from something, but no one has asked. This is not a place where people ask questions like that. That's why it's safe.

It was just a person pausing on their way somewhere else. They weren't looking for me. Probably weren't even looking *at* me. I know I've had a hard time adjusting and convincing myself he won't find us. The world is too big and he's just one man. But I also know what he's capable of. I know what he'd do if he found us. And it is hard to ignore that species of fear.

I back the truck out and idle down Main Street, still looking for anyone walking alone. I would feel better knowing it was my imagination, but there's no one in sight. As I park in the driveway of my son's day care and catch a glimpse of him through the picture window—a bobbing, joyous shape playing with his friends—I tell myself I'm wrong. I've taken every necessary step. I've broken the chain, and there is nothing and no one who could find us now.

"We're safe," I whisper.

Imogen

Lev was waiting in the living room when I got home.

April had dropped me off, giving my hand a squeeze before I climbed out. I was so preoccupied with what was coming, I barely felt it. At least the weekend was finally over.

Mom had heard enough of our conversation to know what we were talking about and had deduced the rest. I'd tried to explain, but when I reached the point where Lev had fallen overboard, she'd held out a hand and turned her head away, eyes closed. *Don't,* was all she'd said, then went outside to rejoin the party.

I went to our room when I was sure Lev had gone. Sat staring out the window until it grew dark. When April had knocked on the door, I gave her an excuse about Lev not feeling well. Who knew what my mother was saying. I guessed she'd only reveal it to Dad and Charlie. Charlie would tell Beth. I couldn't fathom what they'd think of me afterward. Didn't want to. I'd stayed in the room the rest of the night and had bowed out of brunch the next morning before asking April to bring me home.

I told her everything on the way.

She'd listened stoically, not saying anything until I was finished.

"What are you going to do?" she asked as we left the freeway and closed in on my neighborhood.

"I don't know."

"Do you want to stay with me for now?"

"No. I need to figure this out. I can't run from it."

She was quiet for a time before saying, "Are you sure . . ."

"What?"

"Nothing." She'd stared straight ahead the rest of the drive.

Now, standing in the living room doorway, I wondered if I should've taken her up on the offer to stay at her place. Given Lev and me some space. Let us both acclimate to our new reality.

He gazed at me from his chair. I twisted my hands together. With him finally knowing everything, I felt nude. All my protections stripped away. The possibilities of what would come next were overwhelming. Would he leave me? Would he tell everyone the truth? And was this supposed to happen? Was he supposed to remember, and was our marriage destined to crumble from it? Was this the fruition of all my disquiet and worry, my paranoid insecurities? Was it always going to be this way?

"Where's Mox?" I asked, just for something to say.

"Still at Val and Deshawn's."

"Oh."

Lev sat forward, lacing his fingers together. "Were you ever going to tell me?"

I came a step into the room and settled onto an arm of the sofa. "I wanted to. But it was so . . ."

He nodded and looked down at his clasped hands. "When I woke up in the water, it was so dark I didn't know if my eyes were open or not. It was cold. I've never felt that scared or alone before." I wanted to say something, say how sorry I was again, but my throat was constricted so tightly I could barely breathe. "I remember thinking I was going to die."

"Lev—"

"But I remembered something else too." I stiffened, wondering if it was his turn for a confession. "You were so upset before I fell. I thought you were just drunk. I wanted you to come out on the balcony to get some air, and I grabbed your arm. I can see how that might've triggered something for you." There was a flash of Marcus grasping my shoulders, shoving me against the wall, how it felt to be tossed aside by someone stronger. "I shouldn't have done that, I'm sorry."

"I'm the one—" I started, but my voice faltered.

"I know it was an accident," he said. "I don't think for a second you're capable of hurting someone like that intentionally. Hurting me. But I need to know, do you still want this?" He gestured around at our house, our belongings, our life. "Do you still want to do this with me?"

Did I? I thought of all the suspicions. What I did and didn't know. All the things I'd been afraid of. Had walked away from. "Yes," I finally said.

"So do I. But we can't have it unless we trust each other." He pulled out his phone and tossed it onto the coffee table. It landed on a magazine with a dull thud. "Do you want to look through my phone? My computer? Check my emails and messages? Go ahead."

I shook my head again, but I did want to do those things. The part of me that required evidence and solid conclusions was already reaching out to pick the phone up and scan through it. Search it until I was satisfied and could rest.

"Then if we want to move forward, we should say the things that need to be said now."

"Okay."

Lev's brow furrowed and he took a breath. "I want you to start seeing Dr. Rogers again."

"Oh." The suggestion I resume therapy hurt a little. But not nearly as much as falling sixty feet into water and spending the next twelve hours there, bleeding and burned. "Okay. I will."

He relaxed into his chair. "Is there anything you want to say to me?"

I didn't mean to say it, but then the words were tumbling out. Unable to call them back. "Who's Sierra Rossen?"

"Sierra . . ." A shadow passed behind his eyes. He looked away. "Wow. I haven't thought of her in a long time." His gaze came back to me. "She was someone I was with before I met you. But I think you already knew that."

I ignored the remark and forged ahead. Now that things were in motion, I couldn't stop. "Why didn't you ever tell me about her?"

He sighed, passing his hands over his face as if he were just waking up. "A lot of reasons. I suppose the main one is she broke my heart." I settled down into the couch. "We met through a mutual friend. Hit it off right away. I fell for her quick and she took her time." He smiled thinly. "We were together for a couple years. I thought it was going to last. Then she changed."

"Changed how?" I found myself leaning forward, rapt now that I was finally getting some insight into the woman who had been a fixture in my mind from the moment I saw her face.

"She was consumed with her career. Devoted every spare minute to it, and of course she had less time for me. For a while I thought there was someone else, but she always denied it. We started to drift, and I tried everything I could to hold on while she was letting go." He smiled again, sadly this time. "So that was it. We broke up, and then years later she just . . . vanished."

"Vanished?" I sounded believably surprised.

"She went out for a drive one night and never came back. She was reported missing." He barked a quiet laugh. "The cops even interviewed me. I guess that's good—no stone left unturned. But it all didn't really make any sense. Sierra wasn't the kind of person to just pull up stakes and leave. If there was a problem, she faced it head on." His gaze grew distant.

"So what do you think happened?"

"I don't know. Maybe she met someone she couldn't live without and ran away with them. Left everything else behind." He readjusted in the chair and seemed to return from where he'd gone. "I think I didn't tell you about her for the same reason you kept what happened with Marcus a secret for so long. When someone hurts you like that, you want to bury it. You don't want to admit how much you needed them when they didn't feel the same. It's degrading not to be wanted."

He left his seat and knelt in front of me. Took me in his arms. I could feel his breath puffing gently against my neck. We stayed that way for a while, holding each other.

"I thought she was the one," he whispered. "Until I met you."

———

Later, after he'd fallen asleep, I saw Jamie had emailed me. There was a file attached, and he'd written only a brief note, but I could hear every word in his gentle voice.

> Imogen,
>
> Attached is what I was able to find, which wasn't much. I also included the names and addresses of the people closest to her. I hope this gives you some peace of mind. It was hard seeing you the other day, but I'm glad I did. I wish you the very best.
>
> Yours,
> J.

I thought then of how Sierra's name had come out of me without meaning to. How I'd almost been waiting for the chance to say it and see his reaction. I listened to his soft breathing from where I sat at the top of the stairs in the dark of our home. The idea that I'd set things in motion I couldn't stop came again, along with the question of whether I wanted to. Lev knew the worst things I'd done and forgave me. Still loved me. He wanted us to go forward together. No more secrets.

My finger hovered over the track pad, ready to click into the file Jamie had sent. Doing so would be opening yet another Pandora's box. One that could answer certain questions, but would probably only lead to more.

Heart beating hard, I moved the email into a folder marked FINAL QUARTER EVALUATIONS and closed the computer.

If I wanted the life I'd made for myself, I had to stop. There was doubt and there was trust, and I'd been betrayed by both. But one much more so than the other.

I rose and went back to bed and curled in beside my husband, put my hand on his chest, and fell asleep to its slow rise and fall.

Imogen

The Roy project went forward. I got my promotion. Webber won the election.

An undeniable air of buoyancy surrounded us. It was like we'd both turned a corner. It not only had to do with the good news professionally but also from no longer carrying the secret of why he'd fallen. Even so it was difficult accepting forgiveness I didn't feel I deserved.

Lev seemed lighter too. He smiled more. We talked more. In certain moments the uncertainty resurfaced, but it was weaker the further I distanced myself from it. I told myself it was healthy to follow everyone's advice and move forward.

In the wake of the political victory, Lev invited Senator Webber and his wife over for a celebratory dinner. "Are you serious?" I said, a little mortified at the thought of someone with that level of prestige dining in our home.

"Don't worry, he's super down to earth. He grew up in Kansas, for God's sake," Lev had replied, wrapping me in one of his hugs, which had started to feel welcome again. "You don't have to cook; we'll cater it."

"Big Bill's Bodacious Barbecue?"

He laughed and kissed the side of my neck. "I dare you."

When the night arrived, I found myself lingering in the bathroom, retouching my makeup and primping and pulling at my dress. I'd made dinner instead of ordering catering, and it was sitting warm and ready in the oven. In a last-minute decision I'd switched out of the more comfortable dress pants and blouse I'd reflexively put on and found my little black dress hanging lost and lonely in the very back of the closet. It was somewhat flashy and a bit short. In other words, something I normally avoided. But tonight it felt right. It was what the person I was trying to be would unapologetically wear.

Lev appeared in the doorway buttoning the cuffs of his shirt, and froze. "Whoa."

"Too much?"

He approached and leaned close, putting his hands on either side of the vanity, pinning me in. His lips brushed my exposed shoulder and goose bumps spread outward from the spot. He pressed himself against me, and I could feel him through his slacks, hardening.

"Does it feel like too much?" he whispered. I answered by reaching back and squeezing him. He released a groan and started dragging my dress up over my hips. My breath quickened. We hadn't since . . . I couldn't remember exactly. Any sense of intimacy had been bludgeoned by my constant unease. But now I felt myself responding. The final barriers between us breaking down.

"They'll be here any minute," I said.

"Then let's be quick."

I pivoted, boosting myself onto the edge of the vanity and pulled him in close, unbuckling his belt. He raked my dress out of the way, his mouth covering mine, then sliding down to my throat, lingering on my chest, then he was kneeling, his lips grazing the inside of my thigh, tongue hot and slick sliding closer and closer to—

The doorbell rang.

I jolted.

He peered up at me. "If it were literally anyone else, I would not answer the door."

I smiled and nudged him away as he grinned over one shoulder, redoing his pants on the way out of the bathroom. I rearranged my dress, put my hair back in place, tried fanning away the sex-flush from my skin.

What I saw in the mirror flared a brief ember of satisfaction. I looked . . . *good*. I felt good. Desirable. I held on to the feeling as our guests' voices drifted up the stairs and I went down to meet them.

———

"So my uncle says, if I see one more horse wearing a beret, I'm gonna scream!"

Our laughter rebounded off the walls, and Senator Webber shook his head. "And that was the end of my practical-joking days."

"Oh, stop," his wife, Caroline, said, touching my arm. "On my last birthday he filled our entire bedroom to the ceiling with red and pink balloons."

"That was supposed to be a romantic gesture," Webber said, sipping from his whiskey.

"So was taping an air horn to the seat of my office chair supposed to be romantic too?" Lev asked. He and Webber burst out laughing again, and Caroline and I shared a look.

The evening was winding down. It had gone better than I'd hoped. Dinner was a success, and Caroline had complimented my hair and dress. She was a chic woman with gorgeous platinum hair and a warm smile. Webber was a bullish man with a face too honest for a politician. They'd been together since high school and called one another by their pet names. I liked them both off the bat.

"Your house reminds me of our place in upstate New York. It's on a lake, very secluded. So comfortable and homey," Caroline said. "We try going there at least once a month to reset and shed the Washington ick."

"That reminds me," Webber said, snapping his fingers. "Mark your calendar two weekends from now. We decided we're having a private victory lap up at the lake house—just us and the other staff and their wives. Get a game plan for the new session next year. You can meet the rest of the team you'll be lording over."

"Um—" Lev attempted to interject, but Webber carried on.

"And I'll have someone send over that info on the house I was telling you about. It's actually priced right for how close it is to the capital. Extra rooms, too, for when the little ones come along."

"What house?" I glanced from Webber to Lev, who had stilled.

"Well—" Lev started, setting his wine down.

"Oh shit," Webber said. "Did I just spoil something here?"

"No, not at all. It's just, we had a busy week."

My smile faltered. "I think I'm missing something."

Lev shifted toward me. "I meant to tell you earlier, but with everything that was happening—your parents' anniversary, your promotion—I couldn't find the right time."

"Tell me what?"

The room's silence was rigid. Lev cleared his throat. "Carson asked me to become his chief of staff. And I accepted."

I felt like I'd been shoved from behind, mentally pinwheeling for balance. "Oh," was all I could say. Lev looked at me expectantly, like it was my responsibility to save the moment somehow. "That's . . ." I swallowed and raised my glass. "That's amazing." We all drank.

"Apologies to you both," Webber said. "Didn't mean to trod on toes."

"Don't worry," Caroline said. "You'll get used to being blindsided. It comes with the territory."

"That's not exactly fair," Webber said.

"I'm being honest, not fair." She patted my arm again. "Hang with me, honey. I'll show you the ropes. Political wives have to stick together."

Lev gave me a glance, and I feigned a smile and drank the rest of my wine.

———

The front door clicked shut, and Lev stood with one hand pressed against it, the Webbers' footfalls fading as they headed for their car.

I stood in the kitchen, a fresh glass of wine at my elbow. Returning from the entry, he stopped short.

"On a scale of one to ten, how in trouble am I?" He winced. "Fucking twelve?" I gave him a blank stare. "I know it's really fast, but he asked me right after the election, and it took me by surprise."

"Oh, it took *you* by surprise?"

"Let me explain—"

"And what's this about a house with extra rooms for the little ones?"

"Carson mentioned it might be a good idea to rent something closer to the capital to cut down on commute time in case I'm needed on short notice."

"So you're moving to DC in January?"

"I thought it could be our weekday outpost. Then here on the weekends."

"We just bought this place. Now you want to have a second home in the city? And why did you say anything to him about us having kids? We barely know him."

"I know him."

"I don't."

Lev sighed, rubbing his forehead. "Look, I'm sorry. I was going to tell you, but it never seemed like the right time." I shook my head and laughed quietly. "What?"

"You don't even understand why I'm upset."

"Because I didn't tell you."

"Right there—*tell*, not ask, tell."

He frowned, crossing his arms. "I need your permission to accept a career offer?"

"That's not what—"

"Funny, I don't recall you talking to me about your promotion."

"Stop with the false equivalency—this wasn't a promotion. You quit your job and took another one without discussing it with me. And you were well aware I was up for a promotion, which wouldn't change anything about our lives except add more to our bank account along with extra paid time off."

"You're right, a senate chief of staff position is definitely a huge leap from a typical promotion." I stared at him, flames of anger licking higher inside me. He ran a hand through his hair. "Look, let's calm down. I get why you're upset—I didn't communicate. But do you think maybe you're being unreasonable again?"

Again.

I tilted my head. "Do you think you could be any more condescending?"

"I'm just saying you've been . . . stressed, and it's been hard talking to you."

"So which is it? You couldn't find the right time to tell me, or you didn't want to?"

"Given your reaction, I'd say both." Mox walked into the room, head cocked at our raised voices. "Have you made any appointments with Dr. Rogers like you said you were going to?"

I turned away and slugged half my wine. I hadn't, partially because it had been his suggestion. I knew resuming therapy was a healthy decision, but I wanted it to be my own. So I'd kept finding excuses not to schedule any sessions. "Why? You think she'd tell me to calm down too?" Part of me wanted to stop, to de-escalate and try regaining the good feeling from earlier. But I knew I wasn't wrong, and it felt like a betrayal not to stand my ground.

"I don't think you understand what this means." Lev went to the other side of the island and leaned on it, his mouth a flat line. "Carson didn't just win his seat—he destroyed the guy he was running against. And that was in no small part because of my vision for his campaign. It's the only thing people are talking about at the Capitol. There's already been chatter about him being the party's next nominee. There is a very, very good chance he will be in the White House in four years. And if I prove myself, I'll be there with him."

My phone chimed a notification. I ignored it.

"I think that's why you didn't discuss this with me. Because you were going to accept no matter what I said."

"It would be insane not to take the position; the money alone is worth it. Do you know how many doors this could open? I really can't believe we're arguing about this. I can't believe you're not happy for me."

Another notification.

"Have you been listening to yourself? *I, me.* No *us.* All this talk about having kids sooner and your career—you're not including me. In any of it. You're planning our future alone."

"I feel like I'm the only one planning anything. Do you even want this to work?"

"Of course I—"

"Or maybe you wish I'd never been found."

"That's . . . not . . ." All the air in my lungs solidified.

"See? You can't even say you're happy I'm alive." He shook his head, staring at a point over my shoulder. His jaw clenched, the muscles in his cheeks bulging as if to keep from saying what he was thinking. "You know what, you're just . . ."

When he looked at me again, there was some new vacancy in his eyes. It was unlike the other fugues when he was on the brink of a memory. This was a clinical detachment. As if I were no longer his wife but a failed experiment waiting to be scraped away before trying again.

It was so unsettling I had to force myself to keep from taking a step back.

The moment broke.

He made a disgusted sound and headed for the stairs. A few seconds later the guest room door banged shut. Quiet closed in. Mox ambled over to me and nuzzled my leg. I bent to scratch his ears, kissed his head. Tears formed and receded.

I could've kept my mouth shut. Or worse, pretended everything was okay. That his sole decision-making was fine by me. But then, what was to say my input for the future wouldn't continue to be whittled down?

Because no matter what my mother thought, certain concessions were always a surrender.

My phone went off again.

I picked it up, expecting several irritated texts from April. Instead it felt like I'd been struck by a cold fist in my center.

Three Google Alerts lined the screen, all of them shouting some variation of the same thing.

Lyra Markos was missing.

Sierra

I can't stop looking in the rearview mirror on the way home.

As we switchback up the mountainside, I keep expecting a car to appear behind us. For someone to be following. And I'm leading them right to where we live.

"Momma, deer."

He's pointing out the windshield at the doe that's just stepped up from the ditch and is frozen in the middle of the road. I hammer the brakes, and we shudder to a halt. My heart does a double beat, slamming against my ribs. The deer flicks its ears, watching us with black marble eyes. Then it's dashing away, slipping down the opposite embankment and weaving between trees like a slalom skier.

Gone.

I sit staring after it, thinking about signs and instincts. How there's a growing urge inside me to get the go bag I have packed at home with all our necessary things to start over somewhere else and drive out of Maynard tonight. Drive until we're far away, somewhere new and safe.

We're safe.

I keep telling myself this because I have no evidence to the contrary other than my mind jumping at shadows. Is it worth leaving everything I've built—everything my son knows—behind because of unsubstantiated fear? I don't know.

But I do know the cost of lying to myself. And I won't ever do that again.

I resume driving, gravel crackling beneath the tires. The rain's tapered to a light mist, drifting through the trees and across the road.

"Gotta pee, Momma."

"We'll be home in a few minutes."

"Can I have a fruit snack?"

"Did you have one at day care?"

"Ummm . . ."

"That's a yes."

"One more? Pleeeeeaaaase?"

His wheedling makes me smile. "Okay. One more."

We round the last bend, and our driveway appears, snaking its way through the high timber. At the top of the rise, the yard opens up, and Tyler's Jeep is parked in front of the house. Its owner sits on the steps and beside him—

"Zee!" he yells. "Zeezeezee! Zee, Momma! Zee's home!"

When I pull to a stop and release him from his car seat, he's off like a shot to Zee, who trots forward to meet him with slobbery kisses.

"So where was he?" I ask as Tyler rises from the steps, smiling faintly at the boy and the dog.

"At the vet's in Townsend."

"Townsend? That's over thirty miles. How the hell did he get that far away?"

"I guess a couple tourists saw him on the side of Five Twenty. Thought he was lost and picked him up."

Five Twenty is a lonely county road only two miles over the nearest ridge. Zee has ranged that far before and come home. He would have this time if some well-meaning people hadn't stopped and interfered.

"How did you—"

"Started calling around to shelters and vets this morning on the off chance," Tyler says. "Guess I got lucky."

"I never would've guessed he was that far away. Thank you," I add after a beat.

My son is lying on the ground with Zee stretched out beside him, Zee's tongue tickling his face and neck. His high, clear laughter cleanses some of my spirit.

"You're going to get all muddy," I say. "And you better go potty, or you'll laugh so hard you'll pee your pants."

He dutifully gets up and calls Zee to come with him inside. I'm so proud of how well he listens. How polite and thoughtful he's becoming. I've questioned every decision I've made in the last three years, second-guessed myself to no end. But I hold my son's happiness and how he's thrived like a torch in the dark.

"So . . ." Tyler inhales deeply. "Was thinking I'd burn a couple chops on the grill, and you could whip up that coleslaw of yours for dinner."

"Not tonight."

He cocks a half grin like I'm joking. "Really?"

"Today's been . . . just not tonight, okay?" I don't have the bandwidth right now for his plans and expectations of us in bed later.

"I spent an hour on the phone this morning, drove all the way over to Townsend to get the dog, and I can't even come inside for supper?"

"I said thank you. I'll say it again, thank you. But it's just going to be us tonight."

Tyler laughs and shakes his head. "No good deed goes unpunished."

"If you only ever do things for the reward, maybe you should rethink why you're doing them."

His upper lip twists. "You know I don't ask much of you. There are things you won't talk about—fine. Everyone's got their secrets. But I know you're on the run from something. I just thought if I was patient enough, you'd open up. But you're a cold fucking vault. Nothing for it."

"I appreciate your help—"

"Do you? Coulda fooled me."

"—but that doesn't give you rights to my life."

It looks like he's going to try another tack, another shade of guilt, but he must see something in my face. He shakes his head again and starts for his vehicle, offering a parting shot over one shoulder. "Do it all on your own, then. See if you can make it." He tears out, rocks spitting from his tires, frame squeaking as he jounces out of sight.

I stand a for a long moment in the yard, listening to his angry retreat, then to my little boy talking to Zee inside, praising him for coming home. Telling him he can't run away like that. That it scares us.

The rain starts to fall again as I go in and lock the door behind me.

Imogen

A light mist drifted across the water and dripped from the trees lining the river walk.

Moxie's collar jangled as he shook himself and guided us off the concrete into the grass, following the scent of some animal's trail. I let him lead the way. Was barely aware of my surroundings. Given the early hour along with the inclement weather, there were few other people in the park and no one in our vicinity.

I zipped my jacket tighter and flipped my hood up as we neared a lone bench set back from the walking path. I sat and watched Mox snuffle at the ground near my feet, finally bringing my phone out to rest on my thigh.

At first I'd been too shocked by the notifications to read the articles they were connected to. After going upstairs and making sure Lev was still in the guest room, I locked our bathroom door and perched on the closed toilet lid before opening the notices.

Lyra Markos had been listed as a missing person the day before. The article said family members became concerned after their recent attempts at contact went unanswered. Lyra also had stopped going to her place of work without notifying management. A number was listed to call with any information of her whereabouts.

I'd sat stunned for a time, then walked as if in a trance over to the medicine cabinet and took out the Klonopin. Stood staring at the last few pills in my palm before going back to the toilet and dropping them in. I flushed, then lay awake for hours afterward. Mind running a frenetic loop. I'd been afraid Lev would return to bed sometime in the night, but he hadn't. When I slipped out of the house at dawn, the guest door had still been tightly shut.

Somewhere between home and the park, numbness filled me, a mental slogging as if my thoughts were wading through waist-deep cold water. Lyra was missing. What did that mean? For her, for me? I tried sifting back through what I knew, but it was difficult stringing the events together in any sort of order. I'd called Argyros last month, and the manager said Lyra hadn't been in for weeks. If that was true, she'd been missing—

"Since the night on the beach," I said, not intending to say it aloud. But that didn't track, either, because I'd been messaging with her since then. I flicked to my messages and double-checked the dates. Reread the cryptic DMs. Why would she be communicating with me but not her family? The only solace was if she'd disappeared recently, Lev had nothing to do with it. It was a flimsy attempt at comfort, but I clung to it anyway.

The only other question was whether or not to call the tip number and let them know Lyra had been in contact with me. I didn't necessarily want to get involved but realized I already was. I knew something that could be useful to the authorities, and if it helped in any way, I couldn't keep it to myself.

The number rang and rang, then went to voicemail. First Greek, then in English telling me if I had information regarding an active case to please leave the details after the tone. There was a beep in my ear, and I couldn't speak for a second, then it all rushed out in one breath.

"Hello, my name is Imogen Carmichael. I may have information regarding Lyra Markos. I've . . . I've recently been in contact with her." I finished up with my phone number and disconnected, an unpleasant fluttery lightness forming behind my eyes. Since asking Lev about Sierra, I'd been able to brush back thoughts of her whenever they swam to the surface, telling myself he'd been open and forthright about their relationship. I replayed my conversation with April, how she'd disregarded any idea Lev might be involved in Sierra's disappearance. Even Jamie's preface seemed to lean in that direction—*I hope this gives you some peace of mind.*

But then I thought of how he'd looked at me the night before, like I was something subhuman.

Any kind of peace was always won by war, and peace of mind was no different.

I opened Jamie's email and began to read.

———

A little over three hours later I pulled to a stop in front of Sierra's childhood home.

The house was a modest two story, blue with white trim, featuring a quaint front porch complete with swing. It was one of a dozen much like it on the quiet cul-de-sac in New Abbot, Pennsylvania—a town of barely two thousand just across the state's southern border.

I studied the windows and front walk. Took in the tree-shaded yard. Imagined Sierra here as a child, running to catch the bus or riding her bike as the long hot days of summer wound down. Mox yawned loudly in the back seat, and I stroked his ears. "Be just a minute." As I climbed out, the muscles in my legs tried to mutiny, and I had to lean against the side of the car.

When I called the number Jamie had provided for Sierra's parents, it was like I was someone else. A completely different person when Sierra's mother picked up, and I said that I was an independent journalist working on a story concerning missing persons in the tristate area. I'd fully expected a polite brush-off, so when a heartbreaking eagerness came into her voice and she invited me to their home, my stomach turned with self-loathing.

Now I wanted nothing more than to drive away and pretend I'd never called. But even as I hesitated, the front door of the house opened, and a woman with Sierra's blond hair leaned out. She waved, and I started up the walk, caught in regret like a riptide.

"Come in, come in," Sierra's mother said. She was a slight woman who looked like she'd been narrowed by grief. There was an unhealthy thinness to her face and arms as she guided me out of a small entry into a sitting room where her husband sat in an overstuffed recliner.

Jared Rossen was a large man in his early sixties with a sloping belly and wide features. He scowled as he shook my hand, and I hoped he didn't notice how damp my palm was.

"Shirly says you're a reporter of some kind?" he said, resettling into his chair with a grunt as I took a seat opposite him.

"Yes. I do . . . pieces on different subjects." I cleared my throat, wincing at the clumsiness of my reply. "I've wanted to tackle something on missing persons for a while now."

"And who do you work for?"

"I'm independent. I sell stories to different organizations."

He seemed unimpressed and was about to ask another question when Shirly returned with cups of coffee. "We're so glad you called," she said, sitting down in a chair beside her husband. "I tried talking to the *Examiner* about Sierra, but they never returned my emails." Her smile was as brittle as spun glass.

"Right, um . . ." How to begin the charade? I faltered before pulling my phone out to consult Jamie's notes. "So I've learned a little about Sierra online, but I wanted to ask you some questions for background. It looks like she graduated valedictorian from high school, and she was involved in track and swimming?"

"Oh yes," Shirly said. "She was very active. Always on the go. And she barely ever cracked a book but still managed such good grades."

"She sure didn't like studying," Jared said into his coffee.

"And she went to Penn State after high school?"

"Yes. She was—" Shirly began, but her husband talked over her.

"After loafing around Europe for the better part of two years."

"Did she do an exchange program?"

Jared scoffed. "Only exchange was a bunch of money for nothing. She did some bicycle tour and slept on couches."

"She decided to take a little time before college," Shirly added, looking at her folded hands. "Her and a girlfriend lived in Italy and Spain before she came home to go to school."

"I see. And after college?"

"Bummed around. All those loans for a degree and couldn't find work. Or didn't want to," Jared added. "She was a lifeguard for a stint, cleaned hotel rooms, waitressed. Everything but what she went to school for."

"So her degree was in communications, but that wasn't her main interest?"

"She loved everything," Shirly said, brightening. "Even when she was little, she was adventurous, had a passion for anything she read in a book or saw someone else doing. Each week it was something new."

"I told her, time and time again, you can't waltz through life like that," Jared said, sitting forward, pointing in my direction as if I were the one being lectured. "You have to have a plan and execute it. The world doesn't take kindly to people who fly by the seat of their pants. But would she listen? No. Went whichever way the wind was blowing. It's why I wasn't surprised this last time she ran off and didn't come back."

I leaned in. "You mean Sierra disappeared before?"

"Not disappeared," Shirly said. "She liked to travel. If she had time off, she took it and went somewhere."

"Or she'd quit a job once she had enough money and just leave," Jared said, glowering at his wife. "Vanish for weeks, sometimes months at a time without a phone call."

I absorbed this while also thinking if I had a father like him, I wouldn't be rushing to call home either. "Was her interest in travel why she left the insurance firm to start her own business?"

"Seems like you didn't dig too deep," Jared said. "Though I'm glad all that mess isn't public knowledge. And we really don't want it to be, so no putting this in your little article."

"Completely off the record," I said, hoping to keep him talking, but I shouldn't have worried. He seemed all too eager to highlight his daughter's shortcomings.

"She screwed up, and someone got ahold of her passwords. Leaked all kinds of corporate info." He straightened with self-righteousness. "I knew it would happen. That kid always had her head in the clouds." Shirly appeared to have shrunk even more and was looking out the nearest window, brow creased in well-worn lines.

"What about friends?" I asked. "People she dated?"

"The last guy was a real winner," Jared said. "Kyle something or other. Only met him once and once was enough. Seemed like a match for her—just as irresponsible."

"Honey, please," Shirly pleaded.

"Well, he was. They both were."

"What about a"—I pretended to consult my phone—"Lev Carmichael?"

It was Jared's turn to brighten. "Now he was a good guy. Very steadfast. I told her so while they were seeing each other, I said, 'that guy's going somewhere, you should hook your wagon to him.' But of course she didn't listen. I almost think she cut him loose because we liked him." Shirly met my gaze and looked away just as quickly.

"Did she ever say why they broke up?"

"Not to us," he went on. "Just that they weren't compatible. But that's what compromise is for—you gotta work at a relationship. It's give and take all the way."

I blinked, hearing his words comingling with my mother's. "And you don't feel he had anything to do with her disappearance?"

"Lev? Hell no. Solid guy. I wouldn't be surprised if he was doing very well for himself today. He was interested in politics back then, wanted to make a name for himself down in DC."

"And you don't have any idea where she might've gone?"

"None. We've talked it to death. I think she just got bored of things here and went west. She was partial to the West Coast."

"So you don't think there was any foul play involved?" I focused on Shirly, who opened her mouth to say something, but Jared spoke over her again.

"Cops said nothing out of the ordinary. Like she just up and left. My guess is she ran off and found herself some other schlub to shack up with. She's probably scrubbing toilets or bussing tables somewhere and not giving a good goddamn for anyone wondering where she is. Now I have to mow the lawn. Only have one day a week to do it, and that day's today."

Jared stood expectantly, waiting for me to leave before him, but as I rose, Shirly said, "I have a couple photos of Sierra you could use for the article. Would that be helpful?"

I glanced between them. "Yes, it would be."

Jared grunted something and left the room. A moment later a door opened and shut somewhere, and the hum of a garage door rising followed.

"You'll have to forgive him," Shirly said, leading me to an alcove off the kitchen where she pulled out a narrow photo album. The cover was worn, and I was struck by a sudden image of her standing here alone on countless nights, studying the pictures of her only child. "He says those things because he's hurting and doesn't know how to deal with it. Not that any of us do," she added, sifting through the photos before picking out two. One was what appeared to be a business headshot of Sierra, her hair parted on the side, a reserved professional smile on her lips. The other looked to be the real person underneath. She was kneeling in a patch of lush grass, hugging a dark-haired mutt tightly and laughing as it lapped at her chin.

"Thank you," I said, feeling an even greater surge of guilt at taking advantage of a mother's sorrow. "I'll scan these and mail them back to you."

"Keep them. They're copies. I made flyers and hung them everywhere I could after . . ." Shirly smiled painfully again. "When do you hope to be finished with the article?"

"Um . . ." I held the photos awkwardly as we made our way back to the front door. "Probably early next year."

"Oh good. And you'll let us know when it's going to be printed?"

"Of course."

As she opened the door to let me out, I paused, the burr of Jared's push mower loud in the yard. "I couldn't help but notice when I mentioned Lev, you had a look on your face."

Her features darkened slightly. "Well, I guess maybe I didn't connect with him like Jared did. Lev always seemed . . ." I tensed, waiting. "Detached. Not that he was unfriendly, but more like . . ." She searched for a second. "Like an iceberg. Like he kept a lot out of sight." She must've read something in my expression because she said, "Is everything all right?"

"Yes, fine. Thank you so much for talking with me."

"Anything that might help us find her." Shirly smiled again, and tears glistened in the corners of her eyes. She patted my arm, which turned into a gentle hug. She felt like she was all bones beneath her clothes. "It's good knowing people haven't forgotten her."

I had to swallow a thickness in the back of my throat on the way to the car. Doing some online sleuthing to satisfy my anxiety was one thing, but reopening wounds in innocent people's lives was something else entirely. I gave Jared a slight wave on the way by, and he stopped the mower, the engine dying with a cough. "Say, do you have a business card?" he called.

"Um, none with me. Sorry."

"How about a website so we can look at your other work?"

"I'll . . . I'll, uh . . ." I was still moving toward my car, and I couldn't help but pick up the pace. "I'll be in touch," I added quickly, and climbed inside.

As I accelerated down the street, I could feel Sierra's father watching me until I was out of sight.

Imogen

There's an evolution to arguments.

First it's the disagreement itself, petty or otherwise. Then, if the dispute survives its birth, there's a period of distance where both parties retreat to their own moral high ground, waiting for the other to concede. Eventually someone does. Ice is broken. A peace agreement is reached. Most times the reasonable discussion occurs about the original issue, which was the rational choice to begin with. Then comes forgiveness. Until the next argument arises. Ad infinitum.

Lev and I were in the middle stage of avoiding one another. When I returned home after visiting the Rossens, he'd been in the backyard sitting by a small fire. I watched him for a time, letting my imagination off its leash. Let myself sink into the reality of what I was doing, the lengths I was willing to go to prove my suspicions.

No. That wasn't right. What I really wanted was to prove myself wrong. I was making sure my husband was the man I thought and hoped he was. I spent a long time telling myself that, then texted April: If anyone asks, I was with you today. I could almost hear the concern in her response, which took much longer than normal. Is everything all right?

No. I didn't think so.

Even if my secret fears turned out to be unfounded, even if Lev wasn't capable of anything more than brief infidelity, a gap had opened between us I didn't feel could close completely. It was more than the accident. More than distrust. Somehow he had placed his hand on the rudder of our life and was steering it in the direction he saw fit. I wasn't imagining it. If it were up to him, I'd be pregnant and soon we'd be touring rentals closer to the new job he'd taken without telling me.

That night when he came inside, I was already in bed. His footsteps came heavily up the stairs and paused there. I could picture him looking at our closed bedroom door, deliberating. Then he went down the hall to the guest room, and it was quiet.

For the next few days we became ghosts haunting the same house. Seeing signs of one another but never in the flesh. He began staying out late while I would go to bed early. In the mornings there were dirty dishes from his hangover cure in the sink, and his shoes would be askew in the entry since he always kicked them off haphazardly whenever he was drunk. Little things you notice when you've been with someone long enough.

Each passing day I expected a knock at the door or a phone call from the police informing me I was under arrest for falsely impersonating a member of the press, if that was even a thing. But none came. News regarding Lyra was just as scarce. There were no updated notices or info regarding her whereabouts and no response to the message I'd left on the tip line.

As much as I'd ignored Jamie's dossier on Sierra, it now became a rabbit hole I couldn't help crawling further down. Between that and studying her social media accounts, along with what I'd learned from her parents, I'd begun to feel like I was getting to know Sierra the way you get to know a character in a well-told story. I could see her making the decision to go to Europe after defeating high school—bucking the trend of what was expected. Taking the days as they came in a foreign country, no real plan, just trusting her instincts and reveling in the moment, looking forward to the next meal. I imagined her time at college as a whirlwind, one long sequence of parties, men, classes, friends, and shining potential ahead. I sat beside her on planes taking her to places she'd never been and might never return to. I came to think of her as spontaneous in a way I'd never allowed myself to be.

And like any rabbit hole, it became very hard to turn around once I was inside.

Jamie had listed two other contacts besides her parents, one being Kyle Benson—Sierra's most recent boyfriend—and the other was an Ina Wirt. Jamie had typed *close friend* next to Ina's name. During my lunch hour I decided to reach out to her first since Jamie had only provided an address for Kyle. I rehearsed a small speech and punched in Ina's phone number, fully expecting her not to pick up and was at a loss for several seconds when she did.

"Hello? Hello?"

I was sitting outside on a low concrete wall at the rear of the Stanford building, my uneaten sandwich on a wrapper beside me. "Hi, sorry, I'm trying to get in touch with Ina Wirt?"

"This is she."

"Hi, my name is Melody; I'm an independent journalist working on a story about missing persons." I'd come up with the alter ego from the same place I'd named Mox—a childhood cartoon about two mischievous dogs—Moxie and Melody. "I was wondering if you'd be comfortable speaking with me about Sierra Rossen?"

A beat, then, "Oh yeah, Shirly told me about you." My stomach seized. "She was pretty excited and thought you might reach out to me too. So, yeah, anything to help."

"Okay, that's great." I swallowed dryly. "So I understand the two of you were close?"

"Best friends since college. We lived together for a while when we moved to DC."

"How would you describe her?" The question wasn't one I intended to ask. But I wanted to know more about Sierra. Not just her time dating Lev or the facts surrounding her disappearance, but who she was. What made her so different from me.

"Wow, let me think. Vivacious, I guess. Just really alive. She always knew who she was too. Never seemed to go through that awkward finding-yourself stage like I feel everyone else does. I envied that about her. She was thoughtful, kind, clearheaded. Somehow she had the right answer no matter what was happening. She didn't let things overwhelm her."

"She sounds great."

"She was. She really was."

"Can you tell me a little about what happened leading up to her disappearance? Anything out of the ordinary?"

"I mean, not really. I talked to the police after Kyle filed the missing person report. Kyle was her boyfriend, I don't know if you've talked to him yet?"

"No, but he's on my list."

"He'll be able to tell you more. God, poor Kyle. He was devastated. Never the same afterward." There was a pause, and then she went on. "I moved back home a few weeks before she went missing, and we were both so busy we didn't talk a lot right at the end." Some emotion entered her voice. "Now I wish I would've made time, you know? Done anything different. Maybe that would've changed everything." I didn't know what to say to that. I wondered the same thing. There was a soft sniffle. "I guess the only thing was she seemed a little more stressed than normal. She'd had that thing happen at work, which was total bullshit from what she told me."

"The information leak?"

"Right. She said there was no way her passwords got out, that management was looking to cut her department and they used her as a scapegoat for someone else's fuckup. Sorry."

"No, it's fine."

"Anyway, she was upset, but she just rolled with it like always. She'd made some connections and started up her travel business. She was excited about it."

"And was she dating Kyle this whole time?"

"I mean, pretty much." I waited, letting the silence spool out. "They had a breakup a few months before she disappeared. It was kind of weird, actually."

I hunched forward as a sharp gust of wind swept across the empty courtyard. "What was weird about it?"

"She said Kyle had gotten really suspicious and thought she was cheating on him. He said he found a receipt for a hotel room, and she had to show him her credit card statements to prove it was some kind of mistake. But it caused a major rift, and they broke up for a while. She was heartbroken, she really loved him. Then Kyle came around and they got back together."

I took this in, some faint internal bell chiming. "And you don't think she really was seeing anyone else?"

"God no. She wasn't like that. If she wanted to be with someone, she was with them. If not, they were history. It's just the way she rolled."

"So was there anything else odd before she disappeared? Did she say anything to you that stuck out?"

"No, not that I can remember. Just that she had some really bad luck in the last year. Her car broke down and she had to get a new one. Then her dog went missing."

"Her dog?"

"Yeah, it ran away or something, and she was super upset. She'd had him for years, and he went everywhere with her. She and Kyle looked and looked but never found him. It wasn't too long afterward she was gone too."

I was suddenly cold all over. I clenched my jaw to keep my teeth from chattering. Ina's voice filtered in from far away.

"Did I lose you?"

"No, sorry. I was just going back through some notes. I have here she dated a Lev Carmichael for a time? Did you know him?"

"Lev? Oh, sure. They were together for quite a while. I thought they were going to get married. She was really into him."

"What happened?"

"I think they were just going in different directions? I guess he was a little too goal oriented, and she wasn't into it. He got possessive at the end, and that was a deal breaker, so she cut him loose."

"How did he take it?"

"Okay, I guess. He did show up drunk at her place once, and she had to shoo him away. But who hasn't had a rough breakup, right?"

It was a second before I could answer. "Right."

"Say, I'm really sorry, but I have to run."

"Sure, I appreciate you talking with me."

"Of course." Ina was quiet for a beat. "I think about her every day. I wonder where she is. At first I thought maybe she'd just up and left and was starting somewhere new, but she would've let me know. A little over a year after she'd been gone, I just broke down one day out of the blue. I couldn't stop crying, and I realized I was finally mourning her, because inside I'd known for a while she wasn't ever coming home."

"So you think . . ."

"Something terrible happened to her," Ina said, a flatness to her voice. "I can feel it in my bones."

Imogen

I turned the car off and stared up at our house.

It looked different now. Like it belonged to someone else, and I was a stranger here. It was funny to think how circumstance or a single conversation could change the perception of something so familiar. Make it alien and dark.

I'd begun feeling this way more and more, as if I were gradually becoming an intruder within my own life.

After I got off the phone with Ina, Mr. Stanford had let me know the newest project we were undertaking was being helmed by one of the other employees. He mentioned the Roy account as an excuse why he wasn't giving it to me—that I'd be too busy to take on anything else right now. He said all this while looking at a point across the room, and I knew it was because of how I'd reacted the day of the presentation. I'd gotten the promotion, but it had been without fanfare, a perfunctory thing that would've looked bad if he'd withheld it. A fissure had formed between us that wasn't there before, and it felt like everyone knew it.

I didn't feel comfortable anymore. Not at home, not at work. Not even in my own head.

I toyed with my phone, looking for a reason not to go inside yet. Not to enter into the minefield our marriage had become. Telling myself I wasn't going to call while navigating to the number, I hesitated, then tapped the screen.

Jamie picked up on the second ring.

"Hi," he said, and there was a question in the greeting. A hesitancy.

"Hi."

"I was beginning to wonder."

"If I'd call?"

"If you'd call, if you'd gotten my email, if you'd read it, if you'd changed your mind . . ." It sounded like he was somewhere public, a restaurant or train.

"Sorry, you're probably busy, I don't want to bother you."

"No, no it's fine. Just on my way home. So you had a chance to go over what I sent?"

"Yeah. Thank you again, it was all really thorough."

"I hope it was helpful."

"It was. I . . . talked with Sierra's parents. And Ina."

"Did you tell them who you were? Wait, don't answer that. I don't want to know."

"They were very open about everything."

"And . . ."

"And I don't know. It's really strange. I've been swaying back and forth for a while now, constantly questioning myself. I don't know what to think." He didn't reply, but I could tell he was waiting for me to continue. For a second I relished the feeling of him there on the other end of the line. The comfortable background noise. His patience. "You probably think I'm unhinged."

"It's the quality I always admired most about you."

"Asshole." I could almost hear his smile through the phone.

"I think you're coping with some challenges, and you're trying to make sense of how you feel. A lot of people aren't brave enough to do that."

"But you think I'm making something out of nothing."

He sighed. "I won't say that her disappearing isn't weird. But from what I gathered, there was nothing suggesting a crime was committed."

"So you don't think someone could do something to her and not get caught?" I scanned the blank windows of our bedroom. Studied the small gap between the curtains and wondered if the tingling of eyes on my skin was only my imagination.

"It's possible, just unlikely. There're cameras everywhere, cell phone records, eyewitnesses, DNA—"

"But only if the cops consider it a crime, right? They're not going to dig if there's nothing to dig into."

"True."

"So if there was a gun to your head, would you say she disappeared on her own, or did she have help?"

The noise changed on his end, growing louder then receding, and I pictured him leaving the train and walking, head down, one hand shoved deeply in his coat pocket to keep it warm, the cold wind toying with his hair. "I think she liked to travel a lot and sometimes that can become an escape from real life. Some people work fifty weeks a year dreaming of their two weeks of vacation. It's where they hide from their problems and become someone else. So if I had to guess, I'd say something happened between her and her boyfriend, some break she couldn't reconcile. Maybe she didn't have a support system, no one to really turn to, and she just decided to run. People run away from things all the time."

His words hung there like an accusation even though he hadn't meant it that way. Rain began speckling the windshield. "You're probably right. I hope you are."

It was even quieter now on his end, as if he'd stepped in somewhere out of the weather. "I don't mean to intrude, but I feel like I have some ground to stand on since you approached me." He took a breath. "Are you seeing someone? Like a professional?"

"Yes," I lied without hesitation.

"Good. That's good." Silence expanded, filling up the space where things could be said. So many things I could tell him. But I settled for his calm presence. "Well," he finally said. "I should run."

"Yeah, me too."

"But call me if you . . . I don't know, want to talk or anything. We can talk, right?"

"Sure."

"Bye, Imm." Then he was gone, leaving what he'd always called me lingering in my ear.

———

The same odd smell from a few weeks back met me at the door. Something chemical. It jabbed at the junction of my sinuses and throat. I looked for its source, searching for smoke or some residue on the stovetop, but there was nothing. It was only after I quit looking that I noticed dinner had been made and there was a plate wrapped in tinfoil on the counter. A bottle of my favorite wine sat beside it, along with a single glass. Tucked beneath the glass was a note.

Will be home late—Webber had a surprise meeting he needs me at tonight. This is a peace offering and an apology for what I said. I don't want to feel like this. I want to make it up to you. Tell me how.

The sweetness of the gesture was soured by the last three words. If he needed me to explain how to fix things, what was the value in fixing them? I put the food in the fridge, my appetite dwindled to nothing. I opened the wine and poured a glass, stood at the counter drinking it slowly.

I replayed the conversation with Jamie, using what he said like a climber uses their crampons to summit a particularly steep slope. Everything could have an explanation if you wanted it to. As I sipped the merlot, bits of the past few days drifted forward and receded.

Like an iceberg. Like he kept a lot out of sight.

He got possessive at the end, and that was a deal breaker.

Something terrible happened to her. I can feel it in my bones.

All of it was conjecture, small pieces that didn't necessarily fit together. But one thing stood out for me personally—Sierra's missing dog.

I could see how it could be overlooked. Pets run away all the time. It could've been a random occurrence. Nothing to do with her own disappearance. Except I dealt in statistics and probabilities, and another animal in Lev's vicinity had also gone missing recently—Mrs. Miller's cat, Stripes. The tabby that had infuriated him by using our flower beds for a toilet. Slighted him over and over until she was gone.

Where is she?

My mouth was dry, and the wine wasn't helping. I finished the glass, anyway, then stood motionless in the gradually darkening kitchen, waiting to identify what was wrong. Because something was missing. Some integral piece of my day that wasn't present.

Mox.

He hadn't come to greet me like always when I came inside.

"Mox? Moxie?" I started through the house, opening doors, calling his name as panic simmered, then boiled with each passing second the click of his nails didn't respond to my voice. Where? Where could he be? The garage? No. Asleep under the coffee table in the dining room? No. He wasn't upstairs, either, a sliver of hope there and gone at the sight of the closed bathroom door until I opened it to dark emptiness.

"Mox!" I was near tears when a sound so welcome I actually did start crying came from downstairs.

A light scratching at the back door.

He was there in the deepening evening shadows, looking up at me through the sliding glass door, tongue lolling happily. I slung the door open and slumped to my knees, enfolding him in a hug, tears wet on my cheeks. As usual he basked in the attention, licking at my face as the last of the fear dissolved in relief.

"Why were you outside? Huh? What were you doing out there?" The questions weren't just rhetorical. We were always careful about leaving him out for too long. He was very well behaved but curious too. He would wander if left unattended or an interesting smell caught his attention. And given his breed, people tended to overreact seeing him off a leash. Lev must have left him outside before taking off for the evening and forgotten to let him back in his haste to make his meeting.

Or had it been on purpose?

A shot across the bow? Some subliminal power move to let me know one of the most important things in my life could be taken away?

It was getting difficult to think. My thoughts were an unending flurry, a whiteout of the mind. I needed to rest. I was exhausted and getting more so by the minute. The wine had hit hard, and it didn't help I hadn't been sleeping well. Upstairs, I readied for bed, bringing Mox into our room before closing and locking the door. As soon as I lay down, sleep rushed up and dragged me under with unnatural eagerness. I tried fighting it, then surrendered, slipping away into a kaleidoscope of dreams.

My mother dancing in thin air. Never touching the ground.

Hands on my body, groping, pulling in different directions until I came apart at seams I didn't know I had.

A woman's face in dark water—my own. No way to tell if I was surfacing or going under.

Someone standing at the end of the bed.

I lay on my back, frozen in place. The room was pitch black, like being encased in a cube of onyx. But I could tell someone was there. Staring at me. Inches away. I knew I couldn't move. Both physically and because in some innate way I understood moving would mean death. I couldn't let them know I was awake. I closed my eyes. Pretended to sleep.

And woke to my phone buzzing.

Light streamed in around the curtains. It felt like I'd had my eyes open for much longer than I'd been awake. I silenced the alarm and lay staring up at the ceiling. Listening.

Nothing.

The nightmare's hangover was potent. Even with the morning light I was afraid to look at the foot of the bed. Afraid someone would be there, waiting for me to see them before they lunged forward and ended me.

The room was empty.

I rose, feeling like I'd drunk much more than a single glass of wine, but it had been on an empty stomach. Out in the hall the rest of the house was quiet, no sounds from the guest bedroom. When I pushed the door open, the bed was neatly made. There was no water on the bathroom's shower floor. His toothbrush was dry. He hadn't come home last night. For some reason it wasn't as reassuring as it should've been.

I sat at the breakfast counter chewing a mouthful of toast I couldn't taste. I'd readied for work in a haze, muscle memory taking me through the motions until I'd looked at the woman in the mirror, not recognizing her for a half second. I'd always wanted to be someone other than myself in large and small ways. Had tried reshaping who I was to fit in or live up to expectations that weren't my own. There were standards and assumptions and painful truths every woman I knew had to navigate in order to thrive in the world—to survive it at all.

But now I wondered if I was becoming someone else without meaning to.

If the choices I was making were changing my essence. If I got the reassurance I needed so badly, would I ever be able to return to who I was.

And if I'd want to.

I opened Jamie's email and highlighted Kyle Benson's address, then pasted it into my nav app. On the way out the door I called work and let them know I was taking the day off.

"Well of course you should," Bev, the receptionist, said. "I always take my birthday off too."

"Right," I said, then thanked her. I had to double-check the date to make sure she wasn't mistaken.

Around the time I was having the nightmare, I'd turned thirty-six years old.

Sierra

I come awake to the patter of rain and someone standing at the foot of my bed.

It's the shape I'd seen through the bookstore window. His shape. He'd found us. He's here in my room.

The fear is liquid, flowing over every nerve ending.

I'm up and free of the covers before the dream can fully come apart, the shape along with it. I'm reaching toward the lockbox in the bedside drawer containing the handgun I'd convinced myself not to sleep with and punching in the code. The lid pops open, but by then I can see there's no one else in the room. I'm alone. I settle back to the bed's edge, half bent over in relief.

Even as my heart slows I know returning to sleep won't be an option. I'm fully awake, and the fright is still there like the aftereffects of a tainted drug. I pull on a sweatshirt and pause as I go to shut the gun's lockbox, then reconsider and take the pistol with me as I leave the room.

On the way to the kitchen, I peer into my son's room. He's sleeping hard, a soft fan of light from the hall falling across his face, which is losing its baby look. He's left his toddlerhood behind and moves with an exuberant surefootedness I sometimes find myself reaching out to steady or slow. It seems the stages he's growing out of and into are speeding up, and if I'm not careful he'll be five, then ten, then old enough to drive before I know it. Parenthood isn't something you can be told about, though people definitely will. They'll give you hints and advice and warnings, all of it from their own experiences, which they speak from as if there are no variations. But no one says the responsibility for another life can sometimes feel like a beautiful rockslide, both tumbling over and giving way beneath you. That each decision you make for your child feels flawed because it's coming from you, and you don't really know what you're doing because no one does. Not your parents and not theirs either.

Zee's head rises from his bed when I enter the living room. It's so good he's home. Reassuring. I pet him, and he settles back to his side. The security system panel glows a comforting green from beside the doorway. I put on some water for tea and set the pistol on the counter within easy reach. Stand looking out the window into the witching dark until my vision blurs.

How many nights have I done this? Sat awake and watchful, unable to overcome the vulnerability of sleep. A hundred? Two? When Marlene steered me toward this little house owned by her and her brother who lives out of state and never visits anymore even for hunting, it had been every night. I would doze in the evenings after supper, sitting up in a chair in the corner of the living room where I could see the door and out the windows. Before I acquired the pistols from a local hermit who asked no questions and required only cash, I'd balanced an empty beer bottle on the front doorknob and sat with a butcher knife on my lap, going in and out of sleep like a pilot flying through patches of cloud cover.

Eventually, as the days and months passed, a level of reassurance settled over me. The distance, the time, my precautions. All of it adding up to tentative safety. But there were still nights like these where I woke with the terror he was close, right outside the door, watching through the window from the darkness.

I suppress a shiver and pour my tea, take it into the living room along with the gun, and sit in the comfort of the shadows. Zee stretches and yawns. Without meaning to I return to the afternoon and its encounter. Try replaying it to search out any missed details. Anything my panicked mind might've overlooked. But there's nothing but a quasi-familiar shape through rain-smeared glass.

I sip my tea hoping it will thaw some of the cold apprehension lodged in my chest. I try to move on to other thoughts—plans for the next week, what the summer might bring for us in our little lives here in the solitude of the mountains. But I keep being drawn back to the day before. There is something else besides the figure that's bothering me. Something overlooked. I retrace the path from the moment Tyler left in a huff to my waking.

We played with Zee for a while, reveling in his return. I made dinner. We watched TV. Read a book. Had bath time. Read another book before bed. That was it. Nothing more or anything out of the ordinary.

But I'd felt a tingle of unease while Tyler had been here. Initially I'd chalked it up to our disagreement. Now I'm not sure. It was like a sudden frigid wind, finding its way through the gaps in your clothes, chilling, then gone before you had a chance to react.

I turn our conversation over and over, trying to remember his exact words. What it was within them that had sounded my internal alarm.

When I come back to myself, the tea is gone, and I'm holding the gun lightly, its barrel across my thigh. It's still raining, and the very deepest of grays has crept into the eastern sky. I move to the closet where I keep our go bag and consider it. We could leave now with the clothes on our backs and start anew. Run again until it feels safe enough to stop. I'd considered Mexico before; we could try disappearing there with the little savings I have. But how long would it be before the creeping sensation of being watched closed in again? How many times would I uproot our lives on a hunch or seeing some likeness, real or imagined?

Running away never seems to actually get you closer to where you want to be.

On the way back to bed I check on him again. He's rolled over and faces away now, only a tuft of hair visible. My heart trembles thinking of him asking about his father.

Someday, I think, putting the gun back in its box and crawling beneath the covers. *Someday you'll know who your father is. Someday you'll meet him.*

And if the world allows us, maybe then we could be a family.

Imogen

The house Sierra had lived in with Kyle was at the end of a halfhearted development twenty minutes outside of Baltimore.

The homes were mostly one levels with small yards lining one side of a narrow street. The access road leading into the neighborhood continued on to a defunct power plant, which rose in the distance like a gray tower of some decaying industrial kingdom.

I rolled to a stop at the end of the street and verified the address before turning in.

Unlike the neatly kept yards preceding it, Kyle's was overgrown with pieces of rusting patio furniture jutting from the long grass, which was beginning to brown. A chain-link fence surrounded the half acre or so of property, a gate near the front walk gaped open. The house itself was much like its neighbors, but there was a neglectful dullness to it. The windows were dark and dusty, the paint on the siding beginning to peel. A rusting Honda SUV sat in front of a single stall garage. One of its tires was flat.

I stepped out of the car and smoothed my clothes, searching for movement behind the windows. The street was serene, the only noise coming from the highway a mile back in the direction of the city. I made my way up the walk to the front porch, which groaned a little under my weight, and rang the doorbell, inspecting a crusted doormat beneath my feet that read *Welcome to Our Home* in wispy cursive.

All at once the urge to flee came over me. I wanted to be back in the car and driving away from here. The insanity of standing at yet another person's door with the intention of prying into their past was almost overpowering. I'd been walking a line going to Sierra's parents' and calling Ina, but this felt like tempting fate. I was going to get caught and exposed, and everyone would know what I was doing. I could already feel their confusion and disapproval seeping into me, the shaking of their heads, the conversations between family and friends about how I'd come apart in some kind of midlife conspiracy.

As I was taking a step down the stairs, the door opened, and a face swam into view from the house's interior dimness.

Kyle had probably once been a good-looking man. He had sharp features, a strong jaw, and startling green eyes. But now his face was all angles, an unhealthy thinness about him like someone strung out on hard drugs or running on very little sleep.

His eyes took me in, and the door's gap narrowed. "Who are you?" he asked. Kyle's voice was hoarse as if he hadn't spoken aloud in some time.

All at once I knew the story of an independent journalist wasn't going to work. Not on him. There would be immediate questions, and he'd ask to see ID first rather than after the fact like Sierra's father.

"Hi," I said as brightly as I could. "I'm looking for Kyle Benson?"

"I said, who are you?"

"My name is Imogen, I'm—"

"What do you want?"

"I was friend of Sierra's in high school. I just moved to the area—"

"What high school?"

"Terrington."

"How did you find this address?"

"Ina Wirt gave it to me."

"Ina . . . haven't heard from her in years."

"Yeah, we caught up recently and—" Kyle was slowly shutting the door. I was no longer on thin ice; I'd broken through and was sinking.

I made a last Hail Mary. "She told me Sierra's gone. That something bad happened to her."

The effect was instantaneous. Something changed behind his eyes. He glanced past me, scanning the yard and road beyond. "Are you alone?"

"Yes."

He jerked the door open and nodded toward the interior. I stepped inside quickly in case he changed his mind, and immediately felt a pang of regret.

There wasn't a single light burning, and a scent of old food and dirty laundry permeated the air. The entry led directly into an open living room with a small kitchen beyond. A large sectional couch was buried beneath books, papers, clothes, and rumpled blankets. There was no clean, open surface within sight—every table and chair was stacked with magazines, books, or pages of printouts stapled at their corners. Kyle shut and locked the door, then stood near the inside wall studying me. One hand dangled loosely at his side while the other held a compact pistol. My stomach swooped sickeningly.

"Dump out your purse," he said.

"What?"

"Dump it on the floor."

"I don't—" The gun moved up almost imperceptibly. "Okay, okay." I turned out my purse, dumping the contents onto the carpet. Kyle bent and picked through the items. He turned over my wallet, and I stiffened as he looked at the driver's license inside. I didn't know how he'd react to my last name, but he simply set the wallet aside, poked at a scarf and a pack of Kleenex before standing.

"Are you carrying a weapon?"

"No."

"I'm going to make sure."

I almost bolted then, leaving my purse and everything that was in it behind. Ina had mentioned Kyle was never the same after Sierra's disappearance, but that seemed an understatement now. I started to protest again, but then he was patting my waistband down, running his hand along my legs with a smooth efficiency. He swept the small of my back and studied the front of my blouse, which clung tightly to my skin.

"I don't have anything," I said. My hands had come up defensively, and I'd taken a step back. I kept looking from him to the gun. He noticed and glanced at the weapon as if he'd forgotten he was holding it. With a practiced movement he slid it out of sight in the small of his back.

"Turn your phone off."

"Why?"

"Turn it off."

I picked up my phone from the floor and considered the situation I was in. No one knew I was here, and the man I wanted to speak with appeared disturbed and was armed. He glanced from me to the device and back again. I held the power button until the screen went black.

Without another word he stalked to the kitchen, where dingy light seeped through partially drawn curtains. There was a clang of metal on metal, then the pop of a gas burner lighting. "Do you drink tea?" he asked from where he stood at the stove. I gave the front door a lingering glance, then repacked my purse before picking my way across the cluttered room to the kitchen.

Kyle had cleared off a stool, which I perched on, ready to take flight at the first sign of trouble. But he seemed almost oblivious to my presence, readying two clean-looking cups with tea bags as the kettle on the stove heated.

"Ashwagandha," he said quietly. "Powerful adaptogen. Antioxidant too. Helps cut down on all the toxins they put in the air and water. Did you know there are microplastics everywhere? In the ground and water and us." He stopped then, partway facing me, but still not looking my way. He was staring out the slit in the curtains at the gray-cast day. "They don't even know how much a human being can absorb before it causes problems. Or maybe they do. I think they do."

The kettle whistled, and he poured the tea and brought it to the table. The brew smelled terrible, but I thanked him and blew the steam away, cupping my hands around the glass for warmth. The house was uncomfortably cool. Kyle made no motion to clear off another seat and stood by the counter, arms crossed, looking at a place above my head. I tried picturing Sierra here then. What the house might've looked like with her presence. Brighter, I supposed, and cleaner. There were a few paintings on the walls—some of the knowledge from my time with Marcus still remained when it came to art—and from what I could tell, either Kyle or Sierra had a decent eye.

"I like the prints. Are they Cecily Brown?" I said, gesturing at the nearest wall, mostly for something to say.

Kyle's gaze shifted to the paintings, then away again. "I keep meaning to take them down but can't quite get myself to." He drank a few swallows of his tea as if it were iced instead of boiling. "What did you want with Sierra?"

"To catch up. It's been years since I saw her, and I just—"

"Moved to the area, you said that already." He was finally looking at me, and it was unnerving. As if he could tell I wasn't what I said I was.

"I guess I was hoping you could tell me about her," I said, trying to disarm him. "Tell me what happened." Kyle was quiet so long, I started to think he wouldn't answer. Then he took a breath and began to speak, his voice dropping in volume as if there were someone else in the next room who might hear.

"There's a world beneath the world I never knew about. Most people don't. There's what you think you know, and there's the truth. When you have something like this happen, you start to see the cracks. And what's underneath is reality. It's what's waiting if you look past what's presented to you." He paused, listening to something I couldn't hear for a moment, then went on. "I think they started watching her right after the data leak. That was probably what set them off, but it could've been beforehand, I don't know. Maybe she stumbled onto something she never told me about and they got nervous. Secrets, you know? Corporate secrets, the worst kind. If she saw something she shouldn't have, then the whole leak story might've been engineered to frame her. After that they started watching and waiting."

I took a drink of tea, trying to absorb what he was saying. "You think the firm she was working for had something to do with her disappearance?"

"Of course they did. Do you know what kind of contracts that place has? The government kind. The private-defense-contracting kind. The dark-money kind. You have to dig deep to find it, but they underestimated me. I've been peeling the layers back, one by one. The connections are there, down beneath the surface. There are shell companies and fake names and backroom meetings . . ." He trailed off, staring again through the gap in the curtains.

I shifted uncomfortably. "What makes you think she was being watched?"

"She said so." Kyle finished his tea and poured more hot water into his cup. "It was right before they took her. We were drinking one night, and she said she thought someone was following her. She never saw them or anything, but she said she could feel it. Like eyes on her whenever she wasn't looking. At the time I thought it was stress. She was starting up her travel business, working a lot. I brushed it off. But then—"

Kyle cocked his head, listening again. In a movement so quick I flinched, he set his cup down and left the room, moving with an animalistic fluidity to the front window where he peered out. He stood there for a time with one hand on the butt of the pistol, watching what, I didn't know. I couldn't see anything from my point of view. No cars went by on the road. No sounds filtered into the house. Eventually he returned to the kitchen.

"No one followed you, did they?"

"Followed me? No."

"You're sure?"

"No one knows I'm here." My stomach tightened at saying my earlier concerns aloud. Kyle paced around the kitchen, touching certain items on the countertop but never picking them up.

"You thought it was stress, but . . ." I prompted when the silence continued to stretch out.

"There . . . there was someone here," he said, pivoting slowly back toward me. "One day I came home and there was this feeling, like someone had just been standing where I was, breathing the air, touching our things. The doors were locked, but they got in somehow, I know that now. These people are like shadows. Slipping in and out of places. But I've taken precautions. They don't get in anymore."

I nodded. My mouth was dry despite the tea. "Ina said something about Sierra's dog going missing. Do you think—"

"It was them. That's how they got her. They took him from the yard one night while we were watching TV. I let him out like usual, and I know the gate was closed. When Sierra went to call him back in, it was open, and he was gone." Kyle moved forward with the same startling speed, and I shrank back on my seat. There was a manic energy about him now, as if having someone to confide in was spurring him on. "We looked and looked, but nothing, no sign of him. None of the neighbors saw anything. But, see, here's where they made a misstep." He started tapping the cover of the nearest book metronomically. "The day she went missing, there was a call from an unknown number on her phone. It lasted less than a minute. I looked it up later and got nowhere—they'd blocked the number somehow and probably used a burner phone to boot. I told the cops about it, but they wouldn't do anything—the *fuckers*. So here's what I think happened—I think they called saying they found the dog and wanted her to meet them. And she did without hesitation because she loved him so much." He quit tapping the book and straightened. "And then they took her."

Some of the fire seemed to leave him. He leaned against the counter, his shoulders rounded. When he spoke again, he sounded as if he were dreaming. "I went back through all her documents. Her social media, her phone, computer. I went to where her car was found. I posted on every missing-persons site I could find. I've followed up leads and random tips that she'd been seen somewhere. I've driven back and forth across the country three times, looking for anything that would give me a clue as to where they took her or what they did. But there's nothing. The only thing I ever found besides that last phone call was . . ." He swallowed thickly. "The hotel reservation. I thought she was seeing someone. I was sure of it. But that was them too. They *wanted* me to see the reservation. They wanted us to split up, so she'd be alone. Easier to get to. But we got back together." He swiped at the corner of one of his eyes. "Everything was good. We talked about having a family. We'd even started trying."

There was such heartache in his voice, I had to suppress the urge to reach out and touch him, knowing if I did it would break the spell.

"It feels like she was just here. Like she only went out the door a minute ago. But it's been three years. Sometimes I wake up and forget for a second, and I try living in those moments for as long as I can. I think that she's next to me in bed, that if I roll over she'll be there. Or I imagine I can hear her in the shower talking to herself like she used to sometimes when she was trying to work out a problem. I can smell her perfume if I keep my eyes closed. I savor the forgetting until everything rushes back in and I know she's gone."

He lowered his head, chin almost to his chest, and closed his eyes. "I'm so sorry," I said softly. I wasn't sure if he heard me. We stayed that way for a time, a gust of wind moaning in the eaves the only sound. I tried thinking of something else to ask this broken man, but he'd answered any questions I had by revealing the open wound of his loss to someone who would listen.

"At first I thought as long as her body was never found, I could keep going," he finally said, his head still lowered. "It would give me hope that she was out there somewhere. But now I think it might be better to know she's dead. As painful as it would be, uncertainty is worse. I know that now. Purgatory, limbo—that's where I live. That's the real hell."

He raised his head and fixed me with a stare so haunted it seemed to bleed out from his eyes into the air of the room. "The real hell is not knowing."

Imogen

The wind had come up, urging sluggish clouds down from the north as I left Kyle and Sierra's neighborhood.

I drove in silence. Gloved hands on the steering wheel, the heater spilling warmth onto my legs and face. Eyes fastened on the road, gaze turned inward.

I hadn't known what to expect going to meet Kyle. I'd wanted to speak to the man who had loved Sierra, get a sense of her mindset and the last days before she vanished. But what I'd encountered—the depths of paranoia brought on by her absence—was something I'd been unprepared for. Kyle had become a patchwork man with only conspiracy holding him together. He'd been following a trail just as I had, but they led to two very different places.

A drive-through coffee joint appeared on the right, and I swung into it. I was still swimming against a current of fatigue, and a large dark roast sounded like exactly what I needed. I pulled into a vacant parking spot after ordering and sat in the quiet of the car, sipping the brew and willing the caffeine to work faster.

If I had been in my office, I would've been tempted to start a spreadsheet containing everything I knew. Organize it into rows and columns. Facts and suspicions. Pros and cons. Anything to make sense of the chaos my life had become. It was true I'd started in a place of insecurity, and the temptation to find something—anything—wrong to justify running away from commitment and the pain betrayal would cause was still a reality. But despite that instinct of self-sabotage, along the way I'd begun to hope. Hope I was wrong. That I'd find some irrefutable fact that Lev was exactly who he seemed to be—the man I'd fallen in love with. At some point I hadn't been searching for an escape, but a reason to stay.

Except I hadn't found it.

Instead more and more idiosyncrasies had built up, all pointing in a direction darker than I could've imagined. But I still had no real proof. Nothing concrete to substantiate any of my fears.

The traffic continued to glide past on the highway. People going to and fro in their lives. At that moment I would've traded places with any of them to escape. Because Kyle was right.

Not knowing was the real hell.

I picked up my phone, forgetting I'd turned it off at Kyle's request. When it powered on, there were several texts waiting. Two from Lev.

Hey, where are you

Call me. Please.

My fingers hovered over the screen, mind spinning through responses and lies. Before I could type anything, an incoming call from my mother appeared, the phone vibrating with urgency. Shit. My birthday. Of course she'd be calling today. And if I didn't pick up now, it would only be worse later when we finally did talk. I steeled myself and answered.

"Hi, Mom."

There was a long silence in which I thought the call had dropped, but then she spoke, and I knew it was a pause of irritation. "Where are you?"

"I decided to take the day off." When she didn't respond I added, "For my birthday . . ."

"What are you doing?"

"I got my hair and nails done." The lie came as easily as breathing. "Wanted to treat myself a little."

Mom clucked. It was a sound of disapproval I hadn't heard in some time. "Your husband is looking for you. He went to your work to bring you flowers and take you out for lunch. You weren't there, and you haven't been answering your phone."

I closed my eyes. *Shit.* As I scrambled for an excuse, something dawned on me. "Wait, why did he call you?"

"Because he's worried sick. He thought you might be here, and when I asked him why, he said you were fighting. Do you have an aversion to happiness, Imogen?"

"An aversion to happiness?"

"It's like the moment you have something good, you start trying to find a way to ruin it." The harshness of her voice grated against my ear. "Is it sympathy? Are you addicted to it? Is that it?"

"Jesus, mom, no—"

"Because my reserves are getting pretty low in that department. You have all the privileges your father and I could give you, every advantage, and you're trying to throw it all away. Do you know Lev thinks you're having an affair?"

I was struck quiet. Both because Lev had suggested such a thing, along with his reason for doing so. "I'm not having an affair. Listen, Mom, there're some things you need to know."

"More secrets? Hopefully nothing like shoving your husband overboard a cruise ship. Do you understand he could press charges? It's attempted murder."

"It was an accident."

"And was cutting poor Marcus an accident too?"

Poor Marcus. "This has nothing to do with that," I managed. The air was getting close in the car. I cracked a window.

"It's a pattern." When she spoke again it sounded as if she were talking to herself. "This is something we should've dealt with when you were young. Got you psychiatric care. Maybe things would've gone differently."

"I don't know what else he told you, but—"

"Charlie and Beth have noticed it too. They both said you've been off since the cruise. Spacey and odd. I mean look at that disaster of a caterer you booked for our anniversary—God, I was *so* embarrassed. Charlie said he reminded you a dozen times, and you kept forgetting to get someone decent. Or maybe you did it on purpose."

"It wasn't on purpose. There's been a lot going on you don't know about."

"Well I know this; Lev is a good man, and he loves you despite everything you've put him through. So what you're going to do is go back home and ask for his forgiveness. You're going to get some professional help and straighten your life out before it all collapses. I mean, my God, Imogen, when are you going to wake up and realize how good you have it? If I didn't know any better—"

"Why don't you just go ahead and fuck him, Mom? It's obvious you want to."

The words were out before I could stop them. Traveling across the airwaves between us. But in that half second of dead silence before Mom's sharp intake of breath, I realized even if I could, I wouldn't take them back. Saying it hadn't felt like a mistake. It felt *good*.

"What . . . what did you say?" She sounded genuinely confused. As if she couldn't believe her daughter had said it and maybe someone else was on the line. Maybe she was right.

"I've seen the way you look at him. I bet if you had a chance and knew you wouldn't get caught, you'd do it. And you know why?"

"Imogen!"

There was a part of me trying to stop before any more damage was caused, but like a freight train with failed brakes, I barreled onward.

"Because you're miserable in the life you chose. You weren't a good enough dancer to make it professionally, and you settled for Dad because he was a safe bet. But you wanted more, and it's been eating you from the inside out all your life. And you took it out on me."

"You . . . *shut up!*"

I smiled savagely at how her voice wavered. There was a knife in my hands buried somewhere deep in my mother, and I began to twist it. "You talk about therapy, but you would've actually had to give a shit about me for that to happen. And there might've been another reason you didn't get me help, now that I think about it. Maybe you were afraid I would've told them what kind of mother you are—your expectations and disappointment in me when I didn't turn out exactly how you planned because you regretted your own life so much." I paused, teeth gritted and aching. "You say you wanted all these things for me, but you wanted them for you."

I was breathing hard as if I'd just sprinted a mile. My throat and chest were painfully tight, but a wicked joy coursed through me. It was the lancing of a thirty-year-old infected wound I'd only allowed myself to address in periphery. Never straight on because it was too painful. A sound came then from the other end of the line, and it took me a few seconds to recognize what it was.

Mom was weeping.

I'd only seen her cry once before, and that was after her own mother's funeral. She hadn't wanted anyone to know and had gone into the bathroom to mourn privately, but she hadn't locked the door, and I'd walked in. *Get out,* she'd hissed, and fifteen minutes later when she emerged her composure was back—a red puffiness around her eyes the only sign I hadn't imagined the whole thing.

Now I was the reason she was breaking down. Another tributary in a river of disappointments. The fact wiped away any righteousness, and I was filled with sudden self-loathing. I opened my mouth to apologize but realized I couldn't hear her crying anymore. She'd already hung up.

For a while I sat motionless, staring straight ahead with the adrenaline draining away, leaving me feeling as empty as I'd ever been. It wasn't unpleasant. The void was comforting in a way. A blank amnesia-gray blotting out all thought and feeling. I wondered if this was how Lev felt when trying to remember his missing time. I wondered more than that.

Gradually things crept back in, the past weeks falling on me. The weight and stress compounding until it felt as if the car was inside a crusher, the steel and glass compressing around me. Squeezing all the air from my lungs. I tried to swallow, but there was no saliva in my mouth. I couldn't believe I'd said those things to Mom. It was like they'd come from somewhere else, but I knew they'd been there all along, festering inside me. The pressure was suddenly beyond intense. It wasn't only in my head anymore, it was a real physical presence. I couldn't breathe.

I gasped, rolling the window down farther, but there were black dots forming at the edges of my vision. They expanded, a hungry darkness eating outward until they touched each other, the view of the parking lot and highway beyond slowly fading away.

There was a half-full water bottle in the console. I spun its top off, poured a handful of cold water into my palm, and splashed it across my face. Another splash onto my throat. Some air wheezed into my lungs, back out. Another breath, this time easier. My vision brightened. I sat back, eyes closed, focusing only on the oxygen rushing back through my system. It wasn't lost on me I'd used the same trick Lev had taught me the night we met, and I thought of Kyle tortured and alone and how love can either bless or damn us. Sometimes all at once.

When I felt almost normal again, I studied the texts Lev had sent. Pictured him standing at my office feeling foolish, with flowers in his hand and not knowing where I was. Calling my mother in the hope that she'd heard from me. But inversely I saw him doing these things like a charade. Going through the motions as if he were acting out a part in a play. Hitting all the marks and knowing all his lines.

The phone came to life in my hand, and I nearly dropped it. But instead of Lev or my mother calling back like I expected, it was a different number with an area code that sent an internal tremor through me.

Greece. Someone was calling from Greece.

I wavered, both wanting to answer and let it go to voicemail. But something urged me to pick up. As I brought the phone to my ear, I fully expected to hear a woman's voice—Lyra finally reaching out in person. I had no idea what I'd say to her now. If she'd be honest about her and Lev or not. If it even mattered anymore. But when I said hello, I was met by a rough masculine response.

"Mrs. Carmichael? This is Lieutenant Kafatos with the Hellenic Police. I don't suppose you remember me."

For a heartbeat I didn't, but then an image of the compact policeman with the mustache and pointed gaze came rushing back. He'd been the one to notify me Lev had been found and driven me to the hospital. "No, I do," I said, rolling up the car window to hear him better.

"I'm sorry to be bothering you, but something's arisen here I'm hoping you can assist me with." He sounded tired, and, given the time difference, I realized how late he was working.

"Okay?" I tried scanning any possible implications of Lev's fall that might be coming back to bite me, but there was nothing. Lev was alive, and if he were to suddenly press charges, he wouldn't do it through Greek law enforcement.

"It's regarding a Lyra Markos. You know who I'm speaking of?"

Of course. Lyra. Her disappearance. My heart began to kick against the walls of my chest. "Yes," I managed.

"Were you aware that she was missing?"

"Yes." It felt like I was being led to the edge of a tall building with no ledges or railings. Except something stood out in what he'd just said. *Was* missing. Not *is* missing. "Did you find her?"

There was a long pause. "I'm afraid so."

No. I tried to respond, to ask the question blinking in my head like a neon sign, but I was paralyzed. All I could do was wait.

"It appears you were messaging her social media account recently. That's the reason I'm reaching out."

"Y-yes. Is—" I cleared my throat. "Did something happen to her?"

Another span of silence, then a brief sigh from his end. "Her body was recovered late last night. It appears she was a victim of homicide. She has been deceased for quite some time."

Imogen

There was a sprawling beat where I didn't believe him.

There had to be some other explanation. It wasn't actually the Greek detective on the other end of the line. Or I'd heard him wrong. Maybe I'd finally had a break with reality from all the stress and wasn't even speaking to anyone at all. And there was another reason for the dissonance between what he'd said and reality. For a tenuous moment I couldn't grasp it, then I did.

"That's not possible," I said. "I was messaging her, and she was responding less than two weeks ago. There's no—" But even as Kafatos began to speak, I understood what had happened. Or part of it anyway.

"Yes, well, the reason for that is you weren't messaging with Lyra. That was someone else."

"Who?" I blurted.

A tapping came from his end, maybe a pen against a tabletop. Kafatos seemed to be considering something. "An ex-boyfriend of Lyra's. I can't release his identity." I flashed on the picture I'd seen on Lyra's account of her and the handsome young man with the tattoos.

"I don't understand. Why was he pretending to be Lyra?"

"That's part of the reason I called. How did you know Lyra?"

"Well, that's . . . kind of complicated."

"Try and explain. Take your time."

I bit at my lower lip, peeling of a dry strip of skin there with my teeth. "While my husband and I were on our cruise, we ate at the restaurant where she waitressed. I think—" I imagined Kafatos sitting at his desk in a dimly lit station, pen in hand poised above a notepad. "—I think my husband and Lyra slept together."

If he was surprised, he made no sign. "And why do you think this?"

"I noticed them talking at lunch, and later that night I couldn't find Lev on the ship."

"I'm sorry, this was before he fell?"

"Yes. When I couldn't find him, I went ashore to Lyra's restaurant because I had . . . a feeling. And I think I saw them together down on the beach."

"You *think* you saw them?"

"It was dark. I didn't get close enough to see details, but I'm almost sure it was my husband."

"What were they doing?"

"Sitting on a blanket. Drinking."

"And then what happened?"

"It started to storm, and they went into a cave." The tapping began again on his end, louder this time. Insistent. "Is that where they found her?" I swallowed dryly, feeling like I was going to throw up. "In the cave?"

"What did you do then?" he asked, ignoring my question.

"I went back to the ship and . . . went to sleep."

"To sleep?"

"Yes."

"After seeing your husband with another woman on your honeymoon?" Almost imperceptibly I felt a shift. The conversation had become an interview. Maybe it always had been.

"I was exhausted and, well, a little drunk, to be honest. I was going to talk to him in the morning."

"But then he fell overboard."

"Yes."

"And that's when you woke up. Because you heard your balcony door open."

I started to reply, then paused. "No. The door was already open. I woke up because I heard him yell." It wasn't lost on me that Kafatos had intentionally misconstrued my statement. He was trying to trip me up. I could almost feel his sharp little eyes probing across the distance between us.

"Yes, of course, I see that in my notes now."

"I still don't know why Lyra's boyfriend was responding to me," I said, eager to point the dialogue in another direction.

"Ex," Kafatos said. "Ex-boyfriend. They had broken up several weeks before her death, and he was displeased. When she didn't answer his calls or texts and he couldn't find her, he logged on to her social media accounts since he knew her passwords, hoping to get an idea where she'd gone. Seeing your messages, he thought Lyra may have run off with your husband. It seems he was trying to get you to divulge their location."

My head tipped back until it rested on the seat's headrest. All of the weird messages from Lyra made sense now. *Do you know where he is?* Kafatos was saying something I only caught the end of. "I'm sorry?"

"I said, how sure are you it was your husband with Lyra on the beach that night?"

"I don't know, pretty sure." The air was getting close and warm again. Sweat trickled down my chest and pooled near my naval.

"Pretty sure," he echoed quietly.

Something was rising in the back of my mind. A memory from that night. Strangely it was the bored cruise employee at the check-in desk I saw. I could even recall the spray of acne on his forehead. For a second I couldn't understand why I was thinking of him at all. Then it hit me like a cold slap. "The key card," I said.

"What's that?" Kafatos asked.

"The cruise ship—they require everyone to scan their cards departing and boarding. If Lev left the ship that night, they'd have a record." Even with the revelation, I chided myself for not thinking of it earlier. Lev had told me he never left the ship. If I could've somehow verified this, it would've saved me an unknowable amount of worry and grief. Or proved my fears correct.

I could hear Kafatos scratching down a note. "That's very smart, Mrs. Carmichael."

"Please, call me Imogen." I was beginning to dislike carrying Lev's last name and all it entailed.

"You've been extremely helpful, Imogen. May I contact you again with further questions?"

"Of course."

He was quiet for a moment. "Your husband—he has recovered from his fall?"

"Yes."

"And his memory?"

"He's . . . regained it."

"Very good. I'm glad to hear that."

There was a spate of silence in which I almost told him everything. The urge to explain more of my suspicions and incriminate Lev even further in Lyra's death was strong. I'd even tell him what I'd learned about Sierra. He could begin to build a case. I could help.

But then the moment passed, and Kafatos was saying goodbye and he would be in touch. I sat staring at my phone after he hung up, not seeing it. I was still sitting in the seat of my car, but my surroundings might as well have been invisible. In my mind I was standing at the mouth of the cave again in the dark, listening to cries of ecstasy become screams of pain. Hearing the gasp of strangled breath or the heavy thud of a rock cracking bone. Waves rushed around my ankles like the grasp of cold hands trying to drag me into deeper water. I could smell decay, the scent of Lyra's rotting body. Could see what the crabs and other sea life had done to her, could almost feel them scuttling across my skin.

I fumbled for the door handle and managed to lean out of the car to be sick. Sat hunched over awkwardly, spitting the last of my breakfast onto the pavement. When it was over, I collapsed back into the seat, eyes squeezed shut, tears leaking from their corners. I stayed that way for a long time.

The wind gusted, rocking the car on its springs. Traffic hummed past. A couple walked across the parking lot toward the coffee shop, hands linked between them.

When I felt I could drive, I started the car and eased it back onto the highway. I hadn't been able to tell Kafatos everything, but I needed to tell someone. I couldn't be alone in this any longer. It was time to admit something I'd known for quite a while.

I needed help.

Imogen

April answered her door the second time I knocked.

I'd driven by her apartment hoping she'd taken the afternoon off as she did sometimes on Fridays. Seeing her vehicle in the parking lot felt like providence. My oldest and most trusted friend was home. I could tell her anything, and she would listen. She would help me make sense of everything.

April's eyes widened when she saw me. Her hair was damp-dark from a shower, and she was midway through applying makeup. "What're you doing here?" she asked.

I stepped past her into the apartment, feeling a small sense of relief at just being in her presence. "Took the day off." I considered settling into her plush couch but felt sick with energy and walked across to the tall windows instead.

"Well, happy birthday. I was going to call you later and see if you wanted to do something."

I started to say thanks, but what came out was, "The Greek woman—Lyra—she's dead."

April blinked. "What?"

"She was murdered. A detective called and told me. He wanted to know how I knew her since we were messaging." I quickly relayed my conversation with Kafatos as April sank into one of the chairs, the blush she'd applied the only color left in her face.

"God, that's horrible." I waited, but she didn't say anything more.

"I've been looking into Sierra with the information Jamie gave me."

At first it was like she didn't hear me. "What do you mean?" she said after a pause.

"I talked to her parents and one of her friends. I just met with her boyfriend this morning."

"Are you serious?"

I frowned. "You told me to ask Jamie for help."

"I thought whatever he gave you would be enough. That you'd accept it and move on."

"Accept it? It was just basic stuff and some contact information. It wasn't any good to me if I didn't use it."

April stared at me for a beat. "So you still think Lev had something to do with her going missing?"

I nodded. "I was looking for a way to prove to myself he wasn't, but everything I found pointed back to him."

"Like what?"

"Like all the bad things that happened to Sierra after they broke up." I started to pace. "She got blamed for a data leak and lost her job." I thought back to the missing portion of the Roy presentation. How if I hadn't had a triple backup, I would've blown the biggest project of my career. "I think Lev might've had her passwords from when they were together and made it look like it was her fault."

"Or maybe it was actually her fault."

"After that her car breaks down, and she has to get a new one," I said, plunging onward. "Which could be coincidence, but then her boyfriend finds a receipt for a hotel room in her name and thinks she's seeing someone and they split up." April looked at me blankly. I wasn't getting through to her. "Near the end Sierra thought she was being followed. Her boyfriend said someone had been in their house. Then, right before she vanishes, her dog goes missing."

"Okay . . ."

"Do you know the old lady with the dementia across the road from us?" April nodded. "Her cat used to shit in our flower beds. It drove

Lev nuts. After we came back from the cruise, the cat disappeared. It's still gone."

She laughed. "So one of his exes has some bad luck, and the neighborhood cat runs off, and that means he's a murderer?"

I bristled. "I'd say disappearing is more than some bad luck. You should've seen her boyfriend—the guy is destroyed. It ruined his life."

She held up her hands. "Okay, sorry. It's just . . . a little hard to believe. Lev's always been great."

I moved to the windows again and peered out. The day had darkened, and wind bent the trees below as if they were caught in an underwater current. "You don't know him like I do."

"But why? Why would he do all this?"

"He's been shaping our life, guiding it exactly the way he wants it to go. I didn't want to admit it, but now it's obvious. I think he's always gotten what he wanted, when he wanted it. He doesn't like being told no. When Sierra broke up with him, he couldn't accept it because he had their life planned out just like he does ours. When he knew she wasn't going to take him back, he threw everything he could at her to break her down, but she kept going. She left him behind and moved on, and he couldn't stand it. When he realized he wasn't going to get his way—" I faced April. She had her arms crossed, cupping her elbows as if she were cold. There was a look of open concern on her face I didn't care for. "All of it feels like him, like things he'd do. I think he's addicted to control. He can't stand being denied what he wants. And I know how it sounds, but there're other things too. There were times after he fell when it would seem like he was remembering something, but it was all to manipulate me."

April shook her head. "How would he do that if he didn't remember?"

"I don't think he ever forgot."

April stared at the floor for a long moment, then rose and went into the kitchen. She started heating water, then began emptying the dishwasher. I followed her and leaned against the island. "There's this feeling I get sometimes when he looks at me, almost like—" I thought for a moment how to describe it. "Like he's holding something back, some terrible urge. I wonder if that's what happened to Lyra. He saw an opportunity for a release and took it. We were never going back to that island, and he thought he'd get away with it. That no one would ever suspect him." I swallowed dryly. "I wonder how much he knows. I think he's been following me like he did Sierra. I'm afraid. I'm afraid of him."

I took a deep breath and slowly let it out. For a moment it all hung in the air, the only other sound the soft clinking of silverware as April sorted it. I'd expected to feel tired and empty after saying everything I'd been holding in, but if anything, I was even more manic. I couldn't get my hands to stop moving across the granite countertop, sliding back and forth like I was polishing an invisible stain. April still had her back to me, but she wasn't putting away dishes anymore. I noticed then she was wearing a nice pair of slacks and a new top I'd never seen before. Combined with the shower and makeup, I guessed she'd been getting ready to go out. There weren't many Friday evenings she stayed in.

"Sorry," I said, suddenly self-conscious. "I came barging in here and sprang all this on you. It's a lot. I can—" I paused, noticing the set of her shoulders and how they were shaking. April drew in a quick quiet breath.

She was crying.

"Hey," I said, crossing the room. I put a hand on her shoulder and turned her toward me. Tears streamed down her face, eyeliner running in dark streaks as if she were weeping ink. I moved to hug her, but she flinched and pushed me away.

"Stop," she said between sobs. "Just stop."

I was struck silent, a sinking sensation in the pit of my stomach. I'd crossed some sort of line in our friendship without meaning to. Pushed her past a breaking point. When I reflected on the last few minutes, I was reminded of Kyle and the paranoid energy he exuded. I probably sounded just as unhinged. April hadn't really taken my concerns seriously before, and now I'd revealed too much for her to deal with.

"Why?" she said quietly. "Why can't you just let it go?"

"I . . ." But I didn't know what to say. "I'm sorry."

She hunched forward then as if she were going to be sick and put her face in her hands. I wanted to comfort her but knew it would be the wrong thing to do. "This is my fault," she whispered.

"No, I shouldn't have said anything. I'm—"

"Quit apologizing!" she yelled, straightening. I recoiled. "You're always fucking apologizing. Stop it." Anger creased her pretty features, but even as I watched they smoothed to sorrow again. She swiped at her tears. "The way you are is my fault. None of this would be happening if—" Her voice failed.

There was a coiling inside me. Something growing tighter and tighter like a winding spring. "What are you talking about?"

"There's something you don't know." Her breathing came in small gasps. One of my hands reached out and touched the cool countertop, steadying myself against its solidity. I waited, pulse throbbing in my ears. Everything was very still.

"It was me," she finally said, her voice shrunken to that of a child's. "The woman who Marcus cheated on you with—it was me."

Imogen

At first all I felt was confusion.

What she'd said wasn't connecting to anything. It was as if she'd spoken a random phrase in a foreign language. I was lost.

Then the world seemed to shift around me as if its foundations had fractured. I suppose they had. I stared at her, waiting for a smile. The comfort of her laughter. Some hint it was a stupid joke with the worst timing ever. It was the only thing that could save me. Save us. But she just stood across the room, sheet white and breathing in short bursts, eyes streaming more tears.

The pictures from Marcus's phone flashed through my mind.

April. It was April in the pictures. She'd slept with my fiancé in my bed. Not some random woman—my best friend.

The coiling inside me tightened to an unbearable point, then broke. I felt it like something physical. Like the snap of bone. Freezing cold spilled from my center, numbing everything as it flooded outward until I couldn't feel anything.

April drew in a long breath and whispered, "I'm sorry. I'm so sorry."

"Why?" It was a second before I realized I'd been the one who spoke.

She shook her head. Her nose was running and she swiped at it. "I don't know. I was so fucking stupid." She looked at me, then away as if she couldn't stand it. "I was at a bar and Marcus came in. I was already drunk and we started talking. He bought me a few more drinks and asked me to go back to his place . . . I don't know why I did." Her breath shuddered in and out. "We were friends and I don't know what I was thinking. It just . . . happened. And I didn't know he took the pictures until after you found out and—and—" She was hyperventilating. She leaned heavily against the counter and looked down at the floor. A tear fell and landed on one of her bare feet.

Everything seemed to be lagging. Words. Movements. It was as if we were caught in a film on a faulty projector, the frames juttering unevenly.

I turned around and took a step, expecting the floor to give way. For the walls to crumble and fall. For it all to break apart and to wake up from the nightmare it was. Instead I walked smoothly toward the door. April followed.

"Imogen, please stop. Please." I paused with my palm on the handle. "I tried to take care of you after. I did everything I could to make it up to you. But I'm the reason why you're going through this now. It's not Lev—there's nothing wrong with him. What I did, it hurt you so much you never recovered, and now you're destroying your life for nothing." She edged closer, coming into my peripheral vision. She looked very small. "Please, don't throw everything away because of me."

I wanted to say something. Anything to bring back some sort of feeling, even if it was rage. But I was numb. No words could escape the void I found myself in.

When I finally looked at April, she was different. Changed in some fundamental way I couldn't name. I supposed I was seeing her completely for the first time, the hideous scar she'd been carrying finally exposed. I opened my mouth, still hoping for something to come out, but there was nothing. Nothing for me here.

I pulled the door open and went down the hall without looking back.

———

For the next hour or so, I drove without purpose. Drifting along at the posted speed limit on autopilot, thoughts lost in a haze.

Like April herself, everything looked different now. All the colors seemed off, not quite what they should've been. Strange new details leaped out among familiar buildings and streets. Even the wind itself had taken on an uncharacteristic edge, its humming around the car like an alien lullaby.

Gradually what had occurred with April took on a terrible clarity. There was a break in the numbness, and a bolt of anguish so raw overtook me I wanted to not feel again. But like a dam breaking, there was no stopping it. I began to cry so hard I couldn't see the road and pulled into a parking spot on the side of the street. The sobs were unlike anything I'd ever experienced before. They felt autonomic. Necessary. Like breathing.

April had always been there for me. My savior. My protector. Now I knew why. She was driven by a guilt so deep she hadn't been able to utter it all these years. Instead she'd hidden under a cowl of love and support. It was this that hurt almost more than the original betrayal. The hollow falseness of our friendship.

I didn't know how long I cried or when I stopped, but time had slipped even more, and I found myself staring blankly out the windshield at the back of the vehicle in the next parking spot. There was still an uncanny valley feel to the world, and now I realized why.

April's confession had unmoored me in more than one way. Made me question what was real. If any of my concerns were actually valid.

You're destroying your life for nothing.

I wondered if she was right. If the damage done by her and Marcus had set me on a course to this point. All my insecurities and jealous paranoia culminating into a state outside reality. It was what I'd hoped for to begin with—that it was all in my head. But I still couldn't deny the things I'd learned. Not entirely. Not yet.

A knock came from the passenger window, and I jumped.

A municipal cop was looking in at me. She gestured to the unpaid parking meter on the curb and tapped her wristwatch. I nodded and started the car as she ambled off down the sidewalk.

Amid the turmoil raging inside me, I only knew one thing for sure.

I needed to get away.

Sierra

We need to get away.

The thought is on repeat like a catchy song in my head as I shower. As I dress. While I make him breakfast. I'm so distracted he reaches across the table and touches my arm gently to get my attention.

"Momma?"

"Yeah, sweetie—I'm sorry, what did you say?"

"Can I have a cookie?"

"Dessert with breakfast?"

He grins, and there's no point in even pretending I won't give in. "You got me wrapped around your finger, you know that?" His little brow furrows in confusion, and he examines his hand. I burst out laughing and tickle him. Then I give him a cookie. It's time to go.

We need to get away.

I almost take the go bag but force the urge down, refusing to succumb to the resurging fear. I'm tired from the watchful night. The day isn't helping, either, sullen and wet, the clouds low and blackened as if they've been burned. He sings on the way down the mountain, the town below appearing and vanishing as we wind toward it through the trees.

The streets are empty at this hour. Only the mailman starting his rounds. We're a little early to his day care, and Amanda, the redheaded unflappable woman who owns it, doesn't have the door open yet, so we wait until she unlocks it and lets us in. Once he's dumped a small basket of toys in the next room and is playing happily, I ask Amanda if she's noticed anyone new hanging around town.

"You mean like tourists?"

"Could be. But just one man. Alone. Dark hair, good looking."

"Tall, dark, and handsome? No, I'd remember that. Especially around here."

"No strange cars parked out in the street? Maybe longer than they should be?"

"Sierra, what's this about?"

I stand looking into the other room at my son playing with a half dozen or so small figurines. He's set them up in a semicircle and is methodically knocking them over one by one.

"Call the motel if you see anybody you don't recognize," I say, still watching him. Watching the toy men fall.

"Will do." Amanda lowers her voice. "Should I be worried? Is there going to be trouble?"

I don't hear her at first. "No," I say finally, and give her the most reassuring smile I can. "No, I don't think so."

Imogen

There weren't any lights on in the house when I coasted up our street and turned into the driveway.

It was a good sign. If Lev wasn't home, it would be much easier get what I needed and go. Which would only be a small bag of necessities and Moxie. The rest could sit for now or forever as far as I was concerned.

The plan to leave had become all-consuming as I made my way home. It had filled the emptiness left by April's confession like blood clotting a deep wound, and I was glad for it, temporary as it was. It would keep me going for now. If I stopped to think about anything too long, it would be difficult to get moving again. There would be time later for contemplation and the pain that would accompany it, but now it was crucial to stay in motion.

The neighborhood was very quiet, only the wind parading down the street. Mrs. Miller wasn't outside, but there was a humped shadow in one of the windows that could've been her sitting in her wheelchair, watching.

I opened the front door as quietly as possible and slipped inside. The house was silent. I braced myself, waiting for Mox to come running, for Lev to appear in the darkened kitchen. If he was here, I'd just take Mox and go. No questions or answers, only the comfort of distance as the miles grew between us.

"Mox," I said quietly. "Moxie."

Nothing.

I took my shoes off and padded deeper into the house, wanting but not daring to open the garage door to see if Lev's car was there since it would make more noise. I was about to go upstairs when I heard something in the living room.

A whisper. The rustle of clothing.

I stiffened, wanting to run and needing to get Mox at the same time. I moved into the kitchen and stopped. The shades were drawn, and the adjacent rooms were dampened with shadow. It was hard to see if anyone was there. I stood listening at the island, wanting to speak to dispel the fear and knowing the moment I did, something might happen. As my eyes adjusted I noticed a particular shadow against the nearest living room wall. I could only see part of it, but it was manlike, and the nightmare came flooding back—someone standing at the end of the bed watching me—and I wondered if it had been a nightmare at all.

I retreated a single step and reached out, grasping the topmost handle protruding from the knife block as the shadow detached from the wall and stepped forward. At the same moment a half dozen other shapes rose from behind chairs and moved into view from around corners—all of them closing in as the lights suddenly flared brightly in every room.

"Surprise!"

"Happy birthday!"

The cries overlapped and mingled from the smiling people who swarmed around me. They were strangers for a beat, in my house for some reason I couldn't understand, then I recognized them all.

Val and Deshawn. Charlie and Beth. Mr. Stanford. The Millers.

And Lev behind them, eyes shining into mine.

I forced a smile and reset the knife in the block as one after another they swept me into hugs.

Happy birthday, happy birthday, we were waiting forever in the dark, where the hell were you? Happy birthday.

"Thanks, thank you, I can't believe this," I said, hoping I sounded halfway normal.

"It was all Lev," Beth said. "He had everything planned out."

Lev came to me and pressed a brimming glass of wine into my hand. He leaned in close, kissing my temple. "Happy birthday, honey." I squeezed my eyes shut.

"Thank you. You shouldn't have done all this." Sweat beaded between my shoulder blades, tickling as it ran down the small of my back. "Where's Mox?"

"In the garage. He wouldn't stop woofing at Mr. Stanford," Lev said, pulling a charcuterie board from the fridge.

"Must know I'm the boss," Stanford quipped. Everyone laughed. Lev turned on some music and people mingled. I drank my wine, trying to think of how to extricate myself from my own surprise party.

"God, you're old," Charlie said, sipping a beer. "Are you getting mailers from AARP yet?" I flicked him off.

"Be nice, Chuck," Beth said.

"I hate when you call me that."

"I know."

"Where's Mom and Pop?" Charlie said, glancing past me. "Thought they'd beat us here." He drew out his phone and started to text Mom.

"Don't bother her," I said too quickly.

Charlie looked up. "Why? You guys have a fight or something?"

"Or something."

"Jesus, on your birthday? What is it now?"

"I'm going to check on Mox," I said, leaving the party's radius. Mox almost leaped into my arms when I opened the garage door. I petted him and considered just going without another word to anyone. I could do it. Slip outside, pop Mox in the back seat, and be miles down the road before my absence was noticed. I almost started for the overhead door, but then Mr. Stanford was there, smiling at us both. Mox gave him a skittish look before finally licking his hand when he held it out.

"See, I'm not so bad, am I?" Stanford said. "I think he just smelled my own pup on me."

We stood for an awkward moment not saying anything. Then Stanford gestured with the glass of whiskey he was holding. "You know, I hope you don't think there was any confidence lost. After the Roy thing."

I didn't know if he meant the minor hiccup in my presentation or how I'd stood up for myself afterward. I didn't care either way. I was surprised to find I no longer wanted the approval I'd sought from him for so long. Given what my life had become in the last months, career hierarchy and aspirations were nearly meaningless things now. Like toys a child has quickly outgrown.

"I secured a multimillion-dollar project for the company. Why would there be any confidence lost?"

I clinked his glass with mine and drank almost all of my wine. His scowl lines deepened. A man of his age and position probably wasn't used to having an olive branch snapped off in his hand.

I left Stanford in the hallway and went back to the kitchen, the wine making me feel lighter and less afraid. Lev was chatting with the guests, who had formed a loose half circle around the island. The top two buttons of his shirt were undone. His hair had fallen over his forehead. He was smiling and cajoling, the perfect host. Watching him, I could almost believe it was true. That he hadn't done all this for any other purpose than to surprise me and make me happy. But every so often he would glance my way, and something would shift in his gaze—there and gone.

It was like glimpsing someone else looking out from behind his eyes.

I raised my glass but it was empty.

"Where's April?" Beth asked, coming up beside me.

My stomach turned. "I'm not sure. I know she's been super busy with work lately. Maybe . . ." I noticed something strange and shook my head a little. The corners of the room were growing hazy, as if smoke were gathering there. I blinked, thinking exhaustion and lack of food paired with the alcohol was catching up with me. But the edges of my vision continued to soften, a blurriness swarming inward.

"Hey, you okay?" Beth said. Her voice was echoey. Far away. The former lightness was gone, and my body began to feel heavy, like it was being encased in wet concrete.

"I—" My mouth and tongue were fused. I shook my head again, vision wobbling. "Something's wrong." Beth's concerned features swam in and out of view, and I put one hand on the nearest wall.

Through the fog Lev turned to study me.

With a colossal effort, I raised the wineglass and looked at it.

A few white granules were stuck to the bottom.

I lost my grip and the glass shattered on the floor.

I fell next to it.

There was no pain. Only the cool solidity of the hardwood. Then someone was rolling me over. My brother. I tried to say something to him. Tried telling him about what was in my wineglass, but it was getting difficult to breathe.

"Honey? Honey? When did you take your medication?" Lev's face hovered beside Charlie's. "How much did you take?" I tried to say I hadn't taken any. I'd flushed the last of it, but everything was disconnecting, coming apart at the atomic level.

So this is dying, I had the time to think as a veil of darkness drew quickly closed around me, and with it, terror enmeshed with regret. I reached out in one final effort and felt Lev's hand close over mine. I hoped someone saw my finger point at him.

A last accusation as everything slipped away.

Imogen

Thunder.

Muted rumbles far away from an approaching storm. The heaviness of sleep was warm and comforting. I knew when I was able to open my eyes, I would be on my bed in my parents' home waking from an afternoon nap. My window would be open, the white gauzy curtains floating inward from a humid summer breeze ahead of the storm. I would have to get up and shut it soon; otherwise, it would rain in on my books and CDs.

The thunder grumbled again, but now it was different. Quieter. More defined. It sounded like words.

I cracked my eyes open, getting a snapshot before they closed again.

A square room with gray walls. Shades drawn against bright sunlight. Two people standing beside a curtain hanging from the ceiling.

Sleep tugged me back down, but I fought to the surface a second time.

A woman with dark hair in blue scrubs was talking to someone who had their back to me. A tall man. Their murmuring was so low I couldn't make out what they were saying. There was a beeping, and suddenly a blood pressure cuff inflated tightly on my arm. I opened my mouth to speak but there was no saliva. My tongue rasped audibly. The nurse's eyes shifted my way and she abruptly stopped talking. I was fading again, clinging to consciousness like a climber on a sheer drop. The nurse hurried toward me, her mouth moving and her words coming a second later.

"Someone's awake. That's good."

My eyelids fluttered, and before they closed for good, the tall man turned and looked at me.

And smiled.

―――――

The second time I awoke alone. The hospital room was empty, the curtain around the bed drawn aside, the door open to a hallway with the corner of a nurses' station visible. The sunlight had become muted, but it felt like it was the same day as the first time I woke up.

I stared up at the ceiling, letting the memories assemble. They did so sluggishly, with a few blackened parts as if they'd been burned blank.

Visiting Kyle. Mom. The call from Kafatos. April's confession. The decision to leave. The surprise party. Then—

Nothing came at first, but I could feel it hovering just out of sight. When it revealed itself, the heart monitor beside the bed picked up speed until it began to beep intermittently. A few moments later the nurse in blue scrubs from earlier came in, smiling at the sight of me awake.

"Hi, Imogen, I'm Cathy. I've been looking after you. Let's get some water; I bet you're thirsty."

When she handed me a plastic cup filled with ice water, I noticed an IV snaking from my left arm. I drank the entire glass without stopping and wanted more, but the need to speak to her overshadowed my thirst.

"My husband—" I started.

"He's just down the hall with your parents and brother," Cathy said, cutting me off. "Want me to get him?"

"No." She'd already started for the door but froze. "He's the one who did this to me."

Her brow wrinkled. "Maybe I should get Dr. Miter. I think she's next door."

"Don't tell him I'm awake." She gave me a quizzical look, then hurried away.

I assessed how I felt. Tired. Weak. Deeply hungover. My head throbbed and I was breathless, my heart rate still in the 120s but dropping. I tried sitting up and was gratified to find I could. I was inspecting the IV entry point on my arm when Dr. Miter stepped into the room. She was a slender woman with platinum hair tied back in a tight ponytail.

"I'm Tricia Miter. How're you feeling?" she said, taking a peek at my vitals.

"Okay. Shaky."

"That's to be expected. Do you remember what happened to you yesterday?"

"I was drugged."

Miter had been signing in to a computer near the bedside and stopped to glance at me, probably wondering if I was joking or still out of my head. "You're saying someone did this to you?"

"My husband. He put something into my wine."

Miter continued to study me, then resumed typing at the console. "You have a prescription for Klonopin, and that's what we found in your system. A considerable amount of it. Mixed with the alcohol, it caused a loss of balance and a severe depression in your respiration, which we treated you for when you were brought in last night." She turned to me again. "But you're saying you didn't willingly ingest it?"

"No. I don't know how he got it since I flushed the last of my pills down the toilet."

"Why did you do that?"

"I . . . I didn't want to depend on them. I haven't taken them in a long time."

She tapped a few more keys. "It says here your prescription was refilled less than a week ago."

I shook my head. "No, that's not right."

"You use Gateway Pharmacy, correct?"

"Yes but . . ." It registered then what Lev had done. He'd refilled my prescription without me knowing. The process was automated, and no one would bat an eye at a husband picking up a prescription for his wife. I recalled the food and note Lev had left me the night before the party. How hard the wine had hit me. How it had felt like someone had been in the room with me in the middle of the night. Maybe watching to see how affected I was. Like a practice run.

Miter lowered her voice. "I want you to know addiction is nothing to be ashamed of. Klonopin's a powerful benzodiazepine. You're definitely not the first person to become dependent on it."

"I'm not addicted to it—are you listening to me? Lev did this. He tried to *kill* me."

Miter bit her lower lip, and it made her look much younger, almost girlish. "Your family informed me of your recent . . . struggles. It's apparent they all care very much about you, and they're concerned for your well-being. I'm sure you didn't mean to overdo it, but mixing alcohol and your medication is extremely dangerous."

I was stunned silent. This couldn't be happening. But even as I struggled to find a way to explain the truth, I saw how insidiously clever he'd been. How calculated. From the moment he'd fallen from the ship's balcony to now—he'd been maneuvering and manipulating, constantly one step ahead.

It was all Lev. He had everything planned out.

Miter was saying something I only caught the last of. Addiction treatment. They had programs there at the hospital. She would bring in brochures for me to look at.

"For now we're going to keep you for observation and make sure there were no other organ systems affected." She must have mistaken my silence for shame because she squeezed my hand once before leaving the room. "Don't feel like this is the end. It's the beginning of recovery. You can be someone completely different if you want to."

I listened to the soft squeak of her shoes receding down the hallway, thinking of how close I'd come to not waking up. How depthless and empty the time between going under and awakening had been. How easy it had felt not to be.

Someone stepped into the room, and I flinched then relaxed seeing Charlie's familiar features drawn with tension.

"How're you feeling?" he asked quietly, as if his voice could hurt me.

"Where is he? Lev?" I added when he frowned.

"He went down to the cafeteria with Mom and Dad to get something to eat."

I looked past him making sure we were alone. "I know what the doctor told you, but I didn't take any pills yesterday. Lev put them in my wine."

"What? Why?"

"He's not who you think he is. He's done terrible things." Charlie made a small sound in the back of his throat. Something between a sigh and moan I recognized from childhood. He made it whenever he was particularly caught off guard, which wasn't often. He'd made it the day when we were both little and Mom and Dad said we were moving and when I'd had to tell him what happened with Marcus.

"Imm," he began, and my heart slipped in my chest. It was the way he said my name. Like an apology. "We're really worried about you. This shit is serious. You almost died."

I grasped his arm so tightly his eyes widened. Good. "Have I ever had a problem with pills or booze?" He hesitated, then shook his head. "Exactly. Why would I now?"

"Stress? Marriage? Work? I don't know. People overindulge for all kinds of reasons. You've been different lately, we've all noticed it. Mom told me what you said to her yesterday. You don't—"

"He killed a woman on our honeymoon." That shocked him into silence. "Her name was Lyra Markos. She was a waitress at a restaurant we went to and I saw them together the night she was murdered. Lev lied and said he never left the ship, but he did. And I think he killed a former girlfriend too—Sierra Rossen. Look them up if you don't believe me."

Charlie glanced over his shoulder, then leaned closer. "Listen, they're out there discussing whether or not to have you committed. Do you get it? They're going to lock you up for your own good. You need to quit saying shit like this if you want to walk out of here, okay?" I could see he was afraid, but for all the wrong reasons. He straightened and rubbed his forehead. "Just . . . get some rest."

He started away but I snagged his arm again. "Don't trust him, Charlie. Whatever you do, don't trust him." I let him go and he gave me a last look of pity before leaving the room.

I let my head fall back into the pillows and closed my eyes. I was so tired. I felt worn thin enough to see through. Couldn't get my thoughts to align in any sort of shape, couldn't get myself to figure out what came next. When I heard footsteps returning to the room, I was deeply thankful. Charlie coming back to say he believed me, that he knew I hadn't overdosed, that I wasn't losing my mind. But when I opened my eyes, Lev was standing at the end of the bed.

He smiled. "Hi, honey."

Imogen

The air in the room tightened like we were changing altitude. We both felt it, the invisible tension rising until it was unbearable.

I broke it by fumbling for the call button wrapped through the bed's side rails. He crossed the distance in half a step, snagging the button's cord and yanking it away before I could press it. I opened my mouth to scream but stopped short when he drew something from his pocket.

A syringe.

Before I could react, he'd retracted the plunger and inserted the needle into my IV port. There was nothing in the syringe.

"An air embolism happens when an air bubble gets lodged in a vein," Lev said, leaning over me. His voice reminded me of flat water. Calm and dead. "It can cause all kinds of problems like a heart attack or stroke. Not uncommon for someone recovering from a drug overdose."

My whole body had taken on a muted tingling, like I'd been dunked in an ice bath. "I'll scream," I said.

"Not if you don't want to look even crazier than you already do."

I inhaled anyway, ready to release a yell that would bring someone, anyone, running.

His thumb tensed over the plunger, ready to send air into my bloodstream.

I let the scream out in a silent exhale.

"You know, this is almost poetic—last time it was me in the hospital bed and you standing where I am. Funny how things work out."

"What do you want?" I whispered.

Lev's smile was sudden and transforming. It made him look like the person I used to know. The man I fell in love with. "I want you." He came closer while maintaining his hold on the syringe, and I retreated as far as the bed would allow. He reached out to touch my face, and I recoiled. He ignored this. "Everyone's very concerned. So am I. You haven't been yourself lately. We all want to help you."

Footsteps came down the hallway. I tensed and tried leaning forward, but he blocked my view of the doorway, and whoever it was kept going.

"I'm going to make you an offer," he said, sounding as if we were in the middle of a business meeting. "It's a good one. We've built so much together, and I'm not willing to let it all go. The offer is this—you forget everything you think you know, and we move forward. No more questions or doubts, just us together. United. We've got so much ahead of us, and I know you want it as much as I do. The past is nothing compared to the future. It's nothing. It doesn't exist."

I inhaled a long shaky breath. "What if I say no?"

His gaze lost its artificial warmth. "There are dozens of ways someone can lose their life without any suspicion being raised. This is just one of them." He tilted his head toward the syringe. "You could fall down the stairs at home and break your neck. Or next time you succeed in overdosing. Mox could run off for good, or Charlie might be tragically killed in a hit and run." My heart seemed to be much too large for my body, its beating filling the room, pounding off the walls. "I'd say your mother could meet an early end, but that might be doing you a favor."

I stared up at him, insides crawling with revulsion. "Who are you?"

He smiled again, but it was different somehow. A subtle shift. There was no familiarity there now. Nothing to remind me of who I'd once loved and trusted. He was a stranger.

"I'm your husband," he said.

His words hung in the air. The machines around us hummed and beeped. The light shifted as a cloud covered the sun.

"What do you say?" he asked.

"Fuck you." My voice was small. Defeated.

He nodded. "Then let me leave you with something to think about. No matter what you do, you're alone in this. No one believes you. There is no proof of anything. I'm a very careful, meticulous person. I don't want you gone, but if you force me, you will be. Do some risk assessment for yourself, and you'll see it's not worth it. At the end of the day, I'm the only one who can save you from all this."

I brimmed with terror, but there was a part of me that wanted to lash out. Hurt him as much as I could. He must've seen something in my face because he stepped out of reach. "The other night when we were arguing, I held back," he said, smiling faintly. "What I really wanted to say was you're just like the rest of them—ungrateful. Think about all I've done for you, and all I could do to you, before you make your decision."

Someone was coming down the hall, their footsteps slowing.

Lev withdrew the syringe from the port and moved to the open bathroom door as the nurse from earlier stepped into the room. "How're we doing?" she asked brightly.

As I watched, Lev slipped the needle into the locked syringe container mounted to the bathroom wall. Then he stepped into sight wearing his typical dazzling smile.

"We're doing much better, aren't we, honey?" he said.

They both watched me, waiting.

"Yes," I said finally. "Much better."

―――――

I sat looking out the window, watching the world grow dark. I'd had Cathy open the shades before she left while Lev lingered in the doorway.

The patient, doting husband filled with concern. I stared at a place on the wall until they were both gone, the probe of his eyes on my skin like dead fingertips.

For some time I thought of nothing, my mind a slate wiped clean by shock. Everything I'd suspected was true. All my fears confirmed. As my mental gears finally began to mesh, the gravity of the situation continued to gain weight. Lev had carefully alienated me from nearly all aspects of my life—the surprise party being the culmination. Everyone there had witnessed what they thought was a closet addict going over the edge. My boss. My brother and his wife. Our neighbors. The fight with Mom only confirmed I wasn't myself even though that confrontation had been a long time coming. And as terrifying as Lev had been when the mask had slipped, he was right about one thing.

I was alone.

Everything inside me seemed to rise upward, wedging itself into my throat so that it became hard to breathe. I blinked away tears and took a long drink from the water glass beside the bed, then fished some ice out and held it against my throat until it began to burn. I took a half dozen deep breaths, then pressed the nurse call button. Cathy stepped into the room a few moments later.

"What can I get you?" she asked.

"I have to go to the bathroom."

"Do you feel like you can stand? Because you can use a bedpan, it's no problem."

"I can stand," I said, fumbling with the bed rails until she came to help. She released the blood-pressure cuff and unclipped the heart-and-oxygen monitor from my finger. When I rose, she steadied me as the floor shifted under my feet.

"Here," she said, rolling the IV stand along. "Hold this for balance."

"I'm okay."

"Are you sure?"

"I'm fine. I'd just like some privacy."

"I'll wait just in case—"

"I said I'm *fine*." I felt bad at her stricken look, but it was necessary.

"Okay. Well, I'll check on you in a few minutes." She hovered near the doorway until I stepped into the bathroom, then drifted toward the nurses' station. I waited a second before shuffling over to the single cabinet built into the wall. My clothes were inside in a plastic bag, but my purse and phone weren't with them. *Shit.* No time to worry about it, each moment that passed was an opportunity for things to fall apart. I had to hurry.

In the bathroom I peeled off the medical tape from around the IV in my arm, wincing as it came free, then withdrew the needle with a hiss. Vertigo assaulted me as I stripped out of the hospital gown and began dressing in my own clothes, the room swaying like a ship before steadying. I was just lacing my shoes when there was a knock on the door, Cathy's voice filtering in a second later.

"You okay?"

"Doing great."

"Need any help?"

I squeezed my eyes shut. "Nope."

"Okay. I won't be far away."

I listened for the sound of her leaving the room. When it was quiet again, I turned on the tap and finally caught a glimpse of myself in the mirror.

A pale and hollow-eyed woman looked back at me, her hair askew, her clothes rumpled. I'd never considered myself strong. Or truly independent. Or brave. I'd always dreamed of being these things in a different life. Because I couldn't get myself to believe I would ever gain them as time went on through lived experience. It seemed when each challenge came, I fell short and only wore a deeper groove in the path laid out for me. More or less I thought once you reached a certain point in your life, you were who you were. But now I knew there were things that could change you. Alter you in such fundamental ways that you didn't know you were leaving your old self behind until it was already gone.

"Goodbye," I said under my breath, not meaning to speak. Then I opened the bathroom door and slipped out, closing it behind me with the water still rushing quietly into the sink.

The sun had set while I'd been changing, and the room was dimmer, only a single light glowing above the empty bed. I peered out the doorway and clocked Cathy alone at the nurses' station, scribbling something on a pad of paper. I waited until she turned away before swinging out of the room and striding quickly in the opposite direction.

I wasn't deeply familiar with the hospital and took a right out of instinct when I reached the end of the hall, realizing the elevators were the opposite way a second too late. Crossing the main hall again I caught a glimpse of my parents and brother at the far end talking with Cathy. They didn't seem to be alarmed, so I guessed my absence hadn't been discovered yet. But there was something that bothered me as I hurried toward the bank of elevators and punched a down button.

As I stood waiting, a middle-aged couple joined me, their conversation quiet and reserved. Their presence was comforting—I was just like them, another person leaving the hospital at the end of the day. As the elevator arrived a wave of disquiet washed over me, and I realized what had been troubling about seeing my parents and brother talking to the nurse.

Lev hadn't been with them.

The elevator doors opened, and I stepped aside, facing away. The couple stood back as a group of people stepped off onto the floor. I risked a glance and my stomach clenched.

Lev was one of the people exiting the elevator. He had his head down, studying his phone like several of the others, and didn't look up until he was farther down the hall. I watched until he turned at the next junction and headed toward my room.

"Getting on?"

I startled. The couple was standing inside the elevator, the man holding the door open expectantly. "Yes, sorry. Thanks," I said, stepping in with them. As the doors closed agonizingly slowly, I imagined Lev bursting into view and sprinting toward me, eyes ablaze and yelling at the top of his lungs. But the hall remained quiet, and the close silence of the space settled in as we rode smoothly downward.

I hurried across the busy lobby when the elevator opened, still expecting a hospital employee to stop me whenever I passed one, but they were absorbed in their own tasks and didn't give me a second look. I eased between a throng of people waiting in line at one of the intake stations and slipped out the door into the shockingly cold evening air.

Without looking back I started away from the building, wondering if someone were in my room high above realizing I was gone and gazing down at me now. The thought only made me move faster, and by the time I'd reached the nearest street I was running.

Imogen

I had the Uber drop me off at the end of our street and walked the rest of the way.

It was full dark now, gauzy mist drifting beneath the streetlights. I moved quickly, head hunched down, hands tucked in my armpits. After the blessed warmth of the car, the weather felt like an adversary—the breeze pushing me back, moisture trickling coldly down the back of my neck.

The relief from escaping the hospital had quickly faded as soon as I remembered I had no means to call or pay for any type of transportation home. I'd walked nearly a mile, mind whirring through possibilities before the thought of the library's public computers leaped forward. The nearest library was only a few blocks away, and it was a half hour before closing when I rushed inside, logged on to my Uber account, and ordered a car that was two minutes out. Lev, of course, could see what I'd done if he'd known I was no longer in my room at the hospital, but that was a risk I had to take. Now it was a race to see who made it home first.

When the house came into view, there was a light burning in the entry, but we typically left it on when we were out. My car was the only one in the driveway, and I didn't see any movement inside as I crept across the lawn and went down the side of the house to the back door. The spare key was where we always kept it, beneath a cap on one of the deck's corner posts. I unlocked the sliding door but stopped, retracing my steps down to the lawn to pull a rock the size of a baseball from the landscaping before going inside.

The house was still and very dark. I navigated through memory and feel, stopping every so often to listen. Nothing.

"Mox?" I whispered. No response. Panic swelled inside me. Maybe Lev had already done something to him like he'd threatened at the hospital. But I didn't think so; Mox was too valuable a bargaining piece. If he wasn't in the house, he was probably next door at Val and Deshawn's. I clung to the idea as I made my way deeper inside.

The rock was slick with sweat, and I regripped it as I cracked open the garage door and reached inside to turn on the light. All at once I was sure a hand would close over mine and yank me into the darkness. Lev had beaten me here, and he'd been waiting the whole time, knowing I would come back, knowing exactly what I would do, anticipating everything. He would do unspeakable things to me, and then I would disappear just like Sierra had.

My fingers met the switch and flipped it up.

Light filled the garage. It was empty. I was still alone. For now.

Even as I sprinted up the stairs and began filling a small bag with essentials, I was mentally calculating how long I had before his arrival. I might've had a ten-minute head start. Most of that was lost on the walk to the library and waiting for the Uber. Even so, Lev would've had to exit the hospital, gotten to his vehicle, and driven here, which would've taken at least—

A sound came from below.

I froze, the bag half-zipped shut, straining to listen. Had it been the garage door opening and closing? The front entryway? Or something more furtive—the sliding door easing shut.

I waited another thirty seconds, then finished zipping the bag and tiptoed to the top of the stairs. The house was dark and still below. I swallowed, blood surging in my ears. I had to move. If he wasn't already here, he would be soon.

On the main level I paused long enough to assure myself I was still alone, then hunted for my purse and phone. They were both where I'd left them. The phone's screen was lit up with dozens of messages and missed calls, the most recent a text from Lev three minutes ago that simply read, Stay where you are.

Not a fucking chance.

My car keys were in the dish by the front door, and I snagged them as I rushed by, a fraction of my mind noting in a clinically detached way this might be last time I'd ever be in the house. But any sense of loss was overshadowed by how alien it felt now. It was a representation of our marriage, a place hollowed out by lies and misgivings. Something drained of any deeper meaning or sentimentality. It was just a house now.

I threw the bag into the back seat and ran up Val and Deshawn's drive, shooting a look down the still-deserted street. Before I could ring the bell, the door was opening, and Val was there, eyes wide and questioning.

"Girl, what the hell?"

"Do you have Mox?"

"Yeah, yeah, of course. Lev asked us to watch him. Are you all right?"

"Where is he?"

But then Mox had rushed past Val's legs into my arms, as if he knew how much I needed him right then. A surge of emotion nearly overwhelmed me. I bit it back and headed for the car with Mox in tow.

"Hey!" Val followed, her feet bare, arms crossed against the cold. "Imogen? What the hell is going on? Is everything okay?"

"No," I said, opening the back door to let Mox hop inside. "No it's not. I don't have time to explain, but if something happens to me—even if it looks like an accident—Lev did it." I held her gaze, unblinking. "He's a monster, Val."

There were a hundred questions in her eyes, but she could see I was leaving and reached out. I took her hand. Squeezed it tight. A last bit of comfort to carry with me. Then I climbed in the car, backed out of our drive, and sped down the street. Val stood watching me go, a slender shadow in the night getting smaller and smaller until she was lost around the first bend.

I wondered if she believed me. She had no reason to besides our friendship. But I thought maybe that was enough. That and perhaps a deeper kinship most women shared on a subconscious level. Down in that dark place where we all felt small and defenseless sometimes. Where a lying voice whispered about being the weaker sex no matter how many times we proved it wrong. I hoped she felt the weight of our last touch. And if something did happen to me, I hoped she would be careful.

I didn't slow at the entrance to our neighborhood, just glided past the stop sign and accelerated in the opposite direction I knew he'd be coming from. There was a small rise ahead, and I felt if we could just get up and over it, we'd be safe. Safe for now.

The car climbed the hill, and as we crested it, headlights appeared in the rearview mirror and swung hard into the neighborhood.

Then we were out of sight, racing away in the darkness, leaving everything behind.

Imogen

I stopped to make a call at a twenty-four-hour convenience store twenty miles from home.

The halogen brightness of the parking lot along with the steady stream of cars flowing alongside the gas pumps gave me a sense of security. I'd powered my phone off leaving the house, and when I turned it back on, there were two missed calls and three more texts from Lev.

Where are you?

Don't do this. You're not thinking straight. Just come home.

I love you.

I thought of how his eyes had changed—how his true self swam to the surface and then submerged—and shuddered.

He had also frozen our accounts. I found this out when I stopped at an ATM and tried to withdraw the maximum amount of cash. All I got was an error code along with a ripple of alarm wondering if he would be able to see what terminal I'd used. First I cursed myself for not thinking of the ATM earlier, then for not searching for extra cash at home prior to leaving. But in the same moment knew if I'd lingered, even for a minute, Lev would've intercepted me.

I scanned my phone, looking for any tracking apps he might've installed without me noticing and didn't find any. But that didn't necessarily mean they weren't there. Checking the time, I decided I'd keep the call short in case Lev was able to see my location. The ringing on the other end trilled distantly, sounding every one of the miles it was away. I was about to hang up when there was a click.

"Kafatos."

This was my last hope. The final possibility of holding on to what little remained of my life. If I could convince Kafatos Lev had killed Lyra, testify to what I'd seen, get the local authorities reinterested in Sierra's disappearance, there was a chance they could build a case against him, maybe put him away forever, and I wouldn't have to run. Because as much as my life had crumbled, I still didn't want to abandon it.

"Hello?" Kafatos said.

"Lieutenant, it's Imogen Carmichael."

A brief pause. "Hello, Imogen. I'm glad you called. I assume you've had time to look at the picture?"

"Picture? What picture?"

There was a shuffling sound from his end and I saw him at his desk again, this time in the early morning hours before the station began to bustle with activity. "I texted you a photo of a person who was on the cruise ship with you. He and his wife were staying only a few suites down from your own."

"Hold on." Even though I could feel the passage of time like a physical pressure, I flicked to my messages and saw one of them was from Kafatos's number. When I tapped it, a face appeared on the screen. Lev's face. *No, wait.* "I don't understand," I said, switching to speakerphone.

"Your suggestion of checking the ship's boarding logs was a good one. This man exited the ship near the time you said you saw someone on the beach with Lyra and reboarded afterward."

I stared down at the photo.

It was the swinger. The man who had casually invited us to join him and his wife some night. The one who had a passing resemblance to Lev. What had I called it at the time that had made Lev laugh so hard? *He looks like a dollar-store version of you.*

"But . . ." I said, thoughts in free fall. "But Lev left the ship, too, right?"

"No. His card wasn't registered anywhere near that time frame. It was scanned much earlier in the day. That was it."

I looked out the windows at the brightly lit storefront. The highway was alive with traffic even at this later hour. People were coming and going. Talking and laughing. It all looked like a movie to me. False. Not real at all. "He switched them," I said as if in a trance. It felt like I was. "He switched cards with him. That's how he got on and off the ship without scanning his own."

"Mrs. Carmichael—"

"Please don't call me that."

He cleared his throat. "I spoke to your husband late yesterday evening. He told me you had been admitted to the hospital." He let the implication hang. Not saying he knew the reason why I'd been there and not having to. Lev had told him. Of course he had. "Now I'd like you to try and remember—could this man have been the one you saw on the beach? You said it was dark, and I have to say he definitely resembles your husband."

"No, it wasn't him. It was Lev. He killed her. And he killed another woman before that. He threatened to kill me. He's a murderer."

The line was deathly quiet, his breathing the only sign the call hadn't dropped. "Imogen, you haven't been completely honest with me. You weren't asleep when your husband returned to your room that night. You fought, and it became physical. You shoved him, and he fell overboard."

I opened my mouth to refute what he was saying, to lie and stick to my former story, but realized it was useless. Everyone knew the truth now.

The last of my hope was slipping away. It felt like a coarse rope sliding through my clenched hands. Burning.

"Now, I would appreciate your help in this matter since we do have a record of you leaving the ship that night. You've stated you were in the vicinity of Ms. Markos during the last hours she was alive. Are there any more details you'd like to share with me? Anything you'd like to clarify about your story before we proceed any further?"

I hung up.

Powered the phone off.

Sat motionless, but I was reeling internally.

The same thought from the hospital returned like a mantra.

This couldn't be happening.

Any second I'd wake up and the last months would be a nightmare. Or maybe it would be years. Maybe I'd never met Lev. Or Marcus. Maybe I was still a little girl fast asleep in her bed, dreaming terrible things about her future. I would wake soon and be overcome with relief. My life would still be my own. I could change it. Become whoever I wanted to be.

I blinked and looked around at the parking lot. The mist had turned to light snow, drifting down and melting in a thousand specks on the windshield. There was a lull at the pumps, and I drove to the nearest one that was most hidden from the highway. I filled the tank and paid with what little cash I had. The cold air returned some present sense, dispelling the dream fantasy no matter how tempting it was to believe. This was real, and I needed to do something to save myself. No one was going to help me.

As I got back behind the wheel and keyed the car on, I realized that might not be completely true. Mox stuck his head up between the front seats, and I stroked his ears then got him to settle on the floorboards before pulling onto the highway.

A last thread of hope floated ahead in the dark, and I followed it toward the one person who still might be willing to help me.

Imogen

The hallway was dank and echoey—everything old, stained wood from floor to ceiling.

I made my way along it, memories flooding in with each door I passed until I stopped at the very end of the hall, Mox settling to his haunches beside me. I took a deep breath and knocked. Mox licked his chops and whined deep in his throat. He was probably confused as to what we were doing here at this time of night when we should've been settling into bed. If I could've withdrawn cash from our accounts, we would have already been an hour outside of the city, not standing here taking a risk. But I was out of options. I rubbed Mox's head, trying to reassure him as footsteps approached the door from inside and there was a pause while I guessed I was being observed through the peephole, then the rattle of locks disengaging, and the door opened.

Jamie stood looking out at me with something like wonder on his sleep-addled features. "Imogen?"

"Can I come in?"

He looked behind him, and I had the sudden premonition he wasn't alone. But at this point I didn't care. Let whoever he was sharing his life with think whatever they would. I was beyond desperate.

Jamie stepped back and watched us file in like he was dreaming. Mox padded into the small but comfortable living room and flopped down on a rug beside a tidy coffee table. I quickly took in the space, noting not much had changed since Jamie and I were together. The kitchen was clean, its counters clear except for a wicker basket half full of fruit. The worn leather couch where we'd cuddled and watched movies was exactly where it had always been. Even the reading nook under the large windows overlooking the street below was strewn with blankets and pillows, paperbacks lined up along one ledge in teetering piles. I recalled sitting there many rainy mornings with a cup of coffee, reading a novel and pausing to look out at the city beyond. There wasn't any sign another person lived here. The air smelled like Jamie. Comfortable. Safe.

"What's going on?" he asked. Jamie was wearing a pair of gym shorts, which he liked sleeping in, along with a worn Capitals T-shirt. Maybe it was his open concern or the familiarity of the apartment or the fact that I felt more alone than I ever had before in my life, but I wanted to fall into his arms. Wanted him to hold me and stroke my hair and tell me everything would be okay.

Instead I said, "Do you have any coffee?"

He blinked, then without a word went to the kitchen and began to brew some. I checked the time and fingered my phone inside my purse. I hadn't turned it back on since the call with Kafatos and was fairly confident Lev wouldn't be able to track where I was, but out of caution didn't dare power it up again. Besides, there was no one left to call.

"There are other options for coffee besides my place, you know," he said, returning with two steaming cups after a few minutes. "This new thing called drive-through is all the rage. You don't even have to get out of your car."

I tried to smile as I accepted the mug and burst into tears.

He took the coffee back and set both cups down before pulling me to him. I didn't resist.

"Hey, hey, it's okay. You're okay," he whispered. I tucked my face into his neck, wetting his skin with my tears but not caring. After a minute he gently settled me onto the couch and sat with his knees touching mine. When I'd quieted some, he said, "I'm starting to think you didn't come here for the coffee."

I released a strangled laugh, and he offered me my cup again. The coffee was glorious and almost immediately began nudging back the caffeine headache pulsing at the base of my skull. We sat that way for a while, neither of us talking. The snow had thickened and sounded like the soft padding of cat's paws on the windows.

"I think I might be partially to blame for this," Jamie said.

"No, you did what I asked. You helped me."

"Did I?"

I stared into the bottom of my mug. "I was hoping I wouldn't find anything."

"But you did." I nodded without looking up. "Tell me."

I started with going to see Sierra's parents and finished with my call to Kafatos a half hour before, leaving nothing out. He listened, any hints of drowsiness leaving him as I spoke. His eyes only betrayed him once—when I told him about Lev's threat at the hospital, they widened slightly and there was the familiar spark far back in their depths, like twin matches flaring. When I finished my hands were shaking so badly I rose and poured myself another cup of coffee just for something to do before sitting down again.

After nearly a minute of silence, I couldn't stand it anymore. "This is where you tell me I'm overreacting or afraid of commitment, and then I tell you to fuck off."

His eyebrows lifted. "I wasn't going to say that." I studied him, waiting for the "but." Instead he took a long sip of his coffee and said, "You remember my college buddy, Frank Gavin, right?" I nodded. "So Frank's grandmother passed away our senior year, and he got tasked with cleaning out her house since he was the closest grandkid to her. Her place was this turn-of-the-century rickety old thing over near Delaware Bay. He loved staying with her as a kid but always got kind of spooked at night. Said the house gave off a bad vibe even in the daylight. Didn't help his grandma told him a man had been bludgeoned to death in the basement over a bad debt prior to her buying the place. Anyway, Frank's there by himself, and everything's normal and fine, he's making good headway in all the upstairs rooms. Then he starts cleaning out the basement."

Jamie paused and rubbed the scruff on the side of his jaw. "He said he was bent over in one of the very back rooms loading some old jars or something into a box, and the lights went dim. They didn't go out—he made that really clear, they just dimmed like someone had turned them down. Then he saw something coming toward him across the room. He couldn't tell me what it was exactly, just that it moved in kind of a jerky way, like a man with a bad limp. As he tried standing up, something cold pressed itself to the back of his neck. He said it felt like the head of a hammer."

Jamie took a drink of coffee. "I don't believe in ghosts, but I know something happened to him in that house because I've never seen someone so afraid." He looked at me. "Until now."

"You—" My voice failed me. "You believe me?"

"Yes." I felt like weeping again but managed to swallow it down. Jamie took my hand. "What do you need?"

"Cash," I said. "As much as you can spare."

He stood and padded away to his bedroom, returning with a sheaf of bills. "It's a thousand. I can run to an ATM if you want to wait?"

"I shouldn't. I think he'll check at April's first, then maybe Charlie and Beth's, but it won't be long until he finds out where you live and comes here."

"Where are you going to go?"

"I don't know." Until that moment, I hadn't truly considered it. *Away* had been enough of a destination to keep me moving.

"You can use the cabin in Vermont. No one's really been up there since Dad passed."

I shook my head. "It wouldn't be safe."

"There's no way he could—"

"You don't know him, he'd find me. I have to go somewhere . . . else."

Jamie glanced around. "Stay here. I'll start digging again, see if I can find more about Sierra. You'll be safe."

I reached out and touched his face. "I don't want something to happen to you because of me." I dropped my hand to my side, suddenly self-conscious. "Could I use your bathroom before I go?"

"Of course."

The real truth of whether a man has a woman in his life is told in his bathroom, and there was no sign of one here. I could've interpreted Jamie's bachelorhood as a compliment, a testament to the fact he'd never fully moved on from us. But it saddened me more than anything. I hoped he had found love or at least companionship of some kind. He deserved that much as a consolation for me breaking his heart.

Back in the living room Jamie was feeding Mox a piece of beef jerky. Mox licked his chops and flopped gracelessly to his side, letting out a satisfied groan as Jamie scratched his belly. "You know, you really should stay. I mean for his sake." He motioned to Mox. "Look at how comfortable he is. It'd be a crime to take him out in the cold tonight."

I smiled halfheartedly. When we were together, he had always tried to make me laugh. He still was. I gave him a hug and found myself not wanting to let go. Jamie held me. The moment stretched out into something else. We parted just enough to lean our foreheads together.

"Imm . . ." His lips were so close. Then they were brushing mine.

I started to pull away, then kissed him back. Deeply. It was like coming home.

We came apart after a moment, a tear slipping from the corner of my eye. He swiped it away with his thumb. "Stay." His voice was husky and quiet. "Please." It wasn't the first time he'd asked the same things of me, standing in almost the same place. I wished he knew how much I wanted to say yes, then and now.

I squeezed his hands. Tried committing the feeling of his lips against mine to memory. Something I could take with me.

"Goodbye," I said, then let him go.

Sierra

"Goodbye!"

I look up from the blank desktop and return from the dark place I'd gone to see the family waving as they go out the door. They're passing through on their way to the next little mountain town and stopped in for a bathroom break and refreshments—a beer a piece for the mother and father, soft drinks for the boy and the girl.

I feign a smile and raise my hand in return, watching them file out to their hatchback plastered with bumper stickers and climb inside. They pull out of the parking lot, and soon they've disappeared up the street out of sight.

I stare after them longingly.

The urge to flee hasn't faded. It's an undercurrent to everything I've done throughout the day. It followed me as I relieved the night desk worker and began my routine. It was waiting for me in each of the rooms I tidied and cleaned. And now that I've run out of tasks, it's louder than ever, a tornado siren repeating its insistence that we should be gone already. That each passing minute is bringing us closer and closer to ruin.

I snap a ledger closed, and the sound fills the lobby, then it's quiet again. I go to the nearest window and look out. It hasn't rained yet, but the sky is still being held hostage by roiling clouds. It's coming. The storm will break sometime this afternoon and rain well into the dark. I busy myself with vacuuming the long rug running down the hall, and then there's a reprieve as two construction workers stop in for a drink on their way home. Their chatter and flirting is enough of a distraction, I can almost get myself to believe the worry exists solely in my mind.

When they're gone, I turn on the small TV in the lobby. Normally I only have it on when there's more than a few guests staying, and then I keep it muted. Now I flick through the channels, searching for something engrossing until the evening-shift replacement arrives. After several fruitless minutes I'm about to shut it off again when a news station appears on the screen with a chyron that catches my eye.

WEBBER CAMPAIGN CONTINUES STRONG
WHITE HOUSE BID

The scene shifts from the news anchor to Senator Webber giving a speech at a podium, a backdrop of people behind him, and there is a face among them I recognize, and my heart stutters.

It's him.

By the time I manage to unmute the TV, the anchor is back on the screen, his voice pouring from the speakers.

Saturday's event marks just one of the many stops on the senator's busy campaign trail so far this spring. Even with a majority of party leaders voicing that he's on track for a landslide victory, there are still many miles between Senator Webber and the steps of the White House in November.

The news breaks for commercial, and I shut the TV off.

Saturday. The event was on Saturday, and it's now Tuesday. He was in DC a few days ago. That's good. I've kept track of his movements for years, and anytime I can confirm his whereabouts, it's a relief, especially since it's always been on the opposite end of the country. But this time I don't feel the same comfort knowing over twenty-seven hundred miles separates us. Which doesn't track.

Track.

I pause near the desk, the sense of something massive rising slowly toward me. From within me. That word—*track*. Why am I thinking of it? And why is it making me more and more uncomfortable? I settle into the chair and try to be as still as I can. Attempting to force an answer to reveal itself almost never works. It becomes wedged tighter in the confines of the mind. Instead I try to loosen my mental hold, letting go of the wheel and allowing the unconscious to take over.

Track. Track. Track.

On track. The news anchor said Webber might be on track to a landslide victory.

But that isn't it. Or at least not all of it.

I close my eyes and breathe. Slowly. In and out. I ask myself a question: What am I most afraid of?

Him finding us.

What have I spent the better part of the last years preparing for?

Him finding us.

What are my instincts telling me?

He's found us.

How?

I've been over and over my disappearance. Running through the loose ends I left behind, anything I possibly forgot. How meticulous I was in leaving nothing for him to track me.

Track. There it is again. I breathe deep. Release. How could he possibly track us? There is nothing tying us to my former life. There is just me and my son and my dog, and there is no one—

Something in my center clinches so painfully I gasp.

I look around the vacant lobby, scan the parking lot outside. It's empty except for my truck. My fingers and hands begin to tingle unpleasantly as I open a search on the computer and find what I'm looking for after an excruciating beat. Then I dial the number listed on the website and listen to it ring as I sweep the parking lot again. I'm still alone.

"Carhill Veterinary, how can I help you?" The woman's voice is high and pleasant.

"I need to speak to the vet."

"I'm sorry. He's with a client right now. Could I—"

"This is an emergency. I need to speak with him now. Put him on."

My tone must have the right balance of steel and venom. There's a pause before the woman says, "Hold, please."

I pace to the windows. Mist is starting to drift down between the trees. What I can see of Main Street is deserted. My hands are shaking.

"This is Dr. Carhill. What can I help you with?"

"Some people brought my dog to you a couple days ago, and my friend picked him up yesterday. He's a—"

"Yes, of course. I'm glad we were able to get him back to you."

I steady myself and manage to form the question I need to ask. "Before he was picked up, did you scan him for a microchip?"

Within me a slender reed of hope bends beneath a wind of dread.

"Yes, we did, actually. I assumed that was how your friend knew to call us."

The reed breaks. The air throbs. Or maybe it's me. I'm a struck tuning fork, vibrating with fear.

The vet is saying something else but the phone has slipped from my ear. I set it on the counter, the tinny voice still spilling out of it asking if I'm there.

But I'm not.

I'm thousands of miles away, tracing the path that has brought me here. The days and months and years I've spent being afraid all the while reforging and remaking myself. Everything that has led to this.

I get moving, feeling dreamlike as I hurry to the door and step outside, not pausing to lock anything up. Marlene will have to hate or forgive me, there's no time for anything else. We have to go now.

Because despite my careful planning and calculations, I've failed.

He's found us.

Imogen

The blazing lights of the city grew dimmer and began to fade as if I were driving out of a wildfire.

I checked the rearview mirror, glad to see the car behind me I'd been watching for several miles finally veer off onto an exit. Mox lifted his head from the back seat and gave me a long look before resettling again. I was sure he was wondering where we were going. So was I.

After leaving Jamie's apartment, I went right at the sidewalk instead of left, detouring around an entire block before approaching my car in case Lev was watching. I didn't see him or his Audi, but that didn't mean he wasn't there. As soon as we were mobile again, I took turns at random, cruising city streets and gliding through dark and empty brownstone neighborhoods, the buildings like faces of sleeping giants. Once I was sure we hadn't been followed, I got on I-66 and headed west, monitoring any set of headlights lingering too long in my mirrors. As overpasses and medians grew more sporadic, trees began to dot the highway's periphery. Less and less traffic surrounded us until we were mostly alone on the road. As the city receded, so did a measure of my fear. We weren't safe yet, but with each passing mile, I hoped we became more so.

Within the quiet hum of the car and the sprawl of empty highway, my thoughts spooled out. The reality of what had happened settled in slowly, like frost covering a lawn, and just as cold. Everything I knew lay behind me. My family. My friends. My job. My home. The trappings of life I had taken for granted. The gas station I always stopped at. The coffee joint that had the best muffins. Mox's groomer. The wine bar April and I frequented. The backyard and how it smelled after the grass was cut. The tree outside my office window.

It was all gone.

I'd severed my life and cauterized it. Left it burned and smoking in my wake.

But there was no other choice. Lev looked like the rational one, and he'd managed to alienate everyone I could turn to. Except for Jamie. Sweet Jamie.

I was crying and didn't recall when I'd started. It was all too much to comprehend. I knew my next decisions would determine whatever came after, good or bad, but for a time I retreated into a thoughtless void, the only imperative continuing to move.

By the time the sun rose, I'd crossed into West Virginia, leaving the interstate to fill up on gas. I paid with cash and bought a pair of scissors and used them to cut my credit cards up before throwing them in the nearest trash bin. I considered my phone. There were dozens of missed calls and texts. Most from Lev, but some from Charlie and even a few from April. I scanned them, but they all were saying the same thing; *where are you, we love you, come home, come home, come home.* There was a single message from mom, short and succinct—You need help. Don't do anything you'll regret.

"I won't," I said, shutting the phone off and tossing it in beside the remains of my credit cards. "Not anymore." There was a camera mounted above the gas pumps, and I wondered if Lev would see me in this moment sometime in the future. I stared dead into the lens, then climbed into the car and pulled away.

———

I found what I was looking for around midmorning. The used-car lot was a few miles outside a little town called Spring Hills in a field on the corner of two intersecting county roads. Vehicles wound in glittering rows before a small office building with a single picture window in its center. I pulled into the lot and climbed out, releasing Mox from the back seat to sniff at the tires of what must've been dog heaven. Faded pennant flags hung in slack crisscrossing lines. A boat of a Cadillac was parked in front of the office, its paint flawless and shining. Litter clung to a sagging chain-link fence. The air smelled of rust.

I was heading toward the office when an aging man in tweed pants and a dark button-up shirt stepped outside. His hair was pure white and combed straight back. He swept at it with one hand as he made his way over to me, a smile crawling onto his face.

"Good morning, little lady. My name's Vince. How are we today?" He held out a red-palmed hand, which I shook. "In the buying mood, I hope." He smelled slightly of booze.

"Actually in the trading mood," I said, motioning to my car. "If you take trades, that is."

"Wouldn't be much of a used-car lot if we didn't! Now, what are you in the market for?"

"Something older."

"Older. Okay . . . well, let's see." He led me down the first row, pointing out a late-model sedan, then an SUV, chattering all the way. Mox trailed us, nose to the ground, chuffing every so often. I turned in a slow circle, searching across the field of steel and glass.

I'd known I had to dump my car shortly after getting rid of my phone because ditching the device wouldn't matter if there was a way to locate my car. And given its newness, I didn't doubt there was. I could almost sense Lev going through the steps to do so as I stood there in the chill air with the salesman yammering on about antilock brakes.

"What about that one?" I said, walking over to an old Chevy pickup with a stepside box. It was a grayish brown, the color of forgetting. Something the eye would pass over even if you were looking right at it. Its tires were worn, and part of its grill was missing, but I liked the truck's shape, its compact toughness.

Vince laughed. "What would a gal like you want with an old pickup?"

"I'd like to drive away without any record of me being here," I said, facing him.

His features became pinched. "I'm not sure I get you."

"I want to trade straight up for this truck without any paperwork."

"Straight up?"

I nodded, seeing the wheels turning in his head. My car was probably worth ten times the truck's value.

"Well, see, now, I couldn't resell it without a title and paperwork," he said after a pause.

"Not on this lot, no. But I wonder if there wouldn't be someone interested in a clean car at a good price who didn't want the hassle of any paperwork, either?"

Vince shook his head, a shrewdness in his eyes I hadn't noticed before. "No, we don't do that here."

"I'm not a cop."

"Exactly what a cop would say."

"Do I look like a cop?"

"They look like all kinds these days."

I hesitated. "There's someone looking for me. If there was any paperwork done here, he'd know what I was driving. He'd find me. I need to disappear."

Vince studied me, then combed his hair with his fingers, looking out at the rising hills in the near distance. "I won't give anything to boot," he said after a span.

"That's fine."

"Truck's as is."

"It runs?"

"Like a horse with its tail afire."

I pulled my car up to the truck and loaded my bag inside along with the refreshments I'd gotten at the last stop. Vince went to his office and returned with a single key. "You get pulled over and nailed, I'm saying it was stolen and didn't notice it right off."

"What'll you do with the car?" I asked, taking the key from him.

"Oh, it'll end up in a good home."

"I think there's a way to track it."

"Don't you worry about that." Vince hooked his thumbs in his belt loops. "First thing that gets removed."

After some urging, Mox reluctantly hopped up into the truck's cab, sniffing at everything in reach. "Thank you," I said, climbing behind the wheel.

"Best of luck," Vince said. "Sounds like you'll need it."

The truck started with throaty rumble, and as we left the lot, I had the urge to wave, but Vince had already gotten in my car and pulled around the office out of sight.

———

That first night I stopped at the crossroads of a town without a name in the northern Tennessee wilds and got a room at a motel. I was the only guest and pulled the truck around back, though I'd seen only one car go by the whole time I was checking in. The desk attendant was a shrunken woman with the face of a dried apple who didn't ask for any ID and only tapped a wrinkled guest sheet. I signed with a name I plucked out of the air, and she told me not to turn the heat too high in the room. The furnace was old.

In the room's bath, I used the scissors I'd cut up my credit cards with to shear my hair off in a ragged pixie cut. When it was done, I applied the bleaching kit I'd picked up from a pharmacy earlier in the day. The effect was startling. I tried seeing past the changes, but even though I had been the one who'd made them, the woman looking back from the mirror was almost unrecognizable. The last vestiges of who I was were swept away like the dark clippings of hair around the sink.

After a shower I sat on the bed, which creaked like it was haunted, and took inventory. I had approximately eleven hundred dollars. A bag of clothes. My toothbrush and toothpaste, and my wits, if I could count them as an asset. Mox paced around the room, then stood at the door and whined.

"This is home tonight." He gave me a mournful look and uttered a low woof. "Okay," I said. "If the smell in here is bothering me, it must be killing you."

Since there was nowhere to sit outside, we climbed into the pickup bed and watched the sky become a beautiful bruise that blackened until the stars came out. It might've been the prettiest sunset I'd ever seen if I'd really been watching. But I wasn't. I was retracing my steps, pressure-checking every move I'd made since leaving the house. I could feel the fear sealed behind a thin pane of glass. At any second it could crack, and everything would come rushing through. I'd panic and make some kind of mistake, and I couldn't afford that. Logic told me I hadn't forgotten anything. No phone, no credit cards, no car, no main roads, no identity. Leaving the car dealership, I'd turned south and angled southwest as the day wore on, driving the speed limit and avoiding any towns with populations greater than a few hundred. There was no way he could find me here.

I readjusted myself and stared up at the stars. At a certain point their number could've been choices waiting for me—billions of possibilities, and this is where I ended up. Cold and alone in the back of a pickup truck with my dog, on the run from a husband who wasn't what he pretended to be, without another person in the world I could turn to.

I felt like crying again, but I was too tired. I couldn't remember the last time I slept. I pried myself out of the pickup, and we went inside. I lay down on top of the bedspread, fully dressed for more than one reason, and fell asleep almost instantly, cuddling against Mox's warmth.

Hours later I woke to a voice speaking from the shadows of the room. "Come home."

When I opened my eyes, Lev was standing in the corner, one arm reaching toward me. "Come home," he whispered.

I flailed and knocked over the little bedside lamp I'd left on.

The room went completely black.

I couldn't see him anymore, couldn't see anything. I rolled away onto the floor, and Mox woofed loudly, scampering around in the dark. I crawled backward and came up against the bathroom door and fumbled for the light switch until I found it.

The room was empty.

Mox stood on the opposite side of the bed, ears up, head cocked. He looked at me as if awaiting instructions. I was choking and gasping, watching for Lev to reappear from where he'd hidden and then realizing he wasn't here. I'd been dreaming. I was alone. I checked the room anyway and then packed my things, knowing I would never be able to go back to sleep. Not here.

We roared away from the motel into the morning dark and didn't stop again until the sun had fully risen.

———

The next weeks passed in a hallucinogenic liquidity, one day flowing into the next. I drove highways and backroads without true direction, the howl of the truck's tires a soundtrack to our flight. Randomness seemed to be the most crucial compass; if I didn't know where we were going, neither could he.

I spent two days meandering through the autumn hills of Alabama, eventually ending up on an island off the Florida panhandle where the Gulf winds were still sweetly warm. We walked the beaches, and I let the sun tan my skin, but being surrounded by water soon felt the same as being trapped, so we returned to the mainland and headed west again.

Most days we ate little and stopped even less, pausing for only a handful of hours of sleep at motels or in the truck's bed if the weather was nice. Sometimes when the exit sign for a midsize town appeared,

I'd take it and cruise until locating a library. There I would type in certain key words on one of the computers and read about my own disappearance.

There wasn't a lot of public information. Lev had put out a statement and a plea for my return, describing my state of mind as "delicate." A brief online article chronicled my escape with a quote from a source close to me saying my behavior had been "erratic" in the days and weeks prior. In a video Lev had shot sitting at our kitchen table, he spoke directly to me, staring into the camera with sad severity. "Imogen, if you see this—please come home. We all miss you so much, and we want to make sure you're safe. No one is angry with you. We love you." He paused to swallow audibly, looking all of the heartbroken husband he was masquerading as. "I love you. I'll never stop looking for you." Afterward, I went outside and was sick in the tall bushes beside the building. Then I got back in the truck and didn't stop at any more libraries.

One afternoon when we were parked at a wayside rest in southern Arkansas, I came to the realization that for all my running, I was still traveling in a cloud of denial. Because even as I told myself it wasn't possible, a silent part of me continued to hold out hope I would eventually return home. That something would shift, and Lev would be held accountable for what he'd done. How, I couldn't say. I suppose it was my sense of justice in its death throes.

Because what could I really expect? I was one woman who had fled from what appeared to be a perfect life. To the people who knew me, I was paranoid and erratic. To everyone else, I was someone easily written off as unhinged or "delicate."

No, given how calculating Lev had been, I would never be able to go back.

I made myself say it aloud. "I'm never going home."

Now I had to find some way to believe it.

As the miles passed and my funds dwindled, I began rethinking how to spend the remaining cash. I bought a small camp stove at a garage sale along with some scarred pots and pans and started cooking as many of our meals as possible. I purchased a score of canned goods and refilled a large water container at every park we could find, but regardless of my frugality, I knew it wouldn't be long until the money would be gone and we'd be stranded wherever the truck ran out of gas.

In Louisiana, I washed dishes for ten hours a day at a little roadside café for almost a week, splitting tips with the cook and the waitresses.

In a warehouse in South Texas, I swept floors and broke down cardboard boxes for two dollars an hour under minimum wage.

I lost weight and gained new lines around my eyes and mouth.

My hair grew darker roots and became frayed with split ends. I smelled most of the time since showers were sporadic and the use of a washer and dryer was a luxury I couldn't always afford.

There were nights when I didn't have the money for a room, and we slept curled together in the truck, buried beneath blankets. One such night, I woke to a quiet scratching and saw the silhouette of a person outside the passenger door, attempting to pick the truck's lock. I hit the horn and Mox barked, and whoever it was ran. Driving away, I couldn't stop shaking.

We kept moving, never staying in a place more than a week. I became excellent at spotting cameras and made a habit of wearing an old baseball hat and a scratched pair of sunglasses whenever I encountered any type of surveillance. There was no way of knowing what resources Lev had at his disposal, but I assumed there were many. I would never underestimate him again.

———

There was a bottomless supply of hardship while living on the run, but there was also beauty.

On a desolate stretch of Kansas roadway, I witnessed a supercell thunderstorm undulate and flash with purple lightning, its formation and presence like an otherworldly invasion.

In the New Mexico desert, the sky was the merciless white of eternity above magnificent desolation.

I wept watching a valley community's lights gradually bloom as evening descended, thinking of the warmth inside the homes and the comfort of trust.

Whenever I saw a spectacle that gave me pause, I thought of Sierra. I recalled how everyone had described her. I tried embodying her adventurous passion. Envisioned her there beside me, marveling at the wonder and awe of a moment that would never happen again.

―――

The blue infinity of the Pacific spread out before me.

From the vantage of the overlook, I could see for miles up and down the jagged California coastline. Smell stranded seaweed and damp sand. Taste the salt in the air.

I stood in almost the exact same spot I did over ten years ago, watching the white comb of breakers far below. Even though I hadn't admitted it to myself, this was the place I'd been moving toward as I trekked across the country for the last two months. This had always been the destination.

And that was why I couldn't stay.

April and I had come here a few months after Marcus. It had been her idea and her treat—a week of sightseeing and boozing and dancing, all in the name of getting me fully out of my emotional stasis. At the time, it had seemed a heartfelt gesture of an overly concerned friend. Now I saw it for what it was—April's first effort of many to repair the damage she'd caused, and in turn alleviate herself of guilt. Back then I'd loved her for it. In many ways I still did. We'd spent most of our time on the beach, soaking in the sun and marinating in rum. Nights were filled with dinner and club-hopping, the latter a scene I wasn't into but went along with to humor her. At the tail end of the trip, I'd come to this lookout while April was sleeping off the prior night, and the view had unlocked something inside me that the drinks and dancing hadn't been able to.

It was the sense of how small my problems seemed compared to the natural grandeur.

I'd carried the feeling home with me, and that more than anything allowed me my first steps forward.

I'd told Lev all about the trip and how crucial it had been for healing. He would no doubt remember at some point and come looking here on the chance I settled in the vicinity. Knowing that, there was no way I would ever feel comfortable staying in the area, even though it was one of the most gorgeous places I'd ever been. Even this brief stop was a risk, but I had never told him the exact location, and there hadn't been another person in sight the entire time I'd been here.

I closed my eyes and let the past consume me. It could've been then, not now.

Except now I was someone so vastly different, I might as well have been two people.

I opened my eyes, breathed the view in deeply, and walked away.

———

I drove north.

I had never been to the Pacific Northwest. Never mentioned wanting to go there to Lev, never had the inclination. Until now.

As the landscape shifted—trees thickening, hills growing to mountains—a feeling of rightness settled over me. Some innate sense was drawing me onward, and I let it. Mox became more watchful as we drove, seemingly entranced by the lushness surrounding us. When we crossed into Washington, stopped at a wayside rest, and stepped off into the forest, it swallowed us whole. There was the trickle of running water and the glitter of moisture everywhere. Our breath plumed in the cool air.

We kept east of Seattle, and when a mountain pass well north of the city appeared, I took it out of instinct. Snow began to form on the sides of the highway as we climbed, the wet pavement hissing beneath the tires. As the mountains closed in around us, their vastness was unlike anything I'd ever experienced before. The sweeping views were also somehow intimate, as if the valleys were cradles, the peaks walls of safety.

It began to sleet.

Heavy dollops of snow splattered the windshield and melted almost immediately. The gas gauge read a quarter of a tank. It was late afternoon and getting dark. For a time there was nothing but the winding road growing more and more slick, but just as I began to envision a night spent huddled in the cab of the truck on a pull-off, a sign swam into view. I took the turn, and the road narrowed into snakelike switchbacks. We climbed higher and higher.

Just as I began debating whether or not to stop and turn around, faint lights appeared ahead. A small town materialized. It was nestled in a valley tight to the mountainside, a few quaint storefronts still lit. The road bent and rose again, another section of buildings appearing past a growth of mature trees. A neon sign glowed to the left, and I guided the truck into a sparsely filled parking lot and idled to a stop.

I sat looking at the building through the weather. Took in the surrounding trees that were only darker shadows against the gathering night. I shut the truck off and stepped out, listening to the quiet, unbroken except for the whisper of sleet.

"I'll be back in a minute," I told Mox and left him lying on his blankets in the truck.

Inside, there was an unmanned front desk opposite a doorway leading to a dim lounge. Several patrons sat around a table near the back beside the crackling flames of an open fireplace. The bar was empty, and I slid onto the nearest stool. The warmth was intoxicating. I could feel it releasing some of the tension built up from the demanding drive in the higher elevations.

"What can I get you, hon?"

A woman had appeared from a back room off the bar. She was stout, with thick gray coils of hair held back by a headband. She wore a well-loved hoodie with *Slayer* emblazoned across the front.

"Coffee. If you have it," I said.

"Sure do. Want cream or sugar?"

"Cream, please."

"Some weather, huh?" she said, turning away to fix my cup. "Really can't complain, though—this is probably the least snow we've had in the last five years. Hope the drive up the pass wasn't too hairy."

"It was getting a little iffy."

"Well, some go-juice will fix you right up. Especially mine. I grind it fresh every morning." She set a steaming mug before me, and I wrapped my hands around it, relishing the heat. "Where you headed?"

I smiled faintly. "I don't know."

"In that case I won't ask where you're from." She began cleaning some glasses. "Just passing through, or you going to stay awhile?"

"I don't know," I repeated, the smile gone. Steam curled up from the coffee, and I saw pictures in it. My future. More gas in the truck. More roads. More miles. More towns. More hard work for under-the-table pay. More looking over my shoulder. More running. Always running.

I was so tired.

"Do you have rooms available?" I asked before taking a long sip of coffee. She was right: It was rich and strong.

She let out a pleasant cackle. "Do I—yes, we got rooms available. There aren't many weeks out of the year we don't. I don't know if you got much of a look at town with the storm and all, but there isn't a lot here to draw people in. We get a few skiers in the winter and some hikers in the summer, that's about it. Everyone else who knows about this place is either here or dead." She laughed again and went to bring a beer to the table across the room.

I considered what she said and shifted on the stool, thinking of how far I'd come. Everything I'd forsaken. The bartender must've seen something on my face when she came back, because she studied me for a moment before wiping at a particularly clean spot on the bar. "This place ain't much," she said slowly. "Small community built on logging that dried up a long time ago. People who hung around did so because they didn't have any other place to go. But I will say this, the ones who're left are decent folk. Type of people who'll help you if you're broke down on the side of the road but don't care what you're doing as long as you leave them be too. Each to their own—if this place had a motto, that'd be it."

She went down the bar and began refilling garnish containers. I finished my coffee, thoughts whirring. When she came back, I said, "Do you have any pet-friendly rooms?"

"Two. Whatcha got? Dog?"

"Yes."

"Well behaved? Won't shit all over the floor or chew the leg off the bed, will he?"

I laughed. "No."

"Okay, then. How many nights you thinking?"

"One." I paused. "I can only afford one. But I was wondering if you might need some help? I could work off my stay."

She appraised me. "You ever turned rooms before?"

"No."

"Ever worked a front desk?"

"No."

"Ever tended bar?"

I shook my head.

She grunted. "Well . . ."

"But I learn fast. And I'm diligent." I struggled to think of anything else. "I—I could go over your books and marketing. Look at your expenditures and see if there's anything extraneous, give you a corporate assessment." I suddenly wanted her to say yes. It felt crucial to stay.

Mostly because I didn't know if I could get myself to go on. But also because there was something about the mountains, the town, this motel and lounge and the woman across from me. For the first time since leaving Jamie's apartment, I felt the prospect of safety.

The bartender laughed again. "Extraneous expenditures? Assessments? What were you in your past life, an accountant or something?" Caution tingled across my skin. I didn't reply. She studied me for another second, sobering. "Well, I guess it wouldn't hurt to give it a trial. My last manager ran off on me without any notice, and I've been struggling to keep up even with this place as slow as it is. We'll start with cleaning some rooms, then move you on to the desk for a bit if you think you can handle it. Then maybe we'll see about an assessment." She grinned and stuck out her hand. "Name's Marlene Tanner, owner of all you see."

I took her hand, noting the roughness of my own palm matched hers. Somewhere along the way I'd lost most of my softness, both inside and out. Lost so much more. But I'd also gained something invaluable. I'd finally listened to the internal voice calling out, heeding it over the clamor of others. I'd found a reservoir of strength I hadn't known was there and used it to save myself. I'd discovered an ability to survive, to push on when I didn't think I could. I finally understood who I was and what I was capable of.

As Marlene waited expectantly, I thought of another woman who I had never met but shared a kinship with. Lev had stolen from us both, but so much more from her. Taken the most precious thing of all, the beauty of experience. In that heartbeat, I vowed to live for her.

I would live for both of us.

"Sierra," I said, shaking her hand before letting go to touch the slight rounding of my belly and the life growing inside. "My name is Sierra."

Lev

Lev watches his wife walk toward the motel and pause before going inside.

He lowers the pair of compact binoculars and settles to his haunches beside the massive tree he stands under. He is over two hundred yards away, concealed by a lush growth of ferns on the forest floor. He sits listening to the constant drip of water and the faint hum of a car out on Main Street. Everything he wears is soaked. He hates this part of the country, has despised it since coming here on vacation as a ten-year-old boy with his parents. The gray skies and near constant rain, the fog and cool weather. The mountains themselves gave him nightmares for weeks afterward, how they had loomed out of the mist as if they could move on their own and were coming nearer. In sleep their dark profiles became monstrous entities turning their sloped faces toward him, seeking him out through his dreams all the way across the country. He had wet the bed every night for nearly a month.

It is deeply ironic this is where Imogen has settled to hide from him.

Even now it's all he can do to keep from striding to the motel, kicking the door open, wrapping his hands around her throat, and squeezing the life from her. But then it would all be over. His careful planning and efforts would be for nothing. And he isn't like her. He isn't going to throw everything away because he can't control his emotions.

But among the rage he thrums with excitement as well. So long. No progress for so long, then everything had happened very quickly. He'd almost given up, *had* given up on some level he hates to admit, before his last-ditch effort had paid off. Almost like fate, if he had believed in such a thing.

A heavy mist comes down, and Lev flips up his collar, hugging himself against the damp, and waits for his wife to reappear.

———

The night she'd run he'd been one step behind her. When he'd arrived home, he could smell her frantic sweat in the air and noticed her light travel bag was gone. He hadn't bothered to check in with Val and Deshawn; he knew she'd never leave the dog behind. Instead he'd called April repeatedly as he sped toward her apartment, checking the tracking app he'd embedded on Imogen's phone months ago when April didn't pick up. But she'd kept her phone off except for one brief blip at a gas station on the opposite side of the city. By then he'd been knocking on April's door and finding her as drunk as anyone he'd ever seen. Upon seeing him she burst into tears and mumbled Imogen's name, barely making it to her couch before collapsing in a pile of alcohol fumes. He searched the apartment anyway just in case, then sat in his car, mind frantically clicking through options.

It had taken him five minutes to surmise she'd gone to Flanagan's but the better part of an hour to arrive there. Cruising around the area, he hadn't spotted her car, and after watching the building's front door until daylight with no sign of her, he called the police and requested a wellness check on his wife, giving them Flanagan's address. They'd arrived, spent twenty minutes inside, then left. She wasn't there now and hadn't been there. At least that's what Flanagan told them, which to Lev meant that she most definitely had been. He couldn't think of anywhere else she would've gone.

Tracking her vehicle had been equally disappointing. By the time he'd jumped through all the necessary hoops on the manufacturer's website, kicking himself for not having done so prior, the app wouldn't connect with her car. It could only mean she'd disabled it, which he couldn't fathom either. But somehow she'd done it. Somehow she'd been able to slip free without leaving any kind of trail to follow. It had been the second time she'd ever surprised him. The fact kindled a boiling sensation in his stomach that continued throughout the following days and weeks.

Most of the waking hours, it felt like he'd swallowed hot tar.

———

At first visitors came and went in almost wake-like mourning—mostly his parents or Imogen's. Both sets were still completely oblivious and fully believed the narrative he'd crafted; his wife had been a secret struggling addict, crushed beneath the weight of her instabilities and lack of trust. He was just as shocked and saddened as anyone. Their friends had been extremely supportive, along with most of the neighborhood. Charlie and Val Williams, however, were a different story.

He didn't know what Imogen had said to her brother and their neighbor, but it must have been something fairly compelling because the feeling between him and Charlie was no longer the same. He'd seen the other man twice in the following weeks, once at Imogen's parents' and once at home. Both times Charlie had been polite but cool, offering no more than a few words and always exiting the room shortly after Lev entered it. Val, who had never cared for him in the first place, was openly hostile now. She stared him down whenever he went into the backyard or was leaving for work. One morning she'd been sitting on her front steps when he brought the garbage cans out to the curb and had mouthed *I'm watching you* before going inside.

"Watch all you want, bitch," he'd said under his breath. Because no matter what their suspicions, there was no evidence tying him to any of the things Imogen had asserted. Yes, her intuition had been frighteningly on point, but that was all it was—insight and accusations.

Nothing that would even lift a cop's eyebrow. Except maybe for the Greek detective, Kafatos. That man's demeanor was deeply unsettling even over the phone. He hadn't really taken any stock in Imogen's allegations, either, but . . .

Lev didn't like to think about some of the questions he had asked. The detective was curious, and that was the worst kind of person in Lev's opinion. *Curiosity killed the cat,* he thought, looking out at the Millers' house.

For weeks after she'd run, he had expected Imogen to come home. It seemed like the only natural outcome. She had little if any money. She had never been truly on her own before. Where else would she go? Yes, he'd scared her, but it had been necessary. She hadn't been deterred by any of his other gentler warnings, and her insistence on delving into the past hadn't collapsed beneath her own insecurities like he'd anticipated.

One day after work, the knowledge that she wasn't coming back fell upon him all at once. He'd overestimated her weakness, and there was no other choice now but to begin searching himself. If she wouldn't return on her own, he'd assist her. And if she was still unwilling—

Well, then there were other, more serious options if she pushed him to that.

It would be up to her.

———

He began with Flanagan.

If there was anyone she was still in contact with, it was him. Over the years Lev had acquired an above-average skill with lockpicks, and he employed it upon Flanagan's apartment one day when he knew the man was on the opposite end of the city at a meeting. A meeting Lev, of course, had set up anonymously, which would buy him the time he needed.

Once he'd gained access to the apartment, he spent ten minutes sifting through mail and searching for any telltale signs Flanagan was assisting her. When that came up empty, he planted a wireless camera at the back of a bookshelf in the apartment's main area, then left after relocking the door.

Over the following weeks he monitored Flanagan whenever he was home, which was little, but surprisingly the man didn't spend much time on the internet or speaking on his phone. Mostly he read. And looked out the window in silence. Besides his looks, Lev couldn't understand what Imogen had seen in him. But women were bizarre creatures with tastes that changed with the weather. If he'd learned anything, it was never to try making sense of women's choices. There was nothing of value to be gained other than certain patterns that could be exploited.

Other efforts like monitoring her social media accounts and her emails revealed nothing. There'd been no activity since she'd run and no more attempts to access their money either. On the off chance she was being extremely careless, Lev decided to check the property in Vermont Flanagan was associated with—some kind of trust with several other siblings. The place turned out to be a remote cabin on a secluded lake. He'd approached it in the evening through a dense stand of woods and watched through a pair of binoculars for movement behind the windows. The thought that she could be inside staying out of sight sent a shiver of anticipation through him. But as the night wore on and he became restless, he moved closer and verified the place was empty and dusty with disuse.

On the long drive back, he rode in silence, mentally collating a list of possibilities, and wrote them down when he arrived home. Looking at them provided a much-needed sense of progress. He booked his first flight online that night and slept without waking for the first time since she ran.

Details were deeply important.

Lev had known this from a young age and had always paid close attention whenever anyone revealed something personal about themselves. You never knew when someone's soul would slip into view. It was key to be watching and remember its shape.

He began with the two vacation spots Imogen had told him about—places she'd gone with her family as a child that she'd enjoyed enough to recall. One was a resort on North Carolina's Outer Banks, the other a small town high up in Kentucky's Appalachian Mountains. He spent two days canvassing each location, showing her picture to everyone who would look, intuitively seeking out landmarks and neighborhoods Imogen would be drawn to. At every stoplight and street corner he tried setting himself aside, imagining if she were in this very place, what direction she would go. What she would be feeling. If she were hungry, where she would eat. If he was going to find her, he knew he would have to go further than simply thinking like her.

He would have to become her.

After the first two attempts, he took more time planning the next excursion, both because he wanted to be as selective as possible and because he didn't want to raise any further suspicions in seeking her out.

But he soon realized he could take as many trips as his job would allow. To everyone in his orbit, he appeared the heartbroken husband, searching for his deranged wife. Who would fault him for looking for her even if it seemed like a lost cause?

Love, it seemed, was the very best camouflage of all.

High on his priority list was the mid-state Californian town she'd spent a week in with April after the disastrous end of her engagement. And it hadn't been so much the town or the activities they'd pursued, or even April's company that had made the trip special to Imogen. It had been an overlook of the sea that moved her more than anything. *It made me feel small,* she'd said to him with a faint smile. He'd nodded as if he agreed while knowing on some level he'd been fleeing that particular feeling all his life.

The problem was she'd never specified which overlook it had been.

He rented a motel room down by the beach, and after scoping out the town and surrounding area, he began systematically visiting viewpoints south to north. It took him three days before he was sure he'd found it.

The overlook was dramatic in its sweeping panoramas of ocean and land. After spending several days watching and waiting for her to appear, he exited his car and slowly approached the viewpoint. The sun was just setting, and there were no other sightseers to distract him. Lev stood by the railing and gently placed his hands on it, willing the feel of his touch to become hers, the sights flowing in through her eyes, emotions building, pushing first one way then another. He closed his eyes.

You were here. Right here. I can feel it. Where did you go?

He stayed still and silent for a long time, and when he opened his eyes again, the ocean had swallowed the sun, an afterglow all that remained on the water. Shadows leaned and grew, and they might as well have been inside him for how dark he felt.

Nothing. No sense of where she'd gone. There was a time when he'd prided himself on knowing her so intimately he could've operated her from the inside out, and had done so on more than one occasion. But now there was only emptiness. A void where her mind and heart had been. He was lost.

In a brief flicker he saw himself climbing the railing and stepping off into the drop. But that passed as quickly as it came. He was many things, but self-destructive wasn't one of them. There was no satisfaction in that. No balance to be gained.

Lev gave the darkening coastline a final look and went home.

———

He posted more pleas on social media for her return and asked that anyone who saw her please contact him or their local police. He even started a "Find Imogen" page on Facebook, which gained a decent amount of followers without a single sighting. There was some more travel, checking off the last few boxes on his list until none remained. He had held out hope she would return to a familiar place and settle in, and perhaps she had, and he hadn't detected her presence during his searches, but it felt like she'd shed her essence and left it behind, gaining a new scent he couldn't catch wind of.

Day-to-day he functioned like an automaton: arriving on time to work, keeping up with tasks, smiling when it was called for, eating, drinking, shitting, sleeping—all the while a reckoning was taking place inside him.

She had escaped. Beaten him. He had lost.

Out of desperation he even approached Carson about accessing either the DOJ or DHS's facial recognition software to aid in his search. Carson had given him a pained, withering look, part sympathy and part warning, and said, *You know that's not possible. Please don't ask about anything like that ever again.* Lev had promised he wouldn't, but not before imagining sliding a delicately long icepick into the senator's eye.

As more time went by, life took on the quality of a waking dream—living alone in the empty house, its silence like a judgment. A testament to his failure in misreading her. At the sound of an approaching car, he would move to the window and look out, sure he would see her coming slowly up the walk, head lowered in submission, ready to resume her place in their life. In those brief instances something like elation would grip him, then he would see it was a neighbor returning home or a delivery van, and the mental pall would resettle like a burial shroud. It colored his mood to the extent he began revisiting memories, wondering if he could pinpoint the moment where he'd made a misstep and gone astray.

There was a pond in a small park not far from his parents' home where he used to play. An old-growth forest hemmed the park off from the nearest freeway, dampening its sound, and a narrow walking path followed the shoreline, weaving in and out of stands of trees. For an eight-year-old, the park had been a wonderland of delights. He had been able to slip straight out of his backyard, through a brief strip of forest, and onto the walking path, which was popular in the early morning and evening, but throughout the day was mostly deserted.

He had played all sorts of games there alone, bringing toy cars and soldiers in a small pack along with a peanut butter and jelly sandwich for a snack. His imagination the only limits to his adventures.

One day two swans landed in the pond and began paddling along its edge, their long, graceful necks dipping to feed as they glided soundlessly through the water. Lev had watched them for a time coming closer and closer, staying as still as he could. They were entrancing to watch, and as they neared he marveled at the flawless white of their feathers, their charcoal eyes and beaks.

When they were in range he began hurling the rocks he'd gathered at them. The first went wide, and the swans honked in protest, angling away, but his second and third throws were more accurate, thumping solidly onto first one, then the other bird's humped backs. It was satisfying on a level he couldn't articulate. All he knew was that beautiful things cast a sense of smallness over him, and more and more he found himself wanting to destroy them.

"Hey!"

The shrill voice startled him since up until that point he was sure he'd been alone. A woman much older than his mother was hurrying toward him, an ugly puce handbag dangling from one arm with a tiny dog's head poking free of its top.

"You stop that! Right now!" The dog began to yap loudly, mimicking its owner. Lev was so surprised at being caught, he was frozen in place, mind screaming to run into the refuge of the trees. He watched the woman approach, the anger lines in her face becoming more pronounced as she neared.

"I—" he started, but then she'd grabbed him hard by the arm and shaken him.

"Don't you throw rocks at them, you mean little bastard. I ought to find your parents and tell them what you were doing. What's the matter with you?"

Beforehand he'd been aware of his bladder needing to empty but had ignored it when the swans swooped into sight. Now, with the woman's face up close to his, the noxious smell of her perfume invading his nostrils, and the dog's barks filling his ears, he lost control of himself, and wetness spread hotly down both legs.

"Where do you live?" she was demanding, punctuating each word with a shake. "Where do you live?"

Lev broke free then, yanking his arm from her surprisingly strong grip. He raced away, the wind in his ears drowning out the woman's yells and the continued barking of the dog. He hadn't stopped running until his house had come into view, and then he hadn't gone inside. He'd sat on the back stoop, crying quietly with fright but more so anger. The scolding had shot to his core, a bitter humiliation taking root there, growing stronger and stronger until his tears stanched and a stillness fell over him. He felt deeply unbalanced. Like the woman had scooped something out of him that needed to be replaced. Lev sat on the stoop until his face and pants dried, then went inside.

He'd had to wait for five days before seeing the woman again.

The hidden perch was on a small hill above the trail where he'd set up a makeshift blind of branches. Behind it he'd stockpiled rocks ranging in size from a golf ball to one that would barely fit in his hand. Each day he sat for hours waiting and listening for the woman's approach, and at last was rewarded.

As she and her bagdog, as he came to think of the mutt, passed, he threw the first stone. It caught her on the shoulder, and she stopped, glancing straight up at the sky as if the rock had dropped from a cloud.

The second throw landed solidly on her jaw, and she stumbled to the side, losing her balance on the pond's edge and falling into the knee-deep water. The bag and dog therein splashed beside her, and the dog began to paddle with its front feet out of the water. Lev hurled two more rocks in quick succession at the duo before fleeing through the trees, a ripe elation unlike anything he'd ever experienced before carrying him along so that he wasn't sure his feet were touching the ground. The woman shrieked in pain, her cries echoing like peals of music after him as he ran.

It wasn't until he'd safely circled back to his house that he realized he was laughing.

———

There were other events over the years before the culminations of Sierra Rossen and Lyra Markos. But they were minor incidents that he performed reflexively rather than with any real planning.

In the tenth grade a substitute teacher ridiculed his response to one of her questions, the rest of the class laughing uproariously at the slight, the girls' laughter tinkling like shards of glass in his ears. It hadn't been difficult to find the teacher's home address and loosen the oil-drain plug on her car while it sat in her driveway. The following week she was driving a different vehicle, and he overheard her complaining to another teacher about how much it was going to cost to replace her engine.

When he learned the girl he was dating in his junior year of college was cheating on him, he calmly broke up with her, waited almost a year, then followed her to a club and roofied her drink when she wasn't looking. He'd watched from afar as the drug took effect, an electric note of satisfaction chiming within him when she'd wobbled out of the club with a man who wasn't her current boyfriend.

These slights, particularly involving women, always required balancing, otherwise it felt as if a scale were tipping inside him, about to topple. At times it would become so acute, he would feel like he was listing hard to one side, unable to walk straight line.

Meeting Sierra had changed everything.

For the first time he felt he had an equal. A challenge that went beyond sexual conquest. By then he understood his own physical attraction, which did most of the heavy lifting, but he'd also honed his charm to an edge, which cut through any remaining female defenses. Sierra was different. Yes, she found him attractive and witty, but in those categories she more than matched him. He had to strive to keep up instead of leading in a relationship as he was used to. She did things in the bedroom he fantasized about for days afterward, and she had a thirst for life and experiences that at first dazzled him, then aroused a competitive aspect of himself he wasn't familiar with.

With other women he had always been the most important thing in their lives. Not so with Sierra.

When he felt what little influence he had over her begin to slip, he applied certain emotional pressures that had always worked before. She'd responded by putting more distance between them. And the harder he tried to curve their relationship in the direction he wanted it to go, the more steadfast she became.

He wasn't surprised when she finally broke it off with him. But he didn't accept it either.

On the surface he'd taken it well, and they'd parted amicably, while underneath a storm raged, and out of it was born a plan of action. At first it was in an effort to disrupt her life enough to guide her back to him. But it failed. She continued on no matter what hurdle he placed before her, until it was no longer a question of getting her back, but of breaking her.

Except she refused to be broken.

He'd never encountered someone so resilient, and in the end it was this quality that sealed her fate.

He didn't recall the particular details of the evening he'd met her in the empty parking lot pretending to have found her dog. All of it was amorphous, like a fever dream. There was an echo in his memory of her crying out through the gag from the trunk of his car, headlights playing over trees of an access road somewhere hours south of the city, and then the feeling of a shovel in his hands, palms blistering from the work, a hole deep enough that water seeped into its bottom.

Then nothing except the pure bliss of equilibrium returning.

Later, when he had been able to reconcile what he'd done, he'd decided it was of a singular nature. She had been a unique woman who pushed him too far, and he'd had to correct the imbalance. It would never happen again. He would make sure.

When he'd first seen Imogen in the throes of a panic attack at the party, he knew how.

As they grew closer, he became sure she was the perfect counterpart. Intelligent but modest. Sexy but unknowingly so. Pliable, compliant, and broken in all the right ways. He knew he would be able to form her into whatever shape pleased him going forward.

But then he had made the mistake of indulging in Lyra Markos.

It was supposed to be a simple thrill—to see if he could sleep with a woman on his honeymoon without his wife knowing. But throughout the day, the meeting they'd arranged on the beach that night took on a different hue. He'd tried believing it was simply lust coloring the anticipation. But then he'd swapped cruise cards with the swinger, telling himself it was only an added precaution. A darker yearning had built inside him as they ran along the beach in the rain, taking shelter in the cave on the sugar sand within. And when he'd tried to lay her down there where the prior tide had swept a bed for them, she'd resisted. Told him no. Not here. Not now.

He'd receded again like with Sierra—everything slipping out of focus with only flashes of violent clarity filtering through. When he regained control, Lyra was cold beneath him, his hands aching from gripping her throat. There was no remorse, only a vague surprise quickly swept aside by the necessary next steps.

On the way back to the ship, keeping himself as dry as possible beneath the blanket Lyra had brought with her, he watched the lightning fork over the sea and felt the waves throb in his marrow.

He had never felt more alive.

Lev

Now he sits forward as the motel's door opens and Imogen reappears.

Raising the binoculars, he's struck again by how different she looks. Not merely because of the passage of years or by how short and blond her hair is. It's something elemental in the way she moves and the set of her eyes.

He understands now why he wasn't able to find her in all his time hunting.

She hadn't merely changed her appearance, *she'd* changed as well.

She is a different woman.

Imogen stands outside the door, holding a steaming cup of coffee and glancing around, her gaze passing briefly over his position before sliding on. A primal thrill runs through him.

"Don't worry. Everything is going to be okay," he whispers as she gives the surroundings a final look and goes back inside.

———

On Imogen's birthday two years after she vanished, her mother appeared on the doorstep with a bottle of wine.

He'd just gotten off the phone with Carson and was trying to quiet an internal buzzing of alarm the conversation had set off.

"Who's this Jamie Flanagan who keeps poking around?" Carson had asked.

Lev had been semistunned at the question. "One of Imogen's exes. He's obsessed with her as far as I can tell."

"He emailed some information to the office. He's saying this is his third or fourth attempt." *Yes, I intercepted the other times,* Lev thought, listening to the senator breathe. "This looks a little concerning. Something to do with the disappearance of a woman you used to date?"

"It's nothing," Lev said, a familiar hatred stoking for Flanagan. The man's doggedness was beyond infuriating. "She ran away years after we dated. I spoke to the police about it. It's nothing," he repeated.

"And why didn't you mention this before? It's very bad timing as far as plans go."

"Because it isn't pertinent."

"I'll decide what's pertinent and what isn't. I mean, it doesn't look good, what with Imogen—"

"My wife is unstable, and I'm trying to find her," Lev said, regaining some control. "I'll handle Flanagan. He's a second-rate private investigator who slings mud if he can find it. That's all."

Carson grunted. "Well, can't say I'm fond of those oppo-research bastards. Nothing but trouble usually." He paused, then went on. "Campaigns are delicate things, and voters are fickle, you know this. So if this Flanagan keeps making noise, I may have to consider other options."

Lev rested his forehead against the wall. "It won't come to that."

"I hope not. I really don't."

Carson hung up, and Lev resisted the urge to fling his phone across the room, images of Flanagan's body twisted and bound in a hole filling his head. As he was pouring himself a drink, the doorbell rang, and he found Cora waiting outside.

"Mind if I come in and we commiserate a little?" she said, holding up the bottle of wine.

They sat in the living room on the sofa, both sipping from their glasses and talking about the past. Lev spoke a little, Cora a lot. At first she was tearful, talking about Imogen as a little girl, how afraid she'd been of so many things. Then her tone shifted as she discussed the last two years of her absence, a bitterness creeping in.

"I always told her she needed to compromise more. That's what marriage is built on."

"I keep asking myself what I could've done differently," Lev said, half bored. He'd had this same conversation with her and a dozen other relatives more times than he could count.

"Oh, honey, don't blame yourself," Cora said, scooting a little closer. "Some people just don't know how good they have it. I told her over and over, you were the best thing that ever happened to her, but I couldn't see how damaged she was. Not until it was too late. Maybe it was always going to end this way. Maybe there's no helping certain people. You know my cousin was like that—"

He drifted, his mother-in-law's voice background noise. He considered what Carson had said, how it really didn't matter if Flanagan was digging up the truth or not, enough rumors and insinuations floating around the capital, and he would be cut from the senator's staff. He would lose all the progress he'd worked and fought for over the years. His plans would crumble even more so, and all because of a woman's insecurity.

His fists clenched painfully.

"Maybe it's time you cleaned house," Cora said.

That brought him back. He released the tension in his hands. "What?"

"You know, maybe take down some of the things that remind you so much of her. I know if Ted were gone, I'd have to do a cleanse of our place, otherwise it would drive me crazy." He wanted to ask her then why Ted hadn't accompanied her today but held his tongue. "I mean, you haven't even thrown out the dog bed."

He glanced across the room to Mox's empty bed. It was true, he hadn't changed anything since she'd run. First it was to maintain the illusion of a grief-stricken husband, but then it had become a self-flagellation—a reminder of how he'd failed to curb his wife's insolence. How much of a fool she'd made him.

"I guess I can't get myself to. I just really miss her," he said.

One of Cora's hands strayed to his thigh, too high to be simply a touch of comfort. He noticed then she was closer, and much drunker than he'd thought. Her eyes were glassy with wine and something else. She leaned toward him, lips parted. He let her get within inches before pulling back.

"You empty, empty woman," he said in a low voice.

Cora drew in a sharp breath and recoiled, yanking her hand away. Horror brushed her features red as he stared impassively at her. She stood and hurried away, shoulders hunched and shaking. The front door slammed, and he was alone.

He sat motionless until the light slipped from the room. Then he stood and began collecting items from around the house that reminded him of her. All the while feeling as if he were walking a high wire, ready to fall.

At last the only thing left was the basket of Mox's toys and his bed. Lev had tolerated the dog, feeling his feigned connection with Mox ingratiated Imogen more to him. But he wondered if it had been another mistake, letting her keep a pet. Thinking of Sierra's dog, he had to admit they were useful at times.

As he was stuffing the dog bed into the trash, something grazed the back of his mind. He became very still and waited for whatever the thought had been to return. It definitely had to do with the dog, but what he couldn't say. He brought the bed up close to his face and inhaled the old scent of fur. Flicked through all the trappings of owning a pet. Their wants and needs.

The realization dawned and just as quickly shadowed. It was the longest of long shots, but well worth the effort. Lev went directly upstairs and logged on to the computer, then shut it down and went to bed.

The long shot paid off eighteen months later.

Carhill Veterinary Clinic in Townsend was a squat building set on a low hill on the edge of the city. As Lev pulled into the parking lot, he noted only one other vehicle, which could easily have been the veterinarian's. He was tired and wired, having left for the airport less than an hour after receiving the email from the pet-location service.

Your pet has been found! The subject line had paused his heartbeat, then tripled it. He hadn't ever really believed that Imogen would let the ID chip embedded in Mox be scanned by a vet since she'd been so meticulously careful thus far. But there were always unforeseen circumstances, and changing the contact email from her own to his was a simple insurance that paid off hugely. He knew so the moment the vet led him to the back where two dogs were being held in roomy cages.

"I hope we have him," the vet was saying. "This one was brought in yesterday by some tourists. I scanned his chip but didn't hear anything."

Lev stopped in front of the first cage, joy filling him.

Mox was lying to one side of the cage on an overstuffed mat. At the sight of Lev, he rose, sniffed the air, then hurried forward, tail wagging furiously.

Lev studied him for a second, then looked at the dog in the next cage before shaking his head. "Nope. Neither one is mine."

The vet's shoulders sank. "Huh, that's too bad. It kinda looks like this guy wants to go home with you, though."

"I'd take him if I could," Lev replied, giving Mox a final glance before walking away.

———

He surveilled the vet's parking lot from an adjacent business, kept his rental car tucked back mostly out of sight behind a moving van. None of the excitement had dissipated in the hours since verifying it actually was Mox in the vet's office. She was here. She was close. She would come. He just had to be patient. And given he'd waited the better part of three years, what was another day or two.

When the rusted Jeep appeared, he'd sat up straighter, but the occupant had been a roughneck in jeans and a hooded sweatshirt. Except upon leaving, he had Mox in tow.

Lev sat forward, pulse climbing. Imogen wasn't waiting in the Jeep's cab. So this must be the new man in her life, running an errand for her. Either that or she'd lost Mox long ago, and this was a new owner.

No. He couldn't believe that. Not after all this time. The dog was the final thread; all he had to do was follow it.

For much of the drive, he stayed several cars behind the Jeep, but as they wound higher into the mountains and the traffic thinned, there wasn't much choice but to tail in plain sight. The town of Maynard appeared, then faded almost as quickly, the Jeep barely slowing before climbing into a steeper set of switchbacks. Lev put as much distance between them as he dared without fully losing sight of the Jeep.

At the top of a rise in the high timber, the Jeep turned onto a narrow drive and disappeared around a curve. Lev slowed, marking the location on his phone, then cruised on, pulling off a half mile later onto an overgrown logging road.

He made his way quickly through the lush growth, moving at a half run over decaying logs and beneath hanging moss. His sense of direction didn't fail him, and after a few minutes he emerged on a low ridge above a small house and yard. The Jeep was parked beside a leaning shed, the man tweaking something under the vehicle's hood while Mox trotted around the yard's perimeter before settling into a spot near the front steps.

No one came out of the house. The man finished working on the Jeep and began throwing a ball for Mox. Lev watched them, waiting. Imogen didn't appear. A flock of birds swooped low over the treetops, their wing tips whistling. Mox lay down again and the man sat on the steps, scrolling on his phone. Lev withdrew into the cover of the forest and pulled out his own device.

It took him less than a minute to log on to the county's tax site and find the property owner's information.

"Marlene Tanner," he whispered to himself. The name didn't mean anything to him, definitely not something he would associate with Imogen. And as cunning as she'd been, he didn't truly believe she'd been capable of gaining a new identity watertight enough to purchase a home under. *You're renting, probably paying cash,* he thought, feeling the truth in it. *And I'd bet you're working for cash too. But where?*

Scrolling down, he saw Marlene owned another property, this one listed beneath a commercial heading in the town below. He gave the man and the dog a last look, then retreated into the woods and was gone.

––––––

Coming back to town, he'd idled past the motel, parking slightly down the slope beside an enormous stand of pines. And before he could determine the best way to approach the building and get a sense of things, Imogen had stepped out of one of the rooms pushing a cleaning cart.

He'd known it was her despite the distance and the shortened and dyed hair and the work clothes she never would've been caught dead in back in DC. He'd been stunned, entranced by her as she paused to admire the view of the trees as the clouds parted and sunshine flowed through them. He was surprised to feel tears seeping from the corners of his eyes.

Then the sunlight faded, and she'd gone into the next room to clean it.

Lev sat for a few minutes before starting the car and pulling away. As much as he'd longed for this moment, somewhere along the line he'd lost hope it would happen.

Faith fully restored, Lev guided the car deeper into Maynard as the rain began to fall in earnest.

———

After the near miss outside the bookstore he'd backed off, since the last thing he wanted to do was scare her into the wind again. Besides, now he knew where she lived. But he still could hardly believe she'd not only spotted him, but recognized him somehow through the storm, and come running. He'd had to sprint into the nearest stand of trees and press his back against the largest of them as she moved past, searching.

Instead of going straight to her home, he decided to get a feel for the surrounding area in case things didn't go as he planned. After buying a pair of decent hiking boots and a rain slicker at the mercantile, he returned to the logging road he'd parked at earlier. It was still a few hours before full dark, and he set off through the forest, staying well outside the clearing where Imogen's house rested.

From the aerial maps, the home appeared to be completely isolated in almost every direction. A long, narrow lake lay in a nearby valley, and he hiked around its northern edge to the opposite shoreline, moving steadily toward the only other structure he'd seen on the map.

What he'd guessed was a neighboring home on the far side of the lake turned out to be a dilapidated hunting cabin being slowly absorbed by the forest. The sidewalls were stained with mildew and rot, and the roof was swaybacked and furred green with moss. The door swung inward on shrieking hinges, and when he stepped inside, the floorboards groaned and bowed dangerously.

The interior was a single room, a rusting bed frame in one corner. The remains of a table slanted against one wall; the leavings of animals were everywhere. The air was thick with moisture and decay. The scent made him sick, and he was reminded again of how much he despised the wilderness.

Retracing his path around the lakeshore, he felt he couldn't have picked a better setting for them to be reunited. The isolation she'd chosen for safety would soon become his advantage.

Darkness had fallen, and the rain came down heavier as Lev entered the tree line, but he barely noticed.

———

No Jeep. That was the first thing he noticed upon resuming his position on the ridge above the house, which glowed like a ship at sea in the dark.

He'd been afraid the man who had retrieved Mox from the vet would be an issue, but it looked as if he had just done Imogen a favor and moved on, or had been given the brush-off. Lev guessed the latter if he was coming to understand this new version of his wife.

Through the yellow squares of glass, he caught movement from time to time but wasn't at the right angle to see any details. That was okay since what he really desired was a closer look.

Making his way down the pine-studded bank, he paused frequently to listen. There was a half-moon riding overhead, and it coated everything in a satin glow. Lev moved low and fast across the open yard, afraid there were motion lights he hadn't spotted earlier, but the night remained unbroken. He crouched beside Imogen's aging pickup, then circled to the rear of the house where he guessed the bedrooms were.

The first window he peered into was the main bedroom, but it was dark except for a wedge of light falling in from the hall. He sidled on until he was directly under the next window and listened to the low sound of Imogen speaking, her voice plucking at a heartstring. What she was saying was muted through the wall, and he wondered if she were talking to herself. Or perhaps Jeep-guy was still here sans vehicle.

Risking a glance through the bedroom window to find out, he froze.

Imogen sat on the edge of a small bed and was reading to a child. A boy of maybe three, propped on a bank of pillows. He was struggling to stay awake but was losing the battle, his eyelids drooping with each turned page.

Lev felt something dislodge in his chest and free-fall through him.

His legs lost some of their strength, and he sank to his heels, leaning hard against the siding. His breathing was strange, coming in small hitches while one thought repeated in a loop.

A boy. I have a son. And she stole him from me.

The realization was like being struck by lightning. He felt electric with equal parts excitement and rage. This changed everything. He sat marveling at the knowledge he was a father until the boy's light went out. The stars whirled above, and the hoot of an owl became the only sound in the world besides his heartbeat.

Now he knew his attempts at lowering the efficacy of her birth control had paid off—just at the worst possible moment. For months he had placed the packets of pills in the oven on a low temperature whenever he had a chance, baking their life-preventing effectiveness out of them. He could still smell the faint scent of warm plastic. It had always instilled a feeling of bright anticipation.

Lev smiled and closed his eyes.

It was hours later when light sprang on again from inside.

The moon had shifted and the forest was quiet. He must've drifted off at some point. With careful movements he rose and stalked around the side of the house.

Imogen stood at the kitchen counter looking out at him.

His guts shriveled. But no, she wasn't looking at him. She couldn't see him. She was simply lost in thought, staring into nothing.

They stood that way as time stretched out, her looking into his eyes without knowing it, and him looking back.

Then she turned away to make a cup of tea and picked something up from the counter that startled him.

A sleek black pistol.

She took the gun and the tea to a chair and sat, gaze unfocused. Lev watched her for several minutes before moving off in the direction of his vehicle. The night was cool, and his clothes were damp, but an inner fire warmed him, the flames fed by the memory of his son's face. As the dark shape of his car appeared ahead, a single thought pulsed in his mind.

We could be a family if she lets us.

It was her choice.

———

Now he watches as another family exits the motel and continues on their way. Mother, father, son, daughter. Happy and carefree on their trip together. He wants that. Wants everything a life of unity can provide.

Through the motel glass he sees Imogen watching the family depart and wonders if she will finally understand she can't simply walk away from the vows she'd uttered to him. To have and to hold. To honor and obey. She owes him what she'd promised.

And he will have it. One way or another.

Imogen/Sierra

The rain starts to fall as I sprint to the truck.

The disbelief that he's found us, that this is actually happening, is overwhelming. But the veterinarian's confirmation is all the proof I need. Lev must've changed the contact email to his own for the microchip embedded in Zee. I was sure I'd thought of everything—even shortening Moxie's name out of caution—but I'd forgotten the chip. And now it might be our downfall.

I'm looking everywhere except where I'm going, and nearly trip on a crack in the concrete. I stumble and right myself, sliding in behind the wheel. For a terrifying second, I think I've forgotten the keys, but they're in my jacket pocket. The Chevy roars to life, and I drive across the motel's lawn in a wide swath, dropping into the ditch before popping up onto the road.

My instinct is to go straight to the day care and then out of town with just the clothes on our backs, but two things stop me. One, Zee is still at home, and there's no way I'm leaving him behind. The second problem is the truck has only a half a tank of gas. We need money, clothes, supplies, all the things that are in the go bag.

I hesitate, then yank the wheel to the left and speed out of town toward the house.

I'm shaking and breathing so hard, my vision wavers. Have to calm down.

Check the rearview mirrors. Nothing.

No one following.

It kills me to go home first before picking him up, but he's safer there. Amanda's husband is at the day care today, and it's the middle of the afternoon. There are neighbors and cars passing by on the street. Lev wouldn't be stupid enough to barge in and try stealing him, he's too careful. He'll try another tactic, and I'll have to be ready for it.

The windshield smears with rain, and my breath fogs up the glass. I don't slow enough for one of the switchbacks, and the tail end of the pickup slews dangerously toward the slope, then straightens. My mind careens like the truck, swerving through a half dozen scenarios, trying to anticipate what he's going to do.

He found us, he found us, he found us.

The thing I've feared most since settling here has happened. Now we'll have to run again. The thought nearly breaks me, but there's no other choice.

Our drive appears ahead, and I roar onto it, flying around the first bend and then up into the yard. It's empty. I skid to a halt and step out into the rain, hesitant to leave the safety of the truck, which is still idling loudly. I cut the engine to hear better.

The patter of rain.

Wind sighing through the pine needles.

Nothing else. I'm alone.

I take two steps toward the house and think better of it, doubling back to the truck's passenger side. I open the door and reach under the seat for the lockbox and the gun inside. I'll feel so much safer with it in my hand.

It's not there.

I bend lower, stretching my arm out, thinking the rough drive has shifted it farther back, but there's nothing. It's gone.

My insides curdle.

I straighten and turn. The yard's still empty. I need to get inside and get one of the other guns.

I prime myself, heart hammering painfully against my ribs, then launch into motion.

I sprint from the truck to the house, digging my keys out as I go. I can be in and out in less than a minute. Be back in the truck with Moxie and down the mountain to the day care in less than twenty. Out of town in half an hour. I can do it. I can—

Lev steps around the side of the house when I'm two strides away from the door.

I slide to a halt. The sight of him there in a dark rain-slicked jacket, hair plastered to his skull, eyes alight with terrible joy, strikes me so cold I can barely breathe.

"Hello, honey," he says, and smiles.

I retreat a step for the truck, then think better of it and shift toward the leaning shed, which is closer. Lev's smile widens, and he raises one arm. "You thinking about going for this?" He's holding the small revolver I'd stashed in an old coffee can on a shelf in the shed. "I made sure I looked everywhere in there, so I don't think you have another one hidden. I know how you love backing up your work."

He takes a step toward me, and I match it in retreat.

"I can barely believe I'm standing here talking to you," he says. "Do you know how long I waited for this? How far I've come?" His eyes harden with an alacrity that's frightening. "Do you know what you've put me through?"

He's equidistant now between the truck and the house. But it doesn't matter. He's got the gun and I have nothing. I take another step back.

"You don't, do you? You ran and never looked back and left me trying to hold everything together while you started a new life. Right, *Sierra*?"

A few feet to my left is a fallen tree branch that looks thick enough to hurt him with. But there's no way I can pick it up and swing it before he shoots me. And he won't do that until he's finished talking.

"Sierra." He laughs, and it sounds like a high-tension wire at its breaking point. "It's cute you took her name. You thought you could leave who you were behind? Thought you could be her? You could *never* compare to her. She was everything you aren't."

Mox begins to bark from inside the house, his blocky head appearing in the window, but Lev's solely focused on me. The gun rises a little, and I think he might do it then out of pure rage. He looks like he could. But then he seems to restrain himself. He turns the gun over in his hands, a faint smile reappearing. "You know, for all your meticulous planning, this is what your end game was? To kill me if I ever showed up? But how would that look? I'm just a man searching for his disturbed wife. I finally catch wind of where she is, and she shoots me on sight. What would the authorities say? I mean, sure, in today's world, wives might get away with killing their husbands more often, but given your history of instability and violence, do you think a woman like you would?"

A woman like me.

"A woman who tried killing me once already? A woman who breaks promises and runs away?" He pauses. "A woman who kept my son from me?"

I stiffen. My already racing pulse picks up even more speed. "He is not yours."

The dead look comes over him. "But he is. And so are you."

The wind gusts, carrying a swath of rain with it. Even though there's only a dozen feet separating us, we almost lose sight of each other. I tense, then relax as visibility returns.

"So I'll make you one last offer, just like I did in the hospital. Come home, and we'll start over. The three of us. We can tell everyone whatever we want, and they'll believe it. They'll be so happy to have you back. It will . . ." He swallows and squints through the rain. "It will be different. *I'll* be different. I promise."

The gun lowers slightly, and he reaches out his free hand for me to take.

I stare at it as another heavy swath of rain comes down, knowing I only have one choice. I have to do what I'm best at.

Run.

Ducking low, I spin and hurl myself out of the yard. The handgun booms a second later, and even though I'm expecting it, the whine of the bullet as it passes a few feet to my right makes me flinch.

Then I'm hurtling through the trees down the path I've run every morning since I discovered it, familiar trees and logs flying past. My breathing is wet and ragged from adrenaline and inhaling rain.

I jag left and right, feeling his aim on my back.

A second shot explodes the sagging trunk of a leaning tree. Splinters dust my shoulder.

I leave the trail at a curve, sawing through the undergrowth until I meet up with the path again farther downslope. His breathing is loud behind me, and I hope the elevation is taking its toll. I hope his heart explodes and drops him in a heap on the side of this mountain. But hope has only gotten me so far. I'm on my own now.

A shot sings through the branches overhead. And another that goes wide. He's frantic to stop me. Maybe he knows what's ahead. Knows if I reach it, I'll be safe.

Through gaps of greenery is the welcome gray of water.

The lake.

I launch myself down the last stretch and burst from the tree line onto the rocky bank.

Tear my jacket away beneath the weeping sky and dive into the water as soon as my feet touch the shore.

The lake howls in my ears, and I kick hard, propelling myself down. A thin stream of silver curves to my left, and I realize it's his last bullet, cutting through the water, then gone. I manage to pry my shoes off and glide another few yards before surfacing.

Lev stands at the shoreline, chest heaving. He looks out at me where I tread water fifty feet away. The gun dangles loosely in one hand.

He drops it. It looks like he's about to say something, but instead he unzips his rain jacket and lets it fall before unbuckling his pants.

He's going to come after me.

I backstroke farther away, keeping him in sight. He's not a good swimmer, and, if anything, since his fall from the ship, he's become more cautious of water. But there is a dead set to his eyes I can see even across the distance, and I know he's going to try to catch me.

Wearing only his underwear, he hurries into the water and begins to swim toward me.

I paddle away, sure he'll turn back after a few strokes, but he keeps coming. And what's worse is, his form is precise and muscular. *Fast.*

I curse, managing to shuck my pants free, and begin to swim in earnest, letting my own rhythm fall into place.

Stroke. Kick. Breathe. Stroke. Kick. Breathe.

When I risk a glance back, my chest clenches. He's closed some of the gap and is swimming hard.

I turn and focus on my body, letting it become part of the water like I have so many times before. This is what I've trained for. At any second I expect the cold grasp of his hand on my ankle, and then it will be over. He'll drown me here in the middle of the lake, and my son will be alone.

The thought is enough to push me faster. I swim like I never have before.

If I can make the opposite shore, I'll have a chance. And I have to. The only other choice is death.

Lev

The water is like white fire as he dives in.

The old fear of its touch rears, and he fights it down like his swimming coach instructed him to. *We're made mostly of water. We develop in it. We came from it. There's no need to be afraid of it.* He began taking lessons a few months after Imogen ran, partially for something to occupy his time, but mostly because being unable to swim was the weakest aspect of himself, and he hated the vulnerability.

Now a gleeful rage flows through him with each stroke. Pulling him closer to her. She's a strong swimmer, no doubt having swum this particular lake many times, but he's stronger, and faster, and more resolute.

He'll catch her because she is a woman and he is a man.

If he can get close enough to latch on to one of her ankles, it will be all over. He'll hold her under until she quits moving and leave her to float here in the cold, gray water. In fact, it will be the perfect scenario. A tragic drowning. A single mother leaving behind her son. They will write an article up about it in the local paper, and he will happen to see it after returning home to DC. He'll come here again on a hunch and ID her body. He will be utterly stunned to learn he has a son. He will return home, brokenhearted at the death of his estranged wife but dedicated to raising their son in her absence.

It will be perfect if he can just catch her.

But something alarming is happening. His breathing is uneven, and a paralyzing cramp is forming in his middle, boring its way through to his back. This isn't anywhere near the farthest he's swam before, and he can't understand it for a beat. Then it makes sense.

The elevation.

The lack of oxygen is robbing him of power. The gap between them is widening as she continues her steady strokes ahead. He wants to scream, curse her, make her even more afraid than she already is. But that will only use more energy. Instead, he focuses on easing his speed, breathing deeper each time he turns his head. She is nearing the opposite shore, but the cramp is releasing. He keeps moving through the rain-pebbled water.

Imogen hits the shore and stands, wading rapidly onto dry land.

That's fine. There's nowhere for her to go. He'll catch her before she makes it a mile.

His fingers graze rock. He stands, swaying in the lake, then rushing forward, lungs burning. She has made it up the lower bank and into the woods, angling between the massive trees there. He notes she's moving slower, too, and it galvanizes him.

He will catch her. He will restore balance. He will make this all right.

The rocks bite viciously into the soles of his feet, but he hobbles up the bank quickly, deep breaths of oxygen steadying his shaking muscles. He's freezing but invigorated. Alive. So alive.

Through the mossy forest, sticks snapping and falling away. He can't see her for a second, but then she reappears, flashing into view in a small familiar clearing.

The rotting cabin he visited last night.

To his confusion, she moves to its front door instead of continuing on. She glances over one shoulder, their eyes meeting, then pushes inside and slams the door closed.

He nearly laughs. He could put his fist through the cabin's wall easily. She's not safe inside, no matter how she barricades the door.

She's trapped herself.

Lev slows as he approaches the cabin, catching more of his breath.

So this is it. This is where their story ends.

He had no idea all those years ago when he first laid eyes on her that she would lead him through such trial and torment, only to finish in a dreary and remote place like this. He'd had such dreams for them. But he knows now she'd never been the right kind of woman. When this is all over, he will find the person he's supposed to be with. He believes she is out there somewhere. Waiting for him.

Lev takes another deep breath, preparing himself, and kicks the cabin's door in.

Imogen/Sierra

Sometimes I ask myself where it started.

I try pinpointing what was the first thing, the first mistake that changed everything. That put me on this course to the place where I am now.

My mind keeps going back. It's natural—to wonder where things begin. It's an attempt to understand. To find order. If you start at the beginning, you can follow a trail forward like breadcrumbs, or drops of blood.

For me the question is never answered. I have no idea where the beginning was.

All I know is the end.

And this is it.

Somehow I knew this was our destiny. As fast as I can run, he will catch up. As well as I can hide, he'll find me. All that is over now. And I'm ready.

The door flies open behind me, sounding like it's come off its hinges. I didn't barricade it, but I didn't need to.

By the time he made it to the door, I was able to pry the very middle plank of the back wall free and retrieve what I placed there years ago when I'd found this cabin empty and abandoned. Looking all of what it was.

A last resort.

I rip the plastic bag from the revolver I've maintained with a light coat of oil and turn to find Lev striding toward me across the room. He's wearing his true face in all its maniacal victory. He thinks he's won.

At the last second he spots the gun and halts, a look of pure disbelief entering his eyes. His hands come up before him.

"Wait," he says.

I fire twice into his chest.

The reports are cataclysmic in the enclosed space.

The muzzle flashes are like lightning strikes, and in them I see Sierra's face as well as Lyra's.

Lev leans forward as if two .357 rounds at point-blank range aren't going to stop him, but then he steps back, and his legs fold.

He falls in the middle of the cabin floor.

I inhale gun smoke. It tastes bitterly sweet.

He convulses, and I keep the revolver trained on him, but his movements are already slowing as blood pools beneath him. I come closer and stand over him. He's looking everywhere like he might find salvation in one of the cabin's recesses, but finally he focuses on me. His bloody lips part and he blinks, but there are no words. Finally. I kneel beside him, easily nudging away one of his hands as he reaches for me.

"I want you to know something," I say, deeply pleased there is almost no waver to my voice. "I want you to know my son's name." I lean closer. "His name is Jameson. He's named after his father." I watch the recognition bloom far back in his eyes. "He's not yours, and neither am I."

Lev coughs weakly. Bloody rivulets run from each corner of his mouth. His chest wounds suck air, and his back arches slightly; then he deflates, stiffening out. His eyes find me for the last time, and I stare into them until they're empty.

Before my strength leaves me, I crawl to the nearest wall and slump against it, hugging my knees to my chest. I sit there, the only sounds the steady drip of rain through the buckling roof and my heartbeat, growing slower and slower.

———

When I'm sure I can stand again, I set the revolver down and roll Lev's body to the side. The planking beneath him is dark with blood, and I pry it up, five boards in all, revealing the crawl space under the cabin as well as the yawning grave I dug months ago.

I roll the body back over and into the pit without hesitation. It makes a terrible sound when it lands. I climb down into the crawl space and fish around in the dark until I find the shovel I left here and begin filling in the hole.

There are a few other hidden graves and weapons—he was right: I am fond of backups—one such being beneath the shed by the house. But somehow I'd always felt this particular place was where we would end up.

I work without stopping, and before long the hole is filled in, the only sign a slight depression. I climb back up into the cabin and replace the boards, blood-side down, and survey the space. There have been no visitors here for many years, and it will probably stay that way. The structure will continue to rot and eventually fall down on top of an unmarked grave that no one will ever know is there. No one except for me.

I take the shovel with me and retrace my steps down to the lake. The rain has tapered to a mist, and it drifts in whorls like wandering ghosts. I stand listening for any motors or voices, any sign the shots were heard, but there is nothing. Gunfire is not uncommon here and generally ignored if not excessive. I cling to what Marlene told me on the first night I arrived in Maynard—*each to their own*. So far that has proven true. I hope it continues to hold. I hurl the shovel as far as I can into the water and watch it disappear in a rippled splash. There are other necessities I'll need to attend to, like dropping the revolver into the deepest part of the lake and destroying the clothing Lev discarded, along with his cell phone and any other signs of his presence he might have left behind. But that can wait for the moment. I settle onto a large rock and listen to the lap of the waves.

When I'd realized I was pregnant, the strange feeling of my birth control packaging came back to me. It tracked that Lev had been trying to sabotage it in some way—to him, pregnancy was another form of control. Except our intimacy had then become the barrier to getting what he wanted. We hadn't been together since the night of the housewarming, a fact he would've found deeply concerning if he knew how old Jameson was.

I picture Jamie then, and my heart floods with memory.

How I'd told him goodbye in his apartment the night I ran. How he'd taken my hand before I could walk away and pulled me into one last embrace.

How the embrace had led to one more kiss. Then another. And another until we were in his bed and all my worry and heartache had surfaced in a need so profound, it was undeniable.

It had been brief, but so wonderfully sweet. I'd left immediately afterward, him still warm inside me. And a month later the nausea in the early-morning hours led to a pregnancy test in the bathroom of a wayside rest area. In the following weeks, I lay awake at night, wanting to call Jamie and tell him he was a father, knowing all the while it would put us in jeopardy.

So I held my secret as it grew inside me, keeping the hope alive that someday I would be able to tell Jamie the truth.

And now I could.

The reality of what I've done settles over me. Stills me in a way I haven't known in years so that I feel like part of the stone I rest on.

I'm free.

After all the wondering and unease and fear and running and struggle, I'm finally free.

We're free.

I think of Jameson and how I'd left him that morning, playing with careless abandon, safe from the knowledge and danger I'd kept him from his whole life. And now he may never know, and that would be a blessing for us both. I envision what the coming years will bring, how he'll grow and look to me for guidance. And I'll be there to help him become a man who will be worthy of trust.

Because love grows only from trust, and I want both for him.

I rise and go to the water. It laps warmly against my cold skin. The wind gusts, and it sounds almost like a song in the trees. One only I can hear.

I take two steps and dive into the lake and begin to swim back to the waiting shore, and the life I've remade beyond.

ACKNOWLEDGMENTS

As always, I'm beyond grateful to my family for your love and patience since I couldn't do any of this without you. A huge thank-you to my agent, Laura Rennert—I'm deeply lucky to have your unwavering support and guidance. Thanks to Liz Pearsons for continuing to believe in my work and to all the other great people at Thomas & Mercer who make the publishing wheels turn. And eternal thanks to the readers who keep making what I do possible; I am forever in your debt.

ABOUT THE AUTHOR

Photo © 2023 Jade Hart

Joe Hart is the Edgar Award–winning and Wall Street Journal bestselling author of seventeen novels, including *Now We Run*, *Or Else*, *The River Is Dark*, *Obscura*, and *The Last Girl*, as well as many novellas and short stories. His work has been translated into eight languages and has been optioned for film. He lives with his family in Minnesota. For more information, visit www.joehartbooks.com.